FALL

Tiffany Noelle Chacon

WRITE HORSE
Publishing

Contents

Download Off Course: The Equestrian Dreams Prequel

Scan the QR code or go to the link below to download the FREE prequel novella for the Equestrian Dreams series.

tinyurl.com/offcoursebook

For Tyler – you are my beginning, my middle, my end. From first kiss to last breath and beyond. I'm so glad I get to go on this journey with you.

FALL THE NOVEL PLAYLIST:

Scan the QR code or go to the link below to listen to some of the songs mentioned in the novel.

tinyurl.com/falltheplaylist

Glossary of Horse Terms

Broken line—two or more show jumping obstacles jumped in succession that are not in a straight line

Colic—severe abdominal pain which can be life-threatening depending on the cause and severity. Colic is the number one killer of horses.

Clean—to jump over an obstacle without knocking it down. A "clean" round in a show jumping competition means that you completed the round without any faults.

Chip in—to add an extra stride or half-stride before going over an obstacle

Fetlock—a part of a horse's leg, above and behind the hoof

Forelock—the top foremost part of a horse's mane, essentially its "bangs"

Gelding—a male horse that has been castrated/neutered

Girth—a piece of tack that goes under the horse's belly to keep the saddle in place

Grand Prix—the highest level of competition for show jumping, with obstacle heights of up to five foot three inches

Hack/flat—to exercise a horse without jumping them

In-and-out—two show jumping obstacles back-to-back with only one or two strides in between

Jump-off—the second, shorter round in a show jumping competition. The riders who went "clean" in the first round can advance to the jump off. The fastest, clean time wins the event.

Oxer—a show jumping obstacle made of two (or more) poles spread a distance from each other to give the jump width

Rollback—a tight turn from one jump to another

School—to exercise or warm up a horse

Stall—the place in a barn where a horse lives; an individual enclosure for the horse.

Standards—the part of a show jumping obstacle that holds the poles in place. Can be plain or decorative.

Tack—the equipment used to ride a horse. Consists of saddle, bridle, etc. Also a verb—"to tack up" means to put your tack or equipment on your horse.

Triple combination—three show jumping obstacles back-to-back-to-back with only one or two strides in between

Vertical—a show jumping obstacle with poles on top of one another to give it height without the spread or width

1

A Perfect Day

Mila

I press my heels into the gelding's sides and feel a thrill as he surges forward over the grassy field. We're galloping as one, unsure where I begin and he ends. I knot my reins, resting them on his neck as I extend my arms out like I'm flying. And maybe I am.

It's one of those perfect Florida fall days where the sky is bluer than it has any right to be, the air is crisp and breezy, and the scent of hay carries all the way to the field. I take a deep breath as the wind whips past me, and it's as if I'm both bigger and smaller than I really am. Being out here, I feel like I'm part of something *more*—all of my atoms are connected to every other atom in this universe. I am expansive, vast. And somehow that makes me feel small, too. I can sense the enormity of the cosmos thrumming through me—a girl on her horse—and I'm content to just *be*.

I pull up the gelding, a chestnut horse named Harley, and look around at the ViaTech Center for Equine-Assisted Therapy. I can't hold back my smile. We made this place, and it is perfection. The centerpiece of the property is a wood-paneled barn with a gabled roof and charming dormers. The barn has an overhang held up by wooden pillars that gives it a look akin to a wraparound porch. Behind the barn, there are several grassy paddocks and two round pens. Harley and I are at the front of the farm, which has a wide-open field next to a covered ring. The roof of the covered arena is aluminum, and on rainy days when the raindrops ping off the metal, it's my favorite sound in the world.

The back of the property is where Alex and Mrs. Caballero live. It's an adorable little house, with white paneled walls and a black gabled roof to match the aesthetic of the barn. Alex put in carriage lights and flower boxes under the windows with pink petunias for his mom, which led to us dubbing it "The Cottage."

Beside the barn is a wheelchair ramp that allows us to help our patients onto horseback more easily. As we walk back to the barn, a bay mare with long eyelashes named Jasmine, or Jazzy for short, pokes her head out of the stall, a low rumble in her throat. At first, I think the whinny is for me, and then Alex walks up and I realize Jazzy, like every other horse in the world, has a keen Alex radar. Of course he has treats in his pockets that he offers to Jazz. My heart squeezes at the sight of this man in my favorite place in the world—a place we created together.

"Good morning, Mila Kozak," Alex says, pulling me into a hug. I wrap my arms around him and snuggle into his chest as he kisses the top of my head. I wonder if this will ever get old, the feeling of Alex's solid chest beneath my cheek, his heart beating in time with mine. The way he says my name, like it's the most cherished phrase he's ever spoken.

"Good morning." I stand on tiptoe and kiss him briefly. If I had my druthers, it would be for *much* longer, but we have a busy day ahead of us and Anya is wheeling around the corner like her chair's on fire. Anya's straight, dark brown hair is flowing around her shoulders, her sky-blue eyes sparking with energy. A wheelchair cannot dampen my sister's raw beauty—even in the middle of the barn, she looks like she could be on a shoot for Vogue, with her sky-high cheekbones and naturally tinted lips.

The other thing that the wheelchair can't dampen in Anya: her razor-sharp focus.

"Break it up, children," she says with a wave of her hand—a gesture that still sends a thrill through me because a year ago, Anya couldn't move her hand at all. Anya's incredible recovery of movement in her arms is a constant reminder of why we're doing what we're doing at the Center. Coming here is an act of hope. A hope farm, if you will. "We've got a new patient coming in twenty."

Alex and I break apart, sharing a laugh because Anya rarely tolerates displays of affection—or anything she would consider a distraction. Being *unprofessional* is the ultimate insult.

"Tomás ready for the intake?" Alex asks as Harley nuzzles him for treats.

"He actually showed up on time today, unlike someone." Anya gives me a very pointed look.

"I was up super late finishing one of those lame online discussions for my International Finance class," I tell her. I'm in my penultimate semester of my online MBA program at the University of Florida, and I have to say, I'm *so* ready to be done with it. Now that the Center is up and running, trying to juggle grad school, my Center responsibilities, *and* competing on Cyrus—it's a tad much. Of course I'm not going to get much sympathy from my sister, because she's been doing pretty much the same thing (minus competing), except she graduated last semester at the top of her class.

Show-off.

Dad wanted us to 'diversify' our education, so Anya got her MBA from the University of Southern California—she claims she identifies as a California girl after her Stanford undergrad experience. I was thrilled to get into UF, though my dad's top choice was Indiana. I got waitlisted there and ultimately never heard back from them, but it's honestly for the best because I love being a Gator.

I untack Harley and put him in his stall, where he takes a deep drink from the automatic waterer in the corner. Most mornings, I exercise one or two of the horses before the day begins so that they're calm for our patients. Harley might get ridden a couple times today, but only at a walk, so we're both doing each other a favor by having a morning gallop. I stroke his neck and give his cheek a kiss, then head to the lounge area in the center of the barn.

It's a small but comfortable room with wood floors and sparse but cozy seating—most of our clientele are in wheelchairs so we don't need a ton of seats. There's a well-used coffee bar in a cute teal cart beside a stocked mini fridge and a side table with various brochures scattered across it. We recently put up a peg board with pictures of our patients with the horses and some notes and cards that people have written to us. Evenly spaced across the wall are pictures of horses, including one of Cyrus and me that Alex put up when we first built the barn.

Connected to the lounge are two offices—one for one-on-one therapy appointments and the other for Anya, Alex, and me to use when we actually get to sit down and do paperwork or answer emails. Occasionally we use it to complete our schoolwork if there's a lull in the day.

I make a cup of coffee for Anya and then myself, dumping in sugar and flavored creamer until it's practically white. Tomás, our only other full-time employee at the moment—the rest are volunteers or part-time, like our therapist—strolls into the lounge carrying a box of cinnamon streusel muffins. Tommy, as we affectionately call him, is Alex's younger cousin. He showed up at Alex's doorstep seemingly out of nowhere a few months ago, asking for a job. He didn't know much about horses, but he was a quick study and hardworking. He's basically our catchall employee—he helps with the horses, acts as an office assistant, and generally lends muscle when we need it. He's become an essential and pleasant part of our operation.

"Morning," he says, handing the box to Anya. She grabs a muffin, then hands me one and we touch muffins in a 'cheers' like we've done since we were kids.

"How you two don't have diabetes is beyond me," Alex says, shaking his head.

"Just wait thirty years," Tommy says with a coy smile.

"Don't worry, she'll drive him crazy before that," Anya cuts in. But Alex looks at me with a glimmer in his eyes that says he's not going anywhere. And just like that I'm feeling warm and tingly, not at all ready to work. It's been a year and a half of life with Alex, and each day is better than the one before it.

Tommy grabs a bottle of water and chugs it. I don't know anyone in the world with more energy than this guy. He's young and boyish looking, with jet-black hair and wide, brown eyes that I'm sure get him out of a lot of trouble. He walks on the balls of his feet like he's about to break into a sprint at any second, and he's always vibrating with energy and humor. In the months that he's been at the Center, I've come to adore him like the little brother I never had.

He grabs the new client paperwork and clipboard from the office. "Who should I get on the cross ties?"

"Well, let's chat with her first and see what she might need," I tell him, and Alex nods. When we first meet a new client, we like to get a sense of what they need, what their comfort level is with horses, and which of our six horses might be a good fit. Our newest volunteer, Ben, walks in to get himself a cup of coffee. He's a retired FBI agent, with the leathery brown skin of someone who's spent their retirement days outdoors. He's wearing a ViaTech hat to cover his bald head—he claims that for every day he worked in the Organized Crime division, he lost a hair. "After twenty-five years, it's shocking I have anything left," he'd told us.

Our barn cat, Gata, strolls into the lounge like she owns the place. Which, I suppose she does. Of course she goes straight to Alex, curling around his leg. Gata is our resident rat-catcher and she's proud of her prowess. She *does* keep the rats away in exchange for seemingly unending praise from Alex, who's currently speaking to her in Spanish with more affection than he speaks to me.

Anya fills Tommy and Ben in on the day's schedule and what their responsibilities will be. "We're expecting our new therapist, Luke Craig, today as well," she says. "Big day." Our previous therapist resigned after her maternity leave, so Alex had to scramble to find us a replacement while Anya and I were on our annual sister's trip. We haven't met him yet, but Alex has raved about him so much I can't imagine a better fit for the Center.

Anya and I eat our muffins and sip our coffee as the guys discuss a soccer match they watched last night. Anya and I pause, hovering over our coffee cups, when the barn begins to shake with resonating bass from outside. "What is that?" Anya snaps, and we all shuffle out of the barn to see a massive Ford F.350 Super Duty on wheels that might qualify as monster truck status. Blasting from the interior is "Hard Out Here For a Country Boy" by The Cadillac Three, the bass reverberating through my chest as the truck pulls up in front of us. The song cuts off just as the singer is elaborating how hard it is to drink cold beer and love a "hot girl." I glance over at Anya, who may as well have fire coming out of her ears.

"Alex, I swear, if that's our new therapist, I'm going to need a lobotomy," Anya says.

We're all holding our breath as the far side truck door opens, a ramp lowers to the ground, and a man in an aluminum manual wheelchair rolls around the back of the truck.

Our new therapist is wearing a snakeskin cowboy hat, a white button-down shirt with a bull's head bolo tie, jeans, and boots with silver tips. I expect to have to pick Anya's jaw off the ground, but that thing's clenched tighter than an alligator in a death roll.

"Should I schedule your lobotomy for Tuesday or Thursday?" I whisper to Anya.

Luke Craig rolls up to us, then tilts his hat and says, "Howdy, y'all." He's handsome in a quintessentially American boy kind of way, with blonde hair, blue eyes, and a smile that could be on a billboard. My first thought about Luke's appearance is that if he weren't decked out in the cowboy apparel, he'd be just Anya's type. "Didn't realize I had an audience. Would've turned the music up if I'd known," he says with a wink.

It's then that I notice his wheelchair is completely covered in all kinds of faded, peeling stickers. I squint to read one of them with a bucking bronco that says, "I do my own stunts." Yeah, definitely *not* Anya's type.

Anya turns to Alex, glaring flaming daggers at him before muttering, "I need a minute. Alone." And then she wheels off.

Once we've greeted Luke and offered him coffee, Alex sends him on a tour of the farm with Tommy and Ben so we can try to cool down Anya. She's quite literally fuming in our office, and I can practically see the smoke coming off of her as she rants about how unprofessional and vile this cowboy is. But then we hear the gravel driveway crunch outside.

"They're here," Anya says, referring to our new client. She hurries out of the office, wheeling down the ramp out of the lounge, and we file out behind her. In the parking lot, our white transport van with the ViaTech Equine logo is backing up to the barn. We purchased the van a couple months ago when we realized that quite a few of our clients didn't have transportation, especially in the days and weeks after their accident, or whatever other misfortune paralyzed them. Our driver, Nayan, opens the side door and lowers the ramp so that a girl in a wheelchair can exit the van.

"Welcome, Clara," Anya greets our new patient with a forced smile as she rolls down the ramp. She's pale with dark hair and young—eighteen, according to her file, though she looks much younger—and she's looking around at the barn in a wide-eyed, overwhelmed kind of way. Behind her, her mom is hopping out of the van and looks to be as shaken as her daughter. Our clients often arrive like this—jittery, devastated by the trauma they've just experienced, and in need of some TLC.

We escort the pair to the lounge, offer them drinks and muffins, and after a few adjustments to the chairs and wheelchairs so we can all see each other, we're settled and ready to talk.

Alex, in his tender way, asks about Clara's accident, which her mom tells us about through tear-filled eyes. Clara's just sort of staring straight ahead, her eyes glassy, as her mom, Isabella, details her daughter's car accident when she was hit by a drunk driver, the resulting crash damaged her spine at her S2 sacral vertebra. She is paralyzed from the hips down but is experiencing a lot of pain in her lower extremities despite the paralysis.

I glance at Alex during the conversation several times—knowing that his dad died in a car accident—and I wonder how he's feeling as Isabella talks. I'm sure he'd give his right arm to have his dad survive the accident and be in Clara's position. And yet, it's not a fate I'd wish on anyone.

In many ways, this is a key part of the therapy: just talking about the accident. So often, it's easy to get stuck at home and never address the trauma, just like Anya had done. Getting patients out of the house and talking about it is a huge start.

After Isabella is done telling us about the accident and their experiences so far, Anya tells her story and how equine-assisted therapy affected her.

"I saw your story on Instagram," Clara says, and it's the first time she's spoken. As part of our marketing efforts, we recorded Anya's story, along with footage of the barn and Anya on a horse, and paid for ads on social media.

"She wants to be able to move again, like you," Isabella confides, and the idea brings tears to my eyes. I suspect she's not the first client we've had that came here in hopes that they'd have a seemingly miraculous recovery of movement like Anya did. Of course, that's very rare and we haven't seen it happen since Anya, but it's a motivating factor for many people. However, once they're around the horses, our patients reap so many other benefits that it's worth it, even without the miracle. Anya tells Clara and Isabella this as kindly as possible, and Clara's jaw clenches.

Anya reaches out and puts her hand on Clara's. "I struggled for a long time after the accident. I basically stayed locked away in my room for a year. I didn't want to live anymore, but I couldn't do anything about it." Seeing Anya being vulnerable like this makes my heart swell—I know this is a sacrifice for her, and she does it for each and every one of our clients. She opens up her life for them, and I'm proud of her for doing that. "So, I'm proud of you for being here. You're miles ahead of where I was after my accident."

"Do you like horses, Clara?" I ask.

She's silent.

"She's a little...scared," her mom says after Clara doesn't answer.

"That's understandable," I say. "Horses are huge."

"You get scared too?" Clara mumbles.

I nod. "After Anya's accident, I was really scared. And sometimes I still am."

"But she fights to overcome that fear," Alex says, nodding at the picture of Cyrus and me on the wall jumping over a massive CDD Wealth oxer in the International Arena at the Winter Equestrian Festival last season. Clara and her mom glance over and admire the photo. "But don't worry, we won't make you do anything that crazy."

"Not yet, anyway," Anya says with a wink at Clara, and we all laugh.

"So, what goals do you have for yourself, either physically or mentally?" Alex asks, and Clara and her mom just stare at him as if he'd asked them what the square root of 51,389 is. "For example, some of our patients want help getting closer to acceptance of their new life, others need help with movement—they view this as an exercise class of sorts."

Isabella nods. "Acceptance, for sure."

As we talk more with Clara and her mom, my heart is so full because we make such a great team and we are really helping people. I smile at Alex, and he reaches over and squeezes my hand, and my heart is about to burst.

I love my job. And I love my man.

Since Clara is afraid of getting on a horse, we decide to just work on the ground with our miniature horse, Don Juan—named because he charms the socks off of everyone. He's a shaggy palomino with a ridiculously fluffy forelock that's often sticking up in all directions. Clara's demeanor instantly changes when we wheel her up to the cross ties. She's laughing as Don Juan sniffles her lap for treats.

"He's adorable," she croons.

"Good choice, Milly," Anya says, using my hated nickname to poke at me like only Anya can do. I roll my eyes at her and hand Clara a bag of treats for Don Juan. Once Isabella is sure that Clara will be okay, Anya takes her back to the office to talk through the most boring and annoying aspect of our business: insurance. Thankfully, Anya handles all of it. Because seriously, every time she starts talking to me about insurance, I swear I snooze off.

Another client arrives and Tommy goes to get them set up grooming another horse while Alex takes Luke to his office. I show Clara how to curry Don Juan and brush his coat. The nervous energy she was carrying with her when she first showed up starts to dissipate.

"Is he your boyfriend?" Clara asks as she works through the tangles in Don Juan's mane with a hairbrush.

"Alex? Yeah."

"He's cute." Her cheeks redden as she says it, and I hold back a laugh.

"Yeah, he is," I say proudly.

She's quiet for a while and I think she doesn't want to talk anymore when I barely hear her whisper, "I'll never have a boyfriend again." And then there's tears running down her cheeks and she crumples in her wheelchair.

"Oh, sweetheart." I rub her back, wishing Anya or Alex were here. They're so much better at this than I am. "It'll be alright. It's just really new right now."

"Easy for you to say, both of your legs work," she sobs.

I'm racking my brain for something, anything, to tell her, when I land on, "Anya dates, and she has less movement than you."

This stifles the sobs, and Clara looks up at me with red eyes. "Really?" Anya is clearly already her idol—for good reason. What's the harm in exaggerating the truth a bit to help her out?

"Absolutely. She gets hit on all the time," I lie.

"She is really pretty." Clara sniffles.

"So are you." I smile at her, and she smiles back weakly.

"Thanks." She swipes at her cheeks with her hand and then goes back to grooming Don Juan.

"You know, one of the reasons we opened the Center is because horses are the best listeners." They really do offer the non-judgmental feedback that so many of our clients need. "So if there's anything you want to tell Don Juan, he'll be here to listen. I'll sit over there and give you guys some space so you can have some privacy."

Clara presses her lips together and nods. I walk a few feet away and take a seat next to a saddle rack. This is my tack cleaning station, where I give clients some space to pour their hearts out to the horses, but I'm still being productive and close enough to help if they need it. I grab a rag and rub saddle soap into the pommel of a saddle, and I smile when I hear Clara whispering to Don Juan.

That night, when Anya's gone home and I'm packing up to leave too, I overhear Alex and Luke chatting quietly in the lounge.

"Don't worry about Anya," Alex is saying. "She'll come around."

"She's a feisty one, ain't she?"

"She's very...diligent."

"That's one way of puttin' it," Luke chuckles. "But, hey, I can get behind it. In any other setting, I'd say she could spin my wheels if you know what I mean."

My jaw drops open, and I laugh silently. Knowing Alex, he's probably very flustered right now.

"I, uh, don't know what that means," Alex says, and I can practically see the redness in his cheeks with every word. "But you don't need to elaborate, man."

"Today was a good day," I say as I stretch out on the outdoor couch next to Alex. It's nighttime and we're sitting outside in our tranquility garden—a nod to the fountains and gazebos at Zen Elite, where Alex used to work and I've taken lessons for years.

Alex nuzzles into my hair and says, "Every day is a good day," and a thrill goes up my spine. Almost every Thursday, we study at Alex's cottage behind the Center, our books and computers spread out on the kitchen table while Mrs. Caballero cooks and listens to her *Nueva Trova Cubana* music. We just finished having dinner with his mom, and I'm full of arroz con pollo and fried plantains. After the first time she made that meal for us, Alex told her how much I loved it, and now she makes it almost every week. It's still my favorite. I look forward to these sprawling evenings when I get to be around Alex essentially from sunup to well after sundown.

As I look at him, the moonlight glinting off of his dark eyes, highlighting his strong jaw, a current of worry flows through me. In just four weeks' time, he'll have his final hearing for his immigration status. This will be the be-all and end-all for whether Alex can stay in the country or not. His lawyer, Ann, seems positive about it, but every time I think about it, I can't help but wonder *what if.* Of course, it's not something I bring up—for Alex's sake, I choose to be almost obnoxiously cheerful about the whole thing. So instead of talking about the hearing, about my worries and fears, about what he might be feeling, I force myself to bring up something else.

"How did it go with Luke?" I ask. After our initial meeting, our new therapist was busy with clients the rest of the day.

"Really good," Alex says as he twirls a lock of my hair around his finger. "He met with Clara and Santiago, and they both had good things to say about him." He pauses for a moment, glancing at the fountain before saying, "He's definitely a character."

"Can't imagine what would make you say that," I say sarcastically. I look up at him and he's so close, our lips could touch if I moved an inch. The fountain in front of us is trickling peacefully and a horse snorts in the barn behind us. Barn sounds. *My* barn sounds. I could stay here forever.

"One of his stickers says, 'Save a horse, ride a cowboy.'"

"Oh my gosh. Did Anya see that? She would have a stroke."

Alex sighs, rubbing his hand over his face. "She did, unfortunately. She was apoplectic. She gave him a thorough dressing-down after he met with Clara. You could hear her yelling from the covered arena. About how it's unprofessional, and how would a young girl like Clara feel about getting counseling from someone with that on his chair?"

"What did he say?"

"He said it's on the back of his wheelchair so Clara couldn't see it."

"Oh no."

"I think if Anya could walk, she would've grabbed his cowboy hat and thrown it down a well."

"I'm amazed she didn't fire him on the spot."

"I told her not to."

"Why's that?"

"He's really good. I sat in with him and Santiago for a bit, and I learned a lot. Also, he's got so much credibility with the patients since he's in a wheelchair too."

"Yeah, that makes sense."

"Not sure what to do about Anya, though." Alex's lips quirk into a small smile. "He made this comment today, about her, that I just..." he trails off, as if unsure how to describe it.

"Oh, I heard." I laugh, thinking back on Luke's comment about Anya *spinning his wheels*—whatever *that* means. "Can you imagine, Anya with Luke?"

Alex shakes his head. "Not in a hundred million years. I have a feeling we're going to have to do some damage control between them if he stays on."

"We'll just roll her into the closet when he shows up. Lock her in there for a bit." I imagine the feed room stocked with sensory bottles with mesmerizing colored glitter and a book with breathing techniques. "It'll be the calm down closet."

Alex laughs, and the sound makes me feel expansive inside. He traces a finger across my jaw line and says, "I love that you're learning Spanish to talk with my mom. It means the world to me." He tilts his forehead against mine, our noses grazing. "I just wish I could connect with your dad in some way."

"Well, learning Ukrainian is a lot harder than Spanish," I tease, but he doesn't laugh.

"You know what I mean." I do know what he means. The fact that my dad's first interaction with Alex was at the Broward Transitional Center last year when Alex was arrested on false charges didn't exactly set them up for a great relationship. Not to mention that my dad is insanely hard to please. Alex could be the male version of Mother Teresa mixed with Elon Musk and he would only be mildly perturbed he's dating his daughter.

"It's just going to take some time," I tell him, running my hands through the back of his buzz cut. Before he can respond that we've been together for a year and a half and isn't that enough time to prove Alex is a good guy, I say, "Alex?"

"Hmm?" He's looking at me with those dark, knowing eyes, and I wrap my arms around his neck.

"I don't want to talk anymore."

He leans down, brushing his nose against mine. "What do you want to do instead?"

"I think you know." I smile up at him.

A cool breeze whips past us and nips at my bare shoulders, and I shudder. Alex tugs me even closer to him, warming me in more ways than one. "Maybe I want to hear you say it," he says as he bends his head and plants a kiss on my shoulder, and I shiver again, but not from the cold.

"I want to kiss you, dummy," I say tartly and lean toward him to kiss him, but he pulls back.

"Not like that."

I arch an eyebrow at him as if to say, *You're really not going to kiss me?*

"If you ask nicely..."

I scoff and roll my eyes. "Can you kiss me already?"

His lips tilt into a smile, but he doesn't get any closer.

I groan. "Alex, would you *please* kiss me already?"

"There's the magic word," he says and finally angles his head toward me and brushes his lips against mine. I pull at him, wanting him to kiss me more deeply, but this is Alex and he's nothing if not patient. He kisses me leisurely, softly, and I'm a puddle in his hands by the time he leans away.

"I like you," he says, his eyes crinkling into a smile.

"Well, I more-than-like you," I tell him.

He kisses my cheek, and I feel the vibrations of a laugh rumbling in his chest.

I burrow next to him, tilting my head back to look up at the stars, and sigh. Today was a good day. And that's when I realize that with Alex every day really is a good day. My only hope is that after Alex's hearing next month, we can have a lifetime of good days together.

2

Enough?

Alex

It's a typical Tuesday morning as I walk beside a client, Hailey. Hailey came to the Center about six months ago after being diagnosed with Scheuermann's disease, a disc degenerative disease that is slowly causing her back to curve inward. She's riding Jet, one of our oldest and steadiest horses. "What's our goal for today?" I ask Hailey. Right now with our clients we focus on mental health goals, but I'm working on expanding to hippotherapy so that we can have a full-time physical therapist on staff to help with targeted physical goals on horseback.

"Acceptance," Hailey says. She's thirteen years old, her body on the cusp of being deformed by the debilitating disease.

"Acceptance of what?"

"My body," she says.

"Why do you think you should accept your body as it is? As it will be?"

Hailey stares down at Jet's mane, her fingers tangling in the horse's hair. "I don't know," she whispers.

I run a hand down Jet's shoulder. "Jet is an old horse. I don't know if you've noticed, but he has white whiskers and white hairs that are growing around his black hair. He has an old injury on his right cannon bone, on his leg, that makes him basically incapable of doing anything more than walk." I take a breath, glance at Hailey. "What do you think Jet should feel about those things?"

Hailey thinks for a moment, her body swaying gently with each stride Jet takes. "He might be sad about his hurt leg."

"Is it okay for Jet to be sad?"

"Yes?"

"Of course. It's okay to be sad, especially when things change and we're trying to get used to it."

Hailey nods, pressing her lips together. "He's still a good horse."

"He's a very good horse, and no amount of leg injuries or white hairs on his face will change that. Right?"

"Yeah."

"If that's true for Jet, can that be true for you too? That you are strong and beautiful no matter what your body decides to do?"

A smile flickers on the edges of her mouth and she says, "Yeah, I think so."

"I know so. And I want you to tell yourself that: I am strong and beautiful no matter what my body decides to do."

Hailey glances down at me, a skeptical brow raised. I give her an encouraging smile. "It's a positive affirmation, which helps our brains believe what our mouths are saying. You can convince yourself of this, or you can let yourself be convinced that it's untrue—but *you* can change your thinking. It's up to you," I tell her gently.

Hailey thinks about this for a moment and then nods. "I am strong and beautiful," she says quietly, looking down at Jet. "No matter what my body decides to do."

"That's right." I glance over at Luke, who's overseeing the session from the middle of the ring, and he gives me a slow nod. I was able to get the Center approved as part of my practicum for my degree. Since I'm still in the process of getting my degree, a licensed therapist has to oversee any sessions that I give. I'm grateful for Luke, but I can't wait to run my own sessions once I'm licensed. Assuming, of course, my court date goes well and I'm granted legal residency.

I watch as Hailey straightens as she repeats the affirmation, her chin rising and her eyes lifting as she starts to believe what she's saying. And it's these moments that make me fall in love with this place, this job, even more.

That evening, once all our clients and volunteers have trickled out of the barn, I take the time to do some planning for Mila's birthday in a few weeks. To say that I'm anxious about it is an understatement. Because how can I even come close to properly celebrating Mila's birthday? Not to mention that in recent years, Mila has spent a fair share of her birthdays with her ex, Michael. Doing absurdly expensive things like helicopter flights, dinner with a private chef on the balcony of the Ritz Carlton Residences, a catered dinner on a yacht.

How can I possibly measure up to that?

The short answer: I can't.

And it's a painful admission that I can't offer to Mila what Michael did. Not even close.

To make matters worse, I have the constant example of my dad in the back of my mind—the way he went above and beyond to provide for my mom. She never could work because of the severity of her epilepsy, but I'm not sure my dad would've wanted her to work even if she could. He was the Ultimate Provider, taking on the full burden of our family. It's hard to live up to his standard and I often wonder what he would think about how I'm carrying on his legacy.

Even with my regular paycheck from the Center, most of it goes toward taking care of my mom, paying for school, and, as of two weeks ago, replacing the transmission in my beat-up Honda Civic. So things are a little tight this month. Ultimate Provider I am not.

I'm sitting in the office, where Anya's also working at her desk. Mila went home to take an exam for her Corporate Finance class, so it's just the two of us when I spin around in my chair to ask Anya for her advice.

"Look, Alex, the best thing about you is that you aren't Michael." Her silver-blue eyes are almost expressionless, in an impassive look that only Anya can give.

"Uh..?" I'm not sure if this is a joke, or if she expects me to take this as a compliment.

"Don't try to go by his standard. It's not who you are."

"Thanks?"

"Just do something you think she'd like."

I want to say, *Gee, thanks, Anya.* But instead, I say, "Any particular ideas?" *That don't cost as much as my transmission, preferably.*

Anya thinks for a moment, and I can tell she comes up with a few ideas but immediately writes them off—probably because I can't afford them. "She loves dancing with you," she finally says.

"Dancing. Right." We go dancing all the time, though. What would make this time different from any other time? I groan and hang my head in my hands.

"Hey, chin up, Caballero," Anya says. "Mila loves you. Just trust that."

I spend a fair share of the evening researching different places and events in the tri-county area and settle on dinner at the Strawberry Moon, Pharrell's new restaurant poolside at the Good Times Hotel. There's a DJ poolside so we can eat, dance, and swim—which seems like a fun combination. I just hope it's enough.

Two weeks later, things are *really* dire with my bank account. An unexpected MRI for my mom cost us $250, which means I can't take Mila to the Strawberry Moon. I can't even afford drinks there right now.

"I thought this was covered by insurance," I say to my mom, staring at the bill that's just arrived.

"It is. This is the co-pay," she says in Spanish.

I nod, trying to act like this is inconsequential, but inside I feel like someone just torched my lungs.

Meanwhile, Tomás is making a stack of peanut butter and jellies at our kitchen table. "Hey," he says. "I got an idea."

I set the bill down on the kitchen counter and level my gaze at my cousin, whose idea of a good time with a girl is making out in the back row of a movie theater. "What is it?"

"I know this girl. She teaches dance lessons."

"Mila doesn't need ballet lessons, Tomás."

"No, no, not like that. She teaches like salsa and merengue. To couples."

I perk up, because it does sound like something Mila would like. She's mentioned before that she wished she knew how to dance salsa with me. We've had a few impromptu lessons, but I know she'd love this. "Tell me more."

An hour later, I've booked a private lesson with Tomás's friend, Camilla, for free. I can't be one hundred percent sure why she'd do me such a favor, but based on the flirtatious way she laughed at everything Tomás said when we chatted with her over speakerphone, I have a feeling it has something to do with movie theater make-out sessions with my cousin.

My mom agreed to help me make a nice dinner for Mila's birthday so between that and the salsa lesson, I start to feel a little better about her birthday.

On Mila's actual birthday, we go out with her whole family to dinner at Chanson Restaurant on Deerfield Beach. She and I will celebrate next week after Thanksgiving since she's going out of town. Tonight, we're all dressed in our most uncomfortable clothes—Mila's tottering on the highest heels I've ever seen. The Kozak women are all gushing over each other's dresses—the flutter sleeves, the bodice, that ruching—things I've never thought of in my life. Mr. Kozak and I eye each other, he in his sport coat and me in the navy-blue suit he purchased for me when I got into grad school. It wasn't so much of a gift for me as it was a gift for him—helping me get more up-to-par if I was going to run around with the Kozaks.

"Nice coat, sir," I say, since apparently we're at the point of the evening where we all compliment each other's clothing. He pulls at his sleeves, displaying his cuff links. Then he looks me over head to toe and gives a nod.

Conversation over, I guess. I sigh, wishing Mr. Kozak would give me something to work with. Anything.

We're ushered to our table, walking under an aquarium installed in the ceiling filled with colorful coral and exotic fish. I always feel a little like a fish out of water in places like this with Mila. I have the beginnings of a migraine forming, an aching throb beneath my skull. Despite it being November, it was as hot as summer today at the barn and I know I'm dehydrated. When the waitress brings us water, I try to drink as much as possible without looking gauche.

The table seats six people, though we only have five in our party. When the hostess goes to remove one of the seats, Mr. Kozak stops her. "Leave it, please," he says.

Mila leans over, her soft floral perfume wrapping around me as she explains, "We often leave an open seat during special occasions. It's supposed to welcome any unexpected guests or departed spirits." She says this last phrase with air quotes. "Though Anya and I have always said *Tato* would have an aneurysm if an 'unexpected guest' actually joined us."

"I can see where Anya gets her rigidity from," I whisper in Mila's ear.

"Don't you dare say that to her," she says with a conspiratorial smile. I mime zipping my lips and Mila laughs, the sound making me more at ease.

Mr. Kozak reserved the Chef's introduction menu, so plates appear without us ordering anything. We eat shrimp, lobster, and some kind of red meat I didn't catch the name of and probably couldn't pronounce if I did. All the while, Mila's family is making comments about the food that sound like they were ripped from an episode of *Master Chef*:

"The balance of flavors is impeccable." "Very thoughtfully plated." "Such an innovative use of ingredients. I never would've thought to pair this with pears."

It feels insubstantial for me to say, "This is really good." This isn't my first time out to dinner with Mila's family, so I had a few comments in my back pocket, including, "I love the use of seasonal ingredients," which, to be honest, I don't even know if the chef used seasonal ingredients. But Mrs. Kozak hmms and says, "So true," so I think it's a solid comment.

By the time dessert comes around—a deconstructed s'mores that I know Mila will devour in one breath—my headache has faded slightly, but not enough for me to partake in the champagne Mr. Kozak ordered. Champagne has always given me a migraine, and I'm not willing to risk the drink when I already have one forming.

So when Mr. Kozak raises his glass to toast Mila, I lift my water glass. He says the toast in Ukrainian, so I have no clue what he's saying, but when everyone goes to clink glasses, I make my rounds with my water glass. When I get to Mr. Kozak, he withdraws, saying, "It's bad luck to toast with a water glass," and doesn't touch glasses with mine.

I freeze, my glass still raised in his direction. I vacillate between shame that I didn't know that and anger that he would be so exacting with me.

"Anton," Mrs. Kozak chides him under her breath, but Mr. Kozak replies to her in Ukrainian, and I sit there like a child chastened.

Mila squeezes my knee under the table. "My dad is weirdly superstitious," she says as I set down my water glass, glancing at the empty chair next to Mrs. Kozak.

I nod, trying to convince myself that Mr. Kozak's rudeness has to do with his superstitions—and not with me not being good enough for his daughter.

3

A Not-So-Perfect Day

Anya

If I told you I love my life, I wouldn't be lying. I get to work with my sister/best friend doing something meaningful. I have an amazing family who loves me and supports me so much. And every day I get to be around horses. What more could I ask for?

I remind myself of that when I momentarily forget my paralysis and go to stand up, and I can't. Or when I get the urge to be on Cyrus—or any horse for that matter—and just take off. Gallop through a field. Jump over an obstacle—any obstacle. A freaking crossrail would be thrilling.

But then I get to talk with someone like Clara and make a real difference in her life, and it puts things into perspective. Two and a half years ago, I was wasting my life away. But now, because of Mila and Alex, I have so much to live for. And I'm truly grateful.

I steer my electric wheelchair by Jet's stall and he nuzzles the top of my shoulder. Like his name implies, he's a jet-black gelding with no white markings on his whole body, except for the very tip of his muzzle. It looks like he'd dipped his nose in white paint. I sit quietly, petting his nose, soaking in his warmth and comfort. This is not something I would have done before the accident—I was never one to just sit and *be*. I was always too busy. But now, even with running the Center, I know I need these moments. They fill me up, they make me able to pour out to the patients that come here. *They* need me to take these moments. And Jet—like all of the horses at the barn, really—is happy to give them.

I'm toying with the soft skin around Jet's nostrils when I hear him. And all of the calm I'd been feeling a second ago goes out the window. He pulls up in his monstrosity of a truck, blasting some vile country song that most likely revolves around a barefoot girl in booty shorts. I try to take a deep breath, to tell myself that I'll be cordial with him, that

Alex loves him and thinks he's a great therapist so that really must mean something. But Luke Craig is not making it easy. It even irks me that he uses a manual wheelchair—as if the fact that he's incrementally more able-bodied than me is an affront. And now that he's taken off his ridiculous stickers, it's coated with sticker residue, which only serves to bother me more.

Jet nibbles lazily at my fingers, as if to remind me to keep stroking his nose. I give him a kiss and then buzz down the hallway, up the ramp into the lounge, and then into my office. It takes some maneuvering, but I get the door closed and I'm tempted to back my wheelchair against it so Luke can't come in, but I manage to remember I'm not twelve years old.

I'm reading over the benefits of an insurance company that covers equine-assisted therapy centers—we have existing insurance, but it's way too much money so I'm looking for a new one. There's a crashing sound outside the door, and then my office door is flung open and Luke comes cruising in. He's wearing his obnoxious cowboy hat, a plaid button-down which most definitely does *not* match his hat, a pair of faded jeans, and, of course, scuffed cowboy boots with silver tips. I zero in on one of the many stickers on his wheelchair that says, "Real cowboys don't take baths, they just dust off." He's grinning at me expectantly, and it takes everything in me not to roll my eyes at him.

If I want him to be professional, I need to be professional too. But he makes it so ridiculously hard.

"Mornin', darlin'."

I sigh and push my wheelchair back from my desk, unsure of where to start with him. *I'm not your darlin'? Can you please wear something befitting of a licensed therapist? Can you take even a third of your offensive stickers off of your chair?*

"Good morning, Mr. Craig." Of course he's one of those guys with two first names, and it just annoys me even more.

"You can call me Luke," he says with a wink, and I nearly hiss at him. How unprofessional can this guy get?

"How can I help you, Mr. Craig?" I fold my hands in my lap and arch a brow at him. I wait for his smile to fade, but it doesn't. Someone like Luke should have missing teeth, but his grin is frustratingly perfect. Ugh.

"Alex said the schedule for today would be on his desk." He glances around at our three desks as if trying to figure out which one is Alex's. He wheels toward the messy one: Mila's.

"It's that one." I point at Alex's desk, which is tidier than both mine and Mila's, much to my chagrin. The guy is fastidious to a fault, and I wonder if Mila's mess ever bothers him. Otherwise, they seem to be a near-perfect match, but I keep wondering when he's going to rub off on her.

Luke grabs the schedule off Alex's desk, takes a picture of it with his phone, which I'm ninety percent sure is a HIPAA violation, and wheels out.

"Thanks, darlin'."

"Mr. Craig?"

He turns his wheelchair to look at me. "Yeah?" His blue eyes are twinkling mischievously, and I clench my jaw.

"Let's keep things professional here. You can call me Anya or Miss Kozak, but not *darling*."

He nods, tipping his hat at me like we're in a freaking Western, and then says, "Yes, ma'am," and zooms away. As he's leaving, I notice another sticker that says, "If I can't wear my boots, I'm not going." I lean my head into my hands and groan.

How much longer do I have to let him stick around before Mila and Alex let me fire him? I need to get a target date ASAP.

I smile a little at the thought of firing him—shoving all of his unsuitabilities back in his smug, handsome face. The scene plays out in my mind in shocking detail. *You are vile, unprofessional, and careless. Your stickers alone make you incapable of being a mature human being, let alone a competent therapist.* I can't wait to wipe that nauseating grin off his face and watch him tuck tail and leave.

Take that, Luke Craig.

I spent the morning on the phone with several insurance companies and finally found one that will supply what we need at the lowest cost. The only problem? Our current insurance ends on November 30th and the new one won't start until December 3rd. I talk it over with Alex and Mila at lunchtime.

"We could just not have anyone get on a horse during that time? They could come and groom, but we won't get them on?" Mila suggests.

"It's only a few days. I'm sure that would be fine," Alex says.

"Alright, so you guys feel good about that?"

Alex and Mila nod and go back to their lunches.

"There's one more thing I want to discuss."

They glance up at me in expectation.

"Luke?" Mila guesses.

"What do we need to discuss?" Alex asks.

"How much you loooooove him? How you want to jump his bones every time he wheels around the corner?" Mila teases.

I roll my eyes, unable to come back with any sort of witty repartee because Luke really drives me crazy, and I can't think of anything but getting rid of him.

"When is his conditional period over?"

Alex shrugs. "We didn't set a date on it. I told him we'd test it out for six to eight weeks to see if he's a good fit."

"So, six weeks until I can fire him?"

Mila sits back in her seat, looking between Alex and me. We all agreed Alex would oversee the therapists, so this comes under his purview.

Alex takes a deep breath, his gaze steady on me like I'm a spooked horse that he's trying to figure out how to calm. And it just makes me even angrier.

"Do you guys not see how unprofessional he is? Blasting his music—"

"No one was here except us."

"Showing up in boots—"

"We're in a barn."

"He ate all the muffins—"

"Not a reason to fire him. Besides, that was Tommy, not Luke."

"Those reprehensible stickers!"

Alex nods. "Some of the stickers are out of line."

"Thank you!" I fling my hands in the air like I've finally made them see reason, but the way they're staring at me seems to indicate they think I've lost my mind.

"I can ask him to ditch the stickers, or at least the potentially offensive ones," Alex finally says.

"They're *all* offensive. The whole thing is offensive."

"Having stickers is offensive?" Mila says.

"You know what I mean."

"Yeah, I get it—he doesn't float your boat. But that doesn't mean we can't keep him around. He actually is a good fit for the Center, Anya," my sister says with such a measured tone that I feel like I'm being scolded.

"How, exactly, is that?"

"Well, for one, he's in a wheelchair, so he can relate to our clients on a level that very few others can."

"I'm in a wheelchair too." I'm aware at this point that I'm starting to sound dangerously close to a petulant child.

"Right, and that's why you're so great with the patients."

"But you're not a therapist," Mila reminds me.

"Second, he's a horse person too," Alex says. "Which you have to admit is very unique—a therapist who's in a wheelchair *and* a horse person at an equine-assisted therapy center? It's perfect."

Alex is making so much sense, it's infuriating. "Fine. I'll give him six weeks to prove to me that he's a good fit, but I need you to talk to him about the stickers. I want them gone by tomorrow." I know I'm kind of being a brat, but I also believe that I'm protecting our clients—especially the ones like Clara who could be put off by such inappropriate sayings.

Alex nods and takes a bite of his sandwich, but I notice how he and Mila make eye contact briefly, as if they think I'm being way over the top. Which I'm totally not. I just wish they could see that.

The days go by in a pleasant jumble, their pleasantness interrupted only by Luke's continued presence. But life goes on and the Center thrives despite his unprofessionalism. Alex insists that the clients love him, and so far, that's been true whenever I've asked. And I've given *plenty* of opportunities for people to tell me how much of a dud he is, but as of the two-week mark of Luke's employment at the Center, everyone loves him.

Everyone, that is, except yours truly.

No matter. I'm still counting down the days until his six-week mark, and I may or may not fantasize at night about the myriad ways I could fire him. It's become an obsession of mine. One night, I even ordered a mug on Etsy that says, "You're fired," with plans to write in permanent marker all over it the reasons for said firing. It wasn't my proudest moment, I'll admit, but it felt good ordering it, even though I'll probably never give it to him. Or the matching T-shirt.

On Tuesday, our resident jokester—the chestnut gelding, Harley—has escaped his stall again. The first night after we'd purchased him, he let himself *and* all of the other horses out of their stalls with a clever, albeit dangerous, trick with his very adroit nose. Since then, we've put an extra lock on his stall, but sometimes people forget to put it on, and Harley quickly makes his way toward freedom. I want to give the staff and volunteers a stern talking-to, but Mila has a different approach. She gathers everyone at Harley's stall and presents a sign on the outside of Harley's stall.

"When the sign is facing this way, it means the door is not double locked." She reveals the sign, which says, "I solemnly swear I am up to no good." "When you put the double lock on the door, you can flip the sign over to this side." It says, "Mischief Managed."

A few of our volunteers laugh and nod, but Ben goes, "I don't get it."

"It's a Harry Potter reference," Alex tells him.

"Ah." Ben nods. "My kids loved that stuff."

"So, if you see the side that says Harley's up to no good, make sure you put the lock on. Even if you weren't the one to put him away, this sign can alert all of us that Harley might make a run for it." Mila clips the extra lock on the stall door and flips the sign over. "Mischief managed."

I smile at my sister as everyone tells her, *good idea* or *love that sign*, but there's a small part of me that wishes that *I* could be the fun sister for once instead of the serious one. The broken one. The unhappy one. But then I shake my head and tell myself, *Someone has to be the serious one*. And I know that someone is me, and I'll happily play that role for Mila and the Center.

It's a Wednesday morning when Nayan, our Center van driver, drops me off. Typically, my mom brings me to the Center, but she had a doctor's appointment this morning, so I asked Nayan to pick me up. He's quiet and polite, which I appreciate so much more since bringing on Luke. It's a reminder to me that I'll never *not* be a part of a hiring ever again. Sure, when Alex told me that we had an applicant who was in a wheelchair *and* a horse person, it seemed perfect.

Wrong.

Nayan's helping me out of the van when I notice Luke next to his truck, with his shirt off. *Of course* his shirt is off because he'd gone a full twelve hours without doing anything unprofessional. Albeit, the twelve hours were at night when we weren't at the Center, but still. He was on a roll.

I can't help it; I wheel straight up to him. "Mr. Craig," I start to say, but then I catch a glimpse of his half-naked body and, well, I get a bit distracted. Because Luke is more ripped than he has any business being. Not just for a paraplegic, but for *any* man. I count at least an 8-pack, but to be honest, my brain isn't working that well right now, so I may have miscounted. His extremely well-defined chest muscles are covered in just enough hair to make him look manly, but not so much that he would give the impression of an ape.

Much to my chagrin.

Then my eyes make their way back up to Luke's face, where they should have been all along, only to find him grinning at me with all the confidence of a Triple Crown stallion.

"Did you want something?" he says, and I don't know if he intended for it to sound like innuendo or if that's just where my head is at right now, but I gape at him for a second before remembering myself.

"Why on earth are you missing your shirt?"

"Lil' Vicky drenched me while hosing down Harley. Thought you might construe that as *unprofessional* if I went around with my shirt all wet."

I force myself to keep my gaze directed at Luke's eyes and not a millimeter lower. "Put your shirt on, Mr. Craig," I say through clenched teeth.

"I will, Miss Kozak, as long as you're done admiring the view." And then he has the audacity to wink at me. The presumptuous jerk.

"You wish." I roll my eyes—something I'm becoming quite adept at thanks to Luke—but I can feel my cheeks flushing despite all my best efforts. Before I can get caught up any further, I turn my wheelchair and speed toward the barn. I hear him chuckling behind me, and it kicks up equal measures fury and embarrassment. Because one thing is for sure, I definitely was admiring the view. If only for a moment.

In our morning debriefing on November 30th, we all decide it is Clara's day to get on a horse. Ben has brought in a box of chocolate croissants, and I'm picking mine apart while Mila bites into hers whole.

"She's ready," says Luke, whom I would invariably disagree with, but today, I don't. Clara's ready. "It's important for her to overcome her fears. Let's be supportive and positive. Anya, what if we put you on a horse too? That might help Clara."

"That's a really good idea," Alex says, and I'm beginning to think Alex is in love with Luke.

"Yeah, okay."

"We could have you on Rainbow and Clara on Jet?" Mila suggests.

"What about Coney?" Luke asks. "She loves him."

"Coney's mainly for grooming. He's got pony brain."

Luke looks unconvinced. "I'm just telling you, she's gonna ask about riding Coney."

"I got it," I tell him. "You do your job and let me do mine."

He gives me a little salute that feels vaguely patronizing. "I'm here when you need me."

I look toward Alex and tell him, "If Clara hesitates, you should talk to her."

"She likes you," Mila confirms.

"Just bat those long lashes at her," I tease, a long-standing joke between Alex and me that always serves to embarrass him. "She'll do whatever you say."

Alex sighs and shakes his head. "I'll never understand your obsession with my eyelashes."

"Honestly, it's rooted in a deep jealousy because you're a guy and you don't even need them," I say. "So if they're not going to be mine, they might as well be useful."

Tommy cackles, elbowing Alex. "Use those lashes, bro."

Alex, who's flushing at the attention, leans toward Mila, batting his eyes ridiculously. "Is it working?" he jokes. "Are you under my spell now?"

Mila laughs, smacking him on the chest. "I'll ride any horse you want, Mr. Caballero."

"It's not working," Alex deadpans. "She was like that already."

We all laugh, and it makes me happy that Alex is loosening up enough to joke with all of us. Of course, he's still blushing from the attention, but I find it endearing—and clearly so does Mila, because she's looking at him all gaga, and I don't know whether to smile or gag.

"Hey Ben, what are these wires all about?" I ask, wanting to change the subject as I gesture to the wires hanging off of him, wrapping around from his back into his pocket.

"Oh, it's a TENS unit," he says, pulling out the device in his pocket. "Helps my bad back." He explains how the electrical stimulation works, and even puts one of the electrodes on Alex, who squirms like a horse getting clipped for the first time.

"How do you wear that?" Alex says, handing the electrodes back to Ben.

"You get used to it after a while," Ben says with a smile.

"Have you ever tried a TENS unit?" Luke asks me, and I shake my head.

"You should, it might help."

I want to ask him what it'll help with, but we hear Clara pulling up. When she rolls into the lounge, I'm struck by how calm she is, especially in comparison to the bundle of nerves she was the first day.

"Ready to ride today?" I ask her, and just like that, the facade crumbles. Her brown eyes go wide and her already pale face gets even paler. "It's okay, I'm riding with you. It'll be fun. You'll see."

"Can I groom Coney first?"

"Of course. C'mon."

We roll up to the crossties—me in my electric wheelchair and Clara in her hospital-issue one, with her mom pushing her along. Last week we helped her pick out an electric wheelchair as well as assisted in navigating some of the insurance potholes with it. I'm beginning to wonder if I should've gotten an advanced degree in medical insurance—if there even is such a thing. When we first opened the Center, my mom was extremely helpful in learning the ropes, since she had to figure it all out after my accident. It's such a difficult thing to do, on top of navigating a life-altering accident, so I'm happy that we offer help for people like Clara and Isabella and not just therapy.

"Hey, Tommy, can you grab Coney? We're going to do a little grooming before Clara gets on a horse."

"Whaaaat? Getting to ride? That's awesome, man," Tommy says, acting as if he didn't already know she was going to ride today, as he fake punches Clara's shoulder and runs off to get Coney.

Another client, Patty, a 60-something-year-old stroke victim, is grooming Harley with one of our volunteers, Sara. "Don't forget to use your other hand too," Sara gently reminds her. Patty puts the curry comb in her other hand, which has had a hard time gripping since her stroke, and clumsily circles it on the horse's coat.

Tommy's back with Coney, and Clara's crooning over him as she brushes out his mane and then his tail. Coney is a piebald pony with a very long mane that our clients often like to braid, so his mane is typical crimped. He has a wide, inviting face with one blue eye and one brown eye. Our cousin's toddler was around when we first brought him to the Center and we made the—very poor in hindsight—decision to let him name the horse. So he named him Coney, rhymes with pony. That's what happens when you let a two-year-old name an animal. I suppose it could be worse—he could be named Fartbreather or Bubbawubbanubba.

Clara's mom is standing back, watching with a smile as Clara brushes Coney's tail.

"I can't believe how much this has improved her mood."

I smile back at her. "Trust me, I can."

It's moments like this one that makes me so grateful to be here—to have a purpose, to be alive for a reason that isn't just to watch the next episode of *Love is Blind*. It's taken a while since my accident to get to a place of resolve, but here I am, living for something other than myself. And it feels so good.

Clara finishes grooming Coney, and Mila comes to give her the safety debriefing. She shows her the saddle with its special features and safety straps, tells her how she's going to get on, that Tommy and Mila will walk beside her the whole time with Alex at the helm holding Jet.

"Sometimes, when people get on a horse for the first time, they can get anxious. That's normal. It's an opportunity to practice some of that deep breathing and visualizations you've been working on with Luke. Imagine your stress as water droplets coming off of you and dripping onto the horse. Imagine him absorbing—"

"Can I ride Coney instead?" Clara asks, cutting off Mila.

"Coney's not the best for your first ride—"

"But I don't want to ride Jet. I want to ride Coney."

"I understand, Clara. Coney is super cute and sweet, but believe me that Jet is the one you want to be on for your first ride. He's our best horse, he'll take good care—"

"I'm not going to ride unless I can ride Coney."

I can tell Clara is stretching Mila's patience. I watch as my sister grits her teeth and takes a deep breath. "Can you excuse me for one second, Clara?" Mila walks up to Alex and they're whispering to each other. Alex squeezes her shoulders, and it's clear he's calming her down. Then he walks up to Clara, kneels down so he's about eye level with her, and starts talking to her in his Alex way.

"Hey Clara, can you tell me what's going on?"

"I want to ride Coney, but they're not letting me."

"I see. So you're feeling frustrated because you want to ride a horse that you really like, but it's not an option?"

Clara nods.

"I get why that would be frustrating. I would be disappointed if I were excited to ride a certain horse and then I couldn't. How about this? Today I'll give you the choice between riding Jet or Harley,"—he gestures over his shoulder at the chestnut gelding on the crossties—"and if it goes well and you feel comfortable, we'll consider putting you on Coney. How does that sound?"

Clara nods again and Alex gives her a charming smile, which brings a deep blush to Clara's pale cheeks.

He didn't have to bat his lashes, but Alex sure knows how to talk to a girl, that's for sure. Of course, he'd cringe if I ever said that out loud.

Clara decides to ride Harley today, so Tommy gets me situated on Jet. While Clara watches, I roll up the wheelchair ramp as Ben holds Jet. I put my arms around Tommy, and he lifts me onto Jet while Mila arranges my legs from behind. It's a far cry from the first time Alex and Mila tried to get me on a horse, and for that I'm grateful. They put my boots into the stirrups and strap me onto the saddle. Tommy hands me a dressage whip, which allows me to tap Jet into a walk while I steer him. I do a lap around the wheelchair ramp to show Clara how safe it is, then I stop Jet and wait for Clara to get on.

Isabella is holding her phone to her ear and says, "She's about to get on now, honey. I'll call you back after." And then she hangs up.

Tommy is holding Harley while Alex wheels Clara up the ramp. He picks her up the same way that Tommy did with me, and Mila flips her right leg over the saddle. Ben is on the ground on the other side, one hand on Clara's leg and the other on Harley's rump—which strikes me as odd, as if he's stabilizing himself on Harley. I make a mental note to talk with Ben about it later. Alex is trying to straighten Clara in the saddle while Mila rolls Clara's wheelchair to the side of the ramp.

"I don't like this," Clara says suddenly. "I don't like this!" She's shrieking, and Harley flicks his ears back, completely in tune with her fear. He raises his head, nostrils flaring with anxiety, body punching up like he's about to bolt.

"It's okay," Alex soothes, but Clara's crouching awkwardly away from Alex, as if she's going to throw herself off the horse.

"She wants to get off," Isabella is saying, her voice rising as well.

"It's okay," I tell her, but I'm concerned. I've never seen Harley—an otherwise unflappable horse—so agitated. And I can't figure out why.

And then, it all goes south.

Harley has his ears pinned back, prancing in place while Clara is clutching his neck and screaming. Alex is reaching over to grab Clara off the horse, but then seemingly out of nowhere, a huge dog runs toward Harley, barking. Harley spooks, and he tries to take off. Tommy is holding him, so he only takes a few steps, but then he shies to the right, stepping into Ben, who falls over.

Harley, in an attempt to avoid stepping on Ben, kicks up his hind legs. Alex, who was leaning over the wheelchair ramp to hold onto Clara, is balancing precariously as he tries to keep a grip on her. Clara is screaming bloody murder, Isabella is wailing like a banshee and running over to Harley, flapping her hands wildly, which is definitely not helping, as the dog continues to nip at Harley's heels, barking. Harley's eyes are so wide with fear, I can see his whites. Mila jumps down from the wheelchair ramp to try to stabilize Clara from the ground, but this only spooks Harley even more. Isabella's voice is rising, adding to the hysteria, while Clara continues to shriek.

I'm watching, clinging helplessly to Jet, as Clara pitches forward and goes flying head-first into the ground.

4

The Moment You Know...

Mila

"My baby! My baby!" Isabella is screeching as she clutches her daughter's helmeted head. After the fall, I jump into go-mode. I'm not thinking, not feeling—just acting. I tell Tommy to call 911, hand Harley to Alex, send Ben to get the wild dog under control, as I kneel by Clara.

"You shouldn't move her," I say as Isabella rocks Clara's unconscious head back and forth.

"She's dead! She's dead!"

Her words slice through me, but I reach out a tentative hand and press it to Clara's wrist, where I feel a definite pulse. "She's not dead, she's unconscious."

Tommy is talking to a 911 dispatcher, telling them what happened and where we are. Anya sent another volunteer, Sara, inside to get a neck brace and first aid kit so she's still on Jet, pacing around the wheelchair ramp as Isabella and I stare at Clara. Amazingly, Ben gets the dog to calm down pretty quickly—at least one thing is going right.

Isabella is absolutely hysterical, sobbing and wailing over her daughter. I know she shouldn't be moving Clara's head around so much in case she has a neck injury, but Isabella doesn't seem to be hearing anything I'm saying. A flurry of panic comes over me, but I shove it down so I can focus on what's happening.

Then all of a sudden, she turns on me and starts spewing all kinds of things: "This is your fault! If you and your boyfriend hadn't forced her onto that beast, she wouldn't be dead! We never should have come here. We never should have watched that manipulative, fake ad. You are liars. You are thieves. You stole my daughter from me!"

"Isabella, she's alive." I place a hand on her shoulder, trying to get her to listen to me. "Please stop moving her head; she could have a neck injury."

"Don't talk to me!" she shrieks, shoving my hand off of her. "Don't you ever, ever talk to me again."

Sara finally returns with the brace, which she gingerly places around Clara's neck even as Isabella continues to rail on us. She calls down every curse I've ever heard, and some I haven't. Thankfully Luke comes out and starts trying to talk her down, and that's my cue to get out of here and help Anya off of her horse.

Sara holds Jet while Tommy and I get Anya down. She's physically shaking as we lower her into her wheelchair. We stand on the wheelchair ramp, and I'm gripping her hand so hard that I'm certain I'm going to lose feeling in my fingers any minute. Finally, we hear the sound of the ambulance as it speeds down Griffin and turns onto the barn driveway. Alex rejoins us, one hand on my back and the other on Anya's wheelchair, seemingly holding us together.

We watch in silence as the paramedics load Clara onto a stretcher. The whole thing is surreal, like I'm watching a movie instead of real life. Isabella's crying has lessened since Luke started talking to her, and now that the paramedics are here, she's in a stony silence as Alex explains what happened.

Isabella climbs into the back of the ambulance. They shut the doors and take off. That's when Anya and I start to cry. I turn to my sister to hug her, and we just sob. My mind is filled of images of Anya on a stretcher, Anya being loaded into an ambulance, Anya in a hospital bed, unmoving. I weep for Anya, for Clara, for Isabella.

Alex wraps his arms around both of us. He knows we're crying for Clara, but also so much more than that. We're sobbing for the pain of this life. We're mourning the moments that snap your life in half, when you'll never be the same again.

5

Stuck

Anya

We decided someone should go to the hospital, so I volunteer. I don't mind doing the hard-to-face things for the Center—like insurance and difficult moments like this—because I know Alex and Mila would hate it, but also because the Center has given so much to me, and I want to give everything back to it. And, of course, my favorite person in the world offers to come with me, and Alex and Mila think it's a great idea. So that's how I end up in the Center van with Luke. Nayan drives us, all of us sitting in silence, which is perfectly fine with me.

I find myself wanting to blame someone, anyone, for what happened.

Was it Mila's fault for putting her on Harley? But no, she hadn't chosen Harley for Clara—she'd chosen Jet. And Alex had given Clara the option to ride either horse. So was it Alex's fault? All of our horses are incredibly safe horses, so theoretically, Clara should've been fine on any of them. Was it Ben's fault for falling? Clara's for screaming? Isabella's fault for her hysteria? I wish I had an inside view into Harley's brain, to see what he was thinking and feeling. Our horses are bomb-proof—a screaming girl clutching Harley's neck and even a dog yapping at his heels shouldn't have made him quite so spooked, but horses are living beings and therefore hard to predict. He could've been having an off day, but still, something about it doesn't sit right with me.

No matter how I look at it, I can't truly place blame with anyone. It was a freak accident. Something that couldn't be replicated if we tried a thousand times. And yet, it had happened.

I groan and put my head in my hands as I think about what an insurance nightmare this will be. Of course it happened on the last day of our previous insurance coverage. That shouldn't affect anything, should it?

When I look up, Luke is staring at me, and I immediately sit up and look out the window. Why do I have to do this with *him*?

Oh yeah, *Mila*.

It was clear Isabella was most pissed with Mila and Alex. But Luke—who hadn't been there and thereby forfeited whatever blame could be put on him—seemed to have a calming presence before the ambulance showed up. In theory it was a good idea.

Key phrase: in theory.

"Any chance this isn't going to be a disaster?" I mutter.

"Not lookin' good with that perspective."

I roll my eyes, which makes me think that Luke probably knows the whites of my eyes better than anyone else and I've only known him for two weeks.

"Let's go in there channeling peace and empathy." He raises a brow and tilts his head at me. "You do know what empathy is, right?"

"Empathy, empathy," I say, drumming my fingers on my lips. "Is that, like, what you're doing right now?"

"Touché, Miss Kozak. Touché."

An hour later, despite channeling all of our peace and empathy, Luke and I were kicked out of the hospital and threatened with a lawsuit by Clara's very indignant father. We hadn't even made it past the front desk before he met us with his furious coal-black eyes.

"Well, that went well," Luke says as Nayan clips our wheelchairs into place.

"That's a relief," Nayan says.

"It did not go well, Nayan. In fact, it went very badly," I say through gritted teeth. Nayan looks from me to Luke, and the two of them make eye contact and a glance passes between them that seems to imply that I'm being unreasonable. It's enough to make me want to punch the seat in front of me, but instead I fist my hands in my lap and take a deep, shaking breath.

I don't speak the rest of the drive back to the Center, and thankfully neither of the guys try to make me break my silence. I'm outwardly fuming, but really, I'm terrified. What will happen if they sue us? Can they truly make a claim of wrongdoing? Everyone who comes to the Center knows there is inherent risk in working with horses, and of course we discuss that with them and make them sign waivers, but could Clara and Isabella claim negligence on our part? I'm just not sure.

Back at the Center, we gather Alex and Mila and tell them what happened.

"The moment we walked in, some guy we think is Clara's dad started pointing and yelling at us, 'They did this! They did this to her!' And then all these nurses and med techs were yelling too. We backed out of there but not quick enough, because Clara's dad physically shoved Luke's wheelchair out of the hospital."

Mila and Alex are staring at me, ashen faced and quiet. My sister's arms are crossed, holding tight against her chest, but I notice that the tips of her fingers are brushing against Alex's arm. He shifts to hold her hand, and there's something about that that makes me both happy for Mila while simultaneously making me feel utterly alone.

"He's threatening to sue."

"Can he do that?"

"He can certainly try," Luke says.

"What are we going to do?" Mila whispers.

"We should talk to a lawyer. Dad will know one."

Everyone nods at that, and we just sit around staring at the floor for a long time.

"We should talk to the volunteers and clients who were there, who saw what happened. Make sure they're okay," Alex says.

"That's a good idea." Luke presses his wheelchair forward. "I'll go with you."

The two of them leave the lounge and Mila and I are left behind, not saying anything. We sit in silence until Mila leans forward and plucks something out of the trash. "What is this?" she says, holding up what looks like a large sticker with horse hair stuck to it. I lean in, examining it.

"Oh, it's an electrode from Ben's tens unit."

"Why's it got horse hair on it?" she says, looking at the chestnut brown hair plastered on the sticky side of the electrode.

I shrug. "Maybe it fell on the ground or something." Mila looks at it for a second more and then puts it back in the trash, sighing.

After a while, Mila gets out of her seat, kneels in front of me and puts her head in my lap. I stroke her tangled hair and all the loneliness I was feeling a minute ago dissipates. Today was a disaster, but at least I have my sister. At least we get to go through this together.

"I love you, *sestra*," I tell her in our native tongue.

"*Ya tebya looblu, Anochka.*"

That night, when Mila and I get home, my mom is serving up some overcooked, store-bought meatloaf while my dad's on the phone on the patio. I think that my mom started buying meatloaf because she thought that's what you eat in America. I've personally never seen anyone in the States voluntarily eat it, and certainly never heard anyone claim it's their favorite food. Mila says she's not hungry and escapes upstairs to take a shower. My mom is cheerful and overly chatty as she sits down beside me.

"Karen is about ready to pop," she's telling me about her pregnant co-worker. "But she's using it as an excuse to pass off her difficult patients on me. Heck, when I was pregnant with you, I was working the ER at night and let me tell you, nobody was picking up the slack for me there."

What she's saying makes it seem like she's complaining, but she's got a huge smile on her face, and I know she's so happy to be back at work. She starts in on a story about one of her patients when she stops herself.

"Are you okay?"

I shrug, trying to pretend like today didn't shake me to my core. Because if I say it out loud, then it's true. "I'm fine."

My mom raises an eyebrow and gives me a look that says, *I know you're not fine*. I sigh, but don't say anything.

"Sweetheart," she says, taking my hand. "You don't have to have your walls up *all* the time, you know. You can let them fall with me."

I want to say, *I'd rather not*, but instead, I squeeze my mom's hand and say, "Thanks, Mom. I'll let you know when I'm ready to talk about it." I sigh and gesture toward the meatloaf. "I'll take up a plate for Mila."

I grab some food for my sister and wheel away from the table toward the stairs. My new chair, the BRO by Scewo, is nothing short of magic. My dad bought it for me from a Swiss wheelchair company when we started the Center so I could get around on my own more easily. This power wheelchair can climb stairs, has sensors to tell what kind of terrain it's dealing with, and has a seat slider to help me transition to the bed or a stationary chair (or toilet). I back the chair up to the stairs and with a click of a button on the control panel, the chair's tracks lower and start to click up the stairs. It's still thrilling to me to have this much independence—I'm going up the freaking stairs *by myself.*

My mom follows me and helps me get ready for bed—she assists me onto the toilet and helps me get changed. Thankfully, I can brush my teeth on my own now, but I still need her help to bathe and go to the bathroom. It's a long-term goal of mine to work up to being able to do that myself, but I'll need a lot more strength in my arms than I currently have. I'm not even sure it's possible, but I'm learning that hope is the best medicine.

I wish I had hope about Clara's fall—that she'll be okay, that it won't have any implications for the well-being of the Center—but right now, I don't. I just keep seeing her dad's face as he shoved Luke out of the hospital, and it's that image that has me up all night long, tossing and turning.

The next few days at the Center, we keep all our patients on the ground and stick to grooming. A few of our younger patients are sad, but the older ones understand the insurance dilemma.

On Wednesday, Luke brings in lunch for all of us, which I begrudgingly accept. I anticipated he would bring something like Sonny's barbeque or Domino's pizza, but instead he has vegan food delivered from a restaurant called Fresh First. I'm not really sure who he's trying to prove himself to, but even his thoughtfulness irks me.

I'm eating my veggie quinoa bowl when Mila asks, "Are you a vegan, Luke?"

He finishes chewing a bite of his lentil burger and nods. "Don't get this figure for nothing," he says, then he turns his head and winks at me.

This guy.

I snort into my spoonful of quinoa, but Mila and Alex are nodding along like what he's saying is perfectly reasonable. I manage to grumble my thanks to Luke when he pulls out a bag of vegan chocolate chip cookies that are actually quite good.

After our lunch, Mila and Alex escape to the tranquility garden. I often find them there in between responsibilities, cuddled up and whispering to each other. And in the days since the fall, I've spotted them there more than usual. It makes me happy that my sister is so in love, but sometimes it's a little heartbreaking too. Don't get me wrong—I adore Mila and Alex, but being around them so much just highlights how alone I am. How alone I'll be forever. Because, who falls in love with a paraplegic? My own mother could barely take care of me, and she *birthed* me. What man is going to voluntarily choose to spend the rest of his life lugging me onto the toilet?

And since everything with Clara and her mom, my loneliness has only heightened. There's no one for me to whisper all of my worries to, no one to help me carry the weight of this burden. I mean, sure, I have Alex and Mila, but it's not the same. And they have each other—they don't need me in the same way I need them.

I'm so wrapped up in my woeful thoughts that I don't hear Luke wheel up beside me.

"It's nice to see when tragedy brings people together instead of apart. They're a good pair, ain't they?"

I have to agree with him on this, but I don't want to. I glance over at him, ready to see his priggish smile, but for once he's not looking smug. He looks almost...sad. It's such a reversal from his typical sanguine attitude that I nearly ask if he's okay. But I don't. We just sort of stare at each other for a while, until I realize he's waiting for a response from me.

"Yeah, they are."

"You got someone like that?"

His question flares up a whole range of emotions in me—from hurt to infuriated to annoyed. I want to tell him it's not professional to ask me that, I want to shove the question back at him. Instead, I just shake my head and stare at the toes of my Sperrys like they're the most interesting thing in the world.

"It's harder for us," he says knowingly. "Unless someone got stuck with you, it's hard to find love in a chair."

There's a beat of silence as I absorb how true this is, and how strange it is that he can relate with me on something. "Did someone get stuck with you?" I ask before I can stop myself.

I see the glimmer of a sad smile twisting his mouth. "Sure enough."

"That's nice," I say, but even I can hear the envy and surprise in my voice.

"The thing about the stuck ones," he says, "they can easily get un-stuck."

Before I can ask what he means, he dips his hat at me and rolls away. I'm left wondering if whoever got "stuck" with him left him because it was too hard, or if he was just too obnoxious. But mostly I'm taken aback by how we had the semblance of a reasonably deep conversation and I didn't sneer at him, not once.

6

Nacho Salsa

Alex

It's four thirty and I'm heading to my car to get Mila for her birthday celebration when I smell something. I clench my jaw and round the corner of the barn, following the scent. We didn't schedule any clients in the late afternoon, so Luke is gone, Anya's in the office, and Mila's at home getting ready. That just leaves one option...

Tomás.

Sure enough, I find my cousin sprawled on one of the outdoor couches in the tranquility garden, smoking a joint. Gata is curled up next to him as if there's not something illegal happening.

"Tomás!" He jolts up, the joint flying to the ground. Gata shoots off the couch and hurries back to the barn. Tomás gives me a glance and then scrambles to pick up the joint.

"You scared me, cuz."

"You should be scared. What are you doing?"

He looks around like he's trying to figure out what he's doing. When he doesn't respond, I take the joint out of his hand, throw it on the ground and smash it with the toe of my shoe.

He gasps. "Hey! That was a perfectly good spliff!"

I grab him by the collar and haul him to his feet. "And you're going to be out of a perfectly good job if you don't knock it off."

"Alright, alright, alright," he says as he trudges toward the barn. But I catch him checking the ground near my foot to see if the joint is still usable.

"Tomás." I level my gaze at him, and I wish I had more time to chastise him, but I'm going to be late if I don't leave now. "If I catch you doing that again, you're fired. Cousin or not." I lower my voice. "And if Anya smells you, she'll fire you right this second. So go get changed before she sees you."

Tomás gives me a two-fingered salute, which isn't exactly the reassurance I was hoping for, and heads back to the barn. I sigh and run a hand across my face. Tomás is a good kid, but sometimes he does dumb stuff like this, and I doubt whether I did the right thing in hiring him. I pick up the joint and throw it in a trashcan on my way to the car.

I'm on edge as I drive to Mila's house, alternating between my frustration with my cousin and my overwhelming feelings of ineptitude when it comes to giving Mila all that she deserves. Half the time I feel like I'm holding my breath, wondering when she'll figure out she's too good for me. And this birthday celebration is a perfect time for her to get the memo. *Please, God, don't let her figure it out. Not yet.*

We had decided beforehand not to bring up Clara's fall tonight—Mila wants to enjoy her birthday, without thinking about that. I decide it's probably best to not talk about what just happened with Tomás either. Or my upcoming court case. Tonight is about making Mila happy.

I pick up Mila just before five. She's dressed in a short, flowy dress that shows off her legs so much I can't think straight. What was I worried about? What was frustrating me? I have no idea, because there's Mila, looking at me like she's *mine*.

"I still have the tags on"—she gives me a bashful look—"in case you didn't like it." She does a spin, showing off her dress, but I'm looking at everything but the dress.

"If it's on you, I like it."

Her cheeks pink and she smiles up at me, compelling me to kiss her. Though I know this is a slippery slope—I could kiss her forever, so I restrain myself to a quick peck so that we can get to the beach on time for sunset. We get in the car and I put a hand on her unbearably smooth legs, making me immediately regret not kissing her for longer. She shifts in her seat so that her head is on my shoulder and my chest swells. It still feels surreal to me sometimes that I get to do this with Mila.

At the beach, I lay out a blanket and set out the food. We settle down, Mila tucking her long legs underneath her. I lay on my side next to her, sprawling my legs onto the sand as I serve us heaping plates of ropa vieja, white rice, and black beans.

"These are a nice touch," Mila says, picking up one of the flameless candles my mom bought at the Dollar Tree.

I nod and smile, not wanting Mila to realize just how much my mom helped me to pull off tonight. It's nowhere close to measuring up to one of Michael's birthday celebrations, and a wave of humiliation washes over me at the thought. I choke it down, trying to focus on the girl in front of me and not the stupid thoughts swirling through my head.

We dig into the food and I can't help but chuckle as I watch Mila shovel food as fast as she can. The girl is gorgeous, but she has the eating habits of a twenty-year-old frat guy.

"Oh my gosh I love your mom's plantains," she says, plopping one in her mouth with a satisfied noise.

"I helped," I mumble, feeling more and more pathetic by the second.

"Really?" She sounds surprised, and I'm trying not to be offended. "So you can cook *and* dance *and* you're a neat freak?"

"Can't tell you how heartwarming it is to hear your synthesis of my best qualities."

She laughs, the sound getting lost on the ocean breeze, as the wind blows her hair around her face. "I'm serious, Alex. I'm impressed. Marry me, now." She laughs again, tossing her hair over her shoulder.

But I'm stuck on her words. *Marry me, now.* She said them so casually, so nonchalantly. And of course, now I'm overanalyzing them. Was she being facetious? Could there be a hint of desire in there to actually marry me? It's so hard to tell with Mila sometimes, where her playfulness ends and reality begins.

Then I realize she's looking at me, searching my face, and her smile falters. "I'm kidding, Alex." She grips my shoulder. "I'll give you a few more years to decide if you want to spend the rest of your life with me."

Years?? I blink up at her, unable to form words. Why do I always find it so hard to articulate myself around Mila? I thought this would wear off the longer we're together, but sometimes I still find myself stumped.

"Oh! Look!" Mila jumps forward onto her knees, pointing at the ocean. I look over as a pod of dolphins just off the shore dips in and out of the water. It's beautiful, mesmerizing even, but I choose to watch Mila's face light up as she watches the dolphins. It's a better view by far, her eyes reflecting the setting sun, a smile on her pink lips. I let all of my worries slough off as she laughs with glee at the water, and I'm captivated by her. And in that moment, every piece of my heart wants to say, *I* would *marry you now, Mila*.

But of course, I don't, because it's obviously way too soon for that—for her, not for me. So I content myself with watching the breeze play with Mila's long waves, her hazel eyes dancing. For now.

After our beach picnic, we pack up and head to the dance studio on Las Olas Blvd. It takes a while to find parking, and I'm nervous we're going to be late, but when we walk up to the dance studio, the windows are dark and the sign on the front door says, 'closed.' We knock on the door, cupping our hands to look through the window, but seemingly no one is there.

"Let me call her." I dial the instructor, my heart skittering. The call goes to voicemail. I hang up and dial Tomás, but he doesn't pick up either.

"Maybe we got the time wrong?" Mila suggests as I stare woefully at my phone. I notice she says 'we,' as though to soften the blow that *I* could've gotten the time wrong. I don't respond, because I know I got the time right and this is somehow Tomás's fault. I dial my cousin again.

"Hey, cuz," he picks up the phone, smacking obnoxiously on food on the other end of the line.

I turn away from Mila and lower my voice. "I'm here at the studio and no one's here."

"Oh, uhh..." he trails off.

"Do you know how to get a hold of her? Did she say anything to you?"

"About that..." The guilt in his voice is evident and a frisson of anger runs up my spine.

"Tomás, what happened?"

"The thing is, me and Camilla parted ways. It wasn't...friendly."

I run a frustrated hand through my hair, not caring about my cousin's dating bungles at the moment. "Okay, but what does that mean for me and Mila?"

"Well, from what you're tellin' me, cuz, it means she's not doing us any favors."

"You gotta be kidding me, Tomás."

"Sorry, man."

I want to go off on him, to tell him how immature and selfish he is, but Mila's looking at me with a put-on patience, so I hang up.

"I'm sorry," I sigh. "Tomás screwed it up and she's not coming anymore. Probably revenge for whatever he did to her."

"It's okay, Alex." She puts a hand on my chest, and I get the distinct feeling she's trying to comfort me, when I'm the one letting her down. "We can always do this another time. Maybe with someone a bit more...reliable." She gives me a little smile at this, and I can tell she's trying to make light of the situation. But it all just makes me feel worse, because I couldn't even deliver on my *budget* version of her birthday celebration.

I'm racking my mind for what we could do next—I know there's a movie theater close by, but I'm trying to run the numbers in my head to see if I have enough for tickets and whatever Mila might want at the concession stand. And it's just too close and I couldn't stand it if my card got declined while ordering her popcorn and Snow Caps.

I stare down at her, my hand going to her soft waves, wrapping one around my finger. Looking in her eyes, I'm torn in two, because I want to give this girl the world, and all I have as my feeble offering is the man standing in front of her. And I wonder if that's enough.

7

Magical Mundane

Mila

I can tell Alex is mortified that the dance lesson plans fell through. He's embarrassed, and I wonder how much of this has to do with the fact that pictures of Michael and me on the helicopter from my birthday two years ago popped up on my Google photo memories when I was showing Alex a picture of something else. He hadn't said anything then, but the tension in his body was palpable. I'm flashing back to that moment while watching Alex mentally scrambling for what to do next.

I take his hand. "Let's just walk around and window shop," I say as brightly as possible. His other hand is in my hair, and I lean into it, the familiar weight of his palm caressing my cheek. I catch sight of an art gallery across the street and start tugging him in that direction. "C'mon, I've always wanted to go into this gallery."

We walk into MAC Art Gallery, a sleek and modern showroom with bright white walls and gleaming floors. Large canvases line the walls, lit up by overhead lights, and sculptures on pedestals dot the floors. Alex makes a wide berth around one of the sculptures, an orange glass orb speckled with blue. We walk silently around the gallery, until finally I admit, "I don't know anything about art."

"Well, that's alright because I'm an expert." He gives me a half-smile and I smack his arm playfully, relieved that he's relaxing a bit after the hitch in his plans. "I'll let you in on an art secret: the very best art is that which cannot be explained."

I laugh. "Ooookay, Mr. Art Expert."

"So if you look at a piece and say, 'I have no idea what that's supposed to be.' *That* is great art."

"Oooohhh, here I thought it was how complex the art was. I've always judged art this way: does it look like *I* could paint that? If not, it must be good."

Alex shakes his head, his expression sober, like he's disappointed in me. "See, this is why I'm the art expert."

He guides me over to a painting that is mostly black, with a white blob that looks a little like a melting popsicle. "Look at this. Do you see its meaning?"

I shake my head, but then quickly amend it by saying, "I think what it's saying is that it's hot in Florida. Like, *so* hot."

Alex's art expert facade cracks, and he laughs, but then quickly straightens his face and gives a deep sigh. "I am silently judging your artistic savvy."

"Or not-so-silently."

"Oh, no, I always do it silently. Or in passive aggressive comments that make you question your worth as a human."

I poke him in the ribs and he shies away from me, laughing. I pull him against me and kiss him until the sole employee in the gallery clears his throat loudly.

Alex pulls away and whispers in my ear. "I think he's silently judging our artistic savvy."

"Maybe we should get out of here before he starts up on the passive aggressive comments that make us question our worth as human beings."

Alex nods sagely and guides us out of the gallery, making sure to widely avoid the sculptures. Once we're out of the gallery, Alex tugs on me so that I'm pressed to his chest. "Now, where were we?" he says before kissing me again. I wrap my arms around his neck, going up on tip toe to kiss him deeper.

After a moment, I glance into the gallery to find the employee staring at us, looking cantankerous. "He's still watching us."

"Well, he can't kick us out. We're not in there."

"No, but I can *feel* his passive aggressive thoughts from here."

Alex smiles, his eyes crinkling around the edges. "We can't have that, not on your birthday celebration night." He leans down for one more quick kiss and then says, "How about some ice cream?"

"We already had dessert."

"Said Mila Kozak *never*. Are you feeling alright?" He presses a hand to my forehead.

"Just trying to keep my girlish figure," I say as I smooth down my dress primly.

Alex cocks a dark brow at me. "There isn't anything *girl*ish about your figure, Miss Kozak." He wraps an arm possessively around my waist. "You are all woman." I laugh but lean against him as we walk toward an ice cream shop.

That night, when I get home, I take off my makeup, brush my teeth, and settle into bed with the journal Alex gave me when we first got together. Originally, I had filled it with dreams of starting the Center, but now that my dreams were reality, I use it to clear my mind before bed. Which means I mostly write about Alex. I'm not sure when I started it, but I address my journal entries *to* Alex—not that I ever plan on showing him, but it flows out of me when it's like I'm talking to Alex.

Tonight we celebrated my birthday and it was so wonderful. Had dinner on the beach, saw dolphins, laughed a lot. Dance lessons fell through, and I could tell you felt really bad about it. But honestly, we had just as much fun walking around Las Olas. I laugh so much when I'm with you, which is crazy because we also get so deep, unlike I've ever been with anyone else. And I just wonder how can it be both so fun and so intense with you? It's incredible. I made a kind of dumb comment tonight where I said 'marry me now' jokingly, but it was kind of to feel you out to see how you would feel about it. You kind of freaked out—at least that's what your face looked like. It's okay, I know you love me and I know we'll get there eventually, but it's kind of good to know where we stand. We have fun doing even the most basic things together, and I know I could do this with you the rest of my life. There, I said it. I see forever with you. I know you felt some type of way about your plans falling through for tonight, and it made me think about Michael's birthday plans for me in the past. They were always so over-the-top, and tonight just made me realize: Michael needed those crazy plans because there wasn't much true substance to our relationship. At least not anything like me and you have. With you, I don't need the helicopters and yacht rides, because every day is magical with you.

8

The Buckingham of Ocala

Mila

It's Thursday and we're heading up to Ocala to the World Equestrian Center for a horse show this weekend. Trina's new Grand Prix horse sponsor, an uber rich lady named Caterina, got her a suite for the weekend, so we're all crashing with her.

Alex invited Luke to join for some reason I'm suspecting has to do with a budding bromance between the two of them. Anya is none too thrilled about the prospect of spending a weekend with Luke, so we decide to take two cars instead of one—Anya and I are driving together in my car and Luke and Alex in his truck.

Anya is pretty quiet as we drive. "What's going on in that pretty little head of yours?" I tease her.

She sighs heavily, like I've intruded on her thoughts, and then bursts out, "There's no way they're not coming after us, Milochka."

For a moment, I don't know what she's talking about. I glance into my rearview mirror to find Luke's truck still there, but no, she's not talking about that. She's talking about Clara's family, I realize.

"Hmm," I say noncommittally, because I'm not sure it's true. What kind of person sues a therapy center for paraplegics? I mean, c'mon.

Anya sighs and leans her head back onto the headrest, looking up at the ceiling. "You are blessed with the ability to not let stuff like this bother you."

"Are you serious?" *What the heck?*

"Be real, Mila. Has this kept you up at night?"

"That first night after Clara fell, it did. I had nightmares and kept thinking about your accident. It was awful."

"And now?" Everything Anya's saying has a hint of accusation in it, and it's got my hackles up. Does Anya think she's the only one who cares what happens to Clara? To the Center?

"I've been focusing on other things, but that doesn't mean I'm not concerned."

"Exactly. That's a blessing."

"You're acting like you don't have a choice."

"I don't!" Anya huffs. "If something happens from this, it falls on me. Not you."

"It falls on *all* of us, Anya. This Center is not just yours. In fact, it was my idea."

"Yeah, but all you have to worry about is what horse you're going to put someone on."

My jaw drops open because, *wow*, I can't believe Anya just said that. "Are you *serious*?" And now I'm pissed. I'm so mad, I want to swerve my car off the road and have it out with her. Anger is building in me until my face is flush and I feel it prickling down my throat. "Please tell me you're not serious."

Anya sighs again. "No, I'm not serious. I'm sorry, I don't know why I said that."

I'm quiet for a while because I don't know if I'm going to let Anya off the hook so easily. Because what she said was really messed up. But I also understand she's under a lot of stress—if the Center goes sideways, it's true that she has a lot more to lose than I do.

I try to take deep breaths, gripping the steering wheel to channel my anger into something other than Anya.

"I'm sorry," Anya mumbles again after a while.

"It's okay," I tell her, but it still doesn't feel okay. We drive in silence for a long time, and eventually I turn on the radio and Anya closes her eyes and I'm sure she's pretending to be asleep. I'm listening to the music, but mostly I'm repeating what Anya said over and over again. I'm frustrated about Clara's accident, pissed at my sister's response, and I'm even mad at Alex for driving with Luke instead of me. He would've known what to say to Anya to curb this argument before it even started.

When we finally arrive in Ocala, my anger has dwindled and in its stead is something akin to bitterness.

Anya and I walk into The Equestrian Hotel at the World Equestrian Center in Ocala and it takes my breath away. With the vaulted ceilings, wood-paneled pillars, sparkling chandeliers, gold-plated paintings, and elegant furniture, it's unlike any place I've been to before. I'm wondering if their interior designer got this job confused with one for Buckingham Palace.

The best part of it all is that horse people are everywhere in this hotel, walking around with dirt on their boots like this isn't the most expensive carpet they've ever walked on. It's amazing, and I just want to grab Anya and squeal my excitement.

"I texted Trina that we're here," I tell Anya. "She said she'll meet us by the elevators."

She nods and we continue through the lobby, passing a restaurant called The Yellow Pony, which seems almost gaudy in the dignified space with the bright green-and-yellow entryway and the horseshoe-shaped bar. A country singer is crooning from inside, and out of the corner of my eye, I see Anya's jaw clench.

Luke and Alex roll into the lobby thicker than thieves and none more out of place. I'm watching from the elevator hall as Alex quiets, glancing around like he just mistakenly walked back in time to Versailles at the height of French opulence. Luke, however, stares straight ahead and wheels his chair faster through the lobby until he's practically running people over. An older woman in head-to-toe Versace launches herself and her Jack Russell out of his way.

Beside me, Anya's watching them too and shaking her head. "I've never seen anything like it," she mutters.

I can't help but chuckle at how scandalized she is by Luke. "There's something to be said for someone being themselves, no matter where they are."

"Yes, and this is what must be said: he should do it less."

Now it's my turn to shake my head, but I'm smiling because I'm just happy someone else is ruffling Anya's feathers. When Alex gets to us, he puts a tentative hand on my back, like he's unsure how he's supposed to greet me in a place like this. I stand on tiptoe and kiss him, which makes him blush, and I love it.

"How was your drive?" Alex asks.

"It was fine," I say, but I really want to dish on everything Anya said to me, even as I feel her eyes on me. "What about you?"

"We got by," Luke says with a grin.

"Glad to hear you guys are getting along so well," Anya says through gritted teeth. "Now, is there any place a girl can go to the bathroom?"

Luke spins his chair so he's facing Anya. "So you've got an incomplete SCI, then?"

Anya groans like he just asked her the most inconsiderate question. "It does seem that way, doesn't it?"

"Well, if you have control of your bladder, then, yes."

"I don't go around in a diaper, if that's what you're asking."

"I wasn't." And he fixes her with a reprimanding look. "But I know plenty of SCI sufferers have to."

"Guess I'm one of the lucky ones."

"It would seem that way," he says. He's grinning again, and I swear I see him wink at her. Anya huffs and turns her wheelchair a few degrees away from Luke. Alex and I share a glance, and he's barely holding back a smile. It *is* fun to see Luke so successfully poking the beast.

A minute later, Trina steps out of the elevator and gives Alex, Anya, and me a giant hug. I know she's thrilled to be here—she definitely deserves this more than anyone—and her ear-to-ear grin is proof of that. We introduce her to Luke and then head up the elevator.

Her room is huge—apartment would be a better term—with a black tiled hallway with a horse portrait and well-appointed entryway furniture. The entryway opens into a living area with several cushy chairs and French doors that lead to a balcony that overlooks the Grand Arena at WEC. They're dragging the ring, and all the poles are leaning against the jump standards. We all go out onto the balcony—Anya and Luke hovering just inside in their chairs—and this time I really do squeal. This is a horse girl's dream come true.

"This is incredible," I tell Trina. "I'm so glad you convinced us to come."

"It didn't take that much convincing, if I recall."

"True. But I'm still glad you asked." I bump shoulders with her and she smiles up at me.

"I needed an excuse to hang with you guys. I don't see you nearly enough since you opened the Center."

"The only downside, I can assure you," Alex says. Behind us, Anya mutters something under her breath that has Luke snickering and Anya giving him a dirty look.

"I'll show you your rooms," Trina says, pulling me and Alex back through the French doors. We pass a kitchenette and head down a hallway where we pass a room with two king beds. "Here's one room and then the bathroom." She points through another doorway, and I poke my head in and my eyes go wide.

"It's gorgeous." Marble tile brightens the space. A glass-enclosed shower sits in the corner, but the centerpiece is the claw-foot tub. It's massive, and I want to just sink into a bubble bath right this second. Then I remember Anya's comment from earlier and say, "I think Anya and I need a few minutes in the bathroom."

Alex, Luke, and Trina turn aside so Anya can make it into the bathroom. Even in her foul mood, she says, "Wow," as she looks around. "Think we can get one of these at home?" She waves a hand at the tub.

"I think I'd sell my pinky for one of those," I tell her as I help her onto the toilet. Since Anya recovered movement in her shoulders and arms, helping her with everyday tasks like this has been *a lot* easier.

"That seems a bit extreme."

"Well, maybe not my right pinky, just the left."

"Oh, okay. Well in that case, it's perfectly reasonable."

I snort-laugh and then Anya's laughing with me, and for a moment I forget about our fight in the car. Anya leans her head onto my forehead as I hold her upright—and if there isn't a snapshot more sisterly than this, I don't know what is.

After we're settled in our rooms, we head down to the Yellow Pony for dinner. The atmosphere in the restaurant is one hundred percent horsey. Dark wood-paneled walls line the restaurant, and it's almost as if we're inside a tack room. The high-top tables come with saddle seats, some English and some Western. Because of Luke and Anya in their wheelchairs, we opt for the regular height tables. On the wall behind us are a row of polo sticks, and across the room is a poster of a jumping horses that says, "Life is simple: Eat, sleep, ride!" Outside on the patio, a woman in leather pants is crooning old country songs, which makes Anya cringe.

Most of us order burgers and truffle fries, and I'm sure the waiter's expecting Luke to order the "Cowboy Burger," but instead he's the only one at the table who gets a salad. Trina frowns at him like she's trying to figure him out, and I want to laugh and tell her not to bother. Luke is one-of-a-kind, that's for sure.

Anya and Luke exchange barbs across the table throughout the dinner, and it seems like Luke is going out of his way to provoke her. The lopsided grin he's wearing whenever she responds tells me he's enjoying the exchange.

Interesting.

After we finish our dinner, we decide to split a couple desserts. Anya and I order the s'mores brownie and Trina gets the citrus and berry crumble. Alex takes a few bites of both but says he's full, while Luke stoically withholds due to his vegan-ness.

As the singer wails a Carrie Underwood song about a girl getting revenge on her cheating boyfriend by keying his truck, Anya puts her head in her hands and groans. "If she doesn't stop singing, I'm going to key her truck."

"If someone messed with my truck, there'd be misery to pay," Luke says with a playful glint in his blue eyes.

"Don't give me any ideas," Anya grumbles.

"Hide your truck, man," Alex whispers, and Anya smacks him on the shoulder.

"I'm on your side," Alex says to Anya with his hands in the air.

"Yeah, it really seems like it."

"Just trying to keep you out of jail, Anya."

"Whatever," she says, but gives him a little grin.

When the singer switches songs to "Bless the Broken Road," Alex takes my hand and pulls me up to dance. I put my head against his chest as he wraps his arms around me. I steal a glance at the rest of our motley crew at the table and wonder where their broken roads are leading to, and if they'll ever find someone to journey alongside them.

9

Isolation

The horse show weekend alternates between equestrian heaven and asinine levels of frustration with Luke. Since we're not at work, I can't chide him about being unprofessional, and to make matters worse, it seems like everyone else is taken with him. Everyone, that is, but me. Same old story, new location. After dinner, while Alex, Luke, and one of Trina's students, Ryan, play a card game in the living area, Trina, Mila, and I sit on the balcony overlooking the Grand Arena.

Mila starts telling Trina all about Clara's accident—and I barely manage to sit through the conversation. I'm amazed at her ability to blurt the whole story out as if it doesn't bother her.

"They shouldn't be able to sue us, right? They signed a liability waiver," Mila asks.

"Hmm," Trina says, frowning, her brown eyes scanning the arena below us as staff haul flowered standards in and out of the ring. "I've personally never had anyone sue me or the barn for falling, but if she has a serious injury and can prove gross negligence, I suppose it's possible. Do you know if she was badly injured?"

"I don't know. Anya tried to visit her in the hospital, but they kicked her out."

Trina winces as she adjusts her blonde ponytail—and I realize I've never seen her hair down. "If she's fine, it'll blow over, you know? People get freaked out in the moment when they see their kid come off the horse, but as long as they're fine, it's usually okay."

"And if she's not?" I ask, unable to hold back from the conversation anymore.

"I mean, I'm no expert with this legal stuff, but it sounds like you guys do everything by the book. And horses are unpredictable—even the calmest horses freak out sometimes. It's just part of life. The weird thing is the dog. Where did he come from?"

"Honestly, we still have no idea," Mila says, glancing from Trina to me. "Alex and Luke questioned everyone in the barn, and no one took responsibility for him. We brought him to a nearby vet office to see if he was microchipped, but he wasn't. We sent him to the pound."

Trina sighs. "So strange."

I nod, agreeing. I just hope that Clara is fine, and this all doesn't come back to bite us in the rear.

Mila competes in a schooling class with Cyrus on Friday morning and Luke, and I wheel into the stands to watch. We're in one of the indoor arenas, with creaking aluminum bleachers and loud air conditioning units that keep me frigid. Cyrus is fresh, glancing at everything and everyone he passes. As Mila starts to canter him around the schooling area, he keeps kicking out his back legs to show how new this all is.

Sitting beside Luke, watching Mila as she warms up and then waits by the in-gate, I'm flooded with emotions. Of course I'm proud of my baby sister, and I want her to be happy, but there's also resentment bubbling up in me, splashing around like lava in my stomach. To be clear: my bitterness isn't necessarily directed at Mila, just at life. My circumstances. I'm strapped in a chair—literally strapped, so I don't fall out because I can't get myself back in—and she's on a horse, competing in multiple Grand Prix like I never got to do.

I suddenly feel very alone. There are people all around me—horse people, *my* people—but I am utterly by myself. Who in this arena knows how I feel? Knows what I'm experiencing?

Exactly *no one*.

Luke wheels an inch closer to the railing, and the movement catches my eye. Does *he* know how I feel? I wonder. But I tamp the thought down the moment it rears its ugly head. It doesn't matter if Luke can relate to me or not—he's awful.

I think about my conversation with Trina the night before, and a frozen panic grips me as I think about someone trying to sue the Center. Could they take it away from me? I'm finally starting to feel like more of a person and less of a cripple, and now that there's this threat lingering in the back of my mind, it feels like a low-grade dread fever that won't go away.

The rider before Mila leaves the ring, and I see Mila give Alex a kiss and head into the ring. I barely hear the announcer introduce Mila and Cyrus before the buzzer sounds, and Cyrus takes off. I remember when he used to do that with me. I close my eyes and try to remember the sensation of his giant body surging forward, taking me with him. I imagine him soaring over a jump, me on his back, and we're flying. We're free.

I'm sure people assume I wouldn't want to jump again if I could because of the accident. But they're wrong. I would rend my fingernails off one by one if it meant I could jump again like Mila's doing right now—just one more time. And if that sounds extreme, I promise you I'd do way more than that.

The sound of Cyrus's hooves hitting a rail startle me. Luke sucks in air through his teeth and I open my eyes, worried something happened to Mila. But when I look up, the jump is still standing and Mila's pulling my horse into a rollback. His hind legs stumble a bit through the turn and it's my turn to gasp. My hand flies to grasp Luke's arm involuntarily. Cyrus recovers fine and they're over the next jump in a heartbeat, but my hand is still gripping Luke's forearm. He's strong, his muscles ropey underneath my fingertips, with just a dusting of blonde hair. I go to pull away, but he puts his hand over mine and murmurs, "It's okay."

I glance over at him, and for the first time he's not wearing a smirk. His eyes aren't conveying even a hint of mockery. It's then that I notice his blue eyes have flecks of green and gold in them. The kind a girl could fall into and never find her way out of. The moment I realize how aware of him I am, I tug my hand away and force my eyes forward to watch Mila.

Why am I *noticing* Luke? I square my shoulders and tell myself I am allowed to make an objective observation that Luke is attractive. That doesn't mean anything.

The final line in the course is a skinny liverpool, seven strides to an in-and-out right in front of the gate. Cyrus respects the skinny, giving it a wide berth as he launches over it, but then he's charging toward the in-gate and I can tell Mila's having a hard time slowing him down.

"Whoa," Trina's calling from the gate.

Mila's sitting back, practically standing on her toes to pull back on Cyrus, and they're a little disjointed as Cyrus takes off into the in-and-out. He gets over the first jump, but then has to chip in before the second jump, and he barely makes it over, though somehow, he does. Because this is Cyrus and he's a miracle worker like that. Except when it came to me.

Mila's through the timers and we clap, the sound lost in the massive arena. Mila gives Cyrus the reins, and he lowers his head and snorts into the dirt.

"Good boy," she says, rubbing his neck.

At the in-gate, Alex's shoulders visibly slump, like he's relieved her ride is over. I'd never noticed him worried about her before. I guess he has good reason, I think as I look down at my wheelchair.

"Shall we?" Luke says, wheeling toward the exit ramp, but I'm not ready to go anywhere.

"I'll meet up with you guys later," I say. Luke gazes at me for a beat too long for comfort, and I'm afraid he's going to say something to me, try to make conversation with me, but then he just nods and rolls down the ramp.

I sit alone, watching the next several riders, though I'm not really paying attention. I'm wondering if all of this is good for me—being around so many able-bodied people, being around the horses. When the accident first happened and I hid myself away from the world, life was easier, in a way. I didn't *have* to think about other people. I just lost myself in Netflix and whatever audiobook my mom played for me.

But out here, in the real world, I *feel* it *all*. All the things I'm missing. All the things I can't do. And of course I'm grateful for the Center—it gives me purpose, makes me focus on what I *can* do. But it's moments like these where I'm away from the Center that I wish I were back in my room. Hiding. It's why I don't often venture outside of my comfort zone of home and the Center. I've only gone on a handful of trips away from my home in the past two and a half years, and they've all been akin to torture for me. It all just reminds me how different I am, how different my life is from everyone else. I even hate going to physical therapy, even though I know I should be better about going.

Being in the real world is just unbearably hard sometimes.

I feel the bitterness creeping up in me, threatening to take hold of me, and I don't even know how to fight it. How do I accept this reality? Prior to this weekend, I thought I'd come to terms with my limitations, but being in a new place just brings it all back to the forefront. My injuries feel so fresh, so raw.

I don't have a clue what to do about it, and that makes me feel so thoroughly isolated in my pain.

10

Sticky Sticky Bun Bun

Mila

I wake up on Saturday, the morning of the Grand Prix, to find a caramel macchiato, an assortment of pastries in a box from Emma's Patisserie downstairs, and a very bashful Alex holding it all. His dark eyes take me in, with my rumpled morning hair and pajama shorts, and he says, "I could get used to this view every morning."

I smile and stand on tiptoe to kiss him as I take the macchiato from his hand. "Me too," I say, holding up the macchiato, and he laughs. We sit at the table and I inspect the pastries, picking out a sticky bun. It's moist, flaky, and just the right amount of sweet. Despite my seemingly unending desire for sweets, I never want to eat before big competitions. And Alex is always trying to sneak calories into me—though I have to admit that this particular move is working today, because I take several bites before I start to feel my usual queasiness. I push the bun away and take a small sip of water, swirling it around my mouth. I feel the nausea building, the saliva filling my mouth, and glance up at Alex.

"Oh no," he says, realization showing in his eyes at the same time it hits me. I run to the bathroom and empty my stomach with heaves that clutch my abdomen in a death grip. Alex follows me, holding my hair back and applying a cool washcloth to my neck. "I'm so sorry, Mila," he says once I stand with my head against his chest. "I really thought we'd figured it out with that sticky bun."

I groan into his shirt and he strokes my hair, holding me against him. "I may never have a sticky bun ever again."

"You've said that about the last five things I gave you to eat before a Grand Prix, but I'm pretty sure I saw you with a blueberry muffin the other day."

I grunt, the idea of a blueberry muffin making me queasy again, and ask, "Are you ready to give up?"

He gently angles my head back to look at him, the corner of his mouth uplifted into a half smile. "Taking care of you? Never. Making you eat before shows?" He tilts his head back and forth as if considering, "Maybe."

"Quitter."

"Sometimes you gotta know when you're beat."

"Alex, zero. Mila's stomach—what is it, fifteen? Seventeen?"

"Let's not count," Alex says with a groan and rubs a hand across his face. "It's not good for your stomach, or mine."

"True story."

The Grand Prix course at WEC is unlike anything I've seen before. It's truly a work of art. The landscaping alone is noteworthy. There's a stone-lined pond toward the center of the ring as well as several landscaped "islands" dotting the sand with palm trees, shrubs and colorful flowers. They're obstacles in their own right, meant to be navigated around carefully—either as an impediment to your speed or a boon. Each jump has its own landscaping around the edges of the standards, making them seem more permanent than any other jumps I've encountered. There are several massive decorative arches beside the standards, some made of greenery and others covered in white flowers. As Trina and I walk the course, I have to keep reminding myself that I need to learn the course and not just admire it.

"Coming?" Trina calls to me while I'm examining a very solid jump that looks like an arching brick bridge with vines and pink flowers trailing up the columns.

"Oh." I tear my gaze away and jog to catch up with her. "This place is insane." I look up at the Equestrian Hotel—which is the palatial and very elegant backdrop to the Grand Arena.

"Cyrus is going to let it rip in here," Trina says, hyper-focused as usual. "So keep a tight rein and stay steady on these long stretches here."

We count the strides of a long, broken line, Trina going on the outside track while I go on the inside. "It's ten here."

"Eight for me."

"Take the outside if you need to collect him a bit. He's gonna fight you."

I nod, and then I'm taken aback by the decor beside the standards: huge chalice-like vases holding pink blossoms. They're taller than the standards, which means they're taller than me. I have to crane my head back to get a good look at the flowers. I wonder how Cyrus is going to do with all of this stimulation. I can barely handle it.

We finish walking the jump off and I head to the stands to watch a few riders. I send my best friend, Monica, a picture of the ring and text, *What are you up to this weekend?*

She immediately texts back, *Something a million-billion times safer than that.* Then follows up with a picture of herself in bed with her cat curled up beside her.

Don't fall out of bed, I warn her. *You could get a concussion.*

She sends me several eye-roll emojis and then a string of GIFs with people falling out of beds. I laugh and then put my phone away as the first rider comes on course. I watch carefully, counting strides and making note of the turns they make.

Trina comes in the ring after the next rider. She's riding her new Grand Prix horse, Leonidas, a bay Oldenberg gelding with a white star in the center of his handsome face. Today he has button braids dotting the top of his neck, giving him a regal air. He's prancing into the ring, snorting at each jump they pass, until the buzzer goes off and Trina pushes him into a canter. Then he's fixated on the jumps in front of him, his ears pointed forward, intent on his job. They fly over each fence, Trina in perfect form as she navigates her steed. Leo is a scopey jumper, tucking his knees almost to his ears, his neck arching beautifully as they soar from jump to jump.

There's a particularly wide oxer, a colorful fence with hot air balloons on the standards, and Leo has to stretch out in a superhero fashion, and I can't help but gasp and grip the armrests beside me. They glide for several heartbeats over the obstacle, and then they hit the ground and gallop to the next fence. Watching Trina and Leo, I'm reminded of how beautiful and terrifying this sport is. Since Anya's accident, it's been a long while since I've watched someone close to me ride in a class at these heights, and even though it's thrilling, there's an aspect of it that has my heart racing and my breath shallow. When Trina finishes, my body sags with relief.

The whole experience reminds me that there is fear and anxiety lurking in the back of my mind. I may have healed quite a bit in the past year and a half, but the trauma of Anya's accident is still embedded deep in my brain. My therapist, Gwen, has reminded me time and again that it takes time to pave new neural pathways. I'm getting there, but this is a reminder that I'm not quite there yet. And maybe I won't ever be totally free of my fear.

My hands are shaking a bit as I stand up and head to the practice ring, another impossibly small arena with too many horses and riders. Why do they always have to make these rings so tiny?

I see Alex at the edge of the arena, holding Cyrus, looking swoon-worthy with his day-old scruff and ridiculous cheekbones. I have the fleeting thought that someone needs to get over here and carve a sculpture of this guy, because he is so sculptable. When I reach him, I run my fingers across his cheek, feeling the tiny pinpricks of his facial hair on my fingertips. I love when he forgets to shave. And just like that, he's staring down at me with fire in his eyes and hunger in his palms as he pulls me against him.

"Later," Trina calls out as she strides across the ring toward us. "Much, much later." She waves a finger at us, as if to break us up. I laugh and reluctantly extract myself from Alex's grip, but Alex's cheeks are pink and he looks chastened. He still thinks of Trina as his employer and not quite the best friend that I consider her. He gives me a leg up and I start warming up Cyrus, weaving around the other riders. My anxiety drips away with each stride we take, and soon I can't be anything but focused on the jump in front of me.

When we're done schooling, we walk down the breezeway to the Grand Arena entrance and wait for the rider in front of me to finish. It's Aaron Vale on a chestnut gelding with a white stripe down its face.

"Hey Mila," he says as he passes me. I attempt to give a nod, or a wave, or a smile, but fail to do any of those things. When he's past, I lean down to Trina and say, "Aaron Vale knows my name."

Trina laughs and shakes her head. She pats Cyrus's rump and says, "Good luck, chica," and then I'm walking into the ring, thinking about how Aaron Vale rode in his first Grand Prix when he was only fourteen years old, and *where were his parents when he was doing that*? One time, he entered into a Grand Prix with five different horses and won the top five spots. No one has ever done that.

Aaron Vale is a *boss*, and he knows my name. I vaguely hear Anya in the stands call out in Ukrainian, "Keep them up, sestra," her way of saying good luck. The goal of a show jumping competition is to have the fastest time around the course without knocking down any obstacles. Keep them up, indeed.

I barely hear the buzzer go off—but Cyrus does, and he jolts into a gallop like he normally does, and I have to refocus on the course. I point Cyrus at the first fence—a gold jump with cage-like standards that remind me of oversized bird cages. We rocket over it, and it's then that I realize I never gave Alex my obligatory good luck kiss. It's a tradition I started last year when I entered my first Grand Prix, and I've never been in a Grand Prix without it.

It's a thought that freezes me to my core.

I went in without the kiss. *The kiss.*

I'm barely cognizant as we take the broken line in seven strides—not eight like we'd planned—and rollback in front of one of the landscaped islands to jump over the fence with the pink blossoms.

I distantly hear Trina yell out "Whoa!" and it brings me back to the present. I tighten my reins and pull back, trying to slow Cyrus because Trina's right—he's going way too fast. He's fighting me, pulling on the reins and tossing his head, anxious to get to the next jump. But I'm not one hundred percent there—I'm distracted, totally out of it. And even though I know I shouldn't be riding in a Grand Prix like this, I can't seem to get it together.

And suddenly images are flying through my head. Of Anya flipping with Cyrus. Anya in an ambulance. The snapshots tear through me, until I'm shaking with fear, certain I'm going to end up like Anya. I'm not breathing, barely hanging on to Cyrus as he rockets over yet another fence without me being completely present.

We are flying up to the in-and-out when Cyrus chips in at the last second. It cuts our momentum suddenly, and Cyrus can't quite make it over the second fence. I try to lift my hands, giving him the support to make it, but it's not enough. We hit the top rail with a loud smack, but it's not until I'm falling that I realize what's happening.

Everything tilts. The earth is twisting. The sand is speeding toward my face, and for a second it's as if everything slows—I can see myself flying off Cyrus's back, over his neck, and landing on the ground.

Then it all goes black.

11

After the Fall

Alex

How can something happen too fast and be in slow motion at the same time? That's what Mila's fall is like. All of a sudden, she's on the ground, but there it is, so slowly: Cyrus catching the pole between his knees, trying to land, and the pole impeding him. His legs crumple, in painful slow motion, and then Mila's flying through the air, a horse no longer connecting her to the ground. Her arms are outstretched, but that doesn't soften the impact of her head to the ground. Her body collapses, tossed to the sand as if she were a lifeless doll, and my soul rips open. Fear is beating a rhythm in my chest in triple time, and I run. I run to Mila, my hands hovering around her helmeted head, unable to touch her in case it's worst-case scenario.

Her eyes flutter open and focus onto mine. "Alex," she says, reaching for me as she tries to sit up.

"Don't move," I tell her.

"I'm okay," she says. I want her to lay back down, to take an inventory of every inch of her body before she moves, but before I can force her to stop, she's on her feet. Trina's there, dusting off Mila, while I stand aside, my heart still threatening to punch a hole through my chest. Behind her, someone has Cyrus by the reins, and I suddenly feel very useless.

"Do you need to lean on me?" I ask as I wrap an arm around Mila's waist.

"I'm okay, Alex," she says. "Really."

But then, her knees buckle, and my arms are around her, holding her up as she's fighting consciousness again. "Mila," I say, alarm coursing through me as I deliberate if I should pick her up or put her back on the ground. Before I can make a move, her eyes open again, and she's glancing around, a little confused before she says, "I just stood up too fast."

She puts an arm around my waist, gripping onto my shirt as she starts walking out of the ring. "Mila, maybe we should—"

Mila shakes her head and leans into me. "Will you get me out of here?" she whispers. "I just want to get out of here."

Once we're out of the ring, Trina asks if Mila wants to get back on Cyrus, but I wave her off. Mila's shivering, and all I can think about is getting her up to the safety of the room.

Wordlessly, I guide her back toward the hotel. We pass the shops as we head toward the elevator. I'm so intensely focused on Mila that everything and everyone around us blurs away. I'm aware of each step she takes, every breath she inhales, the way she leans against me. Her shaking hands that clasp mine at her waist when we get into the elevator. I unclip her helmet with my other hand, taking off her hairnet and gently tugging her hair tie out of her hair. Her eyes are closed, and I realize she hasn't looked at me since that first flutter of her eyes after she came back to consciousness.

She's squeezing me so tightly, like I'm her only lifeline.

"Almost there," I murmur to her.

In the room, Mila says, "Shower," and I half-carry her down the hall. "Can you help me get my boots off? And then I just want to be alone." I nod, trying not to be offended that she doesn't want me around. Still holding her, I reach into the glass shower stall and turn on the water. I kneel to unzip her boots and gingerly pull them off, though she winces at the right one.

"Where does it hurt?" I ask.

"My hip."

My hand goes to her hip, but then I think better of it, and instead pull down her boot socks and toss them in a pile next to her boots. I stand, moving her curtain of hair to settle my palm against her skin. She still won't look me in the eye.

"Oh no," she moans before she turns into the shower and throws up. I move her hair out of her face, regretting taking it down in the first place, and rub her back as the hot water rushes over her as she heaves. When she's done, she slumps into the corner of the shower, the water misting her so that her sunscreen is pooling on her skin in tiny opaque droplets. I catch one of them with my fingertip, and she finally looks at me.

"I'm so sorry, Alex." And then she sobs into my shoulder.

After the water has run cold and we're both thoroughly soaked but not yet clean, still in all of our clothes, I find out that Mila's distraught not just because she fell—but because she didn't kiss me before she went into her class and that made her ride poorly and *that's* the reason she fell.

"If I'd just kissed you..." she says for seventh time. "I was distracted and it was irresponsible, it's not fair to you—"

"Mila, you know that's not—"

She shakes her head violently, rejecting my stance. We've gone through this already. She feels like she let me down because she didn't kiss me, she rode badly, and therefore took a fall. I'm trying to parse through her logic, trying to get to the core assumption here, but all I can see is Mila's fall. Over and over in my mind.

After what feels like an eternity but could've been twenty minutes, Anya rolls in. "Why don't you get dry," she says to me. I'm hesitant to leave Mila, but I also know that Anya could possibly get through to Mila better than I can. I reluctantly stand up, dripping all over the bathroom while I search for a towel, and then shuffle out of the bathroom, giving Mila one more glance before I leave. She looks so fragile, so breakable, sitting in the shower stall, with the water falling all around her while she stays motionless.

I head to the room I'm sharing with Luke and towel off, changing my clothes. All the while trying to figure out what to say to Mila. She should be shaken from her fall—not because she failed *me* by falling, but because it was scary for *her*. She should be evaluated for a concussion, I realize. Why didn't we think of that right away? I chastise myself. I call Trina, who picks up on the second ring, and tell her what I think. She agrees and thirty minutes later, there's a doctor in our hotel room.

12

Fancy Hat

Anya

Watching Mila's accident, I would've expected to have deja vu or PTSD or some kind of reaction when it happened. Instead, I felt numb. I go through the motions, calling the doctor on call at the showgrounds, talking to Trina about it before heading upstairs. It's concerning that Mila didn't get back on Cyrus after her fall—it's a whole thing with horse people. *Get back on the horse* is a reality when you fall. And Mila's never *not* gotten back on the horse. Which makes me think she's either really hurt, or mentally beaten.

When I get to the hotel room, I sit with Mila, still soaking wet in all her show clothes, pale as her white breeches.

It would be easy for me to jump in, try to solve her problems for her, but I decide to just listen. Now that I'm sitting in front of Mila, I feel shaken—that fall could've taken my sister from me—but I put that aside for now. This is not about me; it's about Mila.

She recounts what happened—how her pre-show ritual was messed up, how she was pre-occupied, and it made her ride poorly. "I just can't forgive myself if I were the one at fault for causing you, and Alex, and Mom and Dad, too, pain." She shakes her head, water dripping from her hair. "How dare I do that? How could I let the distraction, the anxiety, take hold? How could I do that to you guys?"

"Oh, Milochka," I say, reaching out to hold her hand. "We all know there's risk in this business. You can't be perfect, nobody can. We understand that. No one blames you for the fall."

"*I* blame me."

Her words, and the vehemence with which she says them, make me wonder if she blames me for my fall. But again, I decide to put my feelings aside and focus on Mila. We talk for what feels like an eternity, but I can't get through to her. I mentally scroll through my options. Alex isn't helping her see reason. Trina's not exactly the touchy-feely type to work through Mila's emotions with her. So that leaves one option. One I absolutely do not want to take, but I will, for Mila's sake.

Later, I'm sitting at the table, taking deep breaths to center myself for what's to come. I hear him before I see him, his wheelchair whirling down the hallway. I close my eyes and tell myself what I've said to Luke a hundred times since he's started working for the Center: just be professional. That's all this is. It's not a favor, it's not personal. It's just professional.

"Mr. Craig," I say as he wheels past me. He stops and shifts his trajectory to roll up next to me.

"Yes, ma'am," he says, and I'm wondering at his tone—is he being sarcastic when he says 'ma'am'? I mean, I am three years younger than him, so 'ma'am' feels like overkill. Though I am his boss and I did ask him to be professional.

I spit right out with my request. "Will you see my sister in a professional capacity?"

He fidgets with his wheelchair, rolling it back and forth slightly. "Because of her fall?"

I nod. "She seems to have some sort of magical thinking about the fall. That her not kissing Alex before she rode into the ring may have caused her fall."

"I see." He takes off his obnoxious cowboy hat, pushing back his messy blonde hair underneath. This must be his fancy hat, because it's black and doesn't have any snake or alligator skin on it. "Sure, I'd be happy to chat with her. As long as she wants to, of course."

"She does." I smile mirthlessly. "I mean, she will."

13

The Doctor Is In

Alex

We're all congregated around Mila—Anya, Trina, Luke, our barn mate Ryan, and me—watching silently as the doctor examines Mila and asks her questions in a thick Southern accent. What date is it? Where are you? What do you remember from the accident? Do you have a headache? She flashes her pen light in Mila's eyes, watching her pupils dilate, and eventually she sits back and says, "Well, losing consciousness automatically puts you in concussion territory and possibly TBI," the doc says

"What's TBI?" Ryan asks.

"Traumatic brain injury," the doctor says, as if Ryan had asked what the weather's like and she was informing him it was partly cloudy.

"Any grogginess, headache, pressure in your head, vomiting—"

"She did vomit," I cut in.

Mila scoffs. "I vomit all the time." Then, with a quick look at the doctor and then Luke, she amends, "I mean, I usually vomit before competitions. Not, y'know, for other reasons."

"I've seen you eat," Ryan says with a crooked smile. "I don't think you're anorexic."

"Not anorexic," Luke says. "But she could be bulimic." He scratches his chin, like he's putting some pieces together. "It could fit. Binging on the sweets—"

"I am *not* bulimic," Mila says, her voice getting squeaky, which I know she hates. "Alex, tell them." She waves a frustrated hand toward me.

"She's not bulimic," I confirm with a nod. But Luke is still looking at Mila, unconvinced, while the doctor is staring, clearly unsure of what to say.

"I'm fine, you guys. Really," Mila says with a sigh.

"She could have a slow bleed and just not have any symptoms yet," Anya says, staring at her phone as she Googles symptoms for brain bleeds even though there's a doctor right here.

"I don't have a brain bleed."

"Oh really? Can you see in there?" Anya's voice drips with sarcasm.

"I feel fine."

"It couldn't hurt to just pop over and get a quick scan," Trina offers. "What do you think, doc?"

Mila rolls her eyes, and something about the motion comforts me. Would she be able to roll her eyes *so* well if her skull were cracked? "We all know I'd spend the rest of the night in the ER for your 'quick' scan."

"*My* opinion is that you should get a CT scan," the doctor says, staring at Anya as she continues to Google. Anya doesn't look up, so the doctor turns back to Mila. "I can send you the address for the closest hospital."

Mila sighs, looking like she's going to go AMA—against medical advice—and skip the hospital. I put my hands on her shoulders. "We can pick up some pastries from Emma's on the way out," I tell her. "It'll be like a date."

"Fun date," she grumbles.

"Hey, we've never been to the hospital for a date before," I say, trying to keep my tone light even though I'm scared.

"I really think you should go get a scan," Anya says, glancing up from her phone. "This article says you should."

The doctor gives an exasperated groan and stands up, packing her things. "Well, you should obviously go, then. Google declared it."

"Fine," Mila says. "I'll go."

A few hours later, we're back from the ER. Anya decided to join—making it much less of a 'date,' but it's not like Mila bought into that in the first place. I'm sure it was challenging for Anya to go to the hospital after so many traumatizing days spent there after her accident, but I know Mila was grateful to have her there. The ER doctor confirmed that Mila has a concussion, so they did a CT scan to make sure she doesn't have any skull fractures or brain bleeds. Thankfully, that came back normal, so they released her after a couple hours of observation, with lots of instructions about concussion management. Including, but of course not limited to, orders not to ride for a week, which may as well be a life sentence for Mila.

Mila and I are out on the patio as the sun is setting over WEC. A tractor is dragging the Grand Arena below us and we lean on the railing, watching.

"I'm sorry, Alex," Mila says after a while. "For everything today. The hassle."

I turn toward her, taking her shoulders in my hands. "Mila, please stop apologizing. This is not your fault. It was a freak accident caused by something outside of your control. And you're fine. Just stay on the ground for a week and get some rest, you'll be good."

Her eyes are moving back and forth over my face, and I can tell she's trying to find her words, trying to figure out a different way to express what she's told me a hundred times today already—that this is her fault. I wish for a moment I could slip past the mortal barriers between us—skin, bone, cell walls—and be one with her mind, so as to understand what she's feeling. How much easier would that make all of this?

"You don't know what it's like to have your world fall apart when someone you love takes a fall like that."

"That may be true, but I *felt* what that might feel like, if only for a moment today."

A sob chokes out of her, and I know immediately I've said the wrong thing. She closes her eyes, tears streaming out of them. "Yes, and that's *my* fault, Alex. *I* did that to you. I was riding distracted—it's like the equivalent of driving drunk. Yes, I missed the ritual, but it's more than that. I messed up. I couldn't focus. And it could've ended up a lot worse than it did, and I can't shake the feeling that I could've done to you what Anya's accident did to me."

I sigh and scratch my fingertips over my scruff, frustrated that we're back to this and I still have no idea what to say. How can I convince her? "But Mila, you didn't."

"You don't get it," she chokes out. And with that, she storms off of the patio, leaving me alone and utterly baffled.

I take a few deep breaths, looking out into the growing darkness at the Grand Arena. The ring is dragged and ready to go for tomorrow's class, and it's almost as if nothing happened today. I step back inside the hotel room, where I find Anya watching me with wary eyes. She's sitting in her wheelchair at the small, round table that's beside the kitchenette. She's taping her fingers rhythmically on the tabletop.

"I'm guessing you heard all that." I gesture toward the patio.

In typical Anya fashion, she doesn't respond to that. "I sent Luke after her."

I blink at her, not quite comprehending for a moment. "Oh."

"We've all tried. He's our last shot," she says begrudgingly.

I'm surprised Anya trusted Luke enough to let him help her sister, but Luke *is* a good therapist. Even as I think the thought, a flash of guilt hits me, because *I* should be able to help Mila. I may not be a fully certified therapist, but I'm being trained, and I *know* Mila. I should be able to help her through this, better than anyone else.

I sit at the table, tempted to put my head in my hands, but I resist. "I don't know how to help her," I confess into the silence.

"Well, if it makes you feel better, I couldn't figure it out either. She just kept blathering on about the stupid kiss. I mean, we get it. She'll never *not* kiss you again, but it's not like that caused the accident."

"Well, we know that," I say, waving a finger between us. "But she seems to believe otherwise."

Anya shrugs, and I wonder if she's ever had a mythical thought in her life. We sit in silence, not looking at each other, for a long time.

"You can't be everything for her," Anya eventually tells me. I glance up at her, surprised. "You can't always be the one to put her back together."

"I know," I say, but what if I *want* to be everything for her?

14

Feather Pillows and Therapy

Mila

I fall into a comfortable therapist-client dynamic with Luke, which is surprising because I've never seen him as a therapist. But I guess because I've gotten used to talking with Gwen, it's like putting on a comfy pair of sweatpants as I divulge my thoughts to Luke. I'm sitting up on Trina's bed, a pillow in my lap, while Luke is in his wheelchair by the window. I miss the sand tray in Gwen's office that I usually play with mindlessly as we chat. It helps me relax. So now I'm pinching the pillowcase, my fingertips searching for feathers to rub between my fingers as I talk.

I tell him about how I got distracted before I rode into the ring and didn't give Alex my pre-show kiss like I usually do. The shame that gripped me when I realized what I had done. How preoccupied I was as I competed and how sure I was that *that* led to the fall. He listens quietly, nodding with a finger hooked over his chin. Gwen usually asks me questions as I talk, but Luke lets me get all the way to the end before saying anything.

"So obviously your sister's accident has affected you deeply. It seems like you're equating this situation with her accident. Would you say that's true?"

"Well, yeah."

"How would you say that they're different?"

"Well, for one, Anya wasn't responsible for her accident."

Luke leans forward, his elbows propped on his wheelchair arms. "How do you know that?"

"Well, I..." *I have no idea*, I realize. All I know is that Anya's accident wasn't her fault. I can't explain why I think that. I just know it's true. Just like I know that this fall was *my* fault.

"Did your sister have any pre-show rituals? Do you know if she followed through with all of them?"

"I...don't know." I look down at the pillow in my lap, squeezing it until I feel the individual feathers inside. I twirl a couple through the pillowcase between my fingertips.

"If she hadn't followed through with a certain ritual, would you have blamed her for the accident?"

"Of course not."

"Of course?" Luke taps a finger against his chin and gives me a meaningful stare.

"I see what you're getting at."

"What if your sister rode badly and that was part of the reason she had her accident?"

"But that wasn't the case."

"Well, maybe you think that, but what if Anya was convinced of that?"

"I get what you're trying to say."

"Yes, but does it change your thought process?"

I think about this for a moment as I rub the feathers from the pillow in between my fingers and respond honestly, "Not totally."

"Okay, let's try a different way of looking at this." He sits back in his wheelchair and then, using his hands, he pulls his right leg up so that his ankle is resting on his left knee. "If you knew you'd be seriously injured, would you stop riding right now?"

"For my sake? Or their sakes?" I say, thinking of Alex, Anya, my parents.

"Either. Both."

I shake my head. "I don't know."

"What do you think they'd want for you?"

I consider that. Do I wish Anya had stopped riding to prevent her accident? Maybe. But then I think, if that happened, it seems like the outcome would still be the same: a life half-lived. I wouldn't want that for Anya, and I don't think she'd want that for me. And I know for a fact Alex wouldn't want that for me.

"Okay," I say. "I get it. Alex for sure wouldn't want me to give up even if there was a chance of me getting injured."

"Are you sure about that?"

I nod, knowing that Alex wants this for me just as much as I want it. And it hits me that this is what love is: wanting the other person to be happy even more than you want to be happy. Alex would pay the price for my happiness if that meant I was injured show jumping—but he's aware, and so am I. It's a strange thought, equal parts unsettling and peace-giving. "Alex would want me to ride, even if it meant I got hurt."

"Even if it was your fault that you got hurt?"

The question catches me off-guard—I thought I'd settled on the idea he wanted me to grasp, but then he took it one step further. I try to think about what Alex was like after my fall. Was there even a trace of frustration or blame? All I could remember was his hand gripping my waist, leading me to the hotel room, holding me up. Then his face in the shower after he held my hair back when I threw up. The water dripping off his eyelashes, pooling in the divot just above his lip. "He wouldn't want me to stop riding," I say finally. "In a way, he's the reason I'm riding at this level at all. If he hadn't believed in me, hadn't lent me his faith in me, I wouldn't be here."

Luke smiles. "I know. And I love that about Alex. He's a believer."

"He is, isn't he?" And suddenly, I feel like I've got to be in Alex's arms right this second. I excuse myself and run out to the living room, where I find Alex sitting in the dark by himself. He looks up, his eyes conveying a mixture of sorrow and hesitancy. He stands when he sees it's me, and I rush into his arms. And, of course, he catches me. Because that's what Alex does.

15

Thanking the Enemy

Anya

The difference between Mila before and after her session with Luke is stark. She comes out of the room with him, light and bubbly like she'd just downed a bottle of champagne. She throws herself into Alex's arms, and there's a moment when I'm annoyed. Because of course Luke Craig is good at his job. Of course.

But then Mila wraps an arm around me and kisses me on the head. "*Dakuju, sestra.*"

"Anything for you, Milochka." I pat her hand and glance up to find Luke staring meaningfully at us. I open my mouth to say something—thank you?—when Trina blusters in.

"Anyone feel like eating?" she asks the room, but she's looking at Mila. This must be Trina's way of asking how my sister's doing, and I can't help but laugh. Some may accuse me of being made of stone, but Trina's refined steel.

"I'm starving," Mila says, and there's an audible sigh of relief heard around the room. Because if Mila's hungry, that's a good sign.

"Good," Trina says with a quick nod. "Caterina made reservations for us at Stirrups," she says, referring to the fancy restaurant downstairs. "Get your nicest britches on."

"Mine are dirty," Mila says with a taunting grin.

"Darn, left mine at home," Alex teases.

Trina rolls her eyes and disappears into her room before anyone says another word.

Twenty minutes later, we're all wearing the nicest clothes we brought. I stare a little too long when Luke rolls out wearing a nice pair of slacks, a button-down shirt and, most notably, no cowboy hat and no boots. "Didn't realize you owned a pair of dress shoes," I say before I can stop myself.

"You're welcome to come over and go through my closet to get a better assessment of my wardrobe, if you'd like," he says with a lazy smile. I choose not to respond, knowing this is just going to make it harder for me to thank him for helping Mila.

At the restaurant, they have to accommodate for the wheelchairs and of course—*of course*—they put Luke and me next to each other. As if they thought we'd be wheelchair buddies and want to yuck it up all night long.

One positive aspect of being next to Luke all night for this fancy dinner: he'll invariably make a fool of himself at this classy joint and I'll be there to witness it. I smile a little at my good fortune. I feel a little evil at the thought, but a girl has to find something to look forward to, right?

We take a look at the menu and Caterina is recommending things for us to try. "The oysters are always really good," she says.

"Oysters on me," Luke says.

I raise a brow at him. "Have you had oysters before, Mr. Craig?"

"Why, do you need help knowing how to eat them? It can be a little intimidating your first time." He winks at me, and it takes everything in me to not let my jaw drop.

"I've never had oysters before," Alex says on Luke's other side. "I've always thought they'd taste weird."

"Weird is relative," Luke says. "Do you like seafood? It's on the briny side."

Alex and Luke get into a conversation about seafood Alex tolerates or doesn't. The waiter comes and Luke orders oysters for the table and then asks about wine pairings. Luke brings up types of wines I've never even heard of but eventually lands on a bottle of Cakebread. I do a quick scan of the menu to see if he just randomly chose the most expensive wine, but he didn't.

Show-off.

So Luke knows all about wine and oysters. You couldn't have shocked me more if you'd told me Luke was a prima ballerina. I feel miffed, like he's personally offended me with his knowledge of these things. I shake my head, knowing I'm being ridiculous.

When the wine arrives at the table, I take a small sip and almost say, *Wow, this is really good*. But I keep the opinion to myself. It doesn't stop Trina and Caterina from remarking on it, though.

"I thought you were vegan," I say to Luke after everyone praised him for his wine choice. I gesture toward the oysters he's shucked, which are clearly not vegan. I think I've found a fault in his principled facade, something to tease him about.

He shrugs. "I'm more of a pescatarian," he says. "But sometimes people don't know what that means." He takes a sip of his wine. "Don't want to come across pretentious."

I scoff. "I don't think you have to worry about that."

He leans in and whispers conspiratorially. "So the oysters and wine thing didn't impress you much, huh?"

"Were you trying to impress me?"

He shrugs again as if he couldn't care less what I actually think of him. "People aren't always what they seem, Miss Kozak," he says, a glimmer in his eye as he takes a sip of wine.

I want to ask if he's talking about him, or me, but the waiter arrives to take our orders.

We're almost all the way through dinner and I haven't found a single thing to mock Luke for. I also haven't said thank you to him either. Between those two things, I'm starting to feel very annoyed and a little grouchy. I want to talk myself out of it, to enjoy this dinner for Mila and Trina's sakes. At one point, Caterina raises her glass and toasts Trina for her excellent ride on Leonidas.

I should be happy for Trina, for this boon for her career. She hasn't had a reliable Grand Prix horse for almost a decade now. And I *am* happy for her. But there's also an oozy, ugly feeling puddling in my stomach toward everyone else and their able-bodied adventures. And especially toward Luke, though I can't even pinpoint what I'm annoyed at him for right now.

"I have a toast too," Mila says, holding up her water glass. My feelings toward her soften as I think of her fall and her difficulty recovering like she usually does. Mila has less bounce-back than she did before my accident, and that haunts me. Makes me feel like a bad sister, even though I know it's not necessarily my fault. It still doesn't feel good. "I wanted to thank you all for helping me today. It was rough"—she grimaces—"but I'm so grateful to have you all around me to support me." She gestures her water at each one of us, making eye contact and silently thanking us. "Thank you, Luke, for your help today. I really needed that. I'm glad I got to see firsthand how blessed our clients are for having you in their corner."

Luke raises his glass at Mila in thanks. "Happy to help," he says, and then everyone takes a sip. There's a stirring in my chest that's telling me now would be a good time to thank Luke. I take a deep breath and turn toward him, only to find him staring at me. All of my conviction to thank him flees.

"You're a good sister," he says. "You always go above and beyond for Mila. Well, for everybody, really." He says it casually like he compliments people like this all the time. I feel uncomfortable, like someone just put a spotlight on me and expected me to dance a jig.

"Thanks," I mumble before burying myself in my wine glass.

Well, at least I said thanks.

16

Longer > Forever

Mila

After everyone wanders off to bed, Alex and I are sitting on the couch, my feet thrown over his lap. A quietness settles over the hotel suite, and we sit in the stillness until Alex says, "I'm not ready to say goodnight to you."

I glance up at him, the darkened room casting shadows on his face. I line his face with the tip of my finger, from his straight, dark brows to his high cheekbones to his full lips. I run my finger along the edge of his chin, his day-old stubble scouring my fingertips. He watches me, his expression serious yet patient. This is Alex summed up.

My Alex.

And I have this overwhelming feeling that I never want to be without him. That I want a million more days like this, moments like this, where it's just us. I feel greedy for it, like I don't want anyone to take this.

He tugs me into his lap, his hands around my waist, and I lean into him so he can kiss me. "Want to go to the pool?" he says instead.

"Uh." I lean back. "Right now?"

He shrugs. "We leave tomorrow."

What I want to say is, *No I don't want to go anywhere, now just kiss me already*. But instead, I agree to go to the pool, and quietly get changed. We walk to the pool hand in hand without saying anything. A hush has fallen over the hotel, and we respect the quiet.

"You think it'll be locked?" he asks when we get outside.

"You can just throw me over the fence if it is," I tell him. He looks at me, aghast, and I laugh. "You're such a rule follower, Alex."

"Someone has to keep you in line."

We're relieved when the pool is open, and even more relieved when we're the only people there. It's a zero-gravity pool, so we wade in, getting accustomed to the tiny chill the water provides. Once we're waist-deep, Alex dunks under the water and comes up, shaking his wet hair so that droplets fly all over me.

"Hey!" I protest as I'm splattered by the water.

Alex chuckles, a low sound that suddenly seems very suspicious. He's moving toward me, and I realize it belatedly as he wraps an arm around my waist and tugs me under the water with him. "Alex!" I cry out, but my yell is cut off by the water. I can feel his laughter under the water, even as I try to shove against him. He finally lets me up and I come up sputtering and wiping at my eyes. "I didn't want to get my hair wet," I whine.

"You should've told me," he says with a smile.

"Would it have changed anything?"

"Nope."

He pulls me against him, and suddenly, he's serious Alex again. He kisses me then in a way he never has before. Like he's trying to bottle up all of his feelings from the past few hours and express them in a single kiss. I can taste it all—the fear, the pain, the isolation, the relief. And over all of it, the love. The overwhelming love that Alex has for me seeps into the touch of his lips, every brush of his tongue, every sigh that escapes. I try to match him, but soon I'm so flooded by his emotions that all I can do is simply be in this moment. Exist with him.

Finally, he pulls back, his forehead against mine, his breath on my lips. "I'm sorry, I—" he starts, but I cut him off.

"Don't you dare apologize for that."

He sighs and squeezes me tighter against him. "I love you, Mila Kozak."

"And I love you, Alex Caballero." I break away from him, knowing it's time to lighten the mood. "Race me? First one to the other side has to get everyone coffee in the morning!" Before I even finish saying it, I fly back in the water, swimming toward the other side. Alex pulls on my legs, tugging me backward, and then scooping me up in his arms.

"They said to limit your exertion," Alex says, chastising me.

I scoff and roll my eyes. "All they care about is liability. Besides, you and I both know I need to get back on Cyrus tomorrow before we leave."

"Uh, you and I do not know that."

"I'm serious, Alex. You know I shouldn't have left that ring without getting back on."

"You had a concussion, Mila. You were barely conscious."

"It doesn't change the fact that if I don't get back on soon, you know it's going to be that much harder the next time."

Alex shakes his head, seemingly unwilling to argue with me about it, but also not willing to give in. "Can we talk about it tomorrow? After some sleep?"

I nod, and he pulls me closer to his chest, still holding me bride-style with one of his arms under my knees and the other holding me across my back. "You fit really well here," he remarks with his perfect smile.

"I love your smile," I tell him, running my thumb across his lips. "I wish you'd smile more, with other people." I know he feels insecure about his smile, since kids used to tease him for his crooked incisor. But Alex's smile is everything that's good about him—genuine, sweet, and wholly mine.

"Maybe I like to save my smiles just for you," he says with a bashful grin, nuzzling my cheek.

I lean back and straighten my legs so that I'm floating on the water, Alex's palms just barely touching me, keeping me afloat. I close my eyes, relaxing into his hands. "I got you," Alex says, and I smile.

"I know."

I feel light, weightless. The only sound is Alex's breath and the slight rippling of the water against the edge of the pool. I could stay here forever. I can't really tell how long I'm floating for—just that time seems to stand still, and I have this feeling like Alex and I are the only people in the whole world.

Later, once we're dried off and in our pajamas, by some unspoken agreement, Alex and I meet back at the couch instead of heading to bed. His long legs are stretched out in front of him as I curl up beside him, his arm holding me against him.

"I'm glad you're okay," he says.

"Me too."

There's a long stretch of silence before he says, "I know the doctor said you're probably fine, but I'm still afraid of you falling asleep."

I try not to let guilt overtake me and remind myself that Alex chose this life just as much as I did. Last year, he was the one who got me competing in Grand Prix with Cyrus. I look up at him and all the guilt flees, because all I can focus on is the fact that Alex is here and he loves me. "Then stay with me."

His dark eyes search mine for a moment, and then he gives a nod. "I'll stay with you as long as you let me."

I grab hold of his shirt and tug him closer to me so that our foreheads are touching. "Forever, then?"

He runs his thumb over my cheekbone. "Or longer."

"Longer is better."

He smiles. "I agree."

Alex, this weekend we went to WEC and I took a really bad fall off Cyrus. I'm sure you don't need me to go into details—but I went from being so ridiculously happy and quite honestly shocked that Aaron Vale knew who I was to being so hyper-focused on the fact that I'd missed our pre-show ritual of me kissing you. In retrospect, I could've taken it a different way—that I'm strong enough to not need that ritual. I can be brave enough without that ritual. But, I'm not. Not yet, anyway. And between us, I don't know that I ever want to be that brave. I need you, Alex. You are the glue that holds me together. And I always want that. Forever, or longer.

17

Lukey Luke

Anya

The next morning, I wake up to find my sister's bed empty, which sends a chill down my spine. "Mila!" A moment later, Mila comes stumbling in with Alex on her tail. Both looking rumpled, like they just woke up.

"Are you okay?" Mila asks.

"Yeah," I say. *I freaked out when you weren't where you were supposed to be*, I want to say. But now I'm embarrassed for feeling that way since she's obviously fine, so I just say, "I needed help out of bed."

"I got her," Alex says. He lifts me out of bed and into my chair as if I'm no lighter than a pad of hay— which is how I feel getting thrown around here and there by all the able-bodied people in my life. It's gotten somewhat easier in the two years since my accident, but I can't say I'm completely at ease with my neediness.

"I'll order up some coffee," Mila says.

Alex loops an arm around her waist and says, "Coffee's on me, remember?" They exchange conspiratorial smiles—some inside joke I'm left out of—and he kisses her quickly and leaves the room. Mila helps me to the bathroom, and I keep eyeing her as we brush our teeth side-by-side. She seems back to her old self, as if nothing out of sorts happened yesterday. I guess Luke really helped her.

For some reason this bothers me, and I can't quite figure it out. Yesterday, I *wanted* her to be fine. But now that she is fine, I don't like it? What is wrong with me?

Mila helps me get dressed. I dab some makeup on and style my hair. Then we pack up and head into the living area for breakfast. Luke is huddled around a cup of coffee, looking like his life depends on its contents. When I wheel up, he looks at me, his eyes widening in some expression I can't place. "Do you just wake up like that?" he asks.

I stare at him, unsure if he's mocking me or complimenting me. "Do *you* just wake up like that?" I say. His blonde hair is sticking up on the side, his eyes bleary and a day's worth of light blonde scruff dust his cheeks. Even so, he manages to look good. Not that I'd ever admit it.

He gives me a groggy smile and buries his head back in his coffee cup. A moment later, Alex walks through the front door with more coffees and pastries. He hands me my iced mocha, sets down Mila's caramel macchiato, and puts another cup in front of Luke before disappearing to find Mila.

"Another cup of coffee?" I ask, eyebrow raised as I grab a cinnamon roll from the pastry box.

"You don't think I'm my charming self *au naturel*, do you?" The way he says *au naturel*, with his thick Southern accent, has me rolling my eyes.

"It's none of my business if you want to abuse your adrenal glands in order to be 'charming.'"

He leans forward, a smug grin on his face. "You *did* ask." He lifts his cup up in a cheers. "Besides, if we're going to discuss my caffeine intake, that means your sugar consumption is on the table for discussion."

"Oh please."

Luke and I spend the rest of our breakfast in silence, the whole time my subconscious reminding me that I need to thank him for helping Mila yesterday. I manage to ignore the urge until finally Mila and Alex join us. Mila's in her riding clothes, even though she shouldn't ride today. Trina's already on the showgrounds since she had a few students competing early this morning.

"I might hop on Cyrus for a little bit before we leave," Mila says. The whole room seems to tense—or maybe it's just Alex and me—but then Alex takes a bite of his croissant and nods.

"Good idea," Luke says, as if going against medical advice is a normal activity for him. But of course, he's a *cowboy*—they don't even ride with helmets, which is just idiotic.

"That is not a good idea, Mila," I cut in. "You know what the doctor said. Not to ride for a week."

Mila waves a hand dismissively. "The doctor doesn't understand the dynamics here, in our world, between horse and rider. I'll just flat him around the ring, nothing more. I'll wear a safety vest," she says, bargaining with me.

"You can't be on board with this, Alex?"

Alex shakes his head, sighing. "I don't want Mila to get back on Cyrus, but I also understand the need for her to face her fears and ride again while we're still here. You know as well as any of us how hard it is to get back on once you've fallen. It's a principle for a reason."

I glare at Alex, then Mila, then Luke for good measure, too. "I can't believe you guys think this is okay." They're all silent under my scrutiny, so I throw my hands up and say, "Fine, if you're taking part, then I won't be here for it." I leave the hotel room—though being confined to a wheelchair makes it slightly less dramatic of an exit. I have difficulty getting the door open on my own, so Alex has to get up and help me. And I don't even have the satisfaction of slamming the door.

Frustration radiates through me, prickling my skin and accumulating behind my eyes. But I don't want to think about it, don't want to imagine Mila back on Cyrus in that arena. I need a distraction.

On my way out, I pass Mr. Pickles & Sailor Bear Toy Shoppe, where a pair of massive toy giraffes stare at me from inside the shop. I'm tempted to wheel around in there, but one glance tells me it'll be difficult to navigate in my chair without knocking everything down. Instead, I head outside and roll around the side of the hotel toward the Grand Arena. It's a cloudless day, and I close my eyes and tilt my head toward the sun, soaking up its warmth for a moment. *Make me feel better*, I tell the sun. The breeze is mussing my hair, so I put my ice mocha in my cup holder while I throw my hair into a ponytail. It's still relieving to me that I can do this by myself. A year ago, I couldn't even scratch my face, and now here I am, rolling around the showgrounds alone, putting my own hair up. That's something to be grateful for, I try to remind myself.

Beyond the Grand Arena, there's a sweets shop and pizza place. I inspect the colorful mural outside Miss Tilly's Lollipops, with an oversized bear riding a bicycle. I go inside and pick out some treats to take on the drive—cookies, fudge, chocolate covered pretzels. By the time Mila and I get home, we'll have gained fifteen pounds. I tuck the sweets into a side pocket on my wheelchair and head back out. *What do you think of my sugar consumption now, Lukey Luke?*

I wheel over to a statue of a horse and read the plaque. The horse's name is Staff Sergeant Reckless—a mare who served in the Marine Corps during the Korean War. My eyes prick with tears as I think about the bravery of this horse, and I quickly roll away. "Sentimental," I grumble to myself.

I notice someone's in the Grand Arena, even though the classes for the day are over. As I get closer, I realize the horse is Cyrus, and the rider is Mila. My heart freezes in my chest and I stop wheeling over. I know Mila mentioned she might ride, but I didn't realize it would be back in the Grand Prix arena where she had her fall.

Breathe, Anya, I have to remind myself. But my lungs are being stubborn, and it takes a few attempts to get a full breath. I will myself closer to the ring, clenching my jaw to stave off the feelings swelling in me. I roll all the way up to the row of flags at the side of the arena and sit frozen as Mila gallops toward the combination she crashed over yesterday. I'm gripping my wheelchair arms as if I could somehow stop her with the force of my grip, and I hold my breath as she flies over the first jump, then the second. She lands and does a rollback, cantering around the edge of the ring, and then she's heading back to the in-and-out. She jumps it again, then rolls back in the other direction. I realize she's going to keep jumping this same combination, and it's like I'm stuck in a looping nightmare.

I go to back away when I spot Luke, Alex, and Trina standing on the other side of the arena. They're talking and laughing like this is no big deal. There are emotions I can't pinpoint swirling in my chest, threatening to rise like bile in my throat. I turn my chair quickly away and wheel as fast as it can go, and for the second time that day I'm regretting not having working legs—or I'd run.

I'm sitting by one of the paddocks, watching a chestnut mare trotting the fence line, whinnying as she looks for a companion. I wheel closer, my chair bumping along the grass, and extend a hand to the horse's nose. "I'm here," I tell her softly. She snorts into my palm, and for some reason, that's when the tears come.

It wasn't even that I was holding it together before then—I simply hadn't let myself *feel* anything about Mila's fall until this point, when the emotions wouldn't stay stuffed away any longer. I try to remind myself that all riders fall, but the implications of my accident make every tumble seem that much riskier. And the fact that Mila suffered a concussion, a brain injury, makes it that much worse.

And then I realize I'm angry with them—all of them. Alex, Luke, Trina. Angry that they got Mila on a horse, that they let her jump, that they looked so casual about it. The crazy horse-girl part of my brain is saying that it's good for Mila to face her fears, to get back on Cyrus and get back in the ring. And to face the very jump that defeated her the first time—that's epic.

But the sisterly part of my brain, the one whose emotional balance is so fragile that one split hair could upset it—that part of my brain is rioting. How could they? Why would they? How dare they? The thoughts tumble through my brain as I let the tears fall. The mare snorts at me once more, then trots off in search of a better friend.

I let myself grieve and wail, alone and comfortless, as I finally face the fall. I love this sport, despite what it's done to me, but I can't just stand by as it steals my sister, too.

After a while, I realize that my phone is buzzing. I grab it out of the pocket, where it's surrounded by all the treats I bought, and just miss a call from Luke. On my home screen, I see missed calls from everyone—Mila, Alex, Trina, and now Luke. Everyone's looking for me, and I'm over here pouting. I sigh and go to redial Mila, but accidentally call Luke back. I almost groan when his voice is on the line. "Anya," he says, breathless.

"Hi, Luke."

"Where are you? Are you okay?" There's genuine concern laced in his questions, and something about that puts me on edge.

"I'm fine. I just didn't hear my phone. I'm over by the barns. At the paddocks."

"Okay, I'll be there in a minute." I want to tell him not to bother, but he hangs up, and this time I do groan. I do *not* want Luke to swoop in and save me. No, thank you.

I wipe my face, smooth my hair, and spend a moment looking at myself in my phone camera. My eyes are still a little red and puffy, but my sunglasses will cover that. Luke won't notice, and even if he does, I'm not talking about it with him.

His obnoxious truck pulls up a few minutes later, and I steel myself for an annoying trip to wherever Mila is. Then I realize I have no idea how I'm going to get into his truck. I know the truck has been converted to accommodate his wheelchair, but two wheelchairs? I'm not sure how that will work. If he thinks he can toss me into the bed of his truck, he's got another thing coming.

This must clearly be written all over my face, because Luke is looking a little too self-satisfied when I head over to him. His window is rolled down and he's got an arm resting on the truck door.

"Fancy finding you here," he says, his accent dripping in Southern charm. It makes me cringe.

"And how, exactly, do you plan to get me where I need to go?"

He puts his truck in park. "Do you trust me?" he says with a lopsided grin.

"Not even a little bit."

He laughs. "At least we know where we stand." He bangs a hand on his truck door, gives me a wink, and then flips a switch on the inside dashboard. The front and rear truck doors swing out and up, like the falcon-wing doors on a Tesla, and a begrudging part of me has to admit that's pretty cool. Once the doors are out of the way, the platform that's holding Luke's wheelchair swings out and down. He rolls off the ramp, swings around to face me, and then waves a hand toward the ramp.

"You can take it up and then roll to the passenger seat," he says when I don't make a move. I take a sip of my iced mocha, which I immediately regret because it's all watered down now. Then I sigh and direct my chair toward his truck.

"Do you often transport wheelchaired passengers?" I ask as I wheel onto the platform.

"The passenger seat can be added back in," he says as he presses a button on a remote he's holding, and the platform moves me up to the truck cab. "Alex helped me take it out just now so I could drive you. But I had it customized that way initially so that someone could drive me if need be."

I wonder if that 'someone' was the woman who got "un-stuck" from him after his accident. Suddenly I want to ask about this woman, but then chastise myself because, *who cares?*

Once the platform stops moving and I'm firmly inside the truck cab, I start maneuvering my way toward the passenger seat. What should be a two-point turn ends up being more like a three-hundred-point turn. I sigh, anxious to get on with this day.

Once I'm finally on the passenger's side, Luke is heading up to the cab now too. "So the driver's seat can also go back in?" I ask.

"Yes, ma'am."

I raise an eyebrow. "Oh, now we have manners?"

"I've always had manners, Miss Kozak," he says with a half smile as he starts driving away from the barns. "You just might have to look harder to find them."

I actually laugh at this. A true, genuine laugh, which Luke seems to enjoy. There's a moment of peace that ripples between us like a gentle wave, and I think, *I could get used to this.* And then I realize that Luke isn't heading toward the hotel, or one of the barns. He's driving out of the World Equestrian Center.

"Where are we going?" I ask as a sinking feeling collects in my stomach.

He gives me a side-eye and says, "Home, where else?"

"What about Mila? Alex?" Surely they didn't leave me with this bozo for a four-hour car ride.

"They went on ahead. I told them I'd scoop you."

They left me?

All of the so-called 'peace' I'd been feeling toward Luke vanishes. I want to rage. I want to scream. Mila *knows* how I feel about Luke and she *left* me to get 'scooped' by this redneck donkey? I can't even believe it. Can't wrap my mind around a world where my sister—my *best friend*—does this to me. Did I hurt her in some way? Is she trying to get revenge on me for something I unknowingly did to her?

"I know you're thrilled, but there's no need to keep that joy to yourself," Luke says with a twist of his lips.

He's smiling. He's mocking me. He knows how deeply unsettling this is for me and he's making light of it.

If I were able-bodied, I'd have him drop me at the nearest gas station and call an Uber. What would I pay to not have to sit next to Luke—and only Luke—for four hours? Five hundred dollars? One thousand dollars? I decide I'd pay *five thousand* dollars with not even a groan as the money left my bank account.

"Mila and Alex have some things to discuss," Luke says, as if that explains everything.

"They can talk at any time." What could they possibly have to talk about? They've been together all weekend!

"Some things are more pressing than 'anytime.'" He gives me a look like I should know what he's talking about. But I am the queen of bottling up all the 'pressing' matters in my life, so I *don't* know what he's talking about. "Besides, this gives us some time to get to know each other. For example, I don't even know what kind of music you like to listen to."

No, Mr. Craig, you don't. And then, I grin when I think, *I am firing you in just a few weeks. Just you wait.*

I glance up at him, give him my sweetest smile and say, "Anything but country."

Luke let me plug in my phone so I could play my music for the past hour. We don't speak, and I spend my time looking out the window at the countryside rolling by me. Florida is so green, so lush. The trees rush by in a blur, and occasionally we pass long stretches of rolling farmland and my mouth waters at the beauty of it. Oh, to be on horseback, galloping across those grassy fields. I crave it. My body yearns for it.

I decide to get some work done and look over my notes for a Zoom session planned for tomorrow night with people who are interested in learning more about the Center and what we offer. Alex, Mila, and I take turns leading these open sessions, but my sister has hinted at wanting me to take over them completely since prospective clients seem to want to see me more than anyone else. They want to hear about my miraculous recovery in my upper body, to ask if it's possible for them too. And you know how I just *love* being the bearer of bad news. Miracles don't come every day.

At some point, Luke turns down the music and says, "My turn."

"Excuse me?"

"It's my turn to play music." When I don't say anything, he continues, "In relationships, there's this thing called give-and-take. Not sure if you've heard about that."

"We're not in a relationship, Mr. Craig."

"Ah, see. That's where you're wrong. We are in a working relationship."

For a few more weeks, I want to say.

"If I give you some of my candy, will you just please, please not play the country music?"

Luke laughs, a hearty, deep-bellied laugh that makes my cheeks flush with embarrassment for a reason I can't quite comprehend. Is he mocking me again?

"I don't want your candy, darlin'," he says.

"Why? Is it too hoity-toity for you?" I feel a little bad ripping on him for his manners and such, especially after he got us oysters and fancy wine last night. But there's something about harassing him that makes me feel calmer.

He raises an eyebrow and tilts his head at me, as if to say, *Good to know what you think of me.* "Unless you have some vegan candy in that little bag of yours, I'll pass."

"You don't seem like the principled type," I say, and immediately regret it, because even for me and Luke, that's rude. But when he laughs again, I don't apologize.

"Glad I've made such a lasting impression on you."

"Your stickers did that for you."

"Ah." He nods knowingly. "So all of this"—he waves a hand toward me—"is because of my stickers?"

"It's not *only* your stickers."

"I see."

I'm trying to discern what he's thinking or feeling—and wondering why I care—but he doesn't seem offended. He seems amused, which only makes me annoyed. He *should* be offended. I'm his boss and he should care about what I think of him. It makes me want to rip into him, to tell him every vicious thought I've had toward him. Of course, I'm better than that, so all I say is, "You shouldn't have let Mila get back on Cyrus. In that ring."

He's very still for a moment, and I have no idea what he's going to say. "I see."

"Really? That's all you're going to say?"

"Well, it's clear to me that you're projecting your trauma onto your sister, and it's no wonder she had a hard time getting back onto her horse."

"Oh, don't you *therapize* me."

"Am I wrong?"

"I've only ever wanted Mila to be happy. I never wanted her to be negatively affected by my accident."

"I'm sure that's true."

Who does this guy think he is? That because he's a therapist he can magically see into my head and know what I'm feeling? That he's allowed to doubt my motives, to pick at my intentions?

"Look, I understand where you're coming from, but the decision is Mila's. And as a therapist, I'm looking out for her mental health above all, and if she decides to face her fears and get back in the saddle, I want to support that."

I say nothing. I grit my teeth together and stare at the road ahead, the white and yellow lines darting beneath us. How am I going to stay in this truck for three more hours? I might throw myself from the cab if he says one more word.

"I think you like this," he says. "This back-and-forth. It's easier for you than having a real conversation. And I offer you the perfect target."

I scoff, wanting to scrub his words off of me as soon as they land. "Don't try to fix me, Mr. Craig."

"Why would I want to fix you? I like this, too." He smirks at me and something about the way his eyes are glancing over me makes a little tingle go through me. "I've got just as much, if not more, I'm running from than you."

What does *that* mean? His words confuse me and something about them, mixed with the look he gave me, makes me feel jumbled inside. And speechless. Very, very speechless. Of course I always have a good retort—except right this second.

"How about we compromise, hmm?" Luke says after a while, and I have no idea what we could be compromising on. "I'll listen to one of your songs, then you listen to one of mine. Let's try to find some common ground. We'll pick songs we think the other person will like."

"I highly doubt you're going to convince me to like any type of music that advocates women being barefoot, pregnant, and in booty shorts at all times," I say tartly.

"I didn't realize you were such a feminist," Luke says with a grin. "That Nicki Minaj song you were playing earlier would suggest otherwise."

My face flushes and I look away. *I can listen to whatever I want,* I think. But his words strike a nerve.

"I'll make you a deal," I say finally. "If you find a country song that I actually like..."

"Yes?"

"I won't fire you in five weeks when your probationary period is over."

He laughs again, loud and braw, slapping his hand on the steering wheel. But when he looks at me and sees that my face is deathly serious, his smile falters. "Wait, you're serious."

"You can't be surprised, Mr. Craig."

"Pardon me, but hell yes, I'm surprised. Whatever personal issues you have with me, I am good at my job. Let's get that straight."

"Well, let's just hope you can find a country song that doesn't make my ears bleed."

An hour later, I feel nothing but nauseous as Luke plays song after song after song. Rascall Flatts, Luke Brian, Kasey Musgraves, Faith Hill, Garth Brooks, June Carter Cash. Eventually, Luke reaches over and turns off the radio.

"Giving up already?"

He shakes his head, a slight smile playing on his lips. "You're not firing me, Miss Kozak."

"What makes you so certain?"

"Like I said, I'm good at my job. Besides, it's two against one." He gives me a knowing look, and I have to press my lips together to keep myself from doing something embarrassing—like growling at him. "Alex would marry me tomorrow if I asked, and I don't know if you recall, but I helped your sister just a tad back there." He grins at me, and I want to groan because he actually has a nice smile, even if it is smug. "You're stuck with me, darlin'."

"I'm not your darling," I grumble.

"Not yet," he says with a wink, and my mouth actually drops open. The nerve of this guy. "How about we wager something else?"

"Like what?" I ask warily.

"If I find a country song you tolerate…"

"Uh huh."

"You have to go on a date with me."

For the second time in as many minutes, my mouth drops open. "Why on earth would you want to go on a date with me?"

"Well, I would've settled for a cordial coffee with you, but you had to go and threaten to fire me…"

I snort. "You had a better chance when the bet was you keeping your job."

"I like my odds."

"How? How is that even possible?"

"I have faith."

"In country music? Or in me?"

"Definitely country music."

I laugh, shaking my head. I cannot believe the turn this has taken. "Fine. Game on."

"Alright, then this is what you need to know about country music—"

"What is there to know other than the fact that it's annoying, twangy, and decidedly anti-woman?"

"Country music is all about telling a story."

"Okay," I say, drawing the word out.

"That's what makes it the best music. It takes you on a narrative. Weaves a story."

"You are going to have to prove it for me to believe it."

"Get comfy, Miss Kozak." He hands me his phone, which displays the lyrics on Spotify along with the song, and instructs me to follow along.

I roll my eyes and steel my nerves for another irritating song. Sure enough, a twangy female voice comes on the speakers. Reba McEntire sings about a girl named Fancy having one last chance and even though the tune itself isn't for me, I do get a little chill down my back when Reba sings with all her might about how she may have been born white trash but Fancy was her name. Luke doesn't even ask me what I thought about the song, he just moves on to the next one, one by Tim McGraw called "Don't Take the Girl." I cringe at the outdated music but force myself to follow the "narrative."

After the first verse, I comment, "This kid sounds like a jerk. Just let the girl go fishing, geeze."

He smiles over at me and says, "Keep listening."

"Well, that progressed quickly," I say with a laugh when the jerk kid ends up sticking up for the girl in the second verse when they get robbed.

"Just you wait."

At the final verse, I'm yelling, "Oh my gosh! Is she dying? Did she die? Luke! Why did you play this song? It's terrible!"

"But did it make you feel something?"

I don't say yes, even though it did. "That wasn't what the bet was about."

"True enough."

He plays the next song, another old-sounding country tune by Mary Chapin Carpenter called "He Thinks He'll Keep Her."

"Just what I was looking for," I say. "Another chauvinist in a country song."

Luke laughs and shakes his head. "Keep listening."

At the third verse, I say, "Yes! Leave his sorry behind!" Luke smirks at me and I laugh. "I don't *like* the song."

"No, but you're invested. It's very close."

He plays me several more songs with admittedly great narratives, starting with "Goodbye Earl" by The Chicks—a song I laugh at before accusing Luke of being an advocate of murder to solve problems.

"Hey, you wanted a female power song, didn't you?" he says with a laugh. Then he plays "Two Black Cadillacs" by Carrie Underwood.

"All these men are chauvinists," I accuse.

"You want a song with a good guy?" He plays Blake Shelton's song "I'll Name the Dogs," and even though it was a very sweet song, I rebut with, "He's been married three times. The guy's not *that* good." So he plays me Thomas Rhett's song "Life Changes" with the introduction, "This guy's been married to his wife for ten years. Loved her since the second grade. Listen to it, he's an objectively good guy." When we got to the part of the song where Rhett and his wife adopt a daughter from Uganda and then find out they're pregnant, tears prick at the corners of my eyes, and I have to look away to hide them from Luke.

"Are those tears I see?"

"I didn't ask you to make me cry! I wanted a good song!"

"You want a happy song?"

"Yes," I say defensively. He plays a song called "No Bad Days" with Flo Rida and a country artist named Jimmie Allen.

By the end of the song, I'm bobbing my head freely—convinced there's no way this is actually a country song—when Luke goes, "Ha! I got you!"

"This," I say, waving a finger at the radio, "is *not* a country song."

"Google it."

"I will." I tap the words into my phone: "No Bad Days Flo Rida Genre." And there in bold at the very top: COUNTRY. I gasp.

"What does it say?"

I quickly click my screen off and turn my phone over onto my legs. "Nothing."

"Ha!" Luke says again and I hang my head. "Where should we go?" Luke muses, tapping his chin thoughtfully. "The Round Up?" A country and line dancing club in Davie. "Or my buddy has a bluegrass band we can go see..."

"I'm not going on a date with you, Mr. Craig. I'm your boss."

He holds up a finger and waggles it back and forth. "Uh uh, you made a deal."

I roll my eyes. "You know just as well as I do that we shouldn't date. Again, I'm your *boss*." Also, I don't like you *at all* and I don't understand how you could even want to go out with me.

"Well, sort of. Alex is more my direct supervisor, isn't he? Plus, Alex and Mila are dating. It's not like there's a company policy against dating, is there?"

"I just don't understand *why*."

"That's for me to know," he says with a wink, "and you to find out. Soon, preferably."

I groan.

18

The Help

Alex

On the drive home, Mila is chatty and effervescent. I know that facing her fear—getting back in the arena and jumping the very fence that bested her the day before—has got her on a little high, and I try to ride it with her, but find myself trending toward melancholy. Mila doesn't seem to notice. She's too busy talking about how amazing the World Equestrian Center was, how she wants to go back soon and maybe we should go to WEC instead of WEF this season, and so on. I wonder a little about her ability to move on so quickly, and find myself going down a rabbit hole: what if I lose my court case next week? What if they send me back to Cuba? How quickly would Mila move on? The thought stays with me like a thorn in my side.

We stop outside of Orlando to fill up on gas and get a snack at Starbucks. I offer to pay for gas, which Mila accepts, but soon worry I'll have a stroke when the dollar amount keeps going up and up. How much gas does this tiny car take? I'm shocked, and my wallet is literally aching in my back pocket. Next time we go on a road trip, I wonder if I can convince Mila to take my Toyota Corolla—less stylish, but considerably easier on the wallet. I can't help but cringe at the idea of pulling up to a place like the Equestrian Hotel in my beat-up car, with Mila.

We stop at Starbucks and Mila fills up on caffeine—which she definitely doesn't need—and I get her a lemon pound cake, knowing she'll want it later. When we get back in the car, Mila seems to realize my mood.

"Are you okay?" she says, leaning across the center console toward me.

"Just thinking about my court case next week." And then, because we've decided—through unspoken agreement—not to discuss the case, I add, "Can we set a budget for our Christmas gifts to each other?" Considering how I can't even afford Mila's gas, it seems prudent to set a budget so that I don't look like an idiot with a cheap gift while Mila gets me something way outside of my range. "It'll make us get creative with it, you know? Thoughtful things instead of something...pricey."

She nods. "Sure, why not." She lets me set the price at fifty dollars, which seems like a solid middle ground to me. Not cheap, but not ridiculous either.

We listen to music, Mila clearly feeling peppy as she repeats "Superbloom" by MisterWives. I feel bad for not being so chipper with her, for being consumed with anxiety about my court case next week and how useless I felt this weekend with Mila. Eventually, we decide to do some studying. Mila pulls up one of my lectures for me and gives me her AirPods to listen to it. She listens to hers in time-and-a-half speed. I'm not quite sure how she can retain anything her professor is saying when he sounds like a cartoon character on speed, but I've grown used to the sound after many hours of studying with Mila.

When we finally pull up to the Center, I confide in her, "It bothers me that Luke was able to help you and I wasn't."

She furrows her brow and puts a hand on my arm. "Why does that bother you?"

"I don't know—maybe because I'm your boyfriend and I'm going to be a therapist? I should be more capable of helping you than he is."

"Okay, but Luke has been doing this a long time, Alex. And it's not like he's generally helping me with something, he's counseling me. You help me in lots of other areas that Luke couldn't possibly help me with." She teasingly runs a finger across my jaw and then kisses me.

"He better not be helping you like this," I say against her lips. She chuckles and kisses me deeper.

"You're my only...helper...in this department," she says between kisses.

"Good." I laugh and kiss her, but I can't quite shake the feeling that I should be more for Mila. I just wish I knew how.

19

The Question

Mila

In the days after we get back from Ocala, Anya is very weird. She's distant, standoffish, staying in her office and barely coming out. When I ask her about it, she just tells me she stressed or she's tired or she's mad at me for jumping Cyrus or making her drive home with Luke. I can tell she's avoiding him—every time he comes into the office, she wheels off in a different direction as fast as she possibly can.

I convince her to come shopping with me for outfits for our family vacation at the end of the month. It's not as simple as it used to be, shopping with Anya. Of course it's not easy for her to try on clothes, so we don't even bother trying on bottoms. Wheeling around most stores is more of a headache than it's worth, especially since we can easily shop online. After Anya accidentally knocks over an entire display of necklaces with the back of her wheelchair in a Francesca's, we give up. We collapse in a Haagen-Dazs with a cup of Dulce de Leche ice cream. We're both in a melancholy mood, which is exactly the opposite of what I intended with this outing.

"Did something happen in Ocala that you want to talk about?" I ask her, thinking that maybe something happened on the drive home with Luke that's making her so moody.

"You mean other than you going AMA and jumping Cyrus over massive fences when you should've had your two feet on the ground for at least a week?"

My jaw drops open at the unexpected comment—I was waiting for a barrage of loathing toward Luke, not *this*. I thought that Anya would understand how important it is to get back in the saddle, especially after such a bad fall. "Oh, like you've never gone AMA?"

When Anya opens her mouth to bite back, I raise a brow, and she snaps her mouth shut. We're both thinking about last year, when Anya got a pulmonary embolism in part because she refused to go to PT or let Mom do her passive range-of-motion exercises.

"Hey, weren't you supposed to have physical therapy today?" I ask, taking a smug bite of my ice cream.

"Hmm?" Anya acts like she didn't hear me, and I repeat the question.

"I thought I saw that on the schedule," I say innocently.

"Oh yeah," she says. "It got…rescheduled."

I stare at her for a beat, knowing she's lying, but unsure what to do about it. When she changes the subject, I let her. Should I apologize for getting back on Cyrus? It seemed like the right thing to do, but maybe it wasn't considerate of Anya. The whole thing rankles—I feel doomed no matter what I'd chosen. "I should've talked to you more before getting back on Cyrus," I say eventually, hoping this is enough of a compromise for my sister.

Anya nods and takes another bite of her ice cream. I don't feel quite absolved, but Anya doesn't bring it up anymore, so I'm hoping she'll eventually get over it. I'm banking on the fact that we won't have to face this kind of situation again.

I'm looking around the ice cream shop, wanting to make eye contact with anything and anyone other than Anya. Our vibes are still off. It's for this reason that I notice something I might not have.

"Anya!" I whisper-yell at her.

"What?" she says in her normal, annoyed voice.

"That guy is totally checking you out."

She doesn't even look around; she just rolls her eyes. "No one is checking me out, *sestra.* I'm in a wheelchair."

"No, he totally is." I keep looking back at the guy paying for his ice cream, clearly scoping out my sister. He's cute, too, with a head full of dark curls that are falling in his steely gray eyes.

"Mila, hate to burst your optimistic little bubble, but when guys look at me, they don't see a hot girl anymore. They see a poor thing in a wheelchair."

I want to argue with my sister, to call the guy over and get them talking, but by the time I turn around, he's gone. "Dang it, Anya. You missed your chance."

She rolls her eyes as she stabs at her ice cream and says, "Oh yes, I missed my one chance at finding love in a wheelchair."

"I didn't mean it like that."

"Whatever."

A few minutes later, my best friend Monica FaceTimes me. She's living in New York City now, working for Goldman Sachs. When I told my dad about Monica's job, he was practically green with envy. I reminded him that *he* was the one who wanted me to go to grad school and not pursue the workforce yet, which naturally made him feel so much better. (Not.) We exchange a few pleasantries, and all the while Anya must be giving herself a migraine with how much eye rolling she's doing. She's not exactly a fan of Monica.

"Dating any hot guys?" Monica asks, knowing full well that I'm still with Alex. I'm aware of why she's asking this, so I'll reciprocate.

"Are *you* dating any hot guys?" I respond, though not with all the enthusiasm Monica is looking for. She turns the phone to display a shirtless guy asleep on her couch. She waggles her eyebrows and whispers, "That's Emilio. He's my Thursday."

"I see New York has changed you for the better," I say sarcastically.

"Old dogs, new tricks, yadda yadda," Monica says with a wink. Across from me, Anya is groaning in pain from listening to my best friend.

"Mon, I gotta let you go, Anya's having an aneurism."

"Oh! Well," she says. "*Besitos! Besitos!*" She blows me kisses and I wave before hanging up. I glance over at Anya, who's slumped in her wheelchair.

"I'm dead," she groans. "All my brain cells have died listening to her."

I laugh, shaking my head as we leave the ice cream shop. I glance down the sidewalk to see if the guy checking Anya out is anywhere, but he's nowhere in sight. "That guy really looked into you," I insist when we're in the car.

"Drop it, *sestra.*"

By the time I drag Anya back to the barn, I'm really bothered by her perspective on this. Does she really think she has no chance at love in a wheelchair? Sure, I understand it's got its obstacles, but Anya is incredible—surely there's someone out there for her.

It's bugging me so much, I do something almost unthinkable. When we get back to the office, it's time for our daily debriefing from the day. We discuss how it went with clients, any improvements or changes that need to be made, as well as ideas for the future. At the end, Luke or Alex typically lead us in a time of meditation or give us an affirmation to focus on. When you work with people's mental and physical health, it's critical to take care of your own.

Once Luke has finished a meditation on gratitude, after a few moments of silence, we dismiss the staff and volunteers. Tommy, Alex, Luke, and I stay behind, lingering around the coffee station. Anya gets a phone call and wheels out of the lounge, and I see my opportunity.

"Hey," I say. "Let me ask you guys something." I glance at the door to make sure Anya's gone. "Would you date someone in a wheelchair?"

Alex furrows his brows, giving me a look that seems to say, *Are you sure about this?*

Tommy starts asking a ton of questions: "On a scale of 1-10 how pretty is she?" "Does she have a good sense of humor?" "How stuck to the chair is she?" And on and on. I'm regretting my choice when finally he says, "If she were a ten, I'd be down."

Alex rolls his eyes and chuffs Tommy on the back of his head. "What about you?" I ask him.

"If you were in a wheelchair, I'd date you."

"Okay, but just hypothetically, if I were out of the picture, would you consider a girl already in a wheelchair?"

He takes my hand, pulling me to his side in a public display of affection he wouldn't normally show. "There is no world, no universe, where it's not me and you." He kisses my temple briefly and then pulls back so I can see his face. His eyes are dark and earnest. "So I can't answer that question. If you're in a wheelchair, yes. If it's you, I'm in. It doesn't matter what it is. If you lose your hair, or your head is somehow detached from your body and I have to carry it around in a bowling bag—"

"Weird," Tommy cuts in.

"Morbid, but sweet," Luke says with a thoughtful expression. "We get it, though. You don't have to elaborate any further."

Alex's ears pink at the edges, and I know he's embarrassed. I stand on tiptoe to kiss his cheek, which only serves to make his blush deepen. "Thank you for that," I say quietly to him. Then I turn to Luke. "What about you? Would you date a girl in a wheelchair?"

Luke opens his mouth to answer but pauses, mouth ajar, as his eye catches on the door behind me. I swivel, my heart dropping as I see Anya. And the withering look on her face tells me she definitely heard my question to Luke.

A stiffness passes through the room as Anya wheels in, all of us unsure whether to look at Anya or the floor. The only sound in the lounge is the whirring of Anya's electric wheels as she heads toward the office.

"Will you please move, Mr. Craig?" she says in clipped tones to Luke, who is blocking her path.

Luke's hands hover over his wheels, unmoving. "I will if you want me to."

"I do."

Luke holds Anya's gaze for what feels like an eternity. I don't know exactly what I'm witnessing, but I know there's enough tension in the room to fill an Olympic sized swimming pool. Finally, he nods and backs away just enough for her to get by.

Before she reaches the door, Luke turns to me to seemingly answer my question. "If someone wanted to love me, to take on my baggage, I'd let them," he says. Anya stops momentarily, pausing outside the office door, as if she's digesting what Luke has said. And then, without a word, she goes into the office and closes the door.

"Were we talking about Anya?" Tommy whispers to Alex. "'Cause she's definitely a ten. Personality-wise, maybe a six though."

"Shut up, Tomás," Alex says through clenched teeth. We're all still watching the door that Anya went through.

Tommy turns to me and shrugs as if to say, *What? It's true.*

I put my head in my hands and sigh. "I shouldn't have brought that up."

"Yeah, probably not," Alex says honestly.

"It's okay," Luke says. "Anya doesn't need us to tiptoe around her." And then he wheels into his office and closes the door too. Tommy throws up his hands as if we're all too much for him to handle and walks out also, leaving Alex and me alone in the lounge.

"Did we miss something?" Alex says.

"'Let them drive together,' you said. 'It'll be fine,' you said."

"He asked to take her. What was I supposed to say?"

"You were supposed to say no!" I whisper at him.

He wraps an arm around my waist. "Okay, I may have had ulterior motives," he says. "I wanted you all to myself, just for a little bit."

I put my hands on his chest. "You *always* have me all to yourself. I don't belong to anyone else."

He smiles down at me and kisses me, and for a moment I'm glad everyone left the room. Then I hear Anya in the office yell out, "Mila!" and I reluctantly part from Alex, and mouth *Later* to him as I rush to the office. I linger in the doorway, wanting to keep the image of him in my mind's eye as he shoves his hands in his pockets and looks at me with his dark eyes and half-smile that is *so* kissable it's hard to get work done. I love this man. And it makes me feel sad that Anya doesn't think she has a chance at something like this.

Back in the office, Anya says, "I just got a call from Isabella Cardones. Clara's mom."

"Oh my gosh." I quickly sit at my desk, leaning forward so I'm eye level with Anya. "What did she say?"

"She said that Clara had a skull fracture and a subdural hematoma. A brain bleed. She needed surgery."

I gasp, closing my eyes as I absorb this information. "Is she okay?"

"That's all she told me," Anya says, staring down at her phone. "Well, that and the fact that this is all our fault."

I roll my chair closer to Anya and place a hand on her arm. "You know that's not true, though."

Anya sighs. "I know, but it doesn't necessarily make me feel any better."

I pull Anya into my arms, and she lets me hold her, but barely. "It's going to be okay, Anya," I say, but I don't know if it's true.

20

Cell Phone Signals & Heart Flutters

Anya

To say that literally everyone in my life is pissing me off right now would be the understatement of the century. But in the dark moments before I fall asleep, I have to admit—if only to myself—that it's easier to be angry than it is to be sad. To want something I can't have. And Luke's bet to take me on a date broke open the fortress I'd built around my heart after my accident. The knowledge that I was destined to be alone—in my wheelchair—for the rest of my life? I'd come to terms with that.

Sort of.

And then he had to go and make that stupid bet—a bet I thought he'd *never*, not in a million years, win.

Ugh.

And *then* Mila had to go and make it worse by pointing out someone checking me out—I'm convinced there's *no way* that was accurate—and *then* bring it up with the whole barn. How utterly embarrassing. What is wrong with my sister? Why isn't she clued in to how I might be feeling? Leaving me to ride home with Luke and then bringing up that stuff with the barn staff? It was a nightmare come to life. And all at her hand.

And then there's Luke, with his arrogantly perfect smile, his ocean blue eyes, and those stupid abs that I had no business having a visual of. I'd been avoiding him like the plague because there was no way I was actually letting him take me on a date. But when he made that comment earlier today: "*If someone wanted to love me, to take on this baggage, I'd let them…"* Ugh. He thinks he knows what I'm going through—that I'm not *allowing* anyone to love me. But that's the problem, isn't it? There's no one to *allow*. And even before I was in the chair, guys weren't exactly lining up to date me. It's like they instinctively knew I was hot but undateable. That something was inherently wrong with me as a person. Incapable of being loved.

Dan had proven that, hadn't he? My first real boyfriend, the first guy I fell in love with. We'd spend every waking second together, and then he'd disappear for days. I'd have no idea where he went. Then he'd show up like nothing was wrong. And he'd make me feel like there was something wrong with *me* because I wasn't magically okay with him leaving for days and weeks with no explanation. I was so desperate for love, I let him walk all over me. He didn't even dignify our relationship with a breakup—why would he? I hadn't heard from him for a full two months when he'd called me the week before my accident. We had texted late into the night the very night before I was paralyzed, and I had been *thrilled*. Looking back, I feel ashamed of my spinelessness. But then, I couldn't even text him back after my accident. I'd ghosted him, permanently, which in the ultimate act of karma was the worst form of payback because it left me hurting too.

The thought of Dan covers me in a wave of shame and reminds me why I can't go out with Luke. Because I'm broken, not just physically, but on a much deeper level too. I knew what Luke would only soon find out: I'm incapable of being loved by anyone who didn't *have* to love me. Even my own father, my own sister, had wavered in their commitment to me. What would someone like *Luke* do when things got hard?

I squeeze my eyes shut, trying to force myself not to think of Luke in terms of any sort of romantic possibility. I punch a fist into my pillow, fluffing it a little too aggressively. My mind flits to Clara's fall, to the phone call with her mom yesterday. The anger and accusation in her voice. I wallow in that feeling for a while, but then find myself returning to the Luke situation. I have to resolve not to think any more about Luke. I'll tell him tomorrow that I can't go on a date with him. I'll be professional but distant. There's no other way around it. I grab my phone and turn on some music, playing "Numb Little Bug" by Em Beihold, which resonates a little too much when she sings about barely staying afloat.

I turn over and start to drift toward sleep, but the last image that comes to my mind is of Luke's face when he'd said, *"If someone wanted to love me, to take on this baggage, I'd let them."* He'd given me the tiniest glimpse into his soul then. And what I'd seen was not the arrogant cowboy I'd expected. It was a vulnerable, real man who was broken too.

We've been keeping an eye on a tropical storm in the Atlantic—a rare post-season storm that clearly didn't get the hint that hurricane season is over. Two days ago, it looked like it was going to veer off toward Cuba, but last night the winds apparently changed and now we're scrambling to get the barn ready. And of course, Alex's court date is this afternoon.

"There's a tropical storm coming?" Mila asks when she walks into the office.

Alex gives her a quizzical look, as if he can't believe she didn't know about it. She throws her hands up in innocence. "Hey, if it's not popping up on my Instagram feed, I don't know about it."

He laughs and shakes his head, but there's a glimmer of affection in his eyes. "I think this is the part where Anya makes a comment about being a Gen Z-er."

"Yes, insert snide comment about being Gen Z," I say with a wave of my hand, too distracted by the radar to think of something witty.

"Which is hypocritical, because you're Gen Z too, *sestra*."

I scoff without looking up. "That may be technically true, but I don't *act* like one, which is what really matters." I lean back from my computer and glance up at Alex. "I'm surprised they haven't canceled your court date. It's heading straight for us."

"Any word from Ann?" Mila asks Alex, referring to Alex's immigration attorney.

"I called her and she said she hasn't heard anything, so we're still on." He's a jittery mess—which is understandable, since so much rides on this—but Ann keeps assuring us that he should be just fine.

"Look, why don't you guys go get ready for court and me, Luke, and Tommy can take care of everything here?" I say. Mila raises a brow but doesn't express any doubt that the three of us can handle the preparations.

"I hung the buckets in all the stalls, so you just have to fill them up," Alex says. Then he goes to walk out of the office. Mila reaches out and grabs his hand, squeezing it. An unspoken sentiment passes between them, and I look away. There's so much emotion swirling around the barn today, it's oppressive.

Alex walks out and Tommy flies in like he usually does. "What else, boss?" he asks. Mila looks to me, even though technically she's his boss too.

"Can you take the van to the feed store and pick up a couple extra bags of feed and bales of hay? Just to be on the safe side. And then fill it up with gas." I hand him the Center's credit card and he speeds off.

"Anything else you want me to do before I have to leave?" Mila asks.

I shake my head. "No, you've got enough on your plate. I wish I could be there," I tell her, reaching out a hand. "But I think I need to stay and make sure the horses are good to go for this storm."

"I understand." She squeezes my hand and then turns to go. Once she's gone, I realize my mistake. Alex and Mila are leaving and I just sent Tommy on an hours-long errand, which means Luke and I are alone at the barn. I put my head on my desk and groan.

Luke is surprisingly professional as we prep the barn for the storm. He goes all around the property, picking up anything that might fly away in the wind—an exhausting task made all the more tiring by being in a manual wheelchair.

"Would you ever switch to an electric wheelchair?" I ask when he comes back in the barn sweating through his shirt. His familiar crooked smile is back, and today it looks less like a smirk and more like, well, a smile.

"How else would I stay this jacked?" he says, holding up a well-defined bicep. *Spell broken*, I think as I roll my eyes. I turn away, heading into the next stall to fill up the water bucket. We have automatic waterers in each of the stalls, but on the chance that the electricity goes out, we want to make sure the horses have water, so we fill up the buckets. "What about you? Would you ever consider a manual chair?" he asks as he takes off the removable saddle racks lining the aisle, stacking them in his lap.

"Life is hard enough as it is," I say, shocking myself with my honesty. Jet, the horse whose stall I'm in, is nuzzling the top of my head and then nibbling at my shoulder. Most of the horses in the barn are a little antsy—they can tell the storm is coming—but I think Jet is so old, his internal storm radar is broken. I finish filling up his bucket, give him a kiss on his soft nose, and roll out of his stall, tugging the hose behind me. It's not an easy process—I keep rolling over the hose and getting it stuck on the stall doors, but there's a satisfaction in doing this task by myself that I enjoy.

When I come back into the breezeway, Luke is gone, and I wonder if he even stuck around to hear my response to his question. "Typical," I mutter as I wrangle the hose back in its home at the corner of the barn.

"I like the feeling of control it gives me," Luke says, startling me. I straighten up and look at him, and it takes me a moment to realize what he's referring to.

"The manual chair?"

He nods. "So many things feel out of my control," he says, gripping the edges of his wheels and rolling himself back and forth. "But having control over this, I don't know, it helps."

His words resonate with me, flooding my chest with an unfamiliar experience. Camaraderie. I think that's what this is. I understand exactly what he's saying because I've experienced that loss of control too. And scrambled to find even a semblance of it. I put the nozzle over the coil of the hose, just so, and laugh to myself. *Control.* Yes, I get that. Deeply.

But of course I'm not ready to divulge that to Luke—not now, probably not ever. He's not exactly my first choice for friendship, let alone any other kind of *-ship.* "That makes sense," is all I tell him in response.

He wheels closer until our knees are almost touching. "I think it might make more than sense to you," he says, leveling his gaze at me so that his blue eyes are staring fully at me. It's an unsettling feeling. Then he's reaching forward, his hand outstretched toward me, and I'm stuck. I don't know if I should move away or let him touch me. His hand smooths the top of my hair, igniting something both foreign and familiar in my stomach, and then he slowly pulls back. "You had, um..." He waves a finger at the top of his head. "Your hair was, y'know."

Realization dawns that Jet must've made a mess of my hair when he nuzzled my head. And Luke was fixing it. Which was a shockingly intimate thing to do. Or was it? Being stuck in a chair changes how people interact with you—you're not so easy to hug, there's a natural barrier between you and others. And that craving for physical touch, which I normally don't miss, rages through me for a moment like a wildfire.

"Let's check the generator," I say, wheeling away. But not fast enough, because I hear Luke chuckle under his breath, "*Control.*"

Luke inspects the generator while I go through our first aid kit, making sure we have everything we need—bandages, ointment, scissors, and pain relievers for the horses like bute and banamine. I check our toolbox as well to make sure there are wire cutters, a fire extinguisher, duct tape, as well as all the other typical tools we'd need to repair things around the barn.

Luke and I meet back up in the breezeway. "Generator's good to go," he says. "But we don't have a ton of extra gas."

"Tommy's getting some, but he's taking forever." I glance at my phone and realize I've been alone in the barn with Luke for almost two hours without losing my mind. We've actually worked very well together.

"The gas stations are packed, I'm sure."

I try calling Tommy, but it goes straight to voicemail. And then I call Mila to check in with her, and that goes straight to voicemail too. I toss my phone into my wheelchair pocket and give a frustrated groan.

"There's about to be a storm. Maybe the lines are jammed," Luke says.

"Is that an actual thing?" I ask, genuinely curious.

Luke shrugs. "I mean, the signal has to go to outer space."

"Does it? I thought it just had to go to the closest phone tower."

"You know, I said that very confidently, but I actually have no idea." He breaks into one of his wide grins that lights up his whole face, and for a second, I wonder why I thought his smile was arrogant. "I'll stick to therapy."

I laugh and there's a ripple of something flowing between us that I can't quite put my finger on. "And I'll stick to managing the barn. We'll let someone brainier figure out the phone signal thing. Maybe Alex."

He gives a mock gasp and puts a hand to his chest like he's offended. "Are you saying I'm not brainy?" Without meaning to, I follow the movement of his hand, and now I'm mentally tracing the hard lines of his chest through his soaked shirt. I snap my eyes back up to his face, but that's not any better.

"Has anyone ever accused you of being brainy, Luke?" The second his name is out of my mouth, I realize it's the first time I've called him by his first name. How did I slip into this familiarity?

What is going on with me?

He pretends to think for a second, his blue eyes glancing at the ceiling. "Just my mama," he says as he rocks back and forth on his chair wheels. This image of him gives me a glimpse into a different aspect of his personality. He's not unprofessional—he's goofy and sweet. Why didn't I see it this way before?

Another laugh bubbles out of me and it makes him smile. Oh my gosh, are we *flirting*? Honestly, it's been so long since I've flirted with anyone, I can't really remember. Maybe this is just normal conversation. "We should give the horses their dinner," I say, suddenly uncomfortable with whatever this is.

"I'll get the hay." We wheel off toward the feed room. "Then I'll take you home."

My brain takes a minute to unravel what he's just said. There's this weird fluttering in my heart that takes hold when I think, for a moment, he meant that he would take me to *his* home. But then I realize he's offering to take me to *my* home. I chastise myself because I let my mind wander into flirtation territory and now it's gone too far. *Way* too far.

Am I so starved for affection and attention that I'll settle for this? I don't even want to know the answer to this question. So I just won't think about it.

21

Silence & Storms

Mila

On our way to the courthouse, Alex is very quiet and very still. He hardly moves in the passenger seat the entire hour-long drive. I try to think of things to talk about that don't involve his impending trial, but he doesn't take the bait. His mom, who's in the backseat, keeps making comments to him in Spanish, and he only responds with little grunts. I turn on some music, trying to find something soothing, but every song seems to have some sort of implication of pending doom.

When we get there, we park in a parking garage. Before Alex can walk to the stairwell, I grab his hand and pull him to me. "Hey," I say, my hands on his chest. He's dressed in a tailored navy suit my dad insisted on buying him for this occasion. We paired it with a white button down and a textured gray tie. I know he's embarrassed that he couldn't afford the suit on his own, but it doesn't change the fact that it looks incredible on him. I smooth out his lapels, straighten his tie, then look him in the eye. "No matter what happens, it's going to be okay."

He nods and gives me a quick kiss on the forehead before turning away to the stairs. I sigh. I wish I knew what to say. By unspoken agreement, we haven't discussed the case with each other. I've insisted on keeping a positive perspective on it—even when Anya's brought up the possibility of Alex getting deported, I've told her I'm not willing to think about that. Ann says he'll be fine, so he'll be fine. Besides, who in their right mind would want to kick Alex out of the country? He's responsible, gainfully employed, highly educated, and he's making this country better just by being here.

As we walk, I take his hands in mine, squeezing reassurance into him. We go up the steps at the front of the courthouse, walk under the massive salmon-colored archway and then in through the doors of the courthouse. When Mrs. Caballero glances up at me with worry in her eyes, I reach out and pull her into a hug. "*Estara bien,*" I tell her. "*Pronto.*"

She nods, suddenly speechless as well, and then we break up to go through the metal detectors. As Alex's belongings are searched, his phone rings. The guards shuffle him through the line and by the time he gets his phone back, he's missed the call. "It's Ann," he says when he checks the call. He dials her back and is silent for almost a full minute as she talks to him. His face is stony and unreadable. "So, what will we do?" he asks. "Okay, thanks. Yeah, bye." He hangs up and tucks the phone into his back pocket, sighing heavily as he wipes a hand over his tired face. "They're shutting down the courthouse because of the storm."

"What? Wait, so what will happen?"

"Ann's getting it rescheduled, but it'll be a while."

"Oh, Alex." I lean forward to hug him, but his body is stiff, and he barely returns the hug. I let go and wait as he explains to his mom in Spanish. I call my dad, who was meeting us at the courthouse. "Hey, *Tato.*"

"I just got off the phone with Ann," he says. "This isn't good, Milochka."

"Wait, why?"

"The judges are more benevolent around the holidays. It was a good time for Alex's case. But now, who knows when they'll see him."

"*Tato,* don't be so negative," I whisper, cupping my hand around my mouth and the bottom of the phone so that Alex doesn't hear me. "It will be fine. It's just a delay. It has to be fine."

I keep repeating this phrase to myself and anyone who will listen. It will be fine. It has to be fine.

I didn't think the drive home could be worse than the drive to the courthouse. I was wrong. Alex is staring out the window, chewing his thumb. And his mom is doing the same in the backseat. I'm left alone with my thoughts, which is rarely a good thing. And Alex is clearly sinking deep into his own. I want to bridge the gap, to comfort him or ease his anxiety just a bit. But he's untouchable, so distant that it's physically painful.

I'm not used to this Alex. The self-proclaimed eternal optimist has transformed into a brooding ball of nerves, and I have no idea what to do. Time and again, Alex has proved that he knows what to say to me, how to help me, in good times and bad. But now that the roles are reversed, I'm clueless. What does Alex need from me? I reach a tentative hand onto his knee, but he doesn't even seem to notice. "Do you want to talk about it?" I ask about thirty minutes into our drive.

He doesn't move from looking out the window when he says, "Not right now."

We don't say anything for another ten minutes, when we hit traffic. "Can you check Waze for me? See if there's a better way," I ask as I hand Alex my phone. He complies wordlessly.

"*Viene la tormenta,*" Alex's mom says. *The storm is coming.* And I have to wonder if she's simply remarking on the weather, or if she's predicting the future.

22

Need for Speed

Anya

I still haven't heard from Tommy by the time the rain hits. If Luke weren't here, I probably would've freaked out about it, but right now there's something calming about his presence. I chalk up Tommy's absence to the storm—long gas lines, busy phone lines—and let it go. The horses are good for now. Mila texted me fifteen minutes ago, letting me know that they had to reschedule Alex's hearing. Of course they didn't know about it until they *got* to the courthouse, which is in the county north of us. I know it'll take them forever to get back and they'll waste a ton of gas in the meantime.

"Worst case scenario we can always borrow feed or hay from my parents," Luke says as he flings the last pad of hay to Harley.

"Your parents have horses?"

"They own Good Hope Ranch," he says. "I thought you knew."

"The barrel racing place on Flamingo?"

"The one and only."

I try to recall if I knew that Luke came from a horse family. And not just any horse family—one of the horse craziest families in Broward County.

"Was your accident a riding-related one?"

He shakes his head. "Four wheeler."

"I'm sorry."

"Coulda been worse."

"That's true," I say with a mirthless laugh. Our eyes meet then, and I have a hard time looking away because there's something in his eyes that say, *I understand*. And it's something I've experienced so little of since my accident. It's almost a relief.

Once the rain is coming in earnest, Luke says, "We really should get you home."

I glance around the barn, trying to think if there's anything else that could possibly be done for the horses, but Luke's right. We need to get out of here. We wheel to Luke's truck, getting absolutely soaked in the process. When the platform raises me up into the cab, I realize that the passenger seat is back in its normal spot.

"How're we going to work this out?" I yell to Luke over the din of rain. I move my wheelchair as close to the passenger seat as I possibly can, allowing Luke to get into the cab, but we definitely can't drive like this. We're drenched; water is dripping off of Luke's nose onto the steering wheel. I'm sitting in a small puddle in my wheelchair, my clothes suctioning to my body. He hasn't turned the truck on yet, so it's quickly becoming like a sauna in the cab.

Luke curses under his breath. "I forgot my dad put it back in." He looks back and forth from me, to him, to the passenger seat. It feels like one of those impossible riddles—two paraplegics get into a car with one seat...and there's a tropical storm coming. "How about this: if you go in the passenger seat, what if I use your wheelchair to drive and I can fold mine up in the back?"

"It's a good idea," I say, feeling my cheeks flush. "It's just, I can't, you know..." I wave a hand from my lap to the passenger's seat.

"You can't lift yourself?" Luke says. "I see. Okay. Can I lift you?"

"I don't know, can you?"

He laughs, a bit of his arrogance bleeding into his smile. "I know I can lift you. I'm asking if you're okay with it."

"Oh." I sniff. "Yes, that's fine. But, how?"

"Well, it won't be pleasant, but I think we can get the job done." He scoots his wheelchair closer to mine until our forearms are touching. "Can you lift the arm rest? Alright. You trust me?"

Yes. "Not even a little bit."

He grins at me, our faces so close it makes me jittery. "Ready?" He locks his wheelchair, then pulls himself to the edge of his seat, turning toward me. He reaches over and puts one arm around my back and one arm under my legs. My heart is beating way too fast, and I'm not sure if it's because of the proximity to Luke or because I can't quite see how the physics of this transfer can possibly work. "Alright, I'm gonna toss you on three—"

"You're going to *what*?" I grip his neck with my arms.

"Three—"

"Luke!"

"You're going to have to let go for this to work. Two—"

I loosen my grip, but still protest, "I don't think this is—"

"One—"

He doesn't quite toss me, but he does lift me—quite heroically, I might add—up and over my wheelchair arm. He can't quite lower me gently to the seat because of the distance, so I do *plop* onto the seat gracelessly, jostling painfully against the edge of my wheelchair, but I'm here. Before I can even look up, Luke's transferred himself into my wheelchair and is repositioning me in my seat. "How can you do that?" I ask a little too breathlessly.

"A lot of work," he says as he reaches for my seatbelt. I don't even bother telling him I can do that myself. "Are you impressed?" His face is so close to mine, I can feel his breath on my cheek. He smells like cinnamon gum and hay.

Yes. "Not even a little bit."

He chuckles, plugging in my seat belt. "The uncrackable Anya Kozak." I feel equal parts relieved and deprived when he pulls away.

"What am I, a code?"

"I was thinking more like a geode."

I narrow my eyes at him. "You think I'm like a sparkly rock?"

He scans my face. "Well right now you look like a drowned rat," he says with a laugh.

Every ounce of heat I'd been feeling drains from my body. "What every girl wants to hear," I say as I swipe under my eyes where I'm sure my mascara has bled.

"A really hot drowned rat."

"All the better," I say tartly.

He leans over, folding up his wheelchair and tossing it into the backseat like it weighs nothing. It takes him some time to get my wheelchair situated and locked in place so he can drive, but it's a relief once he turns the truck on and gets the air flowing through the cab. I try calling Tommy again as we head down the barn driveway, but I don't get through. I hope he's okay.

Now that we're in Luke's truck, driving through the initial bands of a tropical storm, all of the anxiety I'd sloughed off earlier comes crashing back. I'm gripping the arm rests, trying to see through the windshield as the wipers furiously toss the driving rain back and forth. "Can you see anything? I can't see anything. How can you see?"

"My vision must be better than yours," Luke says, but his face is serious and his eyes don't leave the road. An alert on our phones sounds at the same time, and we both jump at the sound. I check my screen.

"It's a flash flood warning."

Another alert goes off.

"And a tornado warning."

Luke's jaw clenches. "We shouldn't have left the barn so late. I'm sorry."

"It's not your fault. I didn't want to leave when we hadn't heard from Tommy."

"I should've insisted."

"I wouldn't have listened."

"I know." He cracks a smile, but it's not that big and I know he's nervous. "Let's go to my house. It's closer."

"Okay."

"Okay?" He glances over at me for a split second like he's expecting me to have sprouted a second head. "I thought you'd fight me on that."

"I can admit when I'm wrong."

He's silent for a long time, and I don't know if it's because he has to focus so much on driving through the storm or because he doubts my statement. We head down Griffin Road and turn onto Flamingo. The rain is coming in sheets, obscuring the traffic lights so much that they're just tiny green blurs. Finally, we turn down a side street and then a gravel drive, and I have no idea how Luke even knows where he's going— I can't see anything. Finally, we crawl to a halt and Luke puts the truck in park.

"Are we at your house?" I squint at the window, trying to see the structure.

"It's there, right in front of the truck." He points, but I still can't see it. "How wet can this thing get?" He pats a hand on my wheelchair arm.

I bite my lip, trying to remember what the manufacturer said about the electrical components getting wet. "I don't know. I mean, I've been caught in the rain a couple times."

"Yeah, this is a little different than getting caught in a pinch of rain."

"What do you have in mind?"

He unlocks the wheelchair from the driver's seat and maneuvers toward me. "We can go in my wheelchair." He reaches back and pulls his wheelchair from the backseat. I'm increasingly amazed by Luke's independence and strength. Also, his wheelchair is impressive too, as it folds and unfolds so easily. I want to ask him more about it when we're not in the middle of a tropical storm.

"How are you proposing to do that?"

He leans closer to me and gives me a wink. "You're gonna love it."

I think for a second about what he could possibly have in mind. Should I just risk taking my wheelchair? It's already a little wet from earlier. But a small part of me wants to do whatever Luke has in mind. Especially if it means he's going to have to be close to me. I try to ignore the fluttering in my belly at this idea. A tiny, fragile butterfly is emerging from its chrysalis, its delicate wings unfolding. But there's a dragon within me too, looking to incinerate anything that threatens to flutter within me.

I close my eyes and pinch the bridge of my nose. What in the world is happening to me? Why do I want him close to me? Why is he not bothering me so much anymore? Just because he played me a couple heartsy country songs? Because he asked me on a date? Honestly, I liked it better when he bothered me. Things were more straightforward then.

"Look, I'm sorry. I shouldn't have been so cavalier about it." Is he apologizing? Does he think I'm upset? "But I can get us in to the house really fast. You'll barely notice you're on my lap."

On his *lap*?

I should be concerned about how unprofessional this is. How this is totally messing up our working relationship—or lack thereof. But there's another part of me that *wants* to be in Luke's lap. And that's what makes my face flush and words freeze in my chest. I haven't said anything in a long time, and it's getting way past awkward. But I can't find my words, so I simply look at Luke and nod. The teeny, tiny butterfly has somehow multiplied rapidly within me, and the monstrous dragon keeping me safe is nowhere to be found.

Before I know it, he's hoisting me onto his lap. "I need you to hold on to me, because I won't be able to keep you on me while I'm moving us." He turns me slightly in his lap and I put one arm around his neck. And then he's doing something that should be impossible—he's lifting both of us up in the ultimate form of a tricep dip and moving us into his wheelchair. Once we're settled, he pulls me back so I'm flush against him, my back to his front. "You okay?"

I still can't talk, so I just nod.

"Once we get out of the cab, you're gonna want to hold on. I'm gonna go fast."

I nod again, and then he presses the button for the door. Immediately, rain is flying into the cab. The platform lowers us, and even though it's fast for what it is, it feels like an eternity as we're getting pummeled by the rain. But the moment we hit the ground, Luke takes off. I grip the armrest, trying to hold myself in place. It's actually quite thrilling, and even though we're in the middle of a tropical storm and I may fly off this wheelchair at any moment, I'm smiling as the wind whips my hair around my face and the rain stings my eyes.

The wheelchair bumps onto a ramp, and I finally see the front of Luke's house. He rolls to the front door, enters a code into his keypad, and the door opens. I've slid down a bit, so he puts an arm around my waist and pulls me back up. Without realizing it until it's too late, one of my hands goes to his arm, locking him in place around me.

"I need two hands," he says into my ear.

"Oh." I blush, thankful he can't see it, and take my hand off his arm. He rolls us inside and then leans back to close the door. Once we're inside, dripping and panting, Luke starts laughing, the vibrations from his chest spreading into mine, and I can't help but laugh too.

"Nothin' like a little adventure to get the weekend off to a good start," he says.

My heart is still racing from our speedy entrance, and I turn my face toward Luke's. "That was fun."

"Ah," he says. "The lady's got the need for speed, hmm?"

"Something like that."

Suddenly I feel very aware of where I am—and whom I'm *on*. I glance around the house, which is spacious and open. Everything is wood-paneled—and I mean *everything*, from the floors to the ceilings to the wainscoting on the walls. The decor is just north of Spartan—there's a deer head on the far wall (shocking) and a Florida Gators poster, but other than that, there's nothing else on the walls. A massive L-shaped couch situated around a mounted television takes up most of the living area. In the corner there's a Smith machine with tons of weights on it, which explains why Luke can toss me and his wheelchair around like we're nothing. To the right, a hallway leads to the back of the house. On the far side of the living area, there's a kitchen with a small table that has only one chair. I zero in on this chair—this singular chair—and it makes me feel so lonely for Luke. Because someone used to sit in this chair, and they don't anymore. Whoever got "unstuck" from him.

"I have an extra wheelchair in the closet," he says, and it startles me because he's so close, I can feel his breath tickling my ear. "But maybe I should get you on the couch first?"

"Are you going to toss me there?" I joke.

"Only if you want me to." He wheels us so that we're beside the couch and then lifts me under my shoulders onto the couch. It takes some maneuvering between us, but finally I'm on his couch, my wet clothes dripping onto the leather. "Which do you want first, a towel or a wheelchair?"

"Towel, definitely." I smile up at him, and he smiles back, and it's a shock to my system that we've suddenly fallen into this comfortability with each other. I guess sharing a wheelchair will do that to you.

Luke disappears down the hall, leaving a trail of water droplets behind him. I quickly try to shove the butterflies in my stomach to the side. Shouldn't there be a dungeon I can lock them in and throw away the key? Where did my trusty dragon go, and why is she failing me today of all days? A moment later, I hear clattering and a frantic tapping down the hallway before a blur of red-brown streaks into the room and onto the couch. "Incoming!" Luke yells as a fifty-pound dog flings itself onto my lap.

I can't help but laugh as the dog sniffs me wildly. I scratch behind his floppy brown ears. "Hello, you."

Luke comes back in the living room a minute later and the dog goes berserk—he pushes off my lap and sprints over the couch, around the living room, and then skids to a stop at Luke's feet. "Sorry, he's a little nuts."

"You don't say." But I'm laughing because the dog is adorable and I'm happy Luke has a companion. Maybe I should get a dog. A much, much smaller, much less crazy dog. "What kind of dog is he?"

"He's a Vizsla." I've never heard of this kind of breed before—he pronounces it like *veesh-lah*—but the dog strikes me as equal parts regal and zany. Luke rolls up to the couch, the Vizsla on his wheels, and he places a towel and some clothes beside me.

"Alright, Zeke. Show our guest you can behave. Sit." Zeke sits up, his ears piqued at his owner, eyes attentive to his command. "Good boy. Lay down." Zeke quickly complies, never losing eye contact with his owner. "Good dog. Hugs." Zeke jumps onto Luke's lap and throws his paws over Luke's shoulders. I laugh, clapping my hands at them, which excites Zeke. He leaps off of Luke, back onto the couch, disrupting the towel and clothes, and licks my face.

"Good dog. Who's a good dog?" I say, petting him as he gives me kisses. After a while, Zeke decides he needs to take another lap around the living room. "He's like the Flash in dog form."

I glance over at Luke, and he's giving me a strange look. "I never pegged you as a dog person."

"Mila got me this shirt one time that says, 'I like horses, dogs, and like three people' and that's pretty much the gist of it."

"Huh." He leans down and picks up the towel and tosses it to me. "Let me get that wheelchair for you." He wheels off to a hallway closet—of course Zeke clambers after him—and returns with a folded-up wheelchair.

"Where do you get these really compact, lightweight wheelchairs?"

"Oh, I manufacture them."

I stare up at him, surprised. "You make wheelchairs?"

"I mean, we have them manufactured at a facility, but yes." He leans forward with a glint in his eye. "You don't think I can afford that truck just from being a part-time therapist, do you?"

"Why haven't you brought it up? I've never heard you mention it with any of our clients."

"It's a conflict of interest. I wouldn't do that."

"Hmm. So you *are* principled."

"Occasionally. And not just about the veganism." He gestures to me to help me into the wheelchair. I'm not used to a manual wheelchair, but Luke's is so lightweight, it's easy to push. He points me toward the bathroom and I roll down the hall toward it. Everything in Luke's house is wide—the open living room space, the hallways, and even the bathroom. It's as if it were designed for a wheelchair user. And maybe it was. The counters are pretty low, lower than regular countertops. I towel off, trying to get the mascara from under my eyes. I look at the clothes Luke has lent me. But of course he gave me a shirt that says, "Make America Cowboy Again" with a horse and rider silhouetted in an American flag. I crack the door open and shout, "Love the shirt, Luke!"

"Just for you, Miss Kozak."

I close the door, shaking my head. I easily change my top, toweling off my bra as much as possible, but the hard part is the bottoms. I think at the very least I can get them off, though I'm not certain I can get on a new pair of pants on my own. I mean, how much worse would the day be if I had to hang out in a towel all evening long? I laugh mirthlessly at myself, knowing this is not an option, but also not knowing what I can really do by myself. Nothing quite like getting shoved in the pool to teach you how to swim.

It's painstakingly slow, inching my wet pants off. I lift my hip up with one hand and shove my pants down with the other hand an inch at a time. By the time I've got them around my knees, my arms are shaking from the exertion. I understand now why Luke has the Smith machine and why he's so jacked—being independent and in a wheelchair is ridiculously hard. I'm just lucky I don't need to pee right now, or else I'd be stuck.

Finally, my wet pants are on the ground, and I don't even have the energy to try to pick them up. I lean my head back, resting for several minutes before I get the drive to try to put on the sweatpants Luke gave me. Thankfully they're roomy, so once I get them around my feet, I pull them all the way up to my thighs, no problem. Then it's the same game of lifting my hip with one hand and shimmying the pants up with the other. By the time I'm done, I could cry with happiness. I lean forward onto the counter, my head on my forearms, and then I do cry. Because I just put my pants on for the first time in two years by myself. And that deserves a happy cry.

23

Not In My House

Mila

By the time we get to my parents' house in Weston, the dark clouds that followed us from the courthouse have released a torrential downpour. It takes both Alex and me to navigate through the wall of rain, but we eventually make it. Pulling into my parent's garage feels like we've reached an oasis. My dad's Tesla is already parked, so he beat us home, which isn't at all surprising. The reason I've got a lead foot is because I inherited one, and not from my mom.

Inside, my dad is nursing a drink while my mom is preheating the oven. "It's a shame," my dad says to Alex about the case getting rescheduled. "A real shame."

Alex is stoic as he shakes my dad's hand and says, "Yes, sir," but doesn't elaborate. My mom makes a big show of hugging Alex and his mom, offering them drinks and taking Alex's coat. I glance over at what my mom's planning to cook, knowing that she feels insecure having Mrs. Caballero over for dinner. My mom isn't the best cook in the world—sure, she's not the worst, but she's not the best either. Mrs. Caballero, on the other hand, could open her own restaurant with her Cuban food. It's incredible. I've probably raved about it too much to my mom, and now she's always hesitant to have the Caballeros over for dinner. There's a huge casserole of some sort in the oven. I open the trash can and find an Olive Garden bag, and I have to hold back a smile. My mom may be insecure about her cooking, but she's also pragmatic. If you can't do it yourself, outsource it. I grab a few Publix bags and strategically place them in the trash can to conceal the Olive Garden bag.

I know it's torture for Alex to make small talk with my dad right now, so I grab his hand and say, "Alex and I need to check in with Anya." I tug him toward the stairs. "We'll come down when dinner's ready."

My mom says, "Okay," but my dad is giving us what can only be described as a glare.

"Keep the door open, Milochka," he says in Ukrainian so Alex doesn't know what he's saying.

My mom smacks his shoulder and whispers, "They're adults, Anton."

"Not in my house they're not."

I snort and shake my head. My dad doesn't have anything to worry about—Alex won't so much as think of even kissing me under my dad's roof. When we get in my room, I sit on my bed and Alex hovers awkwardly, true to form. Looking around, he finds the stool for my vanity and sits there, keeping a respectable distance. On another day, I'd tease him about this, but everything about Alex is screaming "fragile" right now. I'd wrap my arms around him and kiss him if I thought that would help, but I know right now it'll only make things harder for him.

Outside, the storm is really ramping up—the rain and wind are all-consuming, like if you stepped outside right now, you'd simply cease to exist because of their power. I'm worried that Anya isn't home yet. I call her and I get a busy signal. "Can you call Tommy and see where they're at?"

Alex dials but doesn't get through either. "Maybe we should've gone to the barn first before coming home."

"They should've been back by now," Alex says, his brows furrowing with concern. "Besides, we barely made it here."

"Yeah, so then what're Tommy and Anya's chances of making it back alright?"

Alex doesn't say anything reassuring, just a "hmm," before picking up his phone and dialing Luke. "Does no one think it's important to pick up their phones in the middle of a tropical storm?" he says when Luke doesn't answer.

"Maybe the lines are jammed?"

"It's possible. We should text them; it's more likely to get through." I shoot off a series of texts to Anya, Tommy, and Luke. I almost jump off the bed when a shrill alert sounds on both of our phones. I can even hear the alarm going off on our parents' phones downstairs. For a moment my mind goes someplace wild—it's an alert about something bad happening to Anya—but then I see it's just a flash flood and tornado warning. Which doesn't serve to make me feel any better about Anya. We both swipe out of the alarm and

Alex looks up at me, making real eye contact with me for the first time since we left the courthouse. "She'll be okay," he says.

I step off the bed and sit in Alex's lap. He gives a tentative glance toward the door and then puts his arms around me, sighing. I cradle his head against mine, our foreheads touching. It's just a brooding in silence kind of day, but at least we get to do it together.

24

Your Cracks Are Showing

When I roll out of the bathroom, Luke's banging around in the kitchen and there's a country song playing on the in-ceiling speakers. Luke pokes his head out of the kitchen, sees me, and wheels out with a huge, mischievous grin on his face. We sit there, staring at each other, Luke wearing his obnoxious smile and me with no idea why, until I hear the song he's playing. It's Keith Urban's "You Look Good in My Shirt."

I groan and throw my head into my hands to cover my smile. I'll give him this: he's got a sense of humor. "How long have you been playing this song?" I ask once I've got my face under control.

"Oh, y'know, it's been looping for forty-five minutes."

A laugh breaks out of me at this, and this makes him smile even more. "It only took me forty-five minutes to get my pants on?" I ask, surprised because it felt like at least three hours.

He chuckles. "You tryin' to beat your record or something?"

"I don't know. That was my first time." I feel suddenly very vulnerable admitting that, and I wish I could take it back.

Shock ripples across Luke's features. "That was your first time—since your accident?" He wipes a hand across his face, shaking his head. "I'm such a jerk. I had no idea."

"It's not your fault."

"You gotta tell me more about your injury so I don't keep suggesting things you can't do." He says it earnestly, like he genuinely wants to know. He rolls closer to me, and our knees are just barely grazing each other's. "I mean, at the Center you seem so independent. I just assumed…"

"I can tell you about it if you want. But don't apologize. I'm glad you unknowingly pushed me to do some things I wouldn't normally try to do."

"Like ride in some crazy guy's wheelchair with him?"

I roll my eyes, but I'm smiling. "Like put my own pants on."

"It's really a shame. I would've loved to help you with that."

I scoff and smack him playfully. "I'm still your boss, you know."

He looks up thoughtfully. "I actually think I'm more of an independent contractor."

"I can still fire you. That's pretty much the definition of a boss."

"Hmm, I think we already established this." He leans forward in his wheelchair like he's imparting a secret to me, mock whispering, "You can't fire me. Everybody loves me; you're outnumbered."

"Don't remind me."

"I'll remind me as much as you need reminding." He winks at me. "Darlin'."

I point a finger at him. "Not your darling."

"Not yet," he says with a lopsided smile that, for some reason, makes my stomach swoop. He swings his wheelchair around and grabs a plate from the kitchen counter. "You hungry?"

We head to the table and Luke puts a plate of vegetable stir fry in front of me. "Did you *make* this?"

"Well, on account of there almost bein' a hurricane out there—" Luke gestures toward the window. "Yeah, I did."

I inspect the plate. There's broccoli, peppers, onions, and some other kind of vegetable I can't place in a stir fry sauce over sesame noodles. I twist a bite onto my fork and take a hesitant taste. "Wow," I say when the flavors hit me. "Maybe I *will* be your darling."

Luke's big, braw laughter expands the room. "That good, huh? Darlin'?"

"Just for tonight, anyway." I glare at him. "No one can know about it and I'll fire you if you ever bring it up."

He takes a bite and smiles as he chews. "The uncrackable Anya Kozak, ladies and gents."

"How on earth do you have the energy to do this after everything you did today?"

"Well, you can make fun of me being principled all you want, but that's why."

"You have energy because you're principled?"

"Because of the veganism." He waves his fork over his plate as if to say, *duh*. "Well, that and the Smith machine," he says, nodding toward the weight machine. "My sister calls it the Revenge Press."

"Revenge? And who is the object of your revenge?"

He stabs at a piece of broccoli and says, "My ex-wife, Sienna."

I nod and take another bite. I want to ask more, which is baffling to me—why do I all of a sudden want to know everything about Luke? But I also want to tread carefully and respect his heartache.

"Did it work? The Revenge Press?"

He shrugs. "Can't say exactly. But I'm jacked."

"That's always a good thing."

"Is it?" He gives me a sly look, his blue eyes inviting me to say more, but I keep my mouth shut.

"So, what did you need revenge for?"

"Hooking up with half of Broward County."

I grimace. "Ouch." I realize in this moment how hard it is to know the right thing to say when confronted with another person's tragedy. Do you try to help them see the silver lining? *Well, at least you saw her true colors sooner rather than later*. But I know from experience that this comes across as hollow and dissatisfying. How many times did people try to comfort me by saying, *At least you're alive*? I never wanted to hear that. So I choose the phrase that I usually want to hear. "I'm sorry. That's really challenging."

"Apparently she needed comfort after my accident. Just couldn't get it from me." He says it casually, like he's had this conversation hundreds of times, and maybe he has. Or maybe he's hiding an ocean of pain—something I understand a million times over.

"So she left you for someone else?"

He shrugs. "I don't think it was for one person in particular, more like it just wasn't me."

"Oh." I really don't know where to go from here. All of the annoyance I'd built up against Luke seems to fall away with this revelation. He understands me better than anyone I've ever met. And through his hardships he's become a much better person, which is more than I can say for myself. I'm humbled by the realization.

Luke's phone buzzes and he checks the screen. "Sorry, it's my brother. One sec." He picks up the phone, his ever-present smile playing on his lips despite our topic of conversation. "Hey Mikey." They chat for a minute, and it's clear that his brother is checking in with him to make sure he's okay in the storm. This reminds me to touch base with my parents and Mila, so I quickly call my mom and tell her where I am. We had talked when I was at the barn, but I hadn't updated her since getting to Luke's. She has a hard time understanding how I got here with only Luke to assist me. Which is understandable, because I can hardly believe how I got here myself. It takes some convincing that I'm alright, and we hang up with her assurance that she'll come get me as soon as the storm has passed. But when she passes the phone to Mila, I know I'm in trouble.

"Where have you been? Why aren't you answering my calls and texts?" she practically screams into the phone.

"I've been...busy," I tell her.

"Well while you've been busy, I've been over here worried you're caught dead in this storm!"

"I'm okay, *sestra*. I'm sorry I worried you."

"Are you going to be okay with Luke?"

"I'm fine, Mila."

"You're not going to kill him, are you?" she yells into the phone, and I'm sure Luke can hear her.

"Mila, I'm fine. I'll talk to you when the storm's over."

"Anya, you're not—" I click the 'end' button before Mila can finish her sentence.

Luke is looking at me with a smirk. "You're not gonna kill me, are you?"

I roll my eyes. "Not tonight." I wave a fork at my plate. "Seeing as how you fed me, it seems rude. This time."

He chuckles and forks a bite of broccoli.

"So, all of this"—I wave my hand at the stir fry and then at the Smith machine—"started after your accident, or after Sienna?"

"Mostly after Sienna. It was kind of my wake-up call to take responsibility for myself and my own happiness. I couldn't rely on her or anyone else for that."

"So you never drowned your sorrows in a tub of ice cream, or anything...stronger?"

"Well." He lifts his shoulder in a *What can you do?* motion. "Can't be principled *all* the time, Miss Kozak."

"Apparently not."

"And you? Are you principled all the time?"

No. "What do you think?"

He takes his time answering, taking another bite of his food and chewing as he stares at me thoughtfully. "I'm starting to see the cracks."

I gasp playfully. "In the *uncrackable* Anya Kozak?"

He smiles, a glint in his eyes. "Everybody has cracks, Anya."

"Some more than others."

He puts his elbows on the table and leans toward me. "Which one of us do you think has more?"

Me. "I guess we'll have to see."

After dinner, we head to the couch and turn on a movie. Zeke goes back and forth between Luke and me, curling up beside me with his head in my lap, then going to Luke to do the same. "They call them Velcro dogs," he says. "They stick to you."

"I like that," I say as I play with Zeke's soft ears, and the dog gives a contented sigh. I need a dog like this.

We shuffle through Netflix a bit, and I think there's no chance we'll land on a movie we both will enjoy, but we end up agreeing pretty quickly on a ridiculous yet hilarious movie with Jennifer Aniston and Adam Sandler called *Murder Mystery*. Every time I laugh, Zeke sits up and licks me furiously, which only serves to make me laugh more.

Mila's texting me, seriously concerned about how I'm doing stuck with Luke. She clearly doesn't believe me when I say I'm fine. And maybe I'm not fine, because I'm actually enjoying myself while I'm stuck with Luke.

That's when I realize I'm really in trouble.

About halfway through the movie, the electricity putters out. "Uh oh." I blink into the darkness, and I can't even see Zeke huddled beside me. "You got any candles?"

"I'm a twenty-eight-year-old guy living by himself. What do you think?"

"That you're a responsible adult, prepared for the hurricane season?" I say hopefully.

"Hurricane season ended last month."

"Yeah, tell the tropical storm that, will ya?"

I hear Luke shuffling into his wheelchair, and he rolls past the couch and into the hallway. A few minutes later, he's back with a lantern. He sets it on the ground in front of the couch, and it casts a warm glow around the living room. We sit in silence for a time. Outside, the storm is displaying its power—with the TV off, the sound of the wind howling is louder than ever. Occasionally, lightning rips across the sky, lighting up the room, the thunder shaking the house. I feel strangely calm, though. I'm not even that worried about the horses or the barn.

"Guess that's our cue to go to bed," Luke says reluctantly.

"Yeah, guess so." But strangely, I'm even more reluctant than he is.

"You could, uh, take the bed," he says, and the image of Luke having to take me out of my wheelchair and put me in his bed is just too much. Heat takes hold of me, flushing me from my head to my toes.

"I'm comfortable out here," I say. "Do you have an extra pillow and blanket?"

"I insist."

"I'm not sleeping in your bed, Luke." I try to think of a good reason, but only come up with a lame one. "Besides, I'd like to sleep where the light is."

He chuckles, as if he knows I'm not being fully honest. He rolls away, and for a moment I think he's going to bed, and I feel suddenly hollow. I wasn't ready for him to leave. But he returns almost immediately with a pillow and blanket. "If you lay down, I can cover you with the blanket," he says as he hands me the pillow. "Scooch," he says to Zeke, who slowly stretches and then moves so I can lay down.

Luke's hand finds my side and helps lower me gently to the couch. The moment feels intimate, crackling with a heat I'm trying actively to ignore. His eyes hold mine as he billows out the blanket and covers me with it.

Then he does something that makes me smile. He lifts my feet, wrapping the blanket around them, and then tucks it around my legs. "Snug as a bug," he says, and I don't know if I should laugh or cry.

"Thanks," I whisper.

"Welcome." Luke hovers just above me, and there's something really comforting about his presence. I have this absurd desire to grab hold of his shirt and pull him closer, but of course I don't. I tuck my hands under my pillow, but when he goes to roll away, I say, "Luke?"

"Yeah?"

"Can you not, you know, leave, yet?"

The light from the lantern dances on his face, his smile half-covered in shadows. "Sure." Luke goes to the other side of the couch, pulls himself out of his chair and flops onto the couch. Zeke switches sides to be next to his owner, and soon the dog is snoring.

"You wanna tell me about your accident?" Luke asks, his voice just above a whisper.

With only a little hesitation, I tell him. About getting Cyrus, our first Grand Prix. The excitement I felt, but also a little dread, too. It's like I knew something was going to happen. I remember Cyrus stumbling and then the ground speeding toward me. I can't recall anything else about the day of the accident because I was unconscious. I woke up in the hospital the next day, with the realization—before anyone could even break the news to me—that I was paralyzed. I tell him things I'd never told anyone before—how I wanted to die, how I couldn't face any of my friends or family members who came to visit me in the hospital. I just pretended to be asleep. How I refused physical therapy and occupational therapy because, what was the point? I couldn't move no matter how much therapy they offered me. I didn't even ask my mom about my full diagnosis until months later. I didn't want to know. I simply existed for months, like a shadow person in a useless body. My dad left me, my sister left me. I had only my mom—and she was barely a shell of a person too. The two of us existing side-by-side but not really touching.

I don't even realize I'm crying until there's a small pool of tears on the couch behind my ear. Luke is quiet, letting me finish, and then there's silence. For several beats, we sit in absolute quiet, the only sounds around us are the clash of the storm outside and Zeke's snoring.

Then Luke is back in his wheelchair. He pulls up to my side of the couch and lowers himself to the ground in front of me. He leans his head against mine, his thumb running across my cheek, collecting my tears. "I'm so sorry," he says, and I let myself cry until I don't have any tears left.

25

Baggage Claim

Mila

I'm equal parts livid with Anya for not returning my calls and concerned for her that she's probably going to have to spend the night with Luke. I worry about her sanity, but also about the overall wellness of the Center staff if the two of them are cooped up all night long. She was so pissed about having to drive home from Ocala with him, I don't see how she'll get through tonight. And on top of all that, none of us have heard from Tommy, despite calling and texting him hourly. Between all that and Alex's quiet stoicism, it's a weird night.

We have a delicious dinner of Olive Garden lasagna and salad. I notice my mom accepts compliments on the dish without giving Olive Garden credit—and I don't out her. In a way, I sympathize with her. But she's a full-time nurse anesthetist, a caretaker for a paraplegic, and a wonderful wife and mom—she doesn't need to be a Michelin chef on top of that. That being said, I don't blame her for wanting to give Mrs. Caballero a good meal.

My dad dismisses himself immediately after finishing his dinner, and that relieves some of the tension around the table. Alex clears the plates and together we do the dishes—he rinses, I put them in the dishwasher—while my mom makes coffee. We all meet back at the table for tiramisu and decaf cappuccinos. "I have a puzzle we could do while we wait out the rain," my mom says. Alex leans over and translates for his mom, and she nods. I'm relieved at my mom's thoughtfulness—I'd been wondering if we should do a card or board game, but a puzzle doesn't need any translation. It also doesn't require conversation, which seems to match everyone's mood right now.

We work silently on the puzzle for what feels like hours. I break off to put the finishing touches on my final paper for my Brand Management class, but mostly I find myself staring at the screen without really comprehending anything in front of me. It becomes clear that the storm isn't going to pass over quickly, so my mom offers to get Alex and his mom a change of clothes and put them up for the night. They accept, of course—what choice do they have? We all go our separate ways to get ready for bed. My mom directs Alex to the guest room downstairs and Mrs. Caballero to Anya's room.

I brush my teeth and change into my pajamas in a rush, then hurry down the stairs, afraid Alex will have gone to bed before I get there. But I find him sitting on the couch, and I know he's been waiting for all these hours to talk to me by myself.

I sit beside him, throwing my legs over his lap like I normally do, but he stiffens. "My dad's asleep, Alex."

"I know, it's just…" He shrugs, not finishing his sentence.

"He's obviously okay enough with you for you to come on vacation with us," I say, referring to my family's Christmas vacation in a couple weeks. We'll be at Little Palm Island, a private island resort off the coast of the Keys. I'm sure it was more of my mom's doing to invite the Caballeros to join us, but my dad at least tolerated the idea.

He sighs, wiping his eyes with his fingers. "Mila, you deserve better."

"What are you talking about?"

"You deserve better than this—this day, this whole thing with the immigration and the court case."

"What do any of those things have to do with me and what I 'deserve'?"

"That's what I'm saying. This doesn't, and shouldn't, involve you."

I shake my head. "No, Alex. I know what you're doing, and I need you to stop." I curl my legs underneath me, sitting closer to him as I take his hands. "You know how I was so stuck on the kiss thing when I fell last week?"

"This is very different than that."

"I know it's different, but the principle is the same."

He looks at me warily.

"I choose you, Alex. So that means I choose all of the baggage that comes with you—"

"I don't want that for you." I put a finger over his lips.

"Let me finish. You chose me and the baggage that comes with dating a crazy show jumper." I smile and nudge him, trying to get him to admit we're a little crazy, but he doesn't budge. "It's not right for me to take that decision away from you, so don't take this one from me." I sit on his lap and take his arms one at a time and put them around my waist. "I love you, Alex Caballero." I kiss his cheek. "I love every beautiful thing you bring to my life." I kiss his other cheek. "And every not-so-beautiful thing you bring." I kiss the tip of his nose. "I want every benefit of belonging to you, Alex." I nuzzle my nose against his. "And I accept the very minimal drawbacks there are. So don't take the good away with the bad." I lean in and gently kiss his lips. "Please," I whisper.

He makes a low noise in the back of his throat, which I take as assent, and I run my fingers through his hair and kiss him again.

Alex, today was hard, not being able to have your court case when we thought this thing was going to get solved, but honestly, it doesn't make a difference to me one way or another. I was so sad when you were staring out of the car, not saying anything. I want to be in your head for just a minute, to understand what's going on in there while you're so quiet. Do you think that somehow I'm outta here if things go sideways with your immigration status? You helped me through the hardest time of my life, you were with me at my worst, and somehow brought out the best in me. So I'm with you, Alex, no matter what. Your baggage is mine, and vice versa. Wherever you are, that's where I am. You've become my favorite noun— my favorite person, place, or thing. No one and nothing is more important to me than you are. I wish you would accept that, but something about the look in your eyes tells me you're holding yourself back from believing that. And I wish I knew what to do.

26

Craig Family Compound

Luke and I talk until the storm abates, and then we talk some more. I learn a little more about his life before his accident, his injury and the aftermath, and even a tiny bit about his marriage and its dissolution. We're talking about the Center, and I remember saying something about Clara's accident and how it affected me, but I must fall asleep mid-sentence because the next thing I know, light is streaming into the room. I glance over to where Luke was, and he's gone. Something about his missing form strikes me in a strange way. I rub at my chest to try to get rid of whatever this feeling is.

The next thing that hits me is that I have to pee. Like, *really* badly. I text my mom, and then Mila, the same message: *come get me ASAP.* I send them my location. I'm a little afraid to move because my bladder is so full, I can feel the pressure of it all the way up to my ribs.

I don't see or hear Luke anywhere, and I wonder if he moved to his bed after I fell asleep. I'm attempting to sit up on my own—and failing—when there's a knock at the front door. It's only been a few minutes since I sent my mom and Mila the text to come get me, so I don't think it could be them. I wipe sleep out of my eyes and smooth my hair as much as I can before the door opens and a woman about my age walks in, looking around.

She's trim and graceful with blonde hair with hot pink tips. My first thought is that this must be Sienna, and I loathe her and her pink hair. Then she spots me and a huge,

Luke-like smile breaks across her face. "Mornin'," she says in the cutest Southern accent, and I know this is Luke's sister. "You must be Anya." She butchers my name in a way that would make my *babusya* livid, but I don't mind because she emanates sweetness.

"Are you Katie Jo?" I feel a little awkward laying here while meeting Luke's sister, but I don't have much of a choice.

"The one and only." She draws closer to the couch. "Can I help you?" She reaches out a hand to my shoulder.

"Yes, please." Normally I'd bristle at a stranger's offer to help, but there's something about Katie Jo's spirit that's so unassuming, I don't even think twice about accepting her help. I push up on my arm while she lifts me by the shoulders, and the moment I'm upright, my bladder feels like it's going to explode.

"Katie Jo, I know we just met, but I really need your help with something."

"That's what I'm here for, hun."

It takes me a second to realize what she's implying. "Luke asked you to come?"

"Sent me more like," she says with an eye roll, and I like this girl so much already. "He's at mama's house right now."

"He left?" The words blurt out before I can catch them. I'm genuinely surprised he left me alone.

"He's just next door." She gestures toward the side of the house.

"Oh, your mom lives next door?"

"We're all on the property. Grammy, Mama and Papa, even Mike."

"The Craig family compound, huh?"

"Exactly."

I don't have time to think about the implications that Luke chose to bring us to his house, alone, when he could've taken us to his parents' house where there would be more hands to help. Katie Jo may be slim, but she's horse-girl strong. I was doubtful she'd be able to get me into the wheelchair, but she accomplishes it easily. I don't even have to tell her that I have to pee; she takes me straight to the bathroom. I'm surprised by how straightforward she is about this unenviable task, but she helps me pee no problem and even offers to help me take a shower.

"Do I smell that bad?" I joke.

"I lost my olfactory function before I was in elementary school, on account of livin' with three older brothers."

I laugh as she wheels me out of the bathroom. I expect her to park me in the living room, but she keeps going, and we head outside into the sunshine. "Where are we headed?"

"Mama fixed breakfast."

"Oh." I'm hungry, but I don't know how I feel about meeting Luke's whole family. I glance down at Luke's 'Make America Cowboy Again' shirt and baggy sweats. Not exactly a great-first-impression outfit. I quickly chastise myself for the thought—why do I care what Luke's family thinks of me?

Now that we're outside and it's no longer monsooning, I get a better lay of the land. The Craig Compound is sprawling and gorgeous. We're heading toward a large farm-house, complete with wraparound porch and enough rocking chairs to seat a basketball team. There's a wheelchair ramp at the side of the porch and Katie Jo pushes me into the house.

With Luke's parent's house so close to his, he could've just as easily chosen to bring us here last night—with a plethora of able-bodied people to help move me around—instead of his house, where he had to take care of me alone.

Interesting.

I try—and fail—not to dwell on this revelation as we wheel into the Craig's farmhouse. There's a formal parlor at the front of the house that looks like it hasn't been touched in decades. A long hallway lined with family pictures opens up to an open living room and kitchen. A breakfast nook edges the kitchen, and off to the right side is a formal dining area, where it appears that every member of the Craig family has gathered. I hear them before I see them—they're boisterous and giddy. When we get to the dining room, there's a massive wooden table, the biggest I've ever seen. There's all kinds of plates and food strewn across the table, and each person has a paper in front of them with some kind of doodle. Luke and a guy I assume is his brother are cracking up, tears leaking from their eyes as they talk over one another. Seeing him, I feel suddenly shy—like I don't want him to notice I'm here. Because something transpired last night that I don't want to take responsibility for. A type of intimacy that's different than the crush of bodies together—more like the greeting of minds, the mingling of souls. And that is definitely not the type of relationship I want with Luke Craig, or anyone for that matter.

Mrs. Craig spots us first, her blue eyes lighting up when she sees us in the doorway of the dining room. "Come in, come in," she says, standing up and waving us closer. She's slender, with the ropey, tanned skin of someone who spends their time outdoors for a living.

"Miss Kozak." She extends a hand, shaking mine in both of hers. "I've heard so much about you."

"All lies, I'm sure," I say as I smile up at her.

"Ah, there's the quick wit you told me all about." She glances back at Luke. It's the first time since I've walked in that we make eye contact, and I feel unsteady as his dancing eyes hold mine. Why has Luke talked about me to his family? I grip the armrest of my wheelchair—Luke's wheelchair—and remember that I'm wearing his clothes. I'm covered in all things Luke. So why doesn't it feel more oppressive?

I meet the rest of Luke's family—his dad, Austin; his brother, Mike; his grandma, Viv ("but you can call me Granny like the rest of them," she says); Katie Jo's husband, Atticus, and their son, Rhett.

Luke's mom, Emma, is a fast talker and she covers a range of topics, from the breakfast options to Rhett's picky eating to the weather, all before I'm seated at the table. Almost immediately, I have a plate in front of me piled high with eggs, bacon, biscuits, and something that looks like oatmeal but tastes salty. "I'm just relieved that y'all were safe last night," Emma says, looking at me. "Austin can testify, I was prayin' all night."

"We were at home for almost the whole storm, Mama," Luke says.

"Key word being 'almost,'" I say truthfully. "Luke saved the day yesterday."

"Careful," he leans over, whispering to me. "Everyone can hear you, you know. Can't let them think you actually tolerate me."

I laugh, shaking my head as I smack his arm. Though he has a point. When did I start tolerating Luke? Or, more-than-tolerating him?

Katie Jo watches the interaction with a raised brow and a smirk that makes me put my head down and return to my plate. I take a bite of eggs and check my phone to see if my mom or Mila are coming. I decide to text them: *No rush.*

Mike tells Katie Jo about the game they were playing before we got here. Some kind of drawing challenge where you put a piece of paper on someone's back and draw something, and they have to draw the same thing just by feeling what the person is drawing on their back. Mike had been drawing on Luke's back—he shows us a picture of a truck, albeit poorly drawn and oddly bulbous. "So, then, what'd you draw after this monstrosity?" Katie Jo asks Luke.

Luke holds up a picture of a duck, and Katie Jo giggles. "Well, at least they rhyme."

"I can kind of see the similarities, though," I offer. "I mean, Mike's truck is really...round. Like the duck."

Mike guffaws, slapping the table. "She must like you, bro, if she's sticking up for your duck." And then his statement only makes him laugh even harder.

"Don't embarrass the girl, Mikey," Emma whispers loudly. "She's a filly."

I feel my cheeks redden, and it's like everyone's eyes are on me. *A filly?* Seems like Craig family code for 'she's skittish,' and I grimace. I focus on buttering the biscuit on my plate, though I can sense Luke's eyes on me, and I deliberately avoid them.

"Don't worry about me," I say finally. "I'm not easily flustered." I wait for Luke to laugh, because it couldn't be further from the truth, but he doesn't, and everyone moves on to discuss plans for what they were each bringing for their potluck after church tomorrow.

"Your family isn't vegan," I say to Luke.

"What gave you that idea?" he says with a twinkle in his eye.

"Oh, I don't know." I raise a piece of bacon to my mouth and take a crunching bite. "I just get that non-vegan vibe."

He laughs. "You'll fit right in, then."

"I'm more concerned about their stance on sugar than animal products."

Luke gestures toward his mom, who's debating whether she'll make lemon crinkle cookies or snickerdoodle.

"I thought you were gonna make cinnamon rolls," Luke's dad says.

"That's before church, sweetheart."

"What about chocolate chip, Mama?" Luke asks. "Anya wants some."

"Oh, you comin' to church?" Her face lights up. "I'll make the chocolate chip and the lemon crinkle, then. And if you want cinnamon rolls, you'll come over before church. Better get here early though or Austin'll eat 'em all."

"It's true," Mike and Luke say at the same time.

I glance from Luke to Emma, trying to figure out how to get out of this situation. "I—"

"She's coming," Luke says before I can correct her. Then he leans over and whispers in my ear, his breath tickling my neck. "Think of it as your repayment for me 'saving the day' yesterday."

"Coming to church and eating your mom's chocolate chip cookies is repayment?" I turn toward him, our noses almost grazing. "You drive a hard bargain, Mr. Craig."

"You'll have to call me Luke around here." He nods toward his dad. "That's Mr. Craig."

"Okay." I nod. "Luke."

He doesn't move away, and neither do I, and I wonder what in the world I just got myself into.

27

Last Man Sitting

Mila

The morning after the tropical storm, we get a call from the police station. They found the Center's van on the side of the road, without Tommy. Alex and I head to the barn to check on the horses—they're fine, just hungry. We feed them and then grab the van's spare key and go to the spot the cops told us it would be. Alex has called Tommy no fewer than thirty times this morning, but it keeps going straight to voicemail. We get to the van, which is less than a mile from the Tom Thumb gas station on Griffin Road, and find that it's run out of gas. "So maybe Tommy ran out of gas while he was waiting in line for gas?" I surmise as we drive to the gas station in my car.

"Why wouldn't he call one of us then?" Alex says. While I'm giving Tommy the benefit of the doubt, Alex is quietly seething. I don't quite understand why he thinks his cousin has been up to something nefarious, but it seems unfair to me. He's probably still holding a grudge from when his cousin messed up my birthday dance lessons. I can't imagine Alex nursing resentment for too long, so I let it go. We fill up a two-gallon gas can, drive to the van, fill it up, and then bring it to the gas station to top it off.

Back at the Center, there's a silver Toyota Celica with spinning rims idling in the drive. I pull up beside the car, and Tommy's in the passenger seat, next to a kid who can't be much older than sixteen with a fresh fade and a nose ring. Alex, who pulled up in the van next to us, is staring grimly at the pair of them, but I hurry to where Tommy is getting out of the car.

"You're okay," I say as I throw my arms around him. The moment I hug him, the scent of marijuana and alcohol wallop me. "Whoa." I wave my arms in between us, trying to clear the smell. "Guess I don't have to wonder what you've been up to."

Alex is watching Tommy with a lethal look I didn't know he was capable of. "I'm going to leave you two to chat," I say, backing away toward the barn. I rush to the office and close myself in. That's when I see Anya's text to come get her at Luke's, and then a follow up saying, *No rush*. I assume it's sarcastic because I missed her first texts and I'm obviously not rushing over. I text her back, *Be there in 20*, and then I hover at the office window, watching as Alex reprimands Tommy. I'm sure there's a whole story I'm going to find out about soon enough, but I just wish that Alex were a bit more gracious with his cousin. I wonder if it has something to do with his other cousin getting deported for running a Ponzi scheme or if he's just being protective. I make a mental note to talk about it with him later, once everyone has cooled down.

I pick up Anya at Good Hope Ranch, just a few miles from the Center. She's waiting for me with Luke outside of the most gorgeous farmhouse—it's like it came out of Joanna Gaines' wildest dreams with a wraparound porch, charming dormers, and white pillars between rocking chairs and swinging benches. I'm half expecting a sweet Southern lady to come out and offer me sweet tea.

I put the van in park and hop out. "You survived," I say with a genuine smile.

Anya scoffs and wheels toward me. Luke is missing his signature cowboy hat, his blonde hair ruffling in the post-storm breeze. "Which one of us are you more surprised is still standing?" Luke asks in his sarcastic drawl.

"Sitting, you mean," Anya says, her tone bordering on acerbic.

Luke waves a hand as if to say, *You know what I mean*. "I'm just happy you both are alright," I say, opening Anya's door and pressing the button for the wheelchair ramp.

"Aren't we all," Anya says as she wheels into the van without so much as a backward glance toward Luke. I guess that's how the night went, then. I feel bad for Luke, knowing he doesn't completely deserve Anya's wrath, so before I leave, I go up to him and put a hand on his shoulder.

"Thanks for taking care of my sister," I tell him. "I know she's not always easy."

He smiles up at me, his eyes squinting in the sun. "The best ones rarely are," he says, then wheels away. I'm left wondering at his words—was he being sarcastic? Does he really think Anya is great? I can't imagine a universe where the two of them spent the whole night together and left with anything less than vitriol for one another. I decide he's being sarcastic and leave with Anya.

In the car, I catch Anya up on everything that happened with Alex's court date the day before, including my conversation with Alex last night.

"I don't get it," she says. "Why is he freaking out? Literally nothing has changed about his situation."

"Yeah, I don't know. I think we all had our hopes up that this year-long debacle would be done with, and now that it's not, it's just weighing more heavily on him."

"But to the point where he would say 'you deserve better'? That just seems like a bit of an extreme reaction."

"You think so?" I rub my knuckles across my lips. "Yeah, I thought so, too."

Anya is quiet for a few moments, and then she says, "I wonder if any of this has to do with your birthday."

"My birthday?"

"Yeah, Alex was so freaked out about giving you everything you deserve for your birthday. He felt like he couldn't measure up to Michael and what he'd done for you in the past."

"He talked with you about that?"

Anya nods. I knew Alex felt on edge about my birthday plans, but the fact that he talked with Anya about it shows just how much he was feeling.

"I don't want him to be like Michael," I say. "I just want him to be Alex."

"That's pretty much what I told him."

"What's he freaking out about then?"

"Sometimes you tell guys things and it just gets jumbled in their tiny little brains."

I laugh. "Are you referring to all guys in general, or one guy in particular?"

Anya waves a hand. "It's all the same."

28

Selling Jesus

Anya

Somehow, I convince Mila and Alex to come with me to church. I thought it would be a battle to persuade them, but I guess they're feeling generous now that they've both finished their classes for the semester, which seems like a small miracle in the midst of everything else going on.

As we drive to Good Hope on Sunday morning, Mila's struggling to understand what could've possibly transpired that would make me voluntarily see Luke outside of work. "Did you lose a bet?" she asks.

"No."

"Did he find out something about you that you don't want anyone to know?" She gasps. "Oh my gosh, did you pee yourself at his house and now he's blackmailing you?"

I roll my eyes. "No. But no thanks to you. His sister had to help me go to the bathroom."

"Yeesh."

"It wasn't that bad. She was very professional and sweet."

"Professional. Is that your favorite quality in a person?" Mila teases, and I ignore her.

We're all surprised to find that the Good Hope Church is in a barn. There's hay on the floor underneath the pews and the scent of it wafts heavily through the church. Mila and I are wearing dresses and heels, and Alex is in a button down and slacks with a maroon tie, but when we show up, it's clear we're overdressed by a mile. Everyone is in jeans and boots—even Mr. Austin Craig, who is, come to find out, *Pastor* Craig.

A red-brown blur shoots through the crowd and careens into my lap. "Zeke!" I cry out, scratching him behind his ears.

Luke wheels up a moment later, giving my bare legs a little too long of a glance. I cringe and pull my dress down over my atrophied muscles.

"I can get behind a church that lets dogs in," Alex says, kneeling down to let Zeke sniff him.

"Well, we're very selective about which dogs we allow into service," Luke says. A moment later, three mutts swarm our wheelchairs and he amends his statement. "Alright, we're not selective at all. Church is for all." He pats his leg and one of the mutts jumps up on his lap.

Once we've greeted all the dogs, and a few humans too, Luke leads us to a shortened pew to the right of the stage. Alex and Mila shuffle in while Luke and I get situated in our wheelchairs beside the row. "This is my pew," Luke says.

"So you drew the short stick *and* the short pew?"

"Can't complain," he says with a smile. "I've got a good view at the moment."

His words, paired with the glimmer in his eyes, give my stomach an unauthorized flutter. Thankfully, the worship starts up and I don't have to figure out what to say to Luke. A kid who can't be much older than fifteen takes the stage with his guitar and leads the congregation in a series of twangy hymnals. Luke gives us a book with the lyrics, but I don't even attempt to follow along. I'm just taking in the whole atmosphere of this country church.

Like Luke's house, everything in the church barn is made of wood. Wood walls, wood pillars, wood beams holding up the ceilings, wood floors (at least, I assume there's wood underneath all this hay). There are decorative crosses on each of the beams–crosses made of beads, wood, metal, leather. There's even a cross made of braided horse hair.

After the singing, Luke's dad takes the stage and gives an impassioned speech about a story in the Bible where Jesus healed ten lepers and only one came back to thank him. "All of us want healin'," he says. "Don't we?" A few 'amens' scatter through the audience. "But how many of us are thanking God for what we've already received?"

I glance at Luke beside me, wondering how he reconciles his accident with what his dad is saying. Should he be thankful? Or should he wait expectantly for miraculous healing? I want to ask him about this.

It's interesting—and a little concerning—that a week ago, I couldn't think of a single thing I wanted to talk with Luke Craig about. And now, after a day of being stuck with him, I can think of endless topics of conversation. This is deeply, deeply troubling to me. It makes me want to wheel right out of this church and not look back.

Pastor Craig makes a joke, and everyone laughs. Luke looks over at me with a smile to see if I'm laughing, or to share in the joke, and his look strikes terror in me because I realize something I'd been denying—Luke cares about me. Way more than I want him to. Because I'm broken, incapable of being the object of someone's love. And what can I offer in the way of romantic love, anyway? How could I possibly be what Luke needs?

When Luke's dad instructs the congregation to bow their heads to pray, I'm fighting back tears. Then Luke reaches over and takes my hand. For a moment I'm baffled, and then I realize that he's doing this because we're praying. It's what people do, I guess. But the physical contact is doing nothing to dampen the emotions swirling inside of me. If anything, it's making it way worse because Luke's hand is huge and steady and warm.

Pull yourself together, Kozak.

The prayer ends and Luke squeezes my hand before pulling away. "Ready to eat?"

"That's what we're here for, isn't it?" I say a little too tartly.

"Quick," he says to no one in particular. "Get the lady a chocolate chip cookie before she spontaneously combusts."

I roll my eyes and then I hear Emma Craig from across the church call my name. She calls me something that sounds like '*Ahn-nee*'! Before I know it, I'm getting tackled by Katie Jo's son, Rhett, and not far behind him is Katie Jo and Emma, who hug me tightly and kiss my cheek, leaving lipstick marks that Mila rubs off with her thumb. I introduce my sister and Alex and we're guided over to an outdoor pavilion with a potluck spread. We huddle around a picnic table and pretty soon other church members are joining us, giving us hugs and telling us what to grab–or stay away from–in the potluck line up. Luke disappears and brings us back a plate of his mom's cookies, which we eat first. They live up to the hype–perfectly gooey in the middle and slightly crunchy on the outside with just the right amount of sweetness and a barrage of chocolate chips.

"We can leave now, Mila," I say as I steal two cookies from Luke's plate and put it on mine. "I got what I came for."

Luke puts a hand over mine, which is poised on the button that propels my wheelchair forward. "Not so fast, Miss Kozak. You haven't had any of Mrs. Edwards fried chicken or Katie Jo's mac and cheese."

"I'll be deeply offended if you don't eat my mac and cheese," Katie Jo says.

"It's true," Rhett says. "She cried one time when Mrs. Bucholtz said it was too salty." Katie Jo gives her son a playful smack on the back of his head, but she's laughing.

"I'll make you a plate," Mila says, getting up with Alex. She gives Luke's hand on mine a meaningful glance before turning away to the potluck line.

We spend the better part of the afternoon eating a mishmash of Southern food and chatting with various members of the Good Hope Church and the Craig family. We get invited to every kind of event under the sun, from a Friday night rodeo to a turkey hunt to one member's granddaughter's ballet recital.

"Are these the friendliest people you've ever met," Mila whispers in my ear, "or are they trying to sell us something?"

"Maybe Jesus?"

"Can you sell Jesus?"

"You know what I mean."

When it's time for us to leave, we're bombarded by another round of hugs and kisses, and this time Mila doesn't even bother wiping the lipstick off of me. When it's time for Luke to say goodbye, the distance created by our wheelchairs feels insurmountable. I know on a guttural level that if we weren't in our chairs, he'd wrap an arm around my waist, press his lips against my cheek. But we're stuck in the chairs, so Luke just gives me a wave and a nod. It leaves me feeling empty and twisted up inside.

When we get into the car, Mila whirls on me. "Okay, I need to know right now what happened the other night with Luke."

I don't look her in the eye for fear she'll see right through me and busy myself with putting my seatbelt on. "What do you mean?"

"I was up all night worried about you that night, thinking you were being slowly tortured to death."

"It's true," Alex says. "She wouldn't let it go all night."

"And now you're dragging us to church—"

"I didn't force you to come."

"Hugging his family."

"*They* hugged me."

"His dog is obsessed with you—"

"It's not my fault Zeke has good taste."

"Giving Luke your doll eyes." She fixes me with a no-nonsense stare that I have a hard time rebutting.

"I'm not giving him eyes," I mutter halfheartedly.

"Isn't she giving him eyes?" Mila twists in her seat to ask Alex.

"If she wants to give him eyes, she can give him eyes," Alex says.

"I'm not giving him eyes."

"Okay," Mila says, drawing out the word unnecessarily. "So, what's going on?"

"Nothing," I say, looking out the window. "Absolutely nothing."

I spend the night tossing and turning, wondering what kind of rabbit hole I'm falling down with this, this...whatever this is, with Luke. Where could this possibly lead? We're both in wheelchairs, for crying out loud. I feel a squeeze of regret when I think about the hugs, kisses, and hopeful looks from his mom and sister I got today. It's so clear they want me to be the one to wash away the heartache he experienced at the hands of Sienna. But what they don't know is I'm just too damaged to put anyone back together.

I wake up the next morning resolved to be friendly but professional with Luke. I start to see the weekend's developments as a boon for the Center, rather than a personal one. Luke and I getting along, being friends, can only be good for the Center. I convince myself that whatever feelings I'm experiencing are because I haven't been this close to a guy since Dan. Getting involved with a guy just isn't an option.

This realization doesn't stop me from spending extra time on my hair and makeup, though.

At the Center, I roll into the lounge to find Luke by the coffeemaker. The moment he sees me, he lowers his mug and smiles. "Mornin'."

"Good morning, Mr. Craig." I resist the urge to stop and chat with him, and wheel on through.

"I thought we settled on 'Luke.'"

"We're not at the compound anymore."

"I see." He stiffens, and a shadow crosses his face. The change in his demeanor cuts through me like lightning.

I wheel into my office, shutting the door. I rush to my desk and throw my head into my hands. This is going to be much harder than I thought it would be.

29

Loud and Clear

Anya

It's been a week since the tropical storm and things have settled into a polite tension between Luke and me. I suppose it's only uncomfortable because I feel so aware of him now. Before he was a thorn in my side—now that he's decidedly less thorny, I find myself on edge in a very different way. I can sense whenever he rolls into a room. I can hear him laugh from all the way across the barn. His opinions no longer seem preposterous to me—instead, they're too thoughtful, too astute. It's driving me crazy. So I'm keeping my distance to try to ward off whatever insanity is taking hold of my brain. Mila has noticed and has brought it up at least five times throughout the week.

"He clearly likes you, Anya," she says one night while we're watching *All Creatures Great and Small.*

"Just because we're not at each other's throats doesn't mean he likes me."

"Okay, let's be clear about one thing: *he* was never at your throat. It was just you."

"Fine, whatever."

My tone shuts down the conversation, and we go back to watching Siegfried help a racehorse who'd fallen on the track. He's speaking with the General when Mila says, "I don't understand why you won't give him a chance."

I groan. "What's the point, Milochka?"

"What do you mean 'what's the point'? What's the point in loving someone? In letting them love you?"

"No one's saying Luke loves me."

"I'm saying he could if you let him."

"And then what?"

"And then you love each other!"

"For how long?" My voice raises as frustration courses through my body. "Until he gets tired of me? Until he's fed up with the labor of taking care of a crippled girl? News flash, Mila—he's crippled too. It's not a good match."

"I have a feeling it wouldn't be a good match according to you even if he wasn't in a wheelchair. It's not about that, is it? It's about the fact that you don't want to let someone care for you in case they let you down."

"It's not about that," I say, even though I think it probably is.

"You're in denial, *sestra*."

I don't say anything, and we go back to watching the show. But her words get under my skin, like a splinter that won't go away.

We have our first annual Christmas party for the Center on Friday night. We've pitched a huge white tent with a black-and-white checkered dance floor along with several long wooden tables with gold Chiavari chairs. The caterers are setting up food stations, the DJ is getting his speakers situated, and the florist is setting out the centerpieces with white roses and sprigs of evergreen. We've invited all of our clients as well as our donors and volunteers and anyone else who wants to join at $150 a plate. Mila, who organized the event, hired a local band to play called Mad3 for M3, and they're plugging in their instruments and warming up.

We have a few raffle prizes we're giving away, so I set up the display for those items. I'm conscious of Luke behind me, chatting with the band. They're laughing, and I can picture his effervescent blue eyes, the magnetic pull of his grin. I groan and shake my head, trying to put him out of my mind and focus on the task in front of me. I organize and reorganize a basket of spa products and then a stack of autographed books by a local author.

When the event starts, I'm stuck talking with my dad's partners and various people he wants me to chat up. It's exhausting, even though I know that's what this event is all about. But I can't help but notice that several of our young female volunteers have flocked to Luke and they're fawning over him. I tell myself this shouldn't matter to me, but it does.

When Mila comes over to tell me it's time to say our speech, I snap at her, "I'm not ready."

She puts her hands up as if to remind me that she's innocent in whatever drama she just stepped into. I sigh, pinching the bridge above my nose and say, "Just give me a minute to go over my notes."

I situate myself so that Luke isn't in my periphery and read over my notes, but I don't really need to. My dress feels too tight and itchy, and I feel the need to run out of here. But of course, I can't, so I take a deep breath and give Mila the thumbs up.

I'm barely cognizant of what I'm saying while I give my speech, and I hardly pay attention to the conversation at our table while we eat. Going into autopilot is the only way I'm going to make it through this event. I'm relieved when the band starts up and people get up to dance. Mila must sense my need for it because she brings me dessert.

"Want to talk about it?" she asks, plopping down next to me.

"Nothing to talk about," I say as I cut a piece of the white chocolate raspberry cake with my fork.

"Right, okay." She glances around, zeroing in on Luke who's still surrounded by a gaggle of girls. "So this has nothing to do with Luke and all the pretty girls around him?"

I give her a look that hopefully says, *You're deranged*.

She doesn't seem to get the message because she sighs and says, "Oh Anya, you like him." She says it mournfully, like it's a tragedy. And it is.

She puts her hand on my arm and squeezes. We sit like that for a long time, until Alex approaches our table and says to Mila, "Can I steal you for a dance?"

"You okay?" she asks me. I nod, but the moment she stands up to go off to dance with Alex, I'm blinking away tears like the pathetic loser that I am. I realize that as much as I love Mila, and as much as I know she loves me, she has her own life to live. Her own love to care for. And it makes me feel weirdly distanced from her.

I have to prepare myself for a life alone, I tell myself. And for some reason I can't understand, having Luke around is messing with that reality.

I finish my cake and watch Mila and Alex dancing. The way Alex looks at Mila, with unending devotion, it stirs up a well of envy within me. As much as I'm telling myself I need to prepare for loneliness, I want someone to look at me that way. Doesn't everyone? The band starts playing a song called "More Than Friends" and even though I've avoided looking at him for the past thirty minutes, there's Luke. Right in my line of sight.

He's wheeling away from his entourage, heading right for me. I glance away quickly, trying to enact an air of casualness—like I wasn't staring at him—but when I look back, he's still coming toward me.

The lead singer is crooning, "*You get so close to me I'm paralyzed/You know that you're a dream to me/We could be more than friends/Engaging in more than conversation/I'm wondering how this ends/'Cause with you ya know I got temptation.*"

Luke wheels all the way up to me until my knees are between his. "You want to dance," Luke says, more as a statement than a question.

I don't know what to say—*I can't dance, I don't want to dance with* you—but he's right. I do want to dance. And, if I'm being honest with myself—which, I'm totally not—right now, Luke seems about as good a dance partner as any other. Except for the fact that we're both in chairs. So I don't say anything, I simply shrug in response.

He leans in, his hands on my knees as the song continues, "*The odds ain't in our favor/Don't know if I'll win/This feels like second nature so I'm going all in.*"

"Do you trust me?" he says over the music.

Completely. "A little bit."

His eyes light up with this, and I feel a pang at getting his hopes up. Why am I doing that? "That'll have to be enough for now," he says with a crooked smile.

Then he's reaching out, unstrapping me from my chair, and pulling me onto his lap. It happens so fast I can't even react to what he's doing until I'm firmly in his lap, with my back pressed against his chest.

"Luke," I say, my voice shaky. "What are you doing?"

But his right arm is wrapped around me, his massive bicep squeezing against my stomach, holding me in place.

"You said you wanted to dance."

"I don't think I *said* anything."

"You don't have to say things out loud to communicate them. I got the message loud and clear, Miss Kozak." His breath is warm against my neck, and it sends a shiver down my spine that feels like betrayal. Luke wheels us onto the dance floor and I'm realizing how huge this guy is. He's holding me in his lap like I'm a doll rather than a regular sized human, and it feels good. Of course I knew this from last week when he wheeled us inside during the storm, but that was different. That was necessity. This is madness.

"Stop fighting and just enjoy yourself," Luke says, his lips brushing against my ear. And I give up. It's not like I can get back to my wheelchair by myself, anyway. I lean into his embrace, telling myself that this feels good because I'm not used to this much human contact. This has nothing to do with how attractive Luke Craig is, I remind myself as my heart races.

Luke starts to spin his wheelchair, one arm still tight around my waist. I close my eyes and let the music wash over me. It's then that I notice the speed with which Luke's heart is pounding against my back. I take in everything about him, about this moment. There's his scent, a mix of clean laundry and a musky cologne. The feel of his bicep pressing into my stomach. The tent and all of the people rotating around us. The lead singer's voice carrying up and over all of us. The plucking of the guitar, the bumping of the bass. It's all there, lifting me into the next moment and then the next. I let myself simply exist, to be here, without any thought, any emotion, just taking it all in.

That's when I realize—I like this. A lot. I'm beginning to wonder why I was so opposed to Luke in the first place. That version of Anya seems so distant from this one, the Anya that's so magnetically drawn to this charismatic cowboy. Is this what it feels like to lose your mind?

The band sings two more songs and hands the reins over to the DJ. I glance at Mila, who catches my eye and waggles her brows at me—both she and Alex are smiling at us. On the tomato-to-beet scale of redness, the flush creeping up my neck is off the charts. I'm just glad my dad and the other partners left already. I'm surprised at myself for getting so comfortable in Luke's lap—at a minimum it's unprofessional, something I've been chastising him about since the beginning. I feel myself inching away from him, creating distance between us, even as I'm stuck on his lap.

Just as I'm about to drown in my embarrassment, Luke tilts his wheelchair back a few inches so that I'm thrown against his chest. I'm screeching, grabbing at the armrests while he cackles like a wicked witch. "Luke!" I smack at his arm, but he just laughs.

The DJ starts up the Cupid Shuffle and Luke is tilting his wheelchair back and forth in time with the beat. Then he turns me so that I'm sitting sideways in his lap, taking my arms and placing them around his neck.

"Hold on, Miss Kozak," he says in my ear. I tighten my grip on his neck, all of my self-consciousness fleeing the closer I get to Luke. He tries to follow along with the Cupid Shuffle, which is next to impossible in a wheelchair, and we laugh a lot. Other clients in wheelchairs join us on the dance floor, and we're all freely sweating at this point.

When the song ends, Luke says, "You want something to drink?" We get some water, and I tense just thinking about Luke returning me to my wheelchair and moving on with the night. I'm not ready for this to be over.

Luke downs two cups of water. He's drenched in sweat. I grab a napkin off the drink table and wipe his face. "Thank you, darlin'," he says, and I don't even correct him.

"Oh, I'm not doing this for you," I say. "I'm doing this for me. You're sweating all over me."

He chuckles but then says, "You ready?"

I look at him, frozen with indecision. I don't want to stop dancing with Luke—more than that, I don't want to stop being so close to him. But I also don't want to tell him that I want this. I want this so badly it hurts.

"Hey," he says, misreading the indecision on my face. "It's okay if you're done and want to go back."

I shake my head, looking away as my pride wells in me because I don't want to admit the opposite. "It's not that."

He takes my chin, tilting my face back toward his. He's looking in my eyes, his blue ones searching mine for so long I want to squirm in his lap. "I see," he finally says. And I want to ask, *What do you see*? He starts wheeling away from the drink table, and my stomach is sinking because he's taking me back to my wheelchair.

Until he turns onto the dance floor and starts moving his chair back and forth in time with the music. The song is Harry Styles' "As It Was," and I'm beginning to understand the lyric about being held back by gravity. *There's a lot more than* gravity *holding me back, Harry*. I sigh as I look at Luke, his playful grin on the verge of contagion.

What did he see, just then? My desire to dance? Or my desire to stay with him? The idea unsettles me, makes me feel shaky inside. Luke's voice breaks me out of my thoughts when he says, "Hold on." I tighten my hold around his neck and we're spinning again as Harry sings about it being just us in the world. I do something unthinkable and lean my forehead against the side of his head. I close my eyes and imagine I'm on my two feet, dancing with Luke. It's euphoric, this feeling of spinning, this sensation of dancing. How could I have possibly known how much I missed this? Or how much I needed this?

When the next song comes on, "Crazy What Love Can Do" by David Guetta, Becky Hill, and Ella Henderson, Luke stops spinning us. He's breathing hard, and I know he's tired, but then he starts shimmying his shoulders back and forth and I crack up. He puts a hand around my back, steadying me as he leans us back and forth.

"Do you ever run out of energy?" I ask.

He laughs, and the vibrations from his chest flutter through me. "For you? No."

His words zing down my back like an electric current.

Can someone tell me what is happening to me?

For a moment, everyone drops away—I'm not worried about Clara and the insurance, or Mila and Alex, or anything else but being right here, right now. For a moment, I feel like my whole body can move as Luke moves us together. For a moment, I am not Anya-the-paraplegic. I'm just Anya.

We dance until all of our guests clear out, only taking occasional water breaks. When the DJ announces the last song, my heart drops, and before I even realize what I'm doing, I tighten my grip around Luke's neck. I flush with embarrassment when I recognize what I've done—and why—but am quickly reassured when Luke squeezes me back with his arm around my waist.

Someone else also doesn't want this to end. I smile.

At the end of the last song, Luke wheels us to my chair, and I don't know if he's going extra slow because he's tired or if, like me, he's not ready for this night to end. When we get to my wheelchair, we both just stare at it.

"How did we do this before?" I ask, genuinely unsure how I'm going to get back in my wheelchair, although I'm not too torn up with the idea of staying put.

"Can't remember," Luke says, a little gruffly. "Guess you'll just have to come home with me."

I should say something. But all the words fly out of my head when I glance at Luke and his eyes are burning into mine. My breath hitches as his hand tightens around my waist. My fingers run through the hair on the back of his head, and his sigh makes me inch closer.

There's this moment when I think I'm going to let him kiss me. I *want* him to kiss me.

And then, from somewhere to my right, someone says, "Are you Anya or Mila Kozak?"

I startle, not realizing anyone else was here. That's when I see that Alex and Mila are still here, cleaning up plates from the tables. They venture over when they see the guy dressed in a suit standing beside Luke and me.

I sit up a little straighter, but I'm practically curled up in Luke's lap, so it's hard to do. "Um, yes. I'm Anya Kozak."

The guy in the suit hands me a thick envelope. "You've been served."

30

Aftermath

Mila

In the days after we get served, there are unending conversations about it. With each other, the partners, the insurance company, the reporters who call. I have a permanent tension headache from it, and one glance at Anya tells me she's got it worse than me. Much worse.

My dad has gone into fix-it mode, which puts our entire household in a place of near-permanent strain. I'm not sure why I expected some semblance of comfort from *Tato*—that's not really his style—but I find myself aching for it, nonetheless.

On Monday, the ViaTech partners call us into their office for a meeting. We all put on our best suits and despite all of the nerves I'm feeling, when I see Alex standing in front of the Cottage with his navy-blue suit on, I have a flash in my mind of marrying him—walking down the aisle to him, looking just like *that*. It leaves me feeling shaken in more ways than one.

When we get to ViaTech, it's just my dad and one of the other partners, Hajime Osuke. My dad is dressed down in a Ralph Lauren polo and slacks, and Hajime is in a dress shirt with the sleeves rolled up to his elbows. Hajime's normally sweet, impassive features are collected into a frown today, and it sends a shiver of fear through me. A moment later, a woman in a pencil skirt with cat-eye reading glasses enters the room and my dad introduces her as Nicole, our attorney. We spend the next two hours answering endless questions about the accident, our safety procedures, our insurance coverage, Clara's intake, and our volunteers and staff. By the time Nicole seems to be wrapping up her questioning, we're all sagging in our chairs. Hajime left after an hour, surely doing something, anything, more compelling than this.

Nicole pushes her reading glasses up over her head and says, "Well, my recommendation is to craft a statement. I can help you do that, of course, but we need to be very intentional with how we approach the media." I nod, but my brain is so fried I'm not sure how I could possibly be helpful in 'crafting' anything other than a nap. Nicole glances over her notes and says, "Oh, there is one more thing. The recording."

"What recording?" Anya asks.

My dad leans in and says in the most bone-chilling voice I've ever heard, "They have a recording of Anya telling Alex to flirt with the girl in order to get her on the horse."

I sit back in my chair as if I'd just been punched. "How?" I whisper.

"Does it matter?" my dad says. "They have it, and it's problematic, in more ways than one." He levels his hardened gaze at Alex, and I reach out a hand under the table to squeeze his knee.

Nicole asks several more questions about the recording, Anya answering them in a cool, clipped tone, though I barely comprehend what she's saying. How do they have a recording of that? I barely remember that happening, but of course Anya was being silly, so why would it even matter? I say as much, but my dad responds with, "It doesn't matter what your intention was; it only matters how they hear it."

The sound of his voice is rough like sandpaper, reminding me of how much work we've put into this place and how jarring it feels to have it slipping through our fingers. I don't get to ask who 'they' is, because ViaTech's PR girl comes in the room and we're coming up with a statement for the media. By the time we leave ViaTech and head back to the Center, my brain is more scrambled than eggs. I'm trying to parse through our hours-long conversation with Nicole and my dad, and I can tell Anya and Alex are doing the same.

"Who could've recorded us?" Anya breaks the silence. It's a question I've thought a hundred times since my dad broke the news to us.

"That morning it was us three and Tommy for sure. There was a volunteer there, wasn't there? Who was it?"

"Ben," Alex says.

"And Luke was there, I think."

"Okay, so the options are Tommy, Ben, and Luke?"

"Well, unless someone set up a recording device in the lounge and left it there."

Back at the Center, we tear apart the lounge, looking for some means of recording. We don't find anything, but it puts us all on edge. We all trust Tommy, Ben, and Luke, but this revelation suddenly puts all of that trust into question.

"Let's call a meeting with the staff about this, and we can watch the three of them and see how they react. Get a read on them," I suggest.

"Sounds like something that works in a mystery novel, but not in real life," Anya says.

"We should talk with them regardless," Alex says. "They should know what's going on and go over safety procedures."

"We should tell them not to talk about the fall to anyone," Anya says to Alex and me before the meeting.

"That feels shady, doesn't it?" I ask.

"Or smart," Anya says. "What if they say something that comes back to bite us?"

"Like what?" Alex asks.

"Like we were negligent in some way," Anya says, waving her hand to encompass the fact that they could say literally anything.

"I think we just need to be honest," Alex says. "Tell them the truth, and that there's a chance they could be approached."

"We could tell them they always have the right to not respond," I say.

Eventually, we decide that Anya will make a comment about the lawsuit, and the moment she starts talking to our staff and volunteers, I cringe and immediately wish we'd chosen Alex to deliver the news. Anya is shooting daggers from her eyes, daring anyone to say anything, as she tells them that we're being sued and that they might be approached by the media or opposing lawyers.

The three of us are watching Tommy, Ben, and Luke closely, and I wonder if any of them can feel it. Tommy's fidgeting, shifting from foot to foot and bouncing on the balls of his feet—but he always does that. Ben looks bored, like he's completely zoned out. I wonder how many meetings he's had to endure like this with the FBI. Luke's brow is furrowed with concern, and he asks a few clarifying questions about safety procedures. He's just as invested as the three of us.

I think back to the night of the Christmas party—which was only three days ago yet feels like five years ago. I'd never seen Anya look as free as she did dancing with Luke in his wheelchair. Who would've guessed? Certainly not me, or Anya, for that matter. But what was a glimpse of freedom on that night turned into a landslide of fear and anxiety. And no one feels that more keenly than Anya.

I've paid careful attention to the dynamic between Luke and Anya these past few days, but they're nothing but polite and distant. I don't have the heart to bring it up with her since there's so much else going on. But it pains me to see her denying herself of happiness. I don't get it.

When Alex, Anya, and I reconvene after the staff and volunteers leave, Alex says, "I think it's Tomás."

"I had those vibes too," I say, but Anya shakes her head.

"What? Why do you think that?"

So we tell her about what happened when Tomás ghosted her and ditched the Center van the day of the tropical storm, and then Alex tells us about catching Tommy smoking a joint on the property. Anya is livid, saying, "So Tommy is involved in some kind of sketchy drug-thing and you're allowing him to continue working for us?"

"I'm not positive. It's just a hunch."

"If it's got fur and it roars..." Anya starts.

"It's a bear," I finish.

Alex glances between us, eyebrow raised.

"It's one of our mom's weird sayings," I explain. "It's her version of 'If it looks like a duck and quacks like a duck, it's probably a duck.'"

"I see," he says, not entirely convinced. "So what do you want to do about Tomás?"

"Fire him, obviously," Anya shoots out.

"Well, what if we just pay attention to him? Keep an eye on the things he's doing and see if anything else shady happens?" I ask.

"I recuse myself from the decision," Alex says. "He's my cousin, I'm too involved."

"We're all involved, Alex. This is family, and this is our home that we've built," Anya says, with a touch of sentimentality none of us were expecting.

"Alright," Alex says. "Let's keep an eye on Tomás, and if anything else happens, he's out. But maybe we'll get a clearer idea of how this happened."

We all agree and leave for home, though I can't help but feel like this decision might come back to bite us.

On Friday, we have an event where we're bringing two horses to a memory care facility in Davie. The four of us—Alex, Anya, Luke, and me—pile into Luke's truck with the trailer behind.

"See? This is why we hired you," Alex says.

"Because of my tricked-out truck?"

"Exactly."

"We can get you a truck if you want," I tell Alex.

"I don't need a truck. I just need Luke to drive me around in his truck."

"Ah," Anya says. "That's not weird at all." It's the first thing I've heard her say in five days that's not related to the lawsuit. And even though it's dripping in sarcasm, it warms my heart. That is until she looks down at her phone and says, "Oh no."

"What is it?"

"Another one." She holds up her phone and there's a news article that reads, "Equine Assisted Therapy Center Displays Gross Negligence with Paraplegic."

I wrench the phone from her hand, not wanting Alex to get it first, scrolling through the article. It's terrible. It makes us sound like we purposefully neglected Clara's safety in getting her on a horse. "It says we forced her on the horse. That she didn't want to ride." My heart sinks when I read the part where it says Alex—an 'unauthorized immigrant'—coerced her through flirtatious manipulation. I don't read it aloud. It would rip Alex to shreds. The statement we'd spent an hour working on with the lawyer and the PR girl is mysteriously missing.

"She's not just coming after us financially," I whisper. "She's coming after our character."

"What kind of person does this?" Anya says. "We're a Center for paraplegics, for crying out loud—it's not like we're running a brothel or something insidious. We're trying to help people."

We're all silent at this, because none of us completely understand it. We drive to the memory care facility, the quiet stretching like a tightrope that we're all balancing on.

31

Old Folks

Anya

As I wheel toward the memory care facility, I feel like I'm underwater. Everything feels hazy and blurry. I can't take a full breath. My mind can't form a complete thought. I just go into survival mode when we get there; I'm greeting people, telling them about the horses, chatting with whoever crosses my path. But I'm not really there, not truly present. My body's there, but my mind is somewhere else completely.

The memory care facility have lined up their clients outside, and we bring the horses out. We give some of the patients brushes and they work on Don Juan's mane and forelock. We hand out treats and the horses nibble at their hands. The sight of one patient with Harley sparks a tiny sensation of life in me: Harley lowers his head right into an elderly woman's lap, and she's just holding his head. They look as though they're communicating somehow without saying anything. It's beautiful. I can't believe someone would threaten what we're doing here. I blink back angry tears and go to wheel away, only to run right into Luke.

He doesn't say anything, just looks at me. There's no grin, no wink, no bravado with him right now. He looks as sad as I feel. He reaches out and puts a hand on my knee, and I suddenly wish more than anything that I wasn't in a wheelchair. I could really use a hug right now. "I'm sorry," he says.

"It's not your fault."

"I know, but I know how much this place means to you, and how hard it must be to have someone terrorizing that."

I nod, pressing my lips together to keep the tears from coming. As much as things shifted between Luke and me after the storm—and the dance, but I'm not thinking about the dance—it's not the middle of the night and I can't just cry whenever I feel like it.

I don't say anything for a long time and eventually, Luke says, "You can let me be there for you, y'know."

I want to say, *How?* What would it even look like, practically, for me to allow Luke to 'be there' for me? But instead I say, "What do you think I'm doing?"

He gives a quick laugh. "Puttin' up walls."

"If I had walls up, I wouldn't even let you touch me right now," I say, keenly aware of his hand on my knee. Part of me wants to brush it off. The other part wants it to stay there. For a while.

"Walls take many forms."

"Hmm," I gruff. I feel the push-and-pull of wanting Luke to be close to me, but not too close. It's like a storm inside of me, threatening to pull me apart. It's too much on top of everything else going on. "I like my walls," I say as I back away.

Luke calls out from behind me, "So you can take care of others, but not let anyone take care of you?"

I stop, rotating my wheelchair so I can see him. He has his hands on the wheels of his chair, as if he wants to move closer, but he doesn't. "My mom cared for me nonstop for a year after my accident," I say. "Mila takes care of me. I have no choice."

"Exactly, you have no choice." He sounds almost angry, and I'm not sure why. "Is there anyone you'll let get close enough to care for you in the ways that really matter?"

I grit my teeth as defensiveness takes hold—for who? My mom? Mila? Or...myself? "I am taken care of in every way that matters," I tell him.

He doesn't speak for a while, just simply looks at me, his eyes moving back and forth over my face like he's trying to interpret me. I don't like that he seems to think he knows me—and then I remember that I bared my soul with him on the night of the storm, and I'm really regretting it right now. Finally, he speaks, and I can barely hear him when he says, "You sure about that?"

Before I can blurt the truth, I say, "Yes," and then turn my wheelchair and roll away just as tears are forming behind my eyelids. Because as much as I hate to admit it, Luke is right. Though I'm taken care of physically, there's a void within me. And it's becoming increasingly apparent to me that the only person who can fill that void is the very person I don't want to.

The memory care event lasts well into the evening, and then we have to bring the horses back and feed them. By the time we get home that night, my dad is waiting for us in the living room, in an overstuffed leather chair. It's dark in the house except for a small tiffany lamp on the side table beside him. I immediately tense at the sight of him, knowing that he must have seen the article.

He greets us in his gruff voice. Mila glances back at me, and I know she can sense everything I can. He wordlessly waves a hand at the loveseat beside him, and Mila sits while I roll up beside her. "The partners have called a meeting about this disaster," he says, holding up his phone with one of the articles about Clara's fall.

I nod, waiting for him to elaborate, but he doesn't. "When is it?" Mila asks.

"Mattia is out of town right now and then we leave in a few days for our getaway, but when we're all back, we'll meet first thing."

"Okay, we'll be there," I say.

My dad shakes his head. "No, just partners."

"But it's our business—"

"Funded by us."

"*Tato*, this is not our fault, regardless of what they said in the article. This kind of thing happens around horses. It's just a reality."

"You say 'regardless' as if we could disregard what is written in the news. I'm disappointed in your inability to see this, Anya." I wince when he says my name. "What matters is that this venture was supposed to be good for ViaTech. A feel-good project that brings positive PR. But right now, when you Google our name, this"—he holds up his phone—"is what comes up."

"I'm sorry, *Tato*."

He makes a guttural sound in the back of his throat, but then nods. "I appreciate that. I know it's not your fault, but we have to be intentional about what to do with this."

"We understand," Mila says.

Our dad gets up, kisses the tops of our heads and goes to bed. "*Nadobranich*," he says as he tromps up the stairs.

Mila snorts once he's out of earshot. "As if we could sleep well after that."

"Yeah," I say lamely.

"Seems like a good night for takeout and binging the next season of *Love is Blind*," Mila says, taking out her phone.

"I think I'm just going to go to bed."

"Really? You're not hungry?"

"No." Which is a lie—I am hungry, but the desire to be alone, to shut myself away, is stronger than any hunger pangs.

"You don't want to talk about all this, *sestra*?" Her voice is quiet, barely above a whisper, and it breaks me that I'm pushing my sister away too. That I have no choice but to push her away, because I don't have the bandwidth—or desire—to handle this disaster with anyone but myself.

"No." I wheel toward the stairs. "I'm just wiped. Night, Milochka." I back up to the stairs and turn on the stair climber, carefully avoiding making eye contact with my sister.

I can feel Mila's disappointment, her confusion at me shutting her out, but I can't deal with anyone's pain other than my own right now.

32

The Talk

Alex

It's the day before we're supposed to leave for vacation with the Kozaks, and Mila took Anya to a doctor's appointment using the Center's van. It's almost six o'clock, and I'm returning emails when I hear the horses neighing. At first, I don't think anything of it, but then there's the sound of one of the horses pawing the ground and hitting the stall door. I press 'send' on the email I'm working on, then head out to the breezeway. The horses are typically fed dinner at five-thirty, so when I see all of their heads poking out of their stalls—decidedly not eating dinner—I call out, "Tomás?"

I walk to the feed room, where I expect him to be at least pouring grain into buckets or stacking up pads of hay, but instead, he's huddled in the corner by one of the feed bags. He glances up, whites of his eyes visible in the dark room. The moment he sees me, he fumbles with whatever he's holding—something he pulled out of the feed bag in front of him—and shoves it in his pocket.

I don't know what it is, but a shiver of apprehension goes through me. Whatever Tomás is doing, it's not good. I step closer, and he takes a step back. "Alex," he says, like he's warning me.

I walk to the feed bag, and he tries to block my way, but I shove him to the side. "Alex," he says again, more strained this time. I crouch down and inspect the feed bag, rifling through the pellets only to feel something plastic at the bottom. I pull.

"What is this?" I ask, uncovering a bag with powder in it.

"*Primo*, I can explain—"

I push Tomás against the wall of the feed room, anger rippling through me as I tighten my grip on the bag. "I don't want an explanation. I want a statement of fact. What. Is.

This." I speak through gritted teeth, and my heart is beating wildly, like a caged animal within me.

"It's not anything, it's nothing. It's not mine."

I press my forearm into my cousin's chest, willing him not to move as I hold the bag closer to us, examining it for the first time. It's tightly packed white powder in layers of plastic, secured with clear tape. Rage is exploding through me now; my limbs are shaking with it. I turn back to Tomás, barely able to look at him. "You brought drugs into my facility. You put them in the feed—"

"I didn't put it there—"

"If this bag broke, what would happen? You would feed the horses drugs? What would happen then, Tomás?"

"I wouldn't—"

"You wouldn't deign to do that, but you would bring drugs into this facility? Where's the line, Tomás? Where's the sense in any of this? What could you possibly be thinking?"

"They brought me here for this, *primo*. I had to. They got me here, I owe them."

I release my cousin, stepping back from him. "How much more is in here?" I turn toward another feed bag, ripping it open and pushing my hand through.

"Alex? What are you gonna do?" Vaguely I hear Tomás's voice, but I'm slightly out of my mind and don't have the wherewithal to respond. I rip through bag after bag of feed, finding five more bags of the white powder. I thought that maybe Tomás was just storing the drugs in the feed bags, but this is much bigger than that. Someone is putting the drugs in the feed bags, sealing them, and shipping them here. They're using the feed bags to transport drugs, and I have no idea the scope of this thing, but I know it's much bigger than me and Tomás. I'm shaken by this realization.

I take the bags of powder and shove them into my cousin's chest. I don't know what I should do right now, but I do know that I need Tomás out of here as soon as humanly possible, and I need to never see him again. "Get out of here, Tomás."

"Primo—"

"Don't you dare call me that. This is not how you treat family," I grind out, pointing around the feed room. "You don't get to call me that anymore."

Hurt flashes through his dark eyes—eyes that I know are a mirror of my own. We share the same genes, the same family, and yet he could not be farther from me if he were a stranger on the other side of the world.

"If that's what you want," he says, bending down to grab the other bags.

"Don't come back here."

"Where am I gonna live?" he whimpers like a child.

"You forced me to not make that my problem anymore." When Tomás doesn't move, I shout, "Get out!"

Tomás jumps, startled by my raised voice—something he's never heard before—and leaves the feed room. I stand there, surrounded by torn bags of feed and pellets spilled all over the floor, and let out a guttural yell, the sound raking my throat as it fills the room.

I spend the rest of the evening going through the feed room, taking apart every bale of hay. I don't find any other bags—I'm not even sure what I'd do with them if I found them.

I have no idea what I'm supposed to do. Can I call the cops on my own cousin? Can I embroil the Center in even more chaos? I imagine the headlines—*Equine-Assisted Therapy Center a Drug Den*—and crumple to the feed room floor. I call Mila three times, but she's not picking up. I think about the recording that Clara's lawyer somehow obtained, and I wonder if it was Tomás. He's clearly involved in something so unbelievably wrong. What's one little recording to a drug dealer? What line wouldn't he cross? If he's willing to use the Center to deal drugs, why not betray us even more for a little more money?

I decide to report it to Crime Stoppers from an incognito window on my computer, hoping they are true to what they say about tippers remaining anonymous. I don't mention the Center—only that I found bags of drugs inside horse feed bags. I mention the feed store we got it from, but I don't mention Tomás. I know there are people pulling Tomás's strings, and those people need to be stopped. If what Tomás is saying is true, someone brought him here to do their bidding, and that person is much more dangerous than my cousin. I know it's the right thing to report it, but the whole time I feel like I'm doing something illegal—and maybe I am. I don't even know; I just know I can't jeopardize the Center any more than it already is.

After I've showered, scrubbing my skin until it's red and throbbing, I have to take Mila's car back to her house for her since she took the Center's van to bring Anya to her appointment. I don't know what I'll say to her, how to even explain what just happened, and I debate the issue with myself the whole drive to her house.

When I get there, she's showering upstairs and her dad is alone in the living room. He's sitting at the dining table, nursing a drink as he looks at his phone. I hesitate when I see him, not wanting to talk with him. Mr. Kozak may have been instrumental in my release from the detention center and my employment at the Center, but he's made it clear—to me, at least—that the jury's still out when it comes to his personal feelings toward me. And after everything that's just happened with my cousin and his drug dealing, I might agree with Mr. Kozak if he said I wasn't good enough for his daughter.

When he sees me, he sighs and takes a sip of his drink. "Mr. Caballero," he says, and that's one reason why I know he's not sold on me. I've been dating Mila for over a year and he's yet to call me by my first name. I wonder distantly what he called Michael. I walk slowly toward him, wishing that someone, anyone, would come rescue me from sitting face-to-face with Mila's dad by myself. I send Mila telepathic signals to hurry her shower and get down here.

It doesn't work.

"Sit down," he says, gesturing at the seat across from him. I obey.

"How are you, sir?" I don't mean to sound so hesitant; I know Mr. Kozak values strength and confidence, so I try to exude it. And fail.

"I want to talk about your case getting rescheduled." He's looking down at his phone. He fires off a text or an email and then puts it down, looking me dead in the eye. I'm paralyzed by his stare. "I'm concerned."

"Ann seems positive," I tell him.

"Yes, she does. However, on the off chance it doesn't go your way..." I notice he doesn't say 'our way' and I send more telepathic signals to Mila to hurry up. "I want to discuss what that will mean for you, for the Center, and for Mila."

For Mila? Does Mr. Kozak think he can decide what Mila will do if I get deported? "Yes, sir."

"If the judge decides on removal, I will not pay Ann to fight the case."

"I understand, sir."

"Do you?"

"Yes, sir."

"It wouldn't be a good idea to go back to Cuba. For your sake, and your mother's."

"I agree."

"You should consider Canada," he says. "They're more favorable. I've taken the liberty of getting a visa application for you, in case you need it." He hands me a manila folder with paperwork inside. I don't want to touch it, but I take it from him.

"That's…kind, Mr. Kozak," I say as I page through the application for a visa. Rage is building in me, but I shove it down. This is Mila's dad, I remind myself.

"And as far as Mila goes." He folds his hands, staring at me with his cold hazel eyes. "I think we both know what would be best for her."

"Could you elaborate," I say with a little too much force. "Sir?"

"In the case that you are removed, you need to let her go. That's what is best for Mila. She deserves better."

I stare at him for a beat too long, every part of me railing against what he's saying—I may not be the best, but I know I'm good for Mila. Who else could love her like I do? It makes me wonder if Mr. Kozak actually thinks I flirted with or manipulated Clara. He raises a brow, and I'm certain my stare is rapidly turning into a glare. I need to get out of here before I say or do anything I'll regret. I stand abruptly, gathering the papers.

"Oh, and Mr. Caballero?"

I look reluctantly at Mr. Kozak, not ready for yet another of his unilateral decisions.

"The Christmas vacation should really be family members only, don't you think?" he says, referring to the holiday getaway I'd been formerly invited to. The one that starts tomorrow.

I give one quick nod, unable or unwilling to say anything else. The anger simmering just below the surface will explode if I stay here a minute longer. So I put Mila's keys on the table and leave.

33

"Vacation"

Anya

What does a person do when they're on vacation in which they cannot access television, internet or phones? All they have are the people around them, who are wound just as tightly as you. Do you relax and enjoy the time with zero distractions, or do you let the anxiety overtake every thought, every moment, every inch of your body?

I'll let you guess which one I went with.

Little Palm Island is a private resort island off the coast of the Florida Keys. We take a wood-paneled yacht named Truman, leaving behind our phones and computers on the "motherland," as the yacht driver affectionately named it. My parents have a second-story suite with expansive windows that overlook the ocean, and Mila and I share a thatched-roof bungalow with a massive outdoor copper tub on our private deck.

I try to relax, I really do. I go through the motions of taking a soak in the tub, lounging on the sand with a book, and even going to the spa with my mom and Mila for a round of facials and massages. On our third day, my mom brings in the yoga instructor for a private wheelchair yoga lesson. But I even grit my teeth through that, knowing that I'm getting closer and closer to the Center being ripped from me. Because if I were the ViaTech partners, that's what I would do. Cut my losses and get out of there.

Mila seems just as restless as I am—and though she's concerned about the Center, I know the bulk of her anxiety is over Alex. "I just don't get why he would back out of our vacation so last minute," she tells me one night when we were talking about something completely different.

"I thought *Tato* said it was because his mom isn't feeling well?"

"Yeah, that's what he said but when I tried to call Alex, he didn't pick up. It's just really unlike him. He texted me late last night saying she's fine, but still."

"With her condition, though, I'd understand why he wouldn't want her to be stranded on an island."

"It was just weird because he was supposed to come over that night and hang out with me, but then he just left my keys with *Tato* and didn't even say bye to me."

I think for a moment, suspicion welling in my stomach. "You think Dad said something to him?"

She crinkles her nose. "I don't think so. Do you?"

"He's very protective of you."

"Maybe." Mila sighs and flops over onto her stomach. "I just wish I knew what to say to him right now. He's so worried about his court date and what will happen if it's worst-case scenario."

"I get that. Have you guys talked about what will happen if we...you know, don't win?"

"Not really."

"How come?"

"Neither of us have really wanted to. I dunno, I just want to be positive."

"It's fine to be positive, but Alex might need you to be realistic for a few minutes so you can discuss what might happen *if* worst-case scenario happens."

"Yeah, maybe." She rests her head on her forearms. "I just wish he weren't so in his head about it."

I sigh and close my eyes. "He's not the only one."

The next day, my mom and Mila go out for a kayak excursion, and I decide it's time to talk with *Tato*. We're sitting side-by-side on the beach, books in hand. An attendant shuffles through the sand every time my dad so much as lifts his hand, offering to bring us drinks or towels or whatever we might desire. I can't say this is a particularly beneficial service for my father. So far, in the hour or so we've been out here, he's requested two different drinks, a cold wet towel, an umbrella, a different pair of shoes from his suite, and a plate of chilled shrimp cocktail. I'm doing us all a favor by distracting my dad with conversation.

"So," I say, putting my bookmark in and setting my book down on my chair. My dad, meanwhile, lays his book on its belly, still cracked open, its spine creaking with discomfort. *Monster.* "What do you know about this whole Alex situation? With him not coming on the vacation anymore?"

My dad takes a sip of his drink, ice clinking in the glass as he tips it back. "As much as you do, I suspect."

I rip off my sunglasses and give *Tato* my best glower—which, I have to admit, is pretty good. He matches my gaze. I learned from the best, apparently. "Vacation is for family," he says.

"Alex is practically family."

"If it ever becomes official, he can come on vacation, then."

"If? Or when?"

"If."

"Why did you tell Mila it was because of his mom?"

At this, my dad looks away. I've caught him, and the show of weakness is just enough for me to know he feels guilty about lying. "*Tato.*"

He shrugs. "No one wants to be the bad guy."

"So you're going to let Alex look bad, like he just backed out last-minute? Instead of the truth?"

"It's probably true that his mom shouldn't come to an island like this."

I snort. "That's a stretch, *Tato*, even for you."

"I'm protecting Mila."

"From *Alex*? That's absurd."

"When you have children, you'll understand. You learn to trust your gut on these things."

I stare at my father, waiting for him to realize his gaff. *When you have children.* My ovaries may be fully functional, but that doesn't mean they'll get utilized. I glance over at my wheelchair and grit my teeth. Is my dad irrationally hopeful on my behalf, or deeply insensitive? You can take a wild guess which option I'm leaning toward. I put my sunglasses back on and shift my gaze back to the ocean with its foaming crests and shimmering blue, which does *not* remind me of Luke's eyes. Not at all.

My dad raises his hand, and the attendant comes running. I suppose this conversation is done, and I'm not sure I accomplished anything except just being angry with my dad.

On our fourth day, my mom invites me to lunch with her on the sand. She arranged with the restaurant on site to bring lunch out to us by the water. A lovely table is set with fresh tropical fruit, Key West pink shrimp cocktail, and fresh caught fish tacos.

I'm in my own head as we eat, thinking about the insurance for the Center and how we'll find a new one. Will anyone take us with this lawsuit hanging over our heads? Will the partners continue to back us if we don't have insurance? What could we possibly do without insurance? Basically nothing.

"What was her name?" my mom says softly, and I'm so caught up in my mind, I barely hear her.

"What?"

"The girl that fell, what was her name?"

"Oh, um. Clara."

"Clara. That's pretty." She takes a bite of her shrimp cocktail and looks out at the water. I think we're done with this conversation, and I go back to my mental list of insurance companies I can reach out to when my mom says, "Why didn't you tell me about it? When it happened?"

I think about this for a moment, wondering why I hadn't confided in my mom. I remember that night of Clara's accident, coming home and wanting to unburden to her. But she'd been so happy, talking about work—I didn't want to take her out of that place. And accidents like Clara's mean a lot more to my family, and especially my mom, than the average person. There's a whole boatload of emotions and memories that come with a situation like this. To be transported back to that time, those experiences—it's jarring. And I didn't want that for my mom. I wanted to spare her the pain of thinking about that. "I just didn't want to burden you. You were so happy that night."

"But, sweetheart, I'd happily take that burden for you." She takes my hand, running her fingers over mine. "That's what mothers are for, to share in your pain."

"You've done enough of that."

"There is no end to my love for you and my capacity to uphold you, Anochka."

I smile sadly, tears brimming in my eyes. Because I think my mom wants that to be true, but I know everyone has a limit. Even my unflagging mother.

"I should have said something," I finally say, even though I don't really feel that way. I'm glad I shielded my mom, if only for a time. I'd do it again in a heartbeat.

"I'm here for you, darling." The word darling brings Luke's face to mind, and I think about spinning with him in his wheelchair on the night of the Christmas party. I'd felt so light, so buoyant that night. I look back on that Anya and think she was a fool. She didn't know what was coming. And it makes me that much more determined to guard myself so I don't let my walls down again.

34

Gift Exchange

Alex

Christmas break without Mila was unbearably quiet—and, as an introvert, I like the quiet. Usually. But not the kind of quiet without Mila, apparently. Whenever I'd come down to the barn from the cottage, my mind would automatically search for Mila, even though she wasn't there. Then the reminder of the conversation with her dad would shoot through me, filling me with equal parts shame and horror. Would he let me marry her? If he didn't, would Mila marry me without Mr. Kozak's approval? The thought of my unscheduled court date loomed in the back of my mind at all times, haunting me as I went about feeding the horses, turning them out and cleaning the tack.

And, of course, the pall of Tomás's departure—and all that went with it—follows me through my days. I never had a chance to tell Mila about it, since she left for her vacation where she has no access to the outside world. I feel filthy, like no matter how often I shower, I'll still find traces of the white powder on me. Every vehicle that passes the Center, I worry it's the police. *What would happen to my case if I were arrested?* I wonder. The thoughts are my only real company throughout the week.

I bought my mom a small tree that we decorated with ornaments from the Dollar Tree. My mom *loves* Dollar Tree. She doesn't make many outings by herself, but she always has her weekly Dollar Tree outing. We set up the nativity display under the tree—a small porcelain set my dad got when I was a kid. It's wrapped lovingly in pieces of tissue paper and only comes out for a week each year. On Christmas Eve, or *Noche Buena* as we call it, we make a huge feast of *lechon*—enough to feed us for a month—and exchange a few small gifts. My mom gives me a button down and tie "for when you propose," she tells me. Something about her confidence sits ill with me, making me feel precarious in my hope.

Mila finally gets back on Sunday evening, and I meet her at her house, walking on unsteady legs as I remember the last time I was here, when her dad gave me the Canadian visa papers. The memory sits like a stone in my chest, heavy and unmoving. I suddenly wished I'd had Mila come to the Cottage—but there are bad memories there too, now that Tomás is gone.

When I pull up, Mila runs out as if she was waiting for me and jumps into my arms, looking tan and wind-blown and smelling of the sea. I kiss her, squeezing her against me like I'll never let go—and I'm not sure I will. Thankfully, Mr. Kozak isn't anywhere to be seen, and hope begins to blossom again within me.

Mila pulls me out onto the patio, and we curl up next to the firepit while she tells me in her hyper-animated way about her vacation. Her eyes are lit up, glowing like the sun, as she tells me about the bungalow she shared with Anya, the food, the serene beachfront, the kayak excursions. Part of me is thrilled to see her so happy—if Mila is happy, my soul soars—but there's also a small part of me that is sad she didn't seem to miss me as much as I missed her. Of course it's always harder to be the one left behind—the one at home with nothing to do. But a piece of me twinges with the knowledge.

She asks me about my week, and the first thing I think of is telling her about Tomás, but I don't want to ruin her good mood. So I tell her about decorating the tree with my mom and attempting to watch a dubbed Christmas Hallmark movie with her. "She didn't understand why someone would fall in love with a Christmas tree farmer, why this girl with a good job would quit to go run this tree farm. She was stuck on that the whole time." Mila laughs, the sound bubbling out of her and into me, and I forget about the troubles with Tommy and the Center momentarily. I could listen to her laugh forever.

Eventually, we get to the gift exchange. "Let me go first because I have two," Mila says, which makes my stomach drop because I thought we set a budget? Inwardly, I'm bracing myself for Mila's polite disappointment—a vague smile, a nebulous compliment—at my gift.

"This one's kind of silly, but it made me think of you." She hands me a bag, and I pull out a mug that has two houseplants in a therapy session. One is saying, "It all stems from how I grew up," and the other houseplant is saying, "Now we're getting to the root of it." I laugh and she tells me, "You'll have to bring it with you when you do clinicals next year."

"I will. Thanks, Mila." I kiss her cheek and hand her my gift, my heart hammering against my chest as she unwraps it. It's a custom snow globe with a tiny replica of the Center barn, with its white frame, pillars and gabled roof. A chestnut horse stands in front of the barn, with tiny flecks of glitter falling around it.

"Oh, Alex," she breathes, shaking the snow globe. "This is amazing. It's the Center! Oh my gosh. How did you do this?" The way that her eyes glimmer in the firelight tells me that she approves, and she seals it with a kiss that ends too quickly because she's handing me my next gift. I give her a wary look, and she giggles, knowing that she went over the budget we'd agreed upon.

Inside the gift bag she hands me is a piece of paper. I pull it out—a brochure for AlignerCo. "At home teeth straightening," it says. "What's this?" I ask.

She scoots closer to me, her hand going to my jaw. "Alex, you know I love your smile," she whispers. "But I want you to not just smile for me. I want you to feel confident to smile for other people too."

I take a breath, glancing down at the brochure. It shows before and after shots of people's smiles. And even though this is a very nice gift, something about it doesn't sit right with me. I don't know if it's because of the budget, or something else, but I try to smile and give Mila my thanks. She begins chattering about the process—that I don't even have to go to a doctor's office, it's all at home, I could choose the nighttime only option if I don't want to wear a retainer all the time. I try to take it all in, but it's not until much later that it really hits me why I'm bothered by the gift—it seems to only confirm my hunch that I'm not enough for Mila. I need to be straightened, brightened, smoothed out to be right for her. And it cuts me to my core, because I'm not sure I'll ever be perfect enough for Mila Kozak. Especially not now. Not after getting blamed for manipulating Clara into riding a horse. Or after hiring my drug-dealing cousin and putting us even further at risk.

I set aside the brochure and all the gift wrapping and grab Mila's hand. "I have to tell you something." Mila's eyes widen, catching the rough undertow in my voice. It's an abrupt transition—not at all what I wanted—but I need to tell Mila about Tomás before I lose my nerve. Or my mind. Or both. "I had to fire Tomás."

An awkward chuckle bubbles out of Mila before she realizes that I'm serious. "Tomás? Tommy? *Our* Tommy?"

I nod, running a hand over the back of my neck. It's hard to look Mila in the eye while I tell her what happened, but I force myself to. I tell her everything—from finding the drugs in the feed bags, to kicking him out and reporting it to Crime Stoppers. "I wasn't really thinking straight," I tell her. "I gave him the drugs and told him to get out of there. I just didn't want to touch them, didn't want to have anything to do with them. But I should've taken them to the police. Now they're out there in the world, circling around, and people are using them." I drop my head into my hands and groan. How could I screw up something like this? "I was just so mad; I just wanted him out of there. I wasn't thinking. I couldn't believe—can't even fathom how he could do that. How he could use us like that. What if it got in the feed? What if a kid stumbled on that stuff? I can't believe I let that happen."

Mila is silent as she takes my hand and holds it. We sit there for a long time, and I'm afraid to look up at her, to see what she must think of me.

"Alex?" Reluctantly, I raise my eyes, bracing for impact. But there's no loathing or even frustration in Mila's eyes, only sympathy. "I'm sorry. I know how hard this must be for you. Tommy was like a little brother to you, I can't even imagine—" She cuts off, shaking her head. "I agree that giving the drugs back to Tommy wasn't...ideal. But it's easy to look back and see clearly what we should've done. It's much harder in the moment, with so much emotion and adrenaline going." She puts a hand to my cheek. "We'll figure it out, okay? We'll talk to Anya and make a plan together. But you don't have to carry this on your own. I'm with you, alright?" And then she says something I desperately needed to hear, though I'm not sure it's even true: "It's not your fault."

I shake my head, unable, or unwilling, to accept that.

"It's true, Alex. It's not your fault Tommy was dealing drugs or brought them into the Center. You did what you could. But it's not your fault. We'll decide together what to do next, so it's not all on your shoulders. This is a heavy burden, Alex."

I press my hand against hers and turn my lips to her palm, kissing her hand. I don't know what I did to deserve such an incredible girl, but here she is, holding my hand through it all. And even though the whole situation looms above me like a hovering storm, I'm grateful to have Mila facing it with me.

35

A Week of Bad News

Mila

When we get back from our vacation, Anya is up and ready to go to work before seven o'clock. She shoves me awake. "Let's go, *sestra*."

But not long after we get to the Center, NBC6 goes live with a report on Clara's fall and the lawsuit. The reporter tells the bare details of the accident and makes the claim that our staff includes a man "arrested last year on horse poisoning allegations and currently on trial for improper entry into the United States."

Someone tagged us in the clip on Facebook. We huddle around Anya's phone in the office, watching it again and again. I put a hand on Alex's back and his shoulders are so tight, he feels primed for a fight. After watching it through the third time, Alex says, "I need a minute," and walks out of the office.

"Should I follow him?" I ask, mostly musing to myself.

"Just give him a moment," Anya says.

An hour later, Alex pulls me outside and says, "We need to talk." Immediately, my mind goes in a hundred different directions, all of them bad: *Something happened to his mom. They're deporting him. There's another article out about the lawsuit. The police are arresting him for what happened with Tommy.* But I'm not ready for what he actually says. "I'm going to resign."

"What? Alex, what in the world. Why?"

"I'm obviously causing us more harm than good, and I don't want to draw undue attention to the Center. Between the stuff with the lawsuit and now with Tommy, I think it would be better if I resigned, or if you guys fired me. I'll be the scapegoat."

"Alex, there is no way we are doing that. We're going to figure this out, okay? Just because one stupid article said some bad things doesn't mean we're jumping to worst-case scenario. We'll do what we do with everything here: you, me, and Anya will come up with a plan." I cup his face in my hands. "It will be okay."

He nods, still looking at the ground. "You want me to tell Anya?"

"We'll do it together."

We gather in the office, and Alex and I tell Anya about Tommy. I expect her to ask a million questions, but she sits in silence, staring daggers at her computer. "We need to consult the lawyer," she says finally. "I'll make an appointment." Then she puts her hands back to the keyboard, seemingly ending the conversation.

I look at Alex as if to say, *See, that wasn't so bad*, but the guilt etched in his features tells me he's still thinking of resigning. "Hey, isn't Hailey on the schedule for today? She always loves when you're out there with her," I say, dragging him out into the barn to try to distract him.

On Tuesday, we get an email from one of the rehab facilities that we have a referral relationship with stating that they can't in good conscience keep referring clients to us. I find Anya at her desk, her face pressed into her keyboard. When she sits up, I expect there to be tears in her eyes, but all I see there is fury. A permanent sense of unease settles on the Center, and by the end of the day my shoulders are aching from being so tense.

On Wednesday, Anya is contacted by our former insurance company, stating that they are denying our claim on behalf of Clara.

"How can they do that?" I ask. "Isn't that the whole point of insurance?"

Anya shakes her head, jaw tight with anger. I've watched all week as she fluctuates between livid and utterly dejected.

On Thursday, our current insurance company informs us that our policy with them will be terminated on January 1. We can't operate without insurance, which means we're only days away from the Center being shut down. The thought squeezes in on me like trash compactor walls, and I can barely fight out of the panic that's fisting in my chest.

We also get word that Alex's court date has been rescheduled for January 2nd. My dad insists this is the worst possible scenario for Alex—that judges are more likely to give harder sentences after coming back from vacation. I have no idea if this is true, or if my dad just enjoys being a doomsayer, but either way it doesn't bode well for us.

By Friday, Anya doesn't even bother to get out of bed. When I go to check on her in the morning, she's awake, staring at the wall, barely even blinking.

"Anochka?" I kneel beside her bed, smoothing her hair. "Are you okay?"

She doesn't respond, just closes her eyes. After sitting with her for half an hour without her responding to anything I say, I head to the Center. When I get there, I realize Alex isn't doing any better than Anya, except he's dealing with it quite differently. The barn is spotless—there isn't so much as a speck of hay on the ground, all of the tack has been cleaned until it looks brand new, and I find him in a patch of grass beside the tranquility garden laying pavers for a raised garden bed.

It's not even nine a.m., and his shirt is completely drenched in sweat. "Want to take a break and get some coffee with me?" I ask.

"Maybe in a little bit," he says, barely looking up at me.

I grab some coffee in the lounge and settle in the office, where I find that Alex has gone through our entire stack of mail, organized our outbox, and shredded an entire shredder's worth of paper. *Did he even sleep last night*? I wonder, sighing.

A loneliness settles in my chest because the two people I love the most in the world are falling apart and I have no idea what to do. If the Center crumbles, will they fall too? Waves of despair are crashing into me, threatening to pull me out to sea, and if it were just me, I might let myself be taken. But this is Alex and Anya, and I *have* to do something. To stay strong for them, even when my world is also falling to pieces.

When I hear Luke in the lounge making coffee, I poke my head out and say, "We need to talk."

He nods behind his coffee cup and then settles the cup precariously between his knees as he wheels to my office. "What's going on?"

"We gotta figure out something to do with Anya and Alex."

"What do you have in mind?"

"I think we have to help them remember who they are." I take a deep breath, not wanting to say the next part. I eek out, "Even without the Center."

Luke's eyes twinkle as he raises his cup to me, nodding. "I like the way you're thinking. I'm in."

36

Trail Rides and Cross Ties

Anya

After a weekend spent in bed not looking at my phone, I know I need to go into the Center on Monday. Mila drives me in the Center's van. She greeted me bright and early with a cafe con leche and a guava pastry from a local Cuban bakery, and I feel bad for basically ignoring her all weekend long. I just needed some time to be in denial and not think about the consequences of what was happening, but now I feel more or less ready to face the music. I was supposed to have a physical therapy appointment, but I'm too anxious to get back to the Center to show up for PT today.

When we pull up to the Center, Luke is already there, sitting at the cross ties with Harley. Harley's already tacked up and Luke and Alex are chatting. "Who's scheduled to ride this early?" I ask Mila.

"You'll see," she says with a smile.

When I roll out of the van, Alex moves Harley to the mounting station. In the time it took me to get out of the vehicle, Luke's gotten on Jet. I look from Luke to Mila to Alex. "Is there something I don't know about going on?"

"The horses need some exercise," Mila says. "So you're going on a trail ride."

"Okay," I say, dragging out the word.

"I thought she'd fight me more on that," Mila mutters to Alex.

Once I'm up on Harley and Alex has strapped me to the saddle, I glance back at Mila. "You coming?"

"We'll catch up with you guys later," she says with a mischievous smile. "Alex and I have something we need to do."

Of course Mila has forced me onto a trail ride with Luke by ourselves. I'm tense when we start out, just wanting to get back to the Center and get to work. I need to find a new insurance company and reach out to other rehab centers in the area to get referrals from. Luke seems to understand that I'm not ready to talk, so we walk in silence until we reach the trails.

When we bought this land for the Center, we purposely chose this space because of its opportunity for horse trails. The first few months, Alex and Mila spent hours and hours on end creating these paths for us to ride on. And it's our personal gem hidden on the property. The paths wind through wooded areas, and a calming quiet envelopes us as we enter the trail.

I breathe a sigh of relief, and Harley does the same, snorting toward the ground. I laugh, stroking his neck. Riding gives me a sensation that I no longer get. Simply walking on a horse feels unparalleled because I don't get the experience of plodding over ground like I used to. It's crazy what you take for granted when your legs work. What I would give to take one step, to feel the earth beneath my feet again and to stand on it. Riding gives me back some of that control, and I feel sad that I've neglected to ride these past few weeks.

"Have you gone any faster than a walk?" Luke asks, gesturing toward the horse.

"I can comfortably get to a slow, Western trot," I say. "Not that I wouldn't mind some speed."

Luke grins. "The lady does like to go fast."

I arch a brow at him. "Not in every way."

He chuckles. "Of course not."

"Are you nervous to go faster?" he asks.

"You know, that's the funny thing. I find that I don't have any fear when it comes to being on horseback."

"You trust them still?"

"I do."

"Wish I felt that way about my four-wheeler," he says with a laugh.

"Hard to trust unfeeling machines."

"True enough." He scratches his beard and gives me a side look. "You ever think of competing?"

"Like show jumping?"

"I was thinking more like barrel racing."

"I've never considered it."

"I've seen a handful of paraplegics barrel race. You seen that movie *Walk, Ride, Rodeo*?"

"No."

"It's on Netflix. You should check it out sometime."

"I'll put it on the list."

"You'd look fetching in a cowboy hat," Luke says with a lazy grin.

"You'd like that, wouldn't you? Seeing me barrel race in a ridiculous hat."

"If it made you happy, I would."

For some reason, his words strike sadness in me, and before I can stop myself, I blurt out, "Why do you even like me, Luke?"

"Who says I like you?" For a moment, I think I've gotten it all sideways, read into it all the wrong ways. I whip my head around to look at him, and he's grinning at me. "Fine, okay, I like you. Lord knows it'd be easier if I didn't, but I do." He lifts his cowboy hat, adjusting it on his head, and it's then that I realize he's not wearing a helmet. I shake my head. Cowboys.

It seems like Luke's not really going to answer my question, so we walk quietly, the horses' hooves pattering against the ground. We work our way through the trees, over exposed roots and ducking under branches. We finally round a bend and come into a clearing when I see it: Wolf Lake. The sun shimmers off the surface of the lake, the wind blowing the trees that edge all around the water, and in the distance, I see a horse and rider swimming near the shoreline.

I can't help but smile at the sight, and when I look over at Luke, he's smiling too. Except he's smiling at me. I adjust my gaze to my horse, feeling uncomfortable at the intensity of Luke's gaze. *Why does he even like me?* I've been nothing but rude and nit-picky with him.

And then, as if he'd heard my thought, he says, "I saw you on Instagram before. Well, Katie Jo sent me your story. I'm not really the Instagram type." He gives me a smirk that seems to say, *Cowboys don't do Instagram,* and I laugh. "I dunno. When I heard your story, it spoke to me in a way few others have. You ever have that, an intuition about something?"

"I tend to avoid my intuitions," I say honestly. "Unless they're backed by facts."

Luke laughs his deep belly laugh. "You don't say."

"So you saw my story on Instagram, then came to work for us, then met me and were immediately repulsed because I've been a huge jerk to you?"

"Well, you're not soft spoken, I'll give you that. But what I saw—what I see—in you is a tenacity. You're relentless, Anya."

"And that's attractive to you?" I say in a tone that conveys my disbelief.

"It is. Because so many people give up, let life shove them around. But instead, *you're* shoving life around."

"Hmm."

"Does that scare you?"

"Yes."

"Me too."

I glance over at him, surprised by his response. His normally dancing blue eyes are steady and somber as he gazes back at me. "Thank you," I say.

"For what?"

"For being honest."

"You're not the only one who's scared. Or the only one with reason to be scared."

I nod, digesting what he's saying. He's right—obviously Luke has good reason to be petrified of another person letting him down. It's brave that he's willing to put himself out there. I wish I could do the same.

We've rounded the west side of the lake and reached the shore where you can swim the horses. "Care for a swim?" Luke asks, waggling his eyebrows.

"We'll ruin the tack."

"Maybe not, if we get it clean and dry quick enough." He shrugs. "If we ruin it, I'll buy us new tack."

"How rich *are* you?"

He chuckles. "Maybe if you go out with me, I'll tell you."

"Wealth isn't really a deciding factor for me."

"I know, which is why I'd tell you."

"Why not just tell me now?"

"I don't want it to be *the* deciding factor."

"You're obviously selling a lot of wheelchairs if you're worried that's going to influence me in the right direction."

"Either that, or it's the opposite and I don't want you to know how much of a failure I am until it's too late for you to turn back."

"You think one date is going to be enough to do that?"

"I'm a really good date."

"And so humble, too."

"So are we swimming or what?" He smiles at me, a smile I'm sure has let him get away with murder in the past, but I can't help but smile back.

"Let's go swimming."

I'm so glad I let Luke convince me to go swimming. Feeling the horse swim beneath me is magical. He surges through the water like we're flying, and it's the closest I've gotten to jumping since my accident. It's life-giving. And Luke is in his element too, wahooing like he's surfing, and then splashing me like we're in middle school. It feels good to laugh, to forget everything with the Center and just be with Luke.

We circle the horses along the bank of the lake so that they walk through the water, swim for a few strides, and then walk back onto the bank. The water is cool and refreshing, and we laugh when fish tickle the horses' hocks and they snort at the water.

At one point, Luke unstraps himself from his saddle and lets his legs fall behind him as he holds onto Jet's neck while he swims. Then he flips onto his back, floating while holding onto Jet's pommel. It makes me nervous—what if he loses his grip or Jet freaks out and then how would Luke swim with his legs as deadweight? But seeing his face tilted up toward the sun, his smile open and unhindered—it calms me. Makes me want to do the same, except I don't have the strength or mobility Luke has. So I just watch.

Eventually, Luke gets back in the saddle and says, "You wanna try?"

I should say no, I should be responsible and safe, but instead I say, "Yes." Luke steers his swimming horse toward mine until they're standing side by side in the water, his legs brushing against mine. He leans over, holding the pommel of my saddle in one hand and the back of my saddle with the other. He's so close, he could kiss me. I turn my face away, cognizant of every place our bodies are touching. "Can you help me?" he asks, and I nod because I can't find any words right now. He explains his plan, and we work together to get him in the saddle—with me guiding his leg over Harley's rump while he pulls himself over. Then he's behind me, and the only thing separating us is the back of the saddle. His chest warms my back as he unstraps me, his hands at my waist releasing me from the saddle, and a shudder goes through me.

"You ready?" His voice a breeze in my ear, his breath at my neck. I nod again, still unable to speak—whether from fear or excitement, I'm not sure. "Okay, I'm going to put you fully in the water and then I'm going to pull myself forward, get strapped into your saddle, and then you can let go." He does exactly as he says he's going to—he lifts me up and then brings me to the side so I'm completely off of the horse, floating in the water. "Hold on to me as tight as you can," he says. I put my hands around his waist, gripping him. He keeps one hand on my shoulder, holding me tightly, and then uses his other hand to pull himself into the saddle. It takes both of us to get his straps on—I hold the clip steady while he pushes it in and tightens it. Meanwhile, Harley and Jet are still standing still side by side, seemingly unfazed by all of this. It makes me grateful for these horses. They're unflappable.

Finally, Luke is strapped in. He puts one hand at my waist and one hand at my shoulder and says, "Lean back." I ease my head into the water, soaking my hair. At first, I'm stiff, still trying to hold myself up, when Luke says, "Relax," his voice soft as the breeze flowing through the trees around us. I take a breath, letting the oxygen seep into my limbs, and unwind. I blink up at the blue sky, and then close my eyes, the warmth and sunshine still pulsating behind my eyelids. I let my arms go out by my side, my fingers no longer grasping at anything. I'm simply existing, letting myself *be* in this moment. My hand grazes Harley's neck, his coat smooth beneath my fingertips.

I am weightless.

I am free.

I am.

I find Luke's hand at my waist and press my palm against the outside of his hand. His pinkie comes up and curls around mine, and my eyes flutter open to find his staring back at me. We don't say anything. I float beside Luke and my horse. All the while his eyes are on me, seeing more than I want him to, and simultaneously not enough.

It's pure wonder, and sheer terror, at the same time. Because while I'm letting myself unfurl in the water, I'm also keenly aware that I'm letting Luke past the defenses I said I'd never drop.

37

Panda Express, RadioShack, and Big Lots!

Alex

I spend the day running seemingly pointless errands with Mila. With the week we've had, I want to build a wall around us and never come out. Maybe it'll all go away, or maybe we'll just disappear. I could disappear with Mila in a heartbeat—wherever we end up in the ether, I'd be happy with her. Despite everything that's happened, Mila is determined to be optimistic about it, which is pretty much the opposite of how Anya and I are being. This makes me feel bad for Mila, because not only is she shouldering the burden of what's happening with the Center—she's also shouldering the burden of a miserable boyfriend and sister. So I decide to be buoyant today, to let myself enjoy being with Mila and soak up this moment, because who knows how many of these we have left.

First we go to Big Lots! and find some horse-related decor to "spruce up" the lounge (which is brand new and needs zero sprucing up). Mila picks out a framed picture of a horse, a throw blanket, and a horse LEGO set. "If any kids come in, they can play with the LEGOs," she tells me, and for a moment I envision her buying things for *our* kids. I imagine Mila being a really fun, albeit a little chaotic, mom—the kind that gets into projects with her kids and makes a huge mess but smiles all the way through it because she's having fun.

She glances up at me as she's bent down looking at some throw pillows. "What's that smile for?"

I shrug, feeling like I got caught thinking about something I shouldn't be. But now that I've seen Mila as a mom, I can't unsee it—I visualize her with a huge pregnant belly, knocking over things and nesting like a joyful maniac. And it hurts how much I want that, for her, for us, one day. Not anytime soon, of course. But some day, I want that Mila to be my Mila.

She stands up, hooking a finger through my belt loop and tugging me toward her. "What's going on in that pretty little head of yours?" she teases.

"Just thinking about you," I say, leaning down to kiss her nose.

"What about me?"

"How beautiful you are." I look over her shoulder at the pillows she's tossed around the aisle while looking for something very specific. "And how much of a mess you are," I laugh.

"Yes, but I'm *your* mess," she says.

"Truer words have never been spoken." I run my hand over her hair, smoothing her waves over her back. "My beautiful mess."

After Big Lots! we go to RadioShack and purchase a Bluetooth speaker to play music or white noise in the lounge as a way to offer clients more privacy when meeting with Luke. We get gas even though she's at half a tank and drop off her dad's dry cleaning for a reason that is beyond me because I know he has an assistant who does this for him. Finally, we end up at Panda Express for lunch.

"I didn't know you liked Panda," I say as we stand in line for orange chicken and rice.

"It's a mood thing."

When we sit down, instead of eating her lunch, Mila takes out a stack of papers like she's about to make a presentation. "So, I want to tell you about our errands today."

"Alright?"

"Every place we went today was owned or founded by an immigrant."

"Okay." I nod, taking a bite of my chicken.

"Big Lots! was founded by a Russian immigrant Sol Shenk." She passes me a bio on Mr. Shenk. "Big Lots! now has over fourteen hundred stores and employs over thirty thousand people. Oh, and he was married to his wife for fifty-six years."

"Cool," I say, still not knowing where she's going with all of this, or why it's making me uneasy. She hands me another printout about the history of RadioShack, complete with black and white photos of old buildings and guys I don't recognize.

"RadioShack was founded by the Deutschmann brothers." She points to one of the pictures. "Also immigrants."

She lays out another stack of bios. "The Perng family founded this fine establishment we're currently dining in."

"Let me guess: immigrants?"

"You're a quick study, Mr. Caballero."

"Maybe because I'm an immigrant," I say with an eye roll.

"When Perng and his brother opened the first Panda Inn, they couldn't get people to come eat there. They were practically giving food away to anyone who passed by. But then Andrew Perng's wife, Peggy, joined in and changed everything for them."

"So can Peggy come help us out?"

Mila laughs, shaking her head. "Let me finish. Did you know that immigrants make up approximately thirteen percent of the population, but they own over twenty percent of businesses? And over two hundred of the fortune five hundred companies are founded by immigrants or their children. Fifty-five percent of billion-dollar businesses in the U.S. are founded by immigrants or their children."

I sigh, drumming my fingers on the table. "That's interesting and all, but Mila, my situation is way different from theirs. I'm here illegally—they all came here legally. I might get kicked out of the country in a few days, especially if the Center goes under with everything happening." It's the first time either of us has spoken this truth out loud, and it leaves me feeling exposed.

"Look, Alex, I know there's a lot going on right now with the Center and with your court date coming up, but I just want to take a step back and think about what's possible. These people overcame challenges—sure, they're not the same as ours, but challenges nonetheless—and we're going to overcome, too. And what all these people had in their corner is someone going through it with them. Sol Shenk had his wife of fifty-six years. The Deutschmann brothers had each other. Perng had his wife." Mila reaches a hand across the table, taking mine. "Will you just let me go through this with you? Whatever happens, Alex, I'm in your corner. We'll figure it out and get through it."

I nod and squeeze her hand. I want so much to feel the same level of optimism that Mila feels right now, but I just don't. I do, however, have the hope that at the very least

Mila wants to be with me. That she went to these lengths today to make me aware of how much she's on my side. And that means the world to me. "Thanks, Mila," I say quietly. "I needed this."

"I know."

After we finish our lunch and head back to the Center, I feel lighter. And when I think about the application for residency to Canada sitting in my desk drawer, I'm able to push the thought aside as I take Mila's hand in mine.

That night, as my mom and I are making dinner, I say, "Mama, when the time comes, can I give Mila abuela's ring?"

My mom, who's chopping onions, pauses. Her knife hovering over the chopping board, she turns to me, tears ringing her eyes. And I know they're not from the onions. A slow smile takes over her face and she says, "*Un momento.*" She wipes her hands on a dish towel and disappears into her bedroom. She comes back a moment later, holding a faded red ring box.

Tears are streaming down her cheeks as she holds the box out to me. I take it carefully, waiting to open it until she nods at me, encouraging me. I prop it open, the hinges squeaking. The ring is even more spectacular than I remembered it—not that an engagement ring would ever be all that compelling to a little boy, beyond the fact that it's shiny. The center stone is teardrop shaped and it isn't perfectly clear, with a golden tinge to it that I'd never noticed before. It has smaller diamonds circling the center stone. Etched in the band are tiny swirls and curlicues. It is clearly old and needs to be cleaned—there is a layer of dust and gunk covering it, but nothing that can't be fixed.

My mom watches me admiring the ring, and her smile sparkles through her tears. "Mila will wear this beautifully."

"She will. When the time is right."

I close the box, clutching it in my hands like I might never let go of it.

But then, a thought occurs to me and I ask, "Why didn't we ever sell this to pay for medical expenses? This would've paid for a year of your medicine, Mama."

My mom shakes her head. "Some things are too precious to sell," she tells me in Spanish. She lifts her hand to my cheek and says, "This was always meant for you, *mi hijo.*"

The next day, I call around to local jewelry shops and find one that will do a complimentary cleaning of my mom's ring. When they present it to me later, I'm amazed by how brand new it looks. I can't wait to give it to Mila, but I know I need to get through my court case first, and then I can make plans. For Mila, it has to be the best proposal known to man. Nothing short of breathtaking would be enough.

38

Jeni's Ice Cream For Lyfe

Mila

Later that night, as Anya and I are curled up in her bed watching the reunion episode of *Love is Blind*, I ask her about her trail ride.

"It was good," she says, her eyes glinting in a way that tells me it was a lot more than good.

"Just good?" I ask, eyebrow raised.

She smiles for a moment and then seems to catch herself and sighs. "It was exactly what I needed, and not at all, at the same time."

"Anya..." I pause the show right as Nick and Vanessa are dressing down Shake for the way he treated Deepti throughout the season. "Is this because you're afraid of falling in love with Luke?"

"No," she says, a little too quickly.

"You haven't dated anyone since freshman year."

"I've been strapped," Anya says, voice drenched in sarcasm as she waves a hand at her wheelchair.

"But even before that."

Anya won't meet my eye, and it makes me wonder. "You never got over that one guy, did you?" She scoffs and rolls her eyes, but I can tell I hit a nerve. And right now, everything with Anya is a little nerve-y. "What was his name? Dave?"

"Dan," she squeaks out.

"What did he do to you, *sestra*?" I whisper.

Anya shakes her head, squeezing her eyes closed. A single tear escapes and trickles down her porcelain cheek. I kneel in front of her, taking her hands in mine. "Oh, Anya."

"I gave him everything," she whispers through the tears. "I changed so much for him. At first, it was so wonderful. He was like this Prince Charming sent from heaven—he took me on these extravagant dates, made me feel like I was worthy of so much. And then it was like he ripped the rug out from under me. I mean, it didn't start that way. It was small things, like he'd critique my hair or my clothes. He'd want me to change into a different outfit if he didn't like what I was wearing. And slowly, I became someone else. Someone I didn't recognize. I just wanted his approval so badly, I would do whatever he wanted. And then he'd just leave, completely disappearing like he'd fallen off the face of the earth. Like I wasn't even worthy of an explanation as to what was wrong with me."

I let her talk, spilling out her story with tears and sighs. There's a numbness to her voice as she tells me, almost robotic, like she has to get it out but doesn't want to feel it as it exits her.

When she's done, I hold her for a long time, though she doesn't really hug me back. "I'm so sorry, *sestra*," I tell her as I kiss her hands, then press my cheek against them. "But just because one guy treated you badly doesn't mean they're all bad."

"It's not just one guy," she mumbles.

"Who else?"

She is silent. Unmoving. She won't even look at me, even though I'm kneeling down in front of her at almost eye level.

"Who else, Anochka?"

"You. Dad," she spits out. "Everyone. All of my friends before the accident." Anya takes a shuddering breath, and I ready myself for whatever's coming next. "You left me when I needed you most. I know you're sorry, and you know I forgive you. Things are different now, but that kind of hurt will never go away. I will never forget the feeling of that level of abandonment from the people who should have been there for me. I know my accident was hard for you too, but imagine it, Mila. Imagine what it was like for me to be stuck, to be alone, to be abandoned."

The pain that rips through me makes it hard to breathe. I feel like I'm being buried under an avalanche of guilt and shame. The way I treated my sister after the accident was unacceptable, and I'll regret it until the day I die. But Anya is so untouchable in some ways that I don't always connect with how much I've hurt her. And it hits me then: Anya thinks she's unworthy of love. That's why she's acting this way with Luke. She doesn't want to put herself out there because she's been burned by me, by Dan, by our dad even. Her stupid, shallow friends from before her accident. *Me.* I made Anya feel unloved—worse, unlovable.

I put my head in her lap. "I'm so sorry, *sestra.*" And we cry, because that's all we can do.

When we've both run out of tears, I order us pints of Jeni's Blackout Chocolate Cake and Gooey Butter Cake ice cream via Instacart. "Be right back," I say. "To get the cure for all heartache." I head toward the door to grab the ice cream.

"You bought me a horse?" she jokes.

"Just ice cream this time."

She smiles at me, but it doesn't quite reach her eyes. I run downstairs and grab the ice cream, not even bothering to put it in bowls. Back in Anya's room, we take turns eating straight out of the pints, swapping flavors every few bites.

"I need to say something to you. I don't know if it'll help, but I need to say it," I tell her.

"Okay."

"Just because Dan, or me, or Dad, treated you like you were...disposable"—the word pains me to say it—"doesn't mean that you are. The way that I acted, and Dad acted, after your accident was a reflection on us, not you. We didn't know how to deal—not with you, but with our own selves, our own emotions. So we just ran away." I take a deep breath. "Let me not put this on Dad. I don't know his whole thing, but I can speak for myself. *I* ran away because of *me*, not because of you." I take Anya's hand in mine. "You are the best sister, the best friend, anyone could ask for. Wheelchair or not, heartbroken or not. You are not too broken for love, Anya. It's true that broken people make you feel broken, but you're not too broken for love. Not yet, anyway."

She rolls her eyes through the tears—somehow we both still had more to cry, apparently. Tears must be more of a print-on-demand situation than a warehouse storage type of deal. "I'm so, so sorry that I ever made you feel that way. It's my biggest regret of my life and I'll spend the rest of my days making it up to you."

"Does this mean you'll buy me a horse?"

I laugh and shake my head. "Could we settle for Jeni's ice cream?"

She pretends to think about this for a moment. "It depends. Is it weekly Jeni's ice cream, or daily?"

"Bi-weekly?" I suggest. "Just for the sake of diabetes prevention."

"Ah, yes. We should definitely keep it to bi-weekly. But I want two pints to choose from each week."

"Yes, ma'am."

"Oh gosh, don't call me that," she groans. "Makes me think of Luke."

"Luke!" I squeal. Then I stand up and dance around Anya's wheelchair, chanting, "You want to kiss him, you want to hug him, you want to loooove him."

Anya's laughing and shaking her head and rolling her eyes as I continue to make a spectacle of myself. But I know that deep down, she really wants Luke. And I hope and pray that this conversation will help those walls to fall, just a little.

39

Bewitched

Anya

The next morning, I wake up to find Mila still in my bed, a half-eaten carton of melted ice cream next to her. I smile as I reach over and move the carton to the side table and kiss the top of my sister's head. As painful as it was after my accident for Mila to distance herself from me, I realize that I did let her back in. I've opened myself up fully to her—and it makes me recognize that I can do it again. I can let my walls down for Luke. It's scarier than anything I can conjure in my mind, but it's also thrilling. I think about the adventures I've had with him so far—the night of the tropical storm, swimming the horses in the lake—and I want to keep having those moments with him. I don't want it to stop just because I'm afraid. And I am afraid. Very, very afraid.

I shake Mila awake and have her help me to the bathroom, where I take my sweet time getting ready. I go through what I'll say to Luke in my head over and over. I want to find the exact right words to position myself in the exact right way for him. Usually, I wear my hair straight, but today I curl my hair, my arms aching by the time I've reached the left half of my hair. I finish my makeup, contouring my face to amplify my already-high cheekbones, and end with my favorite lip color: Almost Ready by Kylie. The name is fitting for today, I think.

By the time Mila and I get to the Center, my hands are shaking. I want to see Luke, to talk to him, to finally kiss him—but I'm also terrified too. What if he regrets pursuing me the moment I let him in? Or what if he hates kissing me? It's been so long since I've kissed anyone—what if I'm a terrible kisser? The thought has me checking my teeth in the mirror and digging in my wheelchair pocket for Altoids.

When I roll into the lounge, the second I see Luke, my insides start to quake. I freeze, unable to say anything or move anywhere.

Luke turns from the coffee machine, his lips reaching for his mug, when he stops, too. His eyes find mine, and they widen in appreciation. "Wow," he says. And this is the time where I'm supposed to say something, *anything*. But I'm stuck. My mouth doesn't work, my lungs are frozen, and I'm sure I look like a deer in headlights right now. "You look—"

"I'll be right back," I say quickly, backing out of the lounge and speeding down the barn breezeway as fast as my wheelchair will go. I make it all the way to the tranquility gardens, which are supposed to make me feel *tranquil*, for Pete's sake, but are failing epically. I put my head in my hands, hyperventilating. Why am I overcomplicating this? I don't need to make a big speech. I just need to say, *Luke, I like you*. That's it, that's enough. Why can't I even do that small thing? I groan into my hands.

"Anya?"

It's Luke. Of course it's Luke. I turn slowly toward him.

For the first time since I met Luke, he looks uncertain. And it makes him seem younger, more boyish and vulnerable. "Was there—are you, um, are you okay?"

I nod, a little too emphatically. I am most definitely not okay. The line from Pride and Prejudice flashes through my mind: *You've bewitched me, body and soul.*

I am bewitched.

Oh my goodness. I've lost it. I grip my wheelchair arms as Luke rolls closer to me, my heart thudding helplessly with each inch he advances. He wheels all the way up until my knees are in between his. "Was there something you wanted to say to me?" His voice is extra twangy today, and it should be something I scoff at, but instead it makes my heart tug in my chest.

"Not really."

"No?"

"'Cause Mila said—"

"I like you." I have an absurd desire to squeeze my eyes shut so I don't have to see his reaction, but I force myself to act like an adult, even if I don't feel like one.

Luke's smile starts out slow, spreading across his entire face until it's completely taken over. He leans forward, his hands on my knees, and whispers, "I know." Then he reaches over and flips the switch that locks my wheelchair in place. "May I?"

I nod, ever so slightly, and Luke reaches across the slim barrier between our wheelchairs and unstraps me. Lightning zings through me as the buckles fall to the wayside. He takes my waist in his hands and pulls me gently, slowly, into his lap. I can barely breathe, and yet somehow my arms make their way around him, my fingers tracing the long column of his neck, and then the outline of his jaw. He closes his eyes as I graze my thumb across his cheek, then run my fingers through his hair, thankful he didn't wear a cowboy hat today.

"I like you," I repeat. "A lot. Too much, probably."

"I don't think there is such a thing as liking me too much," he says, his voice raspy as he looks up at me, cupping my face in his hand. "Especially seeing as how I like you way too much too."

The feel of his breath against my lips amps up my fear and anxiety. "I don't know if this can work out," I say. "I'm too broken."

"I'm not inclined to look at all the ways something can't work," Luke says as his thumb brushes gently across my lips. "If I want something, I find the ways it can work. And maybe if you did the same thing, we'd be having a different conversation." He dips my head closer to his, pressing his lips against my jawline. "Or maybe," he whispers against my skin, "no conversation at all."

"I choose no conversation," I say, closing the gap between us as I tangle my fingers in his hair and surrender my lips to his.

Kissing Luke, it's everything. It's life. It's breath. It's freedom.

I yield myself to this moment, to Luke, to *hope*. And it's better than walking, better than show jumping, better than anything I can think of. Because I'm letting myself be loved, and that makes me free.

When I finally manage to tear myself away from Luke, he doesn't put me right back in my wheelchair. Which is a relief. He holds me against him, and we sit like that for what feels like an eternity. Eventually he pulls me away from him just slightly so he can see my face. "Look," he says, "I know we're both busted as a tin house after a tornado"—I laugh at his analogy that's as Southern as he is—"but if we both agree to be broken together, then maybe we can help each other be whole again. Together."

I whirl my fingers through the back of his hair. "I'd like that."

I make a motion like I'm heading back toward my wheelchair, but he tugs me back against his chest. "Not so fast, Miss Kozak." He smiles his wicked grin. "I've waited a long time to kiss you, and I'm not done just yet."

"Good," I say. "Me either." I lean down and kiss him again, my hand fisting into his shirt to pull him as close as possible.

Luke chuckles against my mouth, and I pull back. "What?" I ask.

"You're tenacious," he says, with a glint in his eye. "I like that." He thinks for a second. "Can I stop calling you Miss Kozak now?"

I put a hand over my chest in a mock gasp. "Never!" He laughs, pulling me into him as he nuzzles into my neck, his scruff bristling against my skin.

"Okay, so what, then?"

"You can call me Anya, of course. And sometimes. *Sometimes*. If it's just you and me, I'll let you call me—" I lean in and whisper in a mocking Southern accent, "—*darlin'*."

Luke smiles, a full, genuine smile that makes me feel like I've got feeling in my toes again. "I think you like that more than you let on."

"I'll never say."

"Fine." He gives me a quick kiss, and then leans back, deciding I need another, and kisses me again. "What will you call me then?"

"Mr. Craig, obviously."

He chuckles, shaking his head. "Obviously."

"And Luke."

"On special occasions?"

"Only when I'm deliriously happy." I lean my forehead against his. "Luke."

He makes a low sound in his throat that makes me smile. "A guy could get used to that."

"Oh yeah?" I kiss the tip of his nose. "Luke." Then another kiss on his cheek. "Luke." And another on the other side. "Luke."

And in that moment, I think I'll never stop kissing him, never stop saying his name, because I'll never stop being deliriously happy.

40

Down the Drain

Anya

We're summoned to ViaTech the day after Luke and I kissed. I'm trying to hold on to all the good mojo from that moment, but the second we roll into the boardroom, I know we're facing bad news. My dad has his poker face on, Mattia De Luca looks ready to fight a bull, and Hajime Osuke looks genuinely sorrowful. I steel myself for what's to come.

Thankfully, my dad doesn't waste time, which is fine by me. "After a week of deliberation, we've decided to settle out of court with the Cardones family."

Alex and I take this in silently, but Mila immediately jumps to fight their decision. "We didn't do anything wrong. Settling will just make us look guilty."

My dad shakes his head. "It's not that simple, Mila." He folds his hands in front of him, his long, manicured fingers such a stark contrast from the dirt underneath the three of ours. "Here's the thing. Maybe *you* can take the bad press, but we can't. This was meant to boost our reputation, not hurt it. We need to settle so that we can have them sign a non-disclosure so they'll stop discussing us in the media." He takes a deep breath, looking at each of us in turn. "We also will suspend, perhaps permanently, our funding until you have insurance reinstated. We'll cover the expenses for the horses' care, but that's it. You have eight weeks to find insurance or alternative funding. After that, we will be forced to sell."

I'm breathless, as if all of the air has left the room. Even my heart is struggling to beat, and I can't be sure if it's succeeding. It takes everything in me to not clutch at my chest in panic. Instead, I grip the sides of my wheelchair, staring ahead at my very own father, delivering the Center's deathblow.

Mila asks a million more questions while Alex and I sit in stony silence. How can they do this to us? Without even consulting us? I glance over at De Luca, who is on his phone, probably answering emails instead of being present in this meeting. And that's when I realize: they think we're children with a cute little pet project. And when an adult problem took us all for a ride, they took the reins back. I feel ashamed, heat flaming across my skin.

At one point in the conversation, Mila says again, "But we did nothing wrong."

"They're claiming the helmet you offered is not ATSM approved."

"What?" I can't help but shriek. I purchased the helmets; I know they are top of the line.

"Their lawyer sent us pictures," De Luca says, tossing a photo across the table. It skids into my hand and I scoop it up.

"This is not one of our helmets," I say definitively.

"Well, it's the helmet she was wearing when she fell. Unless you have evidence otherwise, it's our word against this photo," De Luca says, anger biting at each word. "It's enough for us to pull the plug."

Mila opens her mouth to say something and I wave a hand at her, cutting her off. "We're done here, Mila. Let's go." And I wheel out, without a backward glance at my father. Because *he* may be pulling the plug, but the Center is going down the drain because of me.

41

NYE

Mila

After the meeting with the ViaTech partners, I feel murderous. I want to break something—preferably the windows in my dad's precious Tesla—but I settle for grinding my teeth and ordering a dozen guava and cheese pastries from my favorite Cuban bakery. Alex, Anya, and I sit in the lounge of the Center, silently devouring our pastries. Luke rolls in around noon, immediately sensing the mood. He stops his wheelchair, clearly debating if he should wheel out of here or stay and *therapize* us, as Anya calls it.

"Anyone wanna tell me what's happening?" Luke says, evidently choosing to put on his therapist hat.

"No," Anya says.

"Alright," he says, wheeling forward. "Can I at least get a pastry?"

"It's not vegan," I say.

"I was going to loosen my standards for an hour so I could mourn with y'all."

Anya stares at him, wide-eyed. "You're not going to be principled? For us?" The way she's saying it, it's as if Luke is offering to pay for a spa day for us—not eat a delicious pastry.

I hold out the box of pastries and Luke takes one with a smile. "Sometimes," he says, "the most principled people know when to relax their boundaries."

"Uh huh," I say, unconvinced. "You just want a pastry."

We all watch as Luke takes a bite of the pastry and lets out a little groan. "I might need to be a little less principled sometimes," he says.

"Not at the expense of your six-pack," Anya says, and my jaw drops. She looks over at me and shrugs. "What? His being principled has *some* benefits."

I shake my head, unable to contain my shock at Anya's forthright comment. *About Luke.* I guess people can really change. I just wish my dad would too. At least his mind, anyway.

Once the box of pastries is empty and we've licked all the crumbs (okay, it was just me who licked the crumbs), Alex fills in Luke on our meeting. I glance at Anya every once in a while, but she's looking straight ahead, her face masked in calm. I realize she has a lot of practice in pretending difficult things don't bother her. But I know there's a storm rolling inside of her. Once Alex is done, Luke nods grimly and says, "I'm sorry, y'all." He sighs. "I'll think of how I can help."

"I won't go so far as to say we need cheering up, because I don't think that's possible, but we could use some distraction," Alex says.

"Yeah, distract Anya with your six-pack, Luke," I tease, hoping to lighten the mood.

"I'd be more than happy to," Luke says with a half-smile and Anya rolls her eyes. "Tonight's New Year's Eve. I'm not thinking we're up for anything big, but we could do something small with the four of us."

"We could hang here," Alex says. "Maybe get some fireworks. I bet Luke could grill for us."

"I feel like I'm being stereotyped," Luke says. "Just 'cause I look like this, you think I can grill?"

We all take a good, long look at Luke and I say, "Uh, yeah."

"So just 'cause you're Russian, does that mean you can hold your liquor better than the next person?"

"Oh no," Alex says, shaking his head. "Don't call them Russian, man."

Anya's taking a big breath, certainly readying herself for an hour-long tirade about the differences between Ukrainians and Russians, so I put a hand on her shoulder to stop her and say, "Luke, you need to get this right because if you make this mistake again, I'll tell you right now my sister won't stand for it: we're Ukrainians. Very different than Russians."

"Very, very, very," Alex says with a smirk, and I smack his chest.

"And, to your question," Anya jumps in, unable to help herself, "yes, we can hold our liquor better than most. Eastern Europeans have evolved to be able to handle alcohol and fatty foods better than the average person. It's biology."

I press my lips together, holding back a laugh, because Anya knows that I'm a lightweight when it comes to alcohol. But Luke doesn't know this yet, so he holds up his hands in surrender and apologizes to Anya and me. "I'll grill whatever the Ukrainian princesses want," he says with a wink at Anya, who scoffs.

"Alex and I will get the fireworks," I say. "But I don't think we should do this at the barn. With our luck lately, we'll burn this place to the ground."

Anya laughs mirthlessly and we agree to gather at our house later tonight. As we're heading toward the parking lot, Ben pulls in. He gets out holding a platter of Publix cookies. "Thought I'd drop these off, a little New Years' gift. I know it's been rough," he says, handing me the cookies. I'm still full from the guava pastries, but I manage to find space in my stomach for one sugar cookie. Worth it.

"Thanks, Ben," Alex says, shaking the man's hand. "Hey, how's your back?"

"Huh?"

"You know, with the TENS unit," Alex says, gesturing in a looping way around his back.

"Oh, yeah, my back." He puts his hands on his lower back, stretching backward. "It's good, much better. That TENS unit is the real deal. You should check it out one time. Anyway, just wanted to say it's been nice working with you all. I'll be traveling in the coming months, so I won't see you around, but keep up the good work." He waves at us and hops back in his car.

"He's an odd bird," Anya says.

"Aren't we all," I respond as I shove another cookie in my mouth and hand one to Anya, the sugar dulling the sensation that everything is falling apart.

"Some more than others," Alex says, looking between Anya and me as we stuff our faces.

As Alex and I drive to get fireworks, I broach a subject that has taken me far too long to get to, with everything else going on. "Alex, we should call the police." I swallow, steadying my voice. "About Tommy."

Alex is silent, almost as if he's holding his breath.

"Alex?"

"Yeah, sorry. Um, yeah, you're probably right."

"Now that we've settled with the whole Clara thing, it's time. Way past time, but still. Anya talked to the lawyer about it."

Alex nods. "You're right, you're absolutely right. I should've done that before."

"It's okay. I know you were trying to protect us, protect the Center." *But there's nothing to protect anymore*, I almost say. "I know he's your cousin, so I understand if you don't want to be the one to make the call. I can do it."

Alex sighs, rubbing his palms on his pant legs. "No, I'll do it. It's my responsibility."

I reach out and grab his hand, threading my fingers through his. "Not tonight, though. Tonight, we forget about all the terrible things, and just be happy. Or, at least, not be miserable. Deal?"

He ducks his head in a nod, but I know it's not likely that Alex will ever forgive himself for everything that's happened. Even though it's not his fault, he will always feel responsible for Tommy, and for the terrible things the media has said about him with this case. I try to think of what to say to reassure him, but I come up short, and eventually we arrive at the fireworks tent, which I suppose is distraction enough. I decide money will be no object here—whatever firework Alex even glances at, it'll be his. That's what I can do to cheer him up, for now.

Alex, I'm devastated. I'm trying so hard to be hopeful, to be optimistic for you and for Anya, but it's wearing on me. I don't have an ounce of optimism left in the reserves. I'm completely depleted. The meeting with the partners today was just awful. I don't understand how they could just pull the plug on us like that—without even giving us a heads up. I'm so angry with my dad, so angry with Clara and her family. I feel so helpless to fix this. It just feels like everything we worked for is being stripped away, one piece at a time, until all that's left is us. And I just pray that we're still standing at the end of all this.

42

I'm the Problem, It's Me.

Anya

Later that night at our house, Luke showed himself to be adept with the grill. He made us steaks and brats very well, despite his reinstated vegan-ness. He also grilled some zucchini and yellow squash in a balsamic glaze that were quite good. In retrospect, it seemed cruel to make a vegan grill meat for us, but Luke didn't object, and we enjoyed the meats of his labor.

After we eat, Alex and Mila set off the fireworks they'd gotten. We all have a good chuckle at a dragon firework that Alex had picked out, with a firework spewing from its mouth. Mila sets off some more traditional fireworks that pop a little too closely overhead for my comfort. And, of course, Luke takes out his own little box of firework poppers that he throws at Alex's feet to make him dance around. Mila sets off a funny little turtle firework that darts around on the ground, and there's the firework fountain, which sits on the ground and pours out sparks and smoke for what seems like five minutes straight.

"You know," I say to the group, "each year over eighteen thousand house fires are started by fireworks."

"You *would* know that," Mila says.

"Well, I guess we were the lucky ones this year," Luke says with a grin, and the way he's looking at me makes me feel like he's saying that he's lucky. And it might be because of me. I shake that thought off, sure I'm misinterpreting his look, and we head back to the pool deck.

"It's dessert time," Mila says, going inside to grab the Jeni's ice cream I'd ordered, with vegan options for Luke.

"I didn't know what flavors you'd go for," I tell him. "So I just got several different kinds. Dark Chocolate Truffle, Lemon Bar, and Banana Cream Pudding."

He laughs, examining the pints. "I think you got enough ice cream to last me the whole year."

"Oh, don't worry, with me around you'll be done with these in a week."

He glances at me, his eyebrow cocked as if to say, *So you're going to be around?* And I almost regret saying it. Almost.

We devour quite a few pints and even Luke eats his fair share. It's probably the most sugar he's had in the entire year. When we're done, Mila and Alex help me and then Luke into the pool lift, which lowers us into the water. I have a pool float that keeps me buoyed in the water, and even though it's kind of a pain to get in and out of the pool—between the lift and the difficulty of getting out of a wet bathing suit—I feel so free in the water. It's a wonderful feeling and it reminds me that I should be in here more often.

Mila gets Luke a float too, but he mostly sticks to holding onto the edge of the pool. He does the same thing that he did in the lake with the horses, where he holds on to the edge of the pool with one hand and floats on his back. Mila and Alex are sitting on the pool steps, talking, but I stay near Luke. "Can you help me do that too?" I ask Luke when he is upright again. He smiles at me, his blue eyes even brighter in the water.

"I'm happy you asked." He grabs my foot and tugs me toward him.

"Don't make it a thing."

"I won't," he whispers close to my ear. "Darlin'."

I laugh, rolling my eyes as he pulls me out of my float. I hold on to him, my arms around his neck, the side of his body pressed against mine. It feels so good it takes my breath away. "Or we could do this instead," Luke says in a low voice. I feel the vibrations from his chest as he talks. They ripple through me, making me ache to be even closer to him.

I want to say something snarky, to roll my eyes or even push him away so I can maintain some semblance of dignity—especially with Mila and Alex nearby—but I can't. I'm stuck. Not just physically, but mentally. I can't move on from this moment. And, I find, I don't want to.

I breathe him in, taking in every inch of his skin against mine. He's keeping us afloat with one hand on the pool wall, the other wrapped around my back, his fingers splayed out against my skin. It's a beautiful, magical thing.

Then Luke says, "Can you feel that?" And I wonder if he's talking about whatever is sparking between us, but then he pinches my back.

"Ow! Hey!" I go to move away from him, but quickly rethink that strategy and cling to him even harder.

"Sorry. I just felt your back muscles tightening, and I was wondering if you could feel that."

"Of course I feel that." *When you touch me, it's* all *I feel*, I want to say.

"Well, I'll be..."

"What?"

"Can you feel this?" he asks, his finger trailing down my spine, and it's like fireworks are going down my back. I press my lips together, nodding—I don't trust myself to say anything coherent right now.

"Do you feel your muscles tightening when I do that?"

I shake my head.

"It could be an involuntary response. When was the last time you've been evaluated? Or gone to your physical or occupational therapist?"

"I had a doctor's appointment recently, but it's probably been a good four or five months since I've seen my PT or OT."

"Look, I'm no doctor, but what I'm feeling back here seems like possibility for movement."

My heart is quickening, and not just because of Luke's proximity. "What do you mean?"

"I don't want to get your hopes up, but I could feel these muscles back here moving a bit as I held you. They were tensing up. If you still have feeling back here, I think it's possible you could recover some kind of movement."

"I've recovered a lot of movement already—more than we could've ever hoped for," I say, trying to temper my expectations as much as his.

"I know, and you're doing great. I'm just wondering if you're not that far from being able to do more."

I search Luke's face, wondering if *he* needs me to be able to do more. Or if I'm enough just as I am.

"I guess time will tell," I say, feeling guarded.

"Would you be open to doing some workouts with me? Only if you want to."

I glance down, suddenly feeling like maybe my gut instinct was right. Does Luke—the ripped-out-of-his-mind cowboy—need me to be that way too?

"Hey," I hear him say gently. "You know I'm only bringing this up for your sake, right? Heck, I liked you when I thought you could only move your pinky finger," he says, referring to the Instagram video he saw of me before he got the job at the Center.

I laugh and shake my head, but Luke's eyes are on my lips and before I know it, he's leaning even closer. He hums a few refrains from Corey Kent's song "Wild As Her," and when he sings his version of Corey's line, his breath is like a whisper against my cheek. "I ain't tryin' to fix you, I just wanna kiss you," he murmurs. His lips skim my jawline, and the goosebumps that shiver across my skin have nothing to do with the cold. My eyes flutter closed as I wait for his mouth to find mine—but for all of Luke's giddy up personality, the man can take his sweet time. He's placing gentle kisses on seemingly every inch of my face and neck, like he's making up for lost time. When his lips finally connect with mine, it's as if I've been in the desert all my life and someone just offered me water. How did I ever live without Luke? He only kissed me for the first time yesterday and I already can't remember life before him.

I momentarily forget Mila and Alex's presence until Mila starts catcalling from the pool steps. I break away from Luke, flush with embarrassment and something a little more than that. Luke yells something to Alex in a teasing tone, but I don't quite register it as the lightning that's sparking through my whole body starts to calm down. I lean back, trying to return to some semblance of composure.

"I'd be open to working out with you," I say, shoving my insecurity to the side. "It's just, it's hard to want more physically from my body and not be sure if it's even possible. In some ways, it's easier to keep my expectations down so I don't get hurt." The words are like a confession, and for a second I think he's going to assign me some Hail Marys.

"I get it," he says instead. "Is that why you don't like to go to PT?" I look up at him, surprised that he knows this. He shrugs. "I've seen your appointments on the shared Google calendar. You avoid them if you can."

I sigh. I've been found out, again. "I hate going to PT and feeling like a—a..." I struggle to find the right word.

"A paraplegic?"

I nod. "But it's more than that. I don't want to feel like a patient. Like this wounded person."

"Even though you are...?"

"Don't therapize me."

"I'm just asking a question."

"Yes, I don't like feeling that way," I say defensively. "Even though that's what I am," I mumble after a moment.

"I understand."

"You do?"

"To a degree, yes. I mean, my sister is my physical therapist, so I couldn't get away with not going, but yeah. I get it. A little too much."

"Katie Jo is your physical therapist?"

"Yes ma'am."

I laugh at him calling me "ma'am" and then cringe that I ever asked him to refer to me in that way in the first place. I think about Katie Jo—how capable she is, how sweet and trustworthy. "I would definitely go to Katie Jo as my PT."

"Yeah?"

"Oh yeah." I smile at him, feeling a combination of hope and a kind of dread I can't quite explain. Hope is dangerous—but it's also gotten me this far. So why not jump?

Luke returns my smile with one of his own and it sends a shiver down my spine as he leans in and whispers, "Let's do it, then."

43

I Work Out

Anya

Luke picks me up the next morning for my first workout with Katie Jo, and I have to admit, I'm nervous. I've been to my fair share of physical therapy appointments—but not with some guy I'm falling for watching all of my pathetic attempts. Not exactly my idea of a good time.

"Can we put on something with an actual tune?" I say, waving a frustrated hand at the radio. "This is making my ears bleed."

"But you're so cute when your ears bleed," he drawls.

Of course I'm moody and taking it out on Luke, who takes it in stride. He's teasing me, making me roll my eyes and scoff at him. And it makes me wonder, *Does he* like *this?* This back-and-forth thing that we do? I glance over at him, and he's grinning like a fool, and I can't help it—I crack a smile too. He plays a ridiculous country song called "Fancy Like" by Walker Hayes. At one point, I lower the song and tell him, "You do realize that this song is pretty much the antithesis of what I am? I will not be impressed by Applebee's."

"Oh, I don't know, Anya," he says. "I'm not convinced that there's not a little cowgirl trying to get out in there." He waves a hand at me, and I scoff.

"Why in the world would you think *that*?"

"Well, for one, you're here. With me. A cowboy."

"A *vegan* cowboy who can order wine and oysters like you summered in Cape Cod growing up," I clarify.

He chuckles. "So that did get to you. I wondered about that." He scratches his jaw, where he basically has a permanent five o'clock shadow, and I wonder how he does that. Does it just sprout up as soon as he's done shaving?

"Don't flatter yourself," I mutter, all the while wanting to run my fingers through his scruff, wondering what the light blonde hairs would feel like against my fingertips.

"I would never," he says with a mock gasp. "But I'm serious. I'm gonna find that hidden cowgirl in there."

"Good luck with that," I say with an eye roll. I'm beginning to think he *likes* to see the backs of my eyeballs. "If she's there, she's hidden *deep*. Like Mariana Trench deep."

We stop at a red light, and he turns to look at me, his blue eyes twinkling mischievously. "I'll search as long as you'll let me, Miss Kozak."

I should scoff, but instead, tears are inexplicably forming in my traitorous eyes. And I just wonder what I've gotten myself into.

I never thought doing physical therapy—or working out, as Katie Jo and Luke insist we call it—could be so fun. The two of them are a riot together, and I've laughed so much that it's been a workout in and of itself.

"You got nothin' to worry about, Miss Anya," Katie Jo tells me when I first get there. "Unless you're worried about my brother bein' difficult. He could start an argument in an empty house."

"I know you ain't talkin' 'bout me, Katie Jo," Luke yells from the kitchen. His Southern accent really comes out around his family, and I'm starting to like it. Which is only a little bit terrifying. Maybe Luke's right. Perhaps there is a cowgirl hidden somewhere in me. Very, very hidden. So hidden, in fact, that I didn't know about her until just this moment.

Luke comes back with waters for the three of us, then puts on some music—country, of course—and Katie starts me with some light stretching. I tell her about my goal of being able to lift myself out of my wheelchair, which feels more like a confession than anything else. But Katie Jo is straightforward and no-nonsense—she doesn't make me feel like she's pitying me or like my head's in the clouds for wanting to be able to lift myself.

We start with some resistance band exercises, and then Katie Jo shows me how I can do a sort of modified push up off the wall or a table. All of the exercises she's teaching me, I can do at home without any assistance, which is exactly what I wanted without knowing it. We end with some light weighted exercises—shoulder rotations, chest presses, tricep extensions. I would feel self-conscious about the teeny-tiny weights I'm using while Luke slings around weight heavier than me, but Katie Jo is so encouraging it feels like I'm an Olympic weightlifter rather than a paraplegic.

"Luke, I've been meaning to ask you—where'd all your stickers go?" Katie Jo asks as she's rifling through a container of workout bands. "They're all gone."

"Oh, yeah," he says nonchalantly, setting down the weights he's holding. I'm trying hard—and failing epically—not to stare at his biceps. "Had to take them off for work."

"Ain't that a shame," Katie Jo mutters.

"Wait, *why* is it a shame that Luke had to take off all of those inappropriate stickers?" I force my eyes off of Luke's perfectly sculpted form and direct them toward Katie Jo.

"Oh, he didn't tell you?"

"Tell me what?"

Katie Jo looks from me to Luke, who gives her an almost imperceptible nod. "Well, after Luke's accident, he had a hard time, y'know, with the chair. Even after he and Uncle Mark redesigned the whole thing, he just hated being in the chair. It was real bad. But then Mikey and the boys all got together and decorated his chair with stickers so it wasn't such a pain point. I remember when they first showed it to him, he laughed so hard he cried. And then he *really* cried—"

"Alright, Katie Jo, I think she gets the picture."

"So your brother and your friends put all those stickers there?" I say weakly. "To cheer you up about being stuck in the wheelchair?"

Luke ducks his head in a nod. "Somethin' like that."

"And I made you take them off?" I choke out.

"Well," he says with a brashness I'm sure he doesn't really feel, "no one can make me do anything I don't want to do."

"Luke," I say, my voice strangled by regret. "I'm so sorry."

He shrugs, his giant shoulders moving up and down mechanically. "Some of the stickers were inappropriate," he concedes.

"The rest, though—"

"If it makes you feel better, Kozak, you can make it up to me." And the look in his eye makes my stomach drop.

"Uh..."

"I've got just the thing in mind."

"Uh oh," Katie Jo says. "You've done it now, Anya. Best watch yourself."

We end our workout with more stretching, and Katie Jo presents me with a TENS unit. "You're going to be sore after today," she tells me. "This will help with the pain of that." She places the electrodes on my back in between my shoulder blades. "I'll start off with the lowest setting, but you can adjust it here." She shows me how to increase the intensity on the electrical stimulation. It feels like teeny tiny needles of electricity are poking my muscle. It's not necessarily a bad feeling, but I'm not ready to move up the intensity.

After the workout, Luke leads us out to the backyard and informs me that we're going to do some "grounding."

"If this is some kind of personality intervention, I am not at all interested," I tell him. He laughs, informing me that grounding is simply laying on the ground outside, which somehow helps your electrical energy. Whatever that is. Katie helps us get situated on the grass underneath a massive oak tree with Spanish moss dangling in the breeze. "I forgot my water, y'all," Katie says, walking back to the house, and I have a feeling she "forgot" her water on purpose. I'm laying on my back, the grass tickling the backs of my arms and legs. I breathe in, the Florida winter afternoon the perfect temperature for laying outside.

"For a *cowboy*, you certainly have some hippie-dippie tendencies," I tell him, using air quotes around cowboy.

Luke rolls onto his side, propping his head up on his hand. "Don't put me in a box, Kozak. I won't fit."

"That's certainly true," I say, eyeing his impressive bicep. He follows my line of vision and chuckles.

"You're just bothered because there's someone out there who's more principled than you are with something."

I rustle internally at this accusation—some part of it is probably true. "It's just weird. Cowboys eat meat, it's a thing."

"I'm surprised you're so closed-minded. Being vegan's kind of trendy, isn't it? Even Usher is a vegan."

"Usher? The R&B singer?"

Luke hums the first few notes of a famous Usher song and says, "Yeah," just like in the titular song.

I laugh and shake my head. "You're ridiculous."

Luke switches tunes seamlessly. "But you got it, you got it bad."

I smack his chest, almost immediately regretting it because *wow*, it's more chiseled than I remembered. My hand lingers a little too long, and I realize he's right: I do have it bad.

"Maybe," he drawls close to my ear, "I wanted to do this grounding thing so I had an excuse to do this." He wraps a hand around my hip and pulls me against him, enveloping me with his body. And just like that, my breathing is shallow and I can't think of anything except Luke.

"It was a good idea," I manage to get out.

"Yeah?"

"The electrical energy," I say, my mind almost completely numb from his closeness. "It's working."

"And where," he says, his voice low in my ear, "do you feel it working?"

His question shoots straight down my core like lightning sizzling inside of me. I certainly can't answer him directly, so I say, "Everywhere."

"Good," he says, pressing an open-mouthed kiss to my cheek, which serves to double the current effects of the "grounding." All of my cells are buzzing happily, I think they might just all whir away and I'll cease to exist.

"You're glowing," Luke says, fingers brushing across my face.

"It's the sun," I say, glancing up through the branches at the light filtering down on us.

He shakes his head. "It's you. You shine."

My throat is dry. I'm lost for words. The way he's looking at me, I could lose myself there. I *am* losing myself in him.

"I'm sorry about the stickers," I say before I'm a total goner. "I really am."

Luke runs another finger across my cheekbone, which sends a shiver down me. "I forgive you," he says. "It might've been time to move on, anyway. They served their purpose for me, and for that I'm thankful, but sometimes it's time to let go."

I gaze up at him, wondering if he's referring to letting go of anything else. But then he leans closer and whispers, "Don't worry, I'll let you make it up to me."

Katie Jo, who took her sweet time getting her water bottle, comes back out of the house and plops down next to me. I suddenly feel very aware of how close I am to Luke, and if I had all my strength, I'd move away, but I don't. So I lay here next to Luke, trying to convince myself this is normal. Katie Jo doesn't make a deal of it, which I'm grateful for, but I do notice her smiling down at me a little too hopefully. It makes me realize that I'm not the only one who's broken between me and Luke—and he's not the only one offering healing. The fact that we can do that for each other makes me feel whole in a way I haven't felt in over two years.

That night, I go over the day in my mind, recounting every look, each touch with Luke. I can't believe how he's so thoroughly affected me—how he shines through my darkness, lighting me up and making me glow.

I stumble upon a song by Sabrina Carpenter called "Nonsense," which perfectly describes everything I'm feeling now. I listen to it at least fifteen times, and on a whim, I go to send it to Luke. My finger hovers over the "send" arrow, and I debate for an entire song's length, until I finally press send. I clamp the phone to my chest, immediately feeling foolish. When my phone buzzes a few minutes later, I squeeze my eyes shut, unable to look. Why did I send that? I didn't say anything, just sent the song. I suppose I could pretend it was an accident? With that thought, I open the thread with Luke to find that he responded with a song and only this: "You. Today."

I open the song in Spotify, and it's "golden hour" by JVKE. I'm shocked it's not a country song—almost the exact opposite. A swelling piano tune with a man singing about a girl shining, and I don't think I breathe for the entirety of the song. Is Luke sitting around thinking about me? Listening to music, trying to find the perfect song for me? It's hard to believe.

I consider several different texts to send him, but ultimately land on: *You do this to me.*

And, of course, because this is Luke, he replies: *you better believe it.*

I can't help but laugh. *And so humble, too,* I reply.

Luke: *I can just see the eye roll right now.*

Anya: *You think you know me so well.*

Luke: *I do know you so well.*

Luke: *Especially the back of your eyes.*

Anya: *You love it.*

Luke: *Maybe I do.*

I fall asleep smiling for the first time in a long time.

Emergency Slice

Alex

I wake up on the first day of the new year to banging on my door. I glance at the clock. It's just after six in the morning. I throw on a shirt and rush to the door, only to find Tomás there. "Ay *primo*, I need your help."

I go to close the door, but he catches it with his hand. "Please?"

"You have one minute."

"Remember Camilla? We got her car stuck and I need your help to pull it out."

"Why don't you call one of your other friends? The ones who got you here?"

"They're all hungover. Please, Alex. Help me. It'll be really quick." He puts his hands on either side of the door frame. "Her cat is stuck in there; she's moving and her car's packed. The way it got stuck in the ditch, we couldn't get the cat out, so she's stuck in there."

I stare at him for a beat, wanting to go back to bed, to never deal with Tomás again. But the other part of me can't turn away someone—anyone, even my drug-dealing cousin—who needs help. It's an extra low blow that there's an animal involved. He knows that would get me. If he's lying, I'll box his ears. Or worse, tell his mother.

"Fine." I sigh and go back into my room to throw on my jeans. My mom's ring—Mila's ring—is sitting on the bedside table, and I stare at it for a moment. Tomorrow's court case can't come fast enough. Once I'm in the clear, once I can become a legal resident, then I can make plans to marry Mila. I've taken to carrying the ring around, almost like a good luck token. A reminder that there's hopefully some light at the end of all this, as long as I can make Mila mine. I put the ring inside the jewelry pouch they gave me when I went to have it cleaned and stuff it in my pocket.

I grab my keys, intending to follow my cousin in my car, but when I turn the key, I realize I'm almost out of gas. I debate forcing my cousin to follow me to get gas, but then I remember the cat stuck in the car, and sigh. He better not be lying. I put the keys in my pocket and head to Tomás's car.

Camilla is waiting in the back seat of the car, so I get in the passenger seat. We take off down Griffin Road, toward Weston, where her car is stuck. I don't ask any questions. I'm not in the mood for chitchat, and I certainly don't find myself feeling very charitable toward my cousin, or the girl who blew apart my birthday plans for Mila.

We're turning onto Weston Road when lights flash behind us. Cops. Tomás curses under his breath, glancing in the rearview mirror.

"You better not have drugs on you," I say, fear slicing through me. Tomás looks at me, his eyes wide and uneasy. I drop my head into my hands, my heart dropping as well, and I don't know whether I should scream or cry. All I know is that it's entirely possible my life as I know it is over, all because I made the foolish decision to help my cousin rescue a cat in some girl's car—which may or may not even be true.

I expect to feel the car slowing down, but instead, it speeds up. I sit up, looking out at the street, to find the lines blurring beneath the car. "Tomás..."

The speedometer shows we're going seventy miles per hour on a forty mile per hour road. "What are you doing? Tomás!" Behind us, Camilla starts shrieking as well, adding her own anxiety into the fray. My cousin is silent, hands gripped on the steering wheel, leaned forward, eyes fixed on the road. He runs through red lights, hops the curb and skirts the cars in front of him. But still, the police are behind us.

"What are you thinking, man? This only ends badly." I consider trying to stop him, trying to turn the wheel, but now we're going eighty miles per hour, weaving in and out of cars. Camilla and I are both questioning Tomás, trying to get him to see reason, but he's all but gone. He's sweating, shaking, not speaking. Every once in a while, he glances in his rearview mirror, but other than that, his eyes are on the road and his foot is pressed on the gas. Camilla starts offering up loud, erratic prayers. Now we're going eighty-five, ninety miles per hour. I know that soon Weston Road will end in I-75. Is that his plan? To get to the Interstate? Where is the hope of hiding out there, in the middle of the Everglades with only one long highway?

I start praying too. I pray for Tommy to see reason, for this to not screw up everything with Mila, for my mom to be safe. I pray for Mila, for her to be loved her whole long life. I pray for Anya. I pray for Luke. I pray for the Center. I pray until I see I-75 up ahead.

We're going almost a hundred miles an hour, but I know we need to slow down to make this turn onto the Interstate.

Tommy pumps the brakes, but by the time we take the turn, we're still going over seventy. I grip the center console in one hand, and the car door in the other, trying to stabilize myself. We skid through the turn, tires squealing, the scent of melted rubber filling the car. We drift across multiple lanes and into the median beside the highway. A streetlight is right in front of us, and Tomás swerves to avoid it, but then we careen off of the chain-link fence, spinning. Camilla is screaming, the sound swelling to a crescendo. I squeeze my eyes closed, until we hit something, my body shooting forward and then being held back by the seatbelt which razes my chest. And then, we're still.

I open my eyes, breathing hard. Before I can get my bearings, Tomás is opening his door and running. Camilla is still screaming, which at least means she's alive. I glance back, only to find the police right behind us, lights still flashing. So I do the only thing I can think of: I put my hands on the dash and I wait for my arrest.

It's been hours since they put me in cuffs. Hours since I was thrown to the ground and searched several times over. Hours since they took my mother's ring and accused me of stealing it. Hours since Ann showed up and they questioned me, hours since I told them what I know about the drugs they found in Tomás's car. I showed them the proof that I reported it to Crime Stoppers, but what does that even matter now? It's been at least two hours since I called Mila—arguably the worst moment of my life.

I find myself sitting in a holding cell, questioning all of my life's decisions. Why didn't I turn Tomás in when I first found the drugs? Why didn't I fire Tomás the moment I saw him smoking a joint outside the Center? Why did I even hire Tomás? How did I get here, and how can I undo everything?

I just want to go back to having Mila in my arms, to having nothing to worry about except what her lips feel like on mine. It seems as though I'm being taught a lesson, but what it is, I can't exactly say. There is pain in life, and it gets worse. There is joy, and it gets taken away. Is that what I'm supposed to learn from all of this? Or perhaps I'm supposed to learn that I make exceedingly poor decisions and can't be trusted.

If I thought calling Mila to tell her I'd been arrested was the worst moment of my life, I was wrong. When they finally release me, all of my belongings are returned to me, except for the only thing that really matters: the ring. It's unclear to me why they're refusing to give it back to me—I'm not being charged for anything—except for the simple fact that I look like someone who shouldn't have something like that on me. The police officer who's giving me my things insists that I need to return with proof of ownership and they'll give it back. I'm so tired, I barely put up a fight, and the officer gives me a slip of paper that connects me to the ring when I return for it.

Seeing Mr. Kozak waiting for me in the lobby of the police station quickly trumps the horrible moment of calling Mila earlier. We drive to the Center in silence, the tension in the car crackling like a bonfire. Whatever Mr. Kozak thought of me before, it's burned to the ground now. I want to tell him what happened, to explain that I didn't do anything wrong—except for continuing contact with my cousin—but my gut is telling me nothing I say would be productive right now. So I keep quiet, staring ahead as Mr. Kozak steers his Tesla through the night toward the Center.

I'm relieved when we finally pull into the driveway. "Thank you, sir," I force myself to say when I get out. He doesn't respond, and I hurry toward the Cottage. In the safety of my home, my mom is asleep on the couch, Gata purring beside her, clearly waiting up for me. I kiss her on her head, waking her, and she gives me a blurry-eyed hug. She starts to ask me a hundred disjointed questions, but I tell her, "We'll talk tomorrow, Mama." She's so tired, she actually agrees to this.

I pick through the fridge, looking for something to eat, and settle on some four-day-old rice and beans that are almost too dry to eat. I call Mila as I heat the bowl in the microwave, but she doesn't pick up. As much as I want to talk with her, my disappointment is lessened by the fact that I don't want to answer any more questions about today, or tomorrow's court case. I scarf down the rice and beans, then take out an emergency slice of my mom's guava cheesecake. A few months ago, she'd made an extra cheesecake, sliced it up and froze each individual slice so we could eat them one at a time. I've kept this one hidden in the very back of the freezer and have considered it my 'emergency' slice. And this seems as good a time as any to defrost it. A part of me wants to say, *How much worse can it get?* But tomorrow is still a question mark, especially in light of today's events. Even so, I know that my emergency slice of cheesecake won't cut it if tomorrow goes poorly. Not even an entire cheesecake would do that.

As much as I love my mom's guava cheesecake, the emergency slice is disappointing. It's got that plastic taste of freezer burn, and all the moistness of the original cheesecake is gone. And of course, it's not perfectly defrosted, so the outside is warm and the inside is still frozen. Halfway through, I give up and toss it in the trash.

Gata's mewling around my feet, but for once I don't have the energy to scratch her behind her ears. I've got nothing to give, even to the poor cat.

I pace around our tiny living room before I take out the manila folder Mr. Kozak gave me, looking over the visa application for Canada. I sigh, my head and my heart feeling heavier than they've ever been. Before I can talk myself out of it, I sign the forms that Mr. Kozak already filled out, fold them into an envelope, and walk it down to the mailbox.

Somehow, I feel both lighter and heavier once the deed is done. I sit on a tack trunk in the barn, listening to the horses as they swish and stomp. Jet pokes his head over his stall door, extending his nose to rummage at my shirt. I reach in my pockets, and for the first time possibly ever, I don't have any treats. "Sorry, bud," I tell him. "I've got nothing."

I lean my head against the stall wall, close my eyes, and fall into a fitful sleep with recurring dreams about my case tomorrow. Each time I wake up from one of them, I find myself reaching a hand out for Mila, but each time it hits me that she's not there. And maybe I should get used to it.

45

Court

Mila

I wake up on January 2nd at five a.m. I jolt awake, jumbled thoughts of Alex in my mind. I scramble for my phone and see that he called me after midnight last night, and I'm disappointed to not find any texts from him. I try calling him back, but I'm sure he's asleep so I get up, shower, and head out into the pre-dawn. I wait outside the dry cleaner's until they open and pick up Alex's suit. Then I head to our favorite bagel shop and grab a half-dozen options for Alex and his mom and a smoothie for me. I'm too nervous to eat, and throwing up a bagel and cream cheese is way worse than a smoothie. I know this from experience.

When I get to the Center, I find Alex asleep in the breezeway. He's on a tack trunk, leaned against the wall, with his neck at a terrible angle that's definitely going to hurt when he wakes up. Gata, the faithful cat, is curled in Alex's lap. He's got a fragile peace about him that makes me not want to wake him up, so I sit quietly beside him until he stirs.

"You're here," he says, and for a moment I think he's going to cry.

I take his hand in both of mine. "Of course I'm here."

"I'm so sorry, Mila."

"Let's just worry about today," I tell him. "You can apologize to me later." I don't know all the details of what happened yesterday—I called Ann as soon as Alex called me, but she reported back to my dad, not me. And *Tato* has gone into gorilla mode since Alex's arrest, responding with grunts and threatening glares instead of actual words. I didn't even know that Alex was released until my dad disappeared late last night and my mom informed me. I'm not sure who has more explaining to do, my dad or Alex, but today is not the day to do it. Today we just need to get through court.

He ducks his head in a nod, and I know he's swamped with guilt and shame. "I brought breakfast and picked up your suit."

"Thank you." I go to get up, but Alex pulls me back down. "Can we stay here? For a bit?"

I nod and settle beside him, my head on his shoulder. He sighs and leans into me. We sit like that for a long time until the horses start to whinny for breakfast. "I should probably feed them," Alex says. He turns to me and cups my face in his hands, kissing me softly, mournfully. When he pulls away, I wonder why this feels like goodbye.

I drive Alex and Mrs. Caballero to the Palm Beach Courthouse—an unpleasant repeat of our first attempt at Alex's court date. This time, I'm prepared for the silence and have a playlist filled with songs like Walk the Earth's "I'll Be There" and Extreme's "More Than Words." With each song, I try to convey to Alex that we'll get through this, no matter what happens. I have no idea if my point is coming across, but when one of our favorites, Johnnyswim's "Take the World," comes on, Alex reaches across the middle console and takes my hand. I thread my fingers through his and don't let go until we get off the highway and I need two hands to steer.

At the courthouse, we meet up with Alex's lawyer, and the two of them go somewhere to talk while I get coffee for Mrs. Caballero. At half past eleven, my parents, Anya, and Luke roll into the lobby. It's like everyone coordinated their outfits to wear black, and the thought crosses my mind that maybe everyone knew we were going to be mourning today. My stomach clenches at the thought, and I run to the bathroom, barely making it before my smoothie makes its way back up. Tears stream down my face, dripping into the sink as I hang my head over it and heave. My mom comes up behind me, rubbing my back as I cry. She tries to comfort me as I wash out my mouth and wipe down my face, but her words don't make it past my fear.

Eventually we make our way into the courtroom and find seats at the front next to my dad and Luke, with Anya at the end. A minute later, Trina walks in and scoots in beside me. She gives my knee a squeeze, and I notice she also got the memo to wear black.

Another case is going on, and I don't quite get what the case is about before it's over. The judge is a balding Hispanic man with half a halo of hair around his shiny head. He seems bored as he stares down at the papers in front of him. I've only ever seen court cases on TV, and I thought the judge would come in after everything was set up for the case, but here he is. Once the previous defendant and lawyers clear out, Alex and Ann head up to the front to their table. A man announces the case and before I realize it, the case has started. I reach over and take my mom's hand and then, because that's not enough, I take Trina's hand, too.

The charges against Alex are read: that he is not a citizen or national of the United States, that he is a citizen of Cuba, and that he came here without authorization. Judge Alonso doesn't look up from his papers when he says, "Do you wish to designate a country of removal?"

"My client does not wish to return to his country of origin," Ann states. "He requests that his country of removal be listed as Canada."

I look over at Alex, surprised. He'd never mentioned this to me before. Of course, I can barely see his face from where I'm sitting, but I stare at the back of his head as if he can explain telepathically to me what he was thinking with this decision. Next, Ann launches into an explanation of their defense—that Alex wishes to obtain lawful status through Non-LPR cancellation of removal. "My client has lived in the United States for thirteen years, is currently receiving his master's degree at Florida Atlantic University, and has shown good moral character for the entirety of his residence here." Ann continues to explain that Alex's mom is dependent on him for support and medical care. She goes into great detail about Mrs. Caballero's medical condition and her chances for quality treatment in Cuba. She then expounds on his work at the Center. She closes with, "My client is an exceptional young man who will only bring about positive change to his local community and beyond. The United States would be blessed to have someone like Mr. Caballero continuing in residence."

After this, Alex takes the stand and answers seemingly endless questions from Ann and the judge, which are really only repetitions of what Ann previously stated. He's well-spoken yet humble, unassuming yet heartfelt. Pride for him swells in my heart and despite the chaos of the past twenty-four hours, I have hope. Alex steps down and Ann calls Trina to the stand.

"Ms. Powers, thank you for being here today," Ann starts, her hands folded in front of her as she stands in front of the bench. "You were Mr. Caballero's boss at your barn, is that correct?"

"Yes, that's right. Alex worked for me at Zen Elite for over five years."

"And how would you describe Mr. Caballero's work ethic while he was employed at your barn?"

"Alex was a hard worker, always willing to go the extra mile. He treated the horses as if they were his own, and he was dedicated to his responsibilities. I'll probably never have an employee as dedicated as he was."

"That's wonderful to hear. Did Mr. Caballero have any particular skills or talents that stood out while he worked at the barn?"

"Absolutely. Alex had a natural knack for handling the horses. He was patient, gentle, and had a deep understanding of their behavior. We used to joke that he might've been a horse in another life."

Ann gives a generous laugh at Trina's comment, and I notice the judge gives a small smile. "So, would you say that Mr. Caballero was a valuable asset to your barn and an asset to the equine community?"

"One hundred percent. I trusted Alex with the care of my horses, and he never disappointed. He was reliable, responsible, and showed great dedication to his work. He would be an asset in any community anywhere, but he definitely has a special place in the horse world."

"That's great. Can you tell me more about some of the challenges he's faced and why that might have made it difficult for him to pursue becoming a legal resident?"

"Leading," says the opposing lawyer in a bored voice.

"Let me rephrase the question," Ann says. "Can you tell me about some of the difficulties Mr. Caballero has faced in his life?"

"Alex's life has not been easy—of course you already discussed how he came here as a child in a terrifying journey that he couldn't completely grasp the reasoning behind due to his age and maturity. But coming to a new country didn't stop Alex from excelling. He's always done well in school, and even outside of school, he's always educating himself, reading deeply and widely. As you've discussed earlier, Alex's family came here to find medical relief for Alex's mom that simply was not possible in their home country. It was always Alex's intention to pursue a Green card to be here legally. He began working at another barn, Halliday Farm, when he was just fifteen so he could save up to afford an attorney. But unfortunately, Alex's father, who was the primary breadwinner in their family, died about six years ago. And since then, every cent of Alex's work has gone toward caring for his mom since she can't work. What Alex has done is admirable and honorable." At this point, Trina's eyes are watering, and her voice is choked in a rare display of emotion. She takes a shuddering breath and then continues, "He put his mom first, prioritizing her health and wellness at the expense of his own well-being and at the risk of his presence in this country."

Ann is silent for a few beats, to let the power and emotion of Trina's words resonate through the room. Everyone is still, and a palpable relief sweeps through me as I realize Trina just won this for us. "Thank you, Ms. Powers," Ann says. "Your testimony speaks volumes about Alex's character and work ethic. I agree that he is a man worthy of this great nation."

"Ms. Powers," the opposing attorney says, "is it true that while he worked for you, Mr. Caballero was accused of poisoning your horses and causing a potentially deadly bout of colic in your barn?"

"The colic was proven to come from moldy feed, which originated with the feed company itself. Both our vet and myself signed affidavits saying that there is no way, not an inkling of doubt, that Alex could have ever been responsible for the colic." Then she adds, "Anyone with two neurons to rub together would know that Alex couldn't have been responsible."

"Well, someone obviously thought he did it."

"And that person was lacking the aforementioned neurons."

"Is it true that Alex was arrested on these charges?"

"My understanding, and correct me if I'm wrong here"—Trina glances at Judge Alonso—"is that in this country, it's innocent until proven guilty. Getting arrested—on charges that were ill-founded and not pressed by the owner of the barn or anyone with any actual knowledge of the incident—does not make one guilty. And if someone is proven innocent, as Alex was, it is our duty as human beings to respect that. You bringing it up just comes across like a fishing expedition."

"Well, this *is* a fishing expedition, Ms. Powers. For better understanding Alex's character."

"And I am testifying, hand on the Bible, that Alex is one of the most honorable, high-charactered people I know."

"That's all, Ms. Powers."

Trina steps down from the witness stand, and we all watch her as she makes her way back to her seat. When she sits beside me, I clasp her hand in both of mine and I feel her shaking. "Thank you," I whisper.

Next, my dad is supposed to take the stand—a thought that makes me squirm in my seat—but instead of calling him, Ann calls Anya. I watch, wide-eyed, as my sister navigates through the courtroom. She can barely make it through the gate at the front of the room, and it takes a few attempts of her backing up, readjusting and trying to get through. I cast a glance at my dad, frowning at him, but he doesn't meet my eye.

Of course, Anya can't sit in the witness stand, so she just wheels up beside it and turns around, facing us. She looks elegant as usual, but also very serious, a little like a dour Victoria Beckham with blue eyes. Ann questions her along the same lines as Trina. Anya gives details about Alex's involvement in the inception of the Center as well as his day-to-day role there. She discusses the hope for his long-term future there and talks about his rapport with clients. When Ann finishes her questioning, we expect Anya to be done, but then the opposing attorney stands up.

"Ms. Kozak, I understand there was an incident at the ViaTech Center in which Mr. Caballero was involved, and I was hoping you could speak to that."

"You'll have to be more specific," Anya says, a little too tartly. "We've never had any negative incident involving Alex at the Center."

The attorney grabs a stack of papers from his table and waves them at Anya. "It says here that you settled a lawsuit out of court for an incident involving a paralyzed girl who took a fall while under your care."

"It's inherent in this sport that horses are unpredictable, and things like this happen sometimes at no one's fault."

"So then why did you settle?"

Anya raises her chin. "If it were up to me, we wouldn't have."

"Someone obviously felt there was negligence involved or else you wouldn't have settled."

"Well then, it sounds like you'll have to question someone else about it, because I am not of that opinion."

"It states here that the defendant in that lawsuit, Ms. Clara Cardones, accused Mr. Caballero of manipulating her through flirtation to ride a horse she didn't want to ride."

"I'm sorry," Anya says, glaring at the attorney, "are we on trial for a case we settled out of court? I'm confused."

"No, Ms. Kozak," the attorney says with a tight smile. "We are here to determine Mr. Caballero's character and whether he would be a good candidate for remaining in this country. So, please, answer the question."

Anya looks up at the judge with an eyebrow raised, and the judge nods. "Please answer the question, Ms. Kozak."

Anya sighs, pressing her lips together as she considers her words. "Ms. Cardones was hesitant to get on the horse that day. This happens sometimes—people want to get on the horses, that's why they're there, but when it comes down to it, they're nervous. We would never force anyone to get on, though. As a staff, we decided it would be best for Alex to speak with her about it because he had the best rapport with her—"

"Would it be accurate to say that you knew Ms. Cardones had a crush on Mr. Caballero and that's why you chose him to speak with her?"

"No," Anya says adamantly. "We knew Clara felt safe with Alex—"

"So you used your client's feelings to manipulate her into riding a dangerous animal?"

"They're not dangerous—"

"Says the woman in the wheelchair—"

"Counselor!" The judge raps his gavel. "This woman is not on trial. Stick to the case at hand. My apologies, Ms. Kozak."

Anya's stony expression tells us all is not forgiven as she waits for the attorney's next question. "Do you foresee, Ms. Kozak, using Mr. Caballero's 'rapport' with clients in the future?"

Through gritted teeth, Anya says, "Alex has been nothing but professional and has never, not once, conducted himself in an unworthy manner."

A slow smile spreads across the opposing attorney's face and he says, "We'll see about that." And then, he dismisses Anya.

While we're all still reeling from Anya's questioning, the attorney states, "I'd like to call one more witness to the stand, Officer Patrick Etienne."

"We were not made aware of any other witnesses, your honor," Ann says.

"This witness is testifying to events we only found out about this morning that took place yesterday, your honor," the opposing attorney says.

"I'll allow it," Judge Alonso says with a wave of his hand. My heart is pounding so hard, I think it might implode. I don't know what's going to happen, but the anxious knots coiling in my stomach are telling me it's nothing good.

Officer Etienne takes the stand, and I stare at his badge, which is shining at me menacingly. The attorney starts questioning him, and I barely hear it because blood is rushing through my head so loudly, I think I might pass out or throw up. I force myself to focus as Officer Etienne finishes up telling about his job as a beat cop in Weston. My eyes travel up his uniform to his trendy fade haircut with an arcing line shaved into the fade. I follow the path of his haircut, wondering if this is all going downhill just like his linework.

"Can you tell me about how you met Mr. Caballero?"

"Yesterday, my partner and I went to pull over a car that was going fifteen over the speed limit on Weston Road. When we turned our lights on, the driver sped up, attempting to outrun us. Eventually, he hit a fence and the vehicle was forcibly stopped. The driver then exited the car and was attempting to flee on foot when my partner caught him. I approached the vehicle from the passenger's seat and found Mr. Caballero there. When we searched the car, there were drugs with intent to distribute. Mr. Caballero and the driver were arrested."

"Based on your experience with Mr. Caballero, would you consider him an ideal candidate for residency in this country?"

"Objection," Ann shouts. "This is not the Officer's place to make that judgment call."

"I'll allow it," Judge Alonso says.

"If it were up to me, I'd never allow someone into the country that would resist arrest or carry drugs. That's obviously a detriment to society."

"Thank you, Officer Etienne."

Ann stands up and stalks over to the Officer. "Officer, can you clarify something for me?"

"Yes, ma'am."

"Did my client, Mr. Caballero"—she gestures over her shoulder at Alex—"at any point resist arrest yesterday?"

"Well, the driver of the vehicle he was in—"

"Yes, I know the driver resisted arrest, but did my client, that man sitting right there, resist arrest?"

"No ma'am, not technically."

"Is it true that when you approached the vehicle, Mr. Caballero's hands were on the dashboard in plain view and that he complied immediately with every instruction you gave him?"

"I don't recall, ma'am. I've arrested a lot of people."

"How many people did you arrest yesterday?"

"Uh, just the one, ma'am."

"So for the singular person you arrested yesterday, can you clearly recall that he was compliant to your instructions?"

"I believe he was."

"And when you searched my client, did you find any incriminating evidence on his person?"

"The car that we searched—"

"I'm asking you, Officer, if you found anything on my client's actual person. In his pockets, in his hands, hiding in his undies."

"No, ma'am, we did not."

"And once the driver and the other passenger in the car, Miss Camilla Morales, were questioned, did they both not clearly state that my client had no knowledge of his possession of the drugs?"

"I was not there when they were questioned—"

Ann walks to her table, grabs a piece of paper, and hands it to Officer Etienne. "If you'll read this starting at line four."

"*My cousin did not know that I had any drugs in the car. He wouldn't have gotten in if he'd known. He doesn't do that kind of stuff. He's straight edge all the way—*"

"That's good, Officer Etienne. Thank you. So based on this transcript from the driver's interrogation, do you believe that my client had any knowledge of the drugs in the car?"

"I have no way of knowing if this is true or not," Officer Etienne says, holding up the paper.

"Let's just say, for the sake of this conversation, it is true."

"If it's true, then it's true."

"Thank you, Officer Etienne, that'll be all."

"Any more witnesses?" Judge Alonso asks. Both Ann and the opposing attorney say no.

Fear is a wild animal inside me, clawing to be released from her cage. We are all silent as the judge sighs, removes his glasses, and presses his fingertips into the corner of his eyes. I think he's about to dismiss us, to tell us he needs some time to make his decision, but then he says, "Mr. Caballero, I sympathize with your situation, I really do, but I can't in good conscience allow you to stay here after the facts presented by opposing counsel. It's too murky for me." He looks down at Alex, and I can tell he does have sympathy, but clearly not enough to impact his decision. "You will not be granted asylum in the United States. You are required to remove yourself from this country by"—he glances down at his papers— "January twenty-ninth. If you do not leave the country by that date, you will be forcibly removed. If your visa to Canada is approved, you will be removed to that country. If it is not, you will be sent to your country of origin. Do you understand?"

"Yes, sir."

"Very good. Case dismissed." Judge Alonso raps his gavel.

We all sit in stunned silence. I'm gripping Trina's hand tightly, our palms sweating together. My mom's hand is on my knee, her hold almost as strong as mine. I can't move. Especially if it means that once I leave here, Alex has to leave too. So I just don't move.

It's like my heart has been ripped to shreds. It'll never be whole again. How did this happen? I'm still trying to piece it together—why did Alex have to get arrested yesterday of all days? And how did the opposing attorney know about it so quickly? I'm surprised Ann was prepared with the transcript of Tommy's interrogation, but it wasn't enough. I'm not sure anything would've been enough.

And now I'm feeling foolish for believing Alex would get a chance. That *we* would get a chance. How are we going to work this out? We hadn't even discussed it. We'd been too afraid to discuss it. Like fools.

Alex and Ann are talking quietly at their table, and Ann pats him on the back before she walks away. My dad stands at the end of the aisle, intercepting Ann before she leaves, and says something quietly to her. She looks up at him and nods somberly.

Alex is still sitting at the table, his hands folded in front of him. This is the worst-case scenario and I know he's feeling just as wrecked, if not more, than I do.

Then he turns to look at me, and the desolation, the abject misery, in his eyes will forever be burned into my mind. And I am ruined by it.

46

Calm vs Storm

Mila

I drive Alex and his mom back to the Center, and we're silent the whole way. I keep glancing over at Alex, who is staring out the window and refuses to meet my eye since that last look we shared in the courtroom. When I look into the backseat, I see that Mrs. Caballero is doing the same thing. *How is she not crying?* I wonder. But then again, it's entirely possible that she doesn't yet understand what's happening.

We sit in traffic despite being on the expansive five-lane I-95 highway. The radio's playing cheerful pop tunes on Y100, a stark juxtaposition to the mood of the car. I feel suffocated—by the traffic, the sadness, the inability to outthink this situation. By the time we get onto the 869, I feel a hint of relief when I glance at the Everglades stretching out like an ocean of sawgrass. I imagine I'm one of the swallow-tailed kites that swoops effortlessly over the marshland. What if Alex and I could just fly away from here—from all of these problems, from the very law itself? It's a silly, childish thought, but I think it, nonetheless. I crave it.

At the Center, Alex leads his mom to the Cottage, and I wait in the garden at our usual spot. When he comes back, he looks more or less like his normal self, if not a little tired. He plops down on the wicker sofa and pats the cushion beside him. I sit down, tentatively, and he puts an arm around me to pull me close.

"What are we going to do?" I ask, my voice cracking.

"I'm not sure," Alex says in a way that seems to indicate he doesn't want to talk about it.

"We should call Ann."

"Maybe."

"How can you be so calm about this?" I ask after we sit in silence yet again for what seems like forever. All I want to do is talk through solutions, but Alex is giving me absolutely nothing. It's infuriating and terrifying in equal measures.

Alex sighs and rubs a hand across his face. "What other choice do I have?"

"You can scream, cry, break things, I don't know! But this, this acceptance of what's happening, it's not okay."

"Who says I'm accepting it? I'm still processing, Mila. It just happened."

I don't point out that we spent almost two hours driving home in traffic for him to *process*. "You just don't seem that upset that you're leaving me. Maybe forever." I know I'm edging closer to hysteria, and for some reason, his calmness is pushing me to the breaking point.

"Oh, Mila." He pulls me into his lap and wraps his arms around my waist. "There's one thing I know for certain: I'm not leaving you forever."

I push at his chest, but he holds me tight. "You don't know that."

"It's true I can't promise that, but I just know we'll figure it out. Ann says it could only be like a year or two before I can come back."

"A year? Two? Alex, are you kidding me?"

"No?"

I extricate myself from his grasp, standing up. I'm chastising myself—and, yes, him too—for not discussing this sooner. We had been so confident he'd be fine. So confident we didn't bother to even talk about the possibility of deportation. We were so utterly unprepared for this. Doesn't pride come before the fall? And we were falling so far right now. "I'm so confused right now. You're getting *deported*—"

"Removed, yes."

"You're getting forcibly removed from this country for a minimum of a year and you think that's okay?" I spread my hands and look up at the sky, as if to question the universe, *This isn't okay, right?*

Alex is quiet for a long time, and his face is indecipherable in the growing dark. His eyes are scanning me, and I hate that he's probably reading me like a book and I can't tell what's going through his head. Finally, he sighs and says, "Are you not able to wait for me for a year? Is that what you're saying, Mila? That a year is going to break us?" His voice is quiet, pleading.

"That's not what I'm saying, Alex. I'm just honestly shocked that you're so okay with this—"

"To be clear: I am not okay with this. But what are my alternatives? Throw myself on the ground and kick and scream? What good is that going to do me?"

His level tone makes me want to scream. Like he's taken his whole 'radical acceptance' thing too far—but I am not accepting this. "It would do *me* good to know that you actually feel something!"

"Of course I feel something, Mila. I feel something about leaving my mom, about potentially going back to a communist country and not knowing what things will be like there for me, and I most definitely feel something about what *you* seem to be expressing to me—that this situation is too much for you. For us."

"I just need to know that you care."

"That I care? Are you serious? Mila, my whole life revolves around you. This is it for me; there's nothing else."

I squeeze my eyes shut, and tears leak out. "Then why does it feel like you're giving up?" I whisper.

"I'm not giving up on us," Alex says as he stands and puts his forehead against mine. "It's just, sometimes, you lose. And there's not anything to do about it."

There it is. Proof that he is accepting this—radically—when he shouldn't. It feels like a betrayal to me, to us.

"I can't accept that," I say through gritted teeth. "I *won't* accept it."

"Maybe not right now, but you will."

I shake my head. More tears fall down my cheeks. "I need to go."

"Mila."

"I need to get out of here, Alex."

"I don't want to leave things like this."

"I just need some space."

Alex backs away, and the look on his face kills me. A few minutes ago, I couldn't tell what he was thinking, and now, it's so clear. He's hurt, he's disappointed in me and my ability—or lack thereof—to deal with this situation. His lack of emotion about this situation makes it seem like *I'm* overreacting—except I know I'm not. He's under-reacting, and I don't get it. I want to cry, to wail, to bust a hole in something. And I want him to do it with me. The fact that he's not makes me want to run away so I can deal with this alone.

"I'm sorry," I whisper to him as I grab my purse and leave. When I climb in my car, I curl up in the seat, my head on my steering wheel, and sob.

After a very thorough cry, I decide I have to do something. I can't just sit around and wait for Alex to be deported. My first call is to Ann, who picks up on the second ring.

"Is there anything we can do?" I ask her. My graduation tassel from my undergraduate degree is hanging off of my rearview mirror, and I twirl it around my finger until I can feel the blood pumping just below my skin.

"Look, your dad told me he won't continue to pay for me to represent Alex, so I have to respect that. But you could have a different attorney submit a stay of removal. Who knows if they'll approve it; it just depends on the judge. I'll be honest though—it's not looking great. Not with his recent arrest and the Center out of commission."

I nod, even though she can't see me, and I'm fighting back tears as I ask, "What if he doesn't leave? What if he just...stays?"

Ann sighs. "Mila, honey, I know you're desperate right now, but that's not the answer. It'll only make things worse for Alex in the long run. I'll tell you what I told Alex, the best move is to get married. Now I know Alex is—"

"Wait, what?" I let go of the tassel and it swings in the darkness of the car.

"It's what I told Alex. If you two got married, it *could* change the situation."

I'm silent for a long time, breath suspended in my lungs, until Ann says, "Mila?"

"Yeah, sorry. So, you told Alex this?"

"I did."

"And he said...?"

"He said it was unfair to put you in that position, that it's not what he wanted for your relationship—"

"He said that?"

"Look, Mila, don't shoot the messenger here. Alex obviously cares about you a lot, but as you know, a lot of guys are, well, finicky about marriage. I mean, my husband didn't even propose until after I was pregnant—a real romantic, that one—"

"Hey, um, Ann, I got another call coming in," I lie. "Can I call you back?"

"Sure thing."

"Thanks, bye."

I end the call and sit back, gripping my steering wheel as I consider what Ann said. So marriage could possibly save Alex? Why didn't he mention that today with me? I take a deep breath and try to steady my heart rate. What are my options?

I could offer to marry Alex, or I could wait to see if he proposes. I contemplate both, weighing them in my mind.

Two things are certain. One: I want to marry Alex. Not because he's getting deported, but simply because I know I want to spend my life with him. Two: I won't back him into marrying me. So if he doesn't ask me, I don't think I should offer. I remember my birthday dinner on the beach, when I'd made the comment about Alex marrying me. I see his face in my mind in perfect detail, poised on the edge of panic at the idea of marriage. If he'd felt so put off by the idea a couple months ago, how would he feel about essentially being forced into marriage? If he's not convinced he wants to spend his life with me after dating for almost two years, I'm not sure I can face that.

47

Mess is Mine

Alex

I watch Mila walk away, feeling like she's taking my whole world with her. Ever since the judge rapped his gavel, declaring the case closed, I've felt a core-deep numbness that I can't shake. As much as Mila wants me to, I just cannot allow myself to feel all the ramifications of this right now. I need to experience this disappointment on *my* terms, when I'm ready for it and not a moment sooner. I didn't plan for this emotional experience because I didn't think it was going to happen—I foolishly hadn't allocated the appropriate energy reserves for this turn of events.

So our whole drive home, I was spaced out, trying not to feel anything at all. Trying not to think about leaving Mila and what that might mean. And then when Mila seemed to be freaking out, I had to be the strong one. The patient one. The calm one. Which, if I were the type to care about fairness, I would be frustrated by the fact that Mila seems to be making this about her instead of about me. *I'm* the one getting deported—and Mila needs me to have a certain emotional response to make *her* feel better?

As Mila walks away, I know I should sit and parse through whatever this meant, but I can't. I don't even want to go into the Cottage and change out of my suit because I don't want to face my mom. Instead, I go inside the barn and busy myself with the horses—measuring out their dinner, tossing pads of hay into their stalls, flecks of hay sticking to my navy pants. I grab the wheelbarrow and meticulously clean each stall even though I'm in my dress shoes. What do they matter now? I block out any other thought except what's right in front of me. The warmth and companionship of the horses surrounds me, so that I'm not truly by myself, even in my loneliness.

I sweep hay and shavings from the breezeway and then look around for something else to occupy me. A wave of exhaustion crashes over me, and I sit on the tack trunk. I know I shouldn't spend yet another night out here, but I can't find it in me to get up. Eventually fatigue rises up to claim me and I give in.

I wake sometime in the middle of the night and stumble to the Cottage. I check on my mom, asleep in her bed, looking so frail. I change out of my clothes and splash water on my face. My resolve is slipping, and I blame it on middle-of-the-night lack of self-control because the tears come as I stare at my mom, so delicate under her threadbare quilt. How could I possibly bring her back to Cuba? And I know the reality of the situation: once I'm in Cuba, it's near impossible to get back out through legal means. I swipe the tears away with my palms.

Instead of climbing into bed, I sit at the kitchen table with a pad of paper, writing out all of my options. I can go back to Cuba but leave my mom here. We could both go to Cuba. We could apply for visas to other countries where she could receive quality healthcare. I could marry Mila. I could stay, illegally. I cross off that option as soon as I write it. I'm unwilling to do that. I run the pen through the idea of bringing my mom to Cuba. That's not an option either. I pull out my phone and start researching places that we could get visas to easily. I make a list: Canada, Germany, France, Australia. With each country I write, I wonder, *Will Mila follow me here? Would she follow me there?* And I wonder if I can ask that of her.

I've already applied for a Canadian visa, so I start the application for Germany. All the while wondering if I can ask this of Mila after I've made such a mess of everything in *this* country.

48

Stay

Mila

The next morning, after a torturous night of something that couldn't possibly be called sleep, I shower and head to the Center. To Alex. I know we need to talk, and surely we can work something out. I walk through the misty dawn into the barn, where I'm greeted by the low whinny of hungry horses. I go to the feed room, where I find Alex scooping grain into buckets for the horses.

"Hey."

"Hey."

We stare at each other, tension billowing between us until Alex stands up and wraps his arms around me. I sigh, folding into him, relieved to be close to him after the day—and night—we had yesterday.

"I love you, Alex." I pull back, looking up into his dark eyes that seem almost black in the dim feed room.

"And I love you, Mila Kozak." I smile when he uses my full name—something he knows I love—and press my head against his chest, listening to his steady heartbeat.

Outside the barn, Harley paws the ground in his stall, his hoof hitting the stall door so that it sounds like he's pounding on the door for his food.

"We better get them their breakfast," I say. But before we disentangle completely, I take his face in my hands and say, "We'll figure this out, Alex."

He nods, but I can see the doubt in his eyes, and it breaks my heart.

49

The Cockroach

Alex

Mila and I feed the horses and then sit on the tack trunk in front of Harley's stall. "All important decisions should take place on tack trunks," Mila says with a twinkle in her eye that I can't possibly emulate. With all of the bad news and lack of sleep within the past few days, I can barely muster being present.

"Have you made any important decisions on a tack trunk?" I ask, brow raised. To be honest, I want to hear her say that she decided she loved me on a tack trunk—where we spent the night talking before her first Grand Prix.

"Not yet," she says, and kisses me on the cheek before throwing her legs over my knees. "So, I spoke with Ann last night."

"You did?"

She nods, opening her mouth as if she's about to say something, and then she seems to think better of it and closes it.

"What did she say?"

"Well…" She clears her throat, something she does when she feels awkward about something. "My dad told her he's not paying for her to represent you anymore." She grimaces. "I'm so sorry, Alex."

I pat her leg, strangely trying to comfort her even though what she's telling me should wound me more than her. "It's alright. I was expecting that, especially after the arrest." I look down at the barn floor, wondering if I should tell Mila all about the arrest, which seems so small now in comparison to the deportation. I sigh, knowing there's probably no right answer. "Did Ann say anything else?"

Mila clears her throat again, and she's fixing her stare just over my shoulder. I can tell she doesn't want to say something. "She said we could find another attorney to request a stay of removal."

"How much will that be?"

"It doesn't matter, Alex. I'll cover it."

"I can't have you do that, Mila."

"Wouldn't you do that for me, if the situation were reversed?"

"Of course, but—"

"There's no *but*. Let me do this for you. For *us*." She finally looks at me, her hazel eyes shifting back and forth over my face, like she's trying to read me. And I wonder what it is that she's seeing. I'd really like to know. A bum? An *illegal*? A hopeless cause?

"I don't know..."

"Well, I *do* know. Just think of it as me being selfish. I want you to stay here with me forever, so this is what I'm going to do about it."

Something about her words hit me in a disconcerting way. Every part of me wants to get down on one knee right now and ask Mila to be my wife—not because it could save me from deportation, but because I love this girl. But this is not at all how I want Mila to agree to marry me. A girl like Mila should have someone steal the stars from the sky for her—and right now, that's just not something I'm capable of doing. Not when her ring is still in police custody, a fact that burns shamefully in the forefront of my mind. Not when I'm weeks away from being forcibly removed from this country.

I don't know how, but one day I'll find a way to be everything Mila deserves. Today is not that day, though.

I let Mila hire me a lawyer and put in a request for the stay of removal. I feel so low, like a cockroach scuttling over her shoe, but if it means that I get to stay close to Mila, I can humble myself for this. I busy myself with trying to help the Center in any way that I can—I install fans in each of the stalls, plant flowers along the walkway to the tranquility garden, and reach out to other equine therapy centers to see if they've got any advice for us. So far, I haven't heard anything useful yet—only hopeful wishes that it will resolve.

I'm struggling to sleep, which is atypical for me. I'm sitting up, scribbling proposal ideas on a piece of paper—I guess some part of me is still an optimist despite the disaster that is my current life—when there's a knock on the cottage door. I look at the clock. It's after ten, so I'm not sure who it could be if it's not Mila.

When I answer the door, it is most definitely not Mila. Mr. Kozak stares at me from the doorway.

"Oh," I say, unable to hide my surprise. "Good evening, Mr. Kozak." I always feel like I have to be oddly formal with Mila's dad.

"Hello, Mr. Caballero. Can I come in?"

"Yes, sir." I hold open the door, letting him pass through. I'm in an old t-shirt and pajama pants—exactly how I want to be when my boss and girlfriend's scary father comes over in the middle of the night. He heads to the kitchen table, where my list of proposal ideas is out in the open. I quickly grab the paper and fold it up, but when I meet his eyes, his sharp hazel eyes are glaring at me. "Would you like any water? Tea? Whiskey?"

He laughs mirthlessly. "Do you have whiskey?"

"Uh, no, sir." I grip the chair in front of me, hoping I don't fall over from sheer incompetency.

"Then why did you offer it to me?"

Because I'm an idiot? Heat flares through me. "I don't know, sir." I've never called someone *sir* so many times in my life. It's exhausting, but I know the moment I let up, I'm a goner.

"Sit down, Alex." His tone softens toward me, and I slump into the chair across from him. "You probably know why I'm here."

"I can't say that I do." I swallow. "Sir."

"I heard that Mila hired you another lawyer, quite apart from my wishes, and that they put in a request for a stay of removal."

"Yes, sir." I want to crawl under the table.

"I want to be very clear about something, Mr. Caballero."

"I'm listening."

"You are not to use my daughter to stay in this country." His words pound at me until I might as well be fine dust, blown away by the slightest breeze.

"I wouldn't, sir."

"If your stay of removal is denied, which it most certainly will be, you are not, under any circumstances, to propose to her. I will not give my approval. Do you understand?"

I nod, and just like that, I'm blown away. What is left of me? Mila—my heart, my life—might as well be gone for all that Mr. Kozak just said. Out of reach, tucked away under her father's wing. Because I know that Mila wouldn't ever want to go against his wishes. And I wouldn't want to be the splinter in their dynamic—family is too important to me, to us, for me to be the rift.

And then, he's gone. I almost don't realize it until my front door is shutting and he's no longer sitting in front of me. A man of few words, Mr. Kozak. Devastating ones at that. I sit at the table for a long time, wondering what I could have said, should have said. But nothing comes to me. How can I fight for something I don't think I should have? And, in my truest heart, I agree with him. I should never, ever use Mila for my own gain. But to leave her...I would die a thousand deaths to protect her, to give her everything she deserves. And I know that I'm good for Mila—*to* Mila—and there's something to be said for that. We make a good team—at least, we did. Before the Center fell apart and I ruined my chances at residency. We could've been everything. But this? Loving her, and then abandoning her without at least exploring the other options—it leaves a bitterness in my stomach that gnaws away at me through the night. Because right now, every time I think of Mila, I see her father too.

50

The Super Bowl of Cows

Anya

In the days after Alex's court date, there's a sense of unraveling that follows me everywhere I go. The Center is empty of clients since we still don't have insurance. Mila and Alex are shadows of their former selves, and no one knows what to say to make it right—least of all me.

To make matters worse, Luke is gone for two weeks at the National Western Stock Show in Colorado—what he called the "Super Bowl" of stock shows. The analogy immediately conjured an image of cows battling it out on a football field, though what they're *actually* doing at a stock show is beyond me.

He sends me pictures of the event each day—sadly, there are no cows in football helmets—along with the occasional rodeo GIF and a few songs that he thought I might like. He sends me a cover of "Fast Car" by Luke Combs, which is quite good but nowhere near the original, and I tell him as much, with as much sarcasm as I can muster, which isn't a lot these days.

Luke: *I found you a sad song since you seem to like those.*

I almost tell him that I never *liked* sad songs, I just listened to them because I was sad. But that feels like too much to reveal through a casual text message, so I just say, *Someone has to listen to the sad songs.*

I listen to half of the song he sends, "Something in the Orange," by Zach Bryan. I shut if off when he keeps singing about someone never coming home—which strikes too close to home with Luke out of town and Alex about to be deported. In response, I send him a Fail Gif of someone falling off a horse, face first into a mud puddle. He seems unfazed by my rejection of his sad song, sending me another, not-so-sad one immediately after.

Luke: *I thought this one would resonate with you.*

It's Kenny Chesney's "She Thinks My Tractor's Sexy." I'm glad Luke isn't here to listen to the barking laugh that comes out of me at the chorus of this absolutely ridiculous song.

They put this song on the RADIO??? I text.

Luke: *If you think I look good in my truck, imagine me on a tractor.*

He sends me a series of GIFs, the first of a shirtless hillbilly with a mullet waggling his eyebrows, and then another of a buff guy driving a tractor.

Luke: *Just imagine it.*

Me: *I'm actively trying not to.*

Later, Luke sends me a picture of him and Katie Jo with someone named Martha Josey. When I confess I don't know who she is, Luke is shocked.

Luke: *Magnificent Martha?? The Cowgirl Queen??*

Me: *No clue.*

People assume that if you know about one horse discipline, you know about them all. I know *a lot* about show jumping, but not a clue about horse racing or rodeo events or three-day eventing. When people find out that I'm a horse person, they usually ask me about the Kentucky Derby—but I don't even know when it takes place. Luke of all people should know this, even though he's giving me a hard time about not knowing who Martha Josey is.

Me: *Oh, so you know all about Beezie Madden? Laura Kraut? McLain Ward?*

Luke: *Touché, Miss Kozak.*

I appreciate how he's trying to stay connected with me while we're apart, but the distance seems to bring to the forefront all of my insecurities. Luke hasn't left me in any way like Dan did, but in the back of my mind I wonder if while he's there he'll realize that I'm not a good fit for him. All of those cowgirls in their brightly colored Wrangler jeans, walking around on two perfectly good legs, and he's going to choose *me*? I'm unsettled by the thought. The fact that Luke would choose me feels like trying to fit a square peg in a round hole.

Not to mention that we haven't quite addressed whatever this is—am I his girlfriend? Luke's been married, for crying out loud—a fact I'd very much like to forget. I'm not even sure what that means for this relationship. Will he find all the typical girlfriend-boyfriend stuff tedious? Redundant?

My phone buzzes with another text from Luke, and I shake my head, trying to get rid of all the insecurities swirling there. Luke hasn't given any indication that he's anything but all-in with me. And I know I need to trust him, but I'm still scared. If I had to put a percentage on it, I'm sixty percent invested, withholding a bit so I can maintain some semblance of dignity if things go sideways like they usually do for me.

With the time distance between us, I'm up later than normal one night talking with Luke when I hear a car door close in our driveway. I check our Ring video doorbell and see my dad coming in. It's well after midnight—much too late for *Tato* to be out. An uncomfortable feeling unfurls within me, a suspicion that things are not as they should be.

If my legs worked, I'd be down the stairs and confronting my dad in a heartbeat. But I can't put myself in my wheelchair—not *yet*—so I simply listen as *Tato* pours himself a drink and then trudges up the stairs.

I lay awake in my bed for far too long, my mind filled with all sorts of scenarios in which my father isn't home when he's supposed to be. And I wonder what I'm supposed to do about it.

51

Thin Ice

Alex

A week later, all of us have spent every moment at the Center calling every single insurance company we can find, without any success. Anya is so frustrated, she's making all of our lives miserable. Not that we needed any extra help in that department—our baseline is misery. I've been careful to avoid going to Mila's house—I can't afford any more run-ins with Mr. Kozak.

Despite how badly everything is going, Mila seems to maintain a quiet optimism that crushes me a little bit every time I notice it. I don't have the heart to tell her how unlikely it is that my stay of removal will get approved. She's unaware that I spend my nights applying for visas to Germany, France, Australia, and now the UK and Spain.

We're in the office searching for new insurance companies when Mila's phone rings. "It's Mr. Rodriguez," she says, referring to the attorney she hired to put in my stay of removal. I clench my teeth, readying myself for whatever news he's bearing. Mila puts him on speaker phone, and the sound reverberates through the room, settling into my chest.

I'm not even breathing when he says, "Mila, Alex, I'll be quick. The stay of removal was denied."

Denied. The word skips through me like a broken record. Denied, denied, denied.

I was expecting it, and yet it's still a blow. I can't even look at Mila because I know she's destroyed. I phase out as she speaks with the lawyer for a minute longer, asking him questions I don't have the capacity to hear the answers to. When she says goodbye and hangs up, I can feel her eyes heavy on me. We sit in silence, and I know she's waiting for me to say something.

It's then that I realize: no amount of hardships or tragedy will prepare you for the blow of disaster. Even when you're bracing for impact, it still hurts.

"What do you want me to do, Alex?" she asks, standing to come next to my desk. And I notice she doesn't say "what are we going to do" or "how can we fix this"—I would've had immediate answers for those questions: I don't know. We can't. But her question? I don't know how to answer it.

She's hovering in front of me, as if she's unsure whether to hug me or not. What do I want her to do?

Don't leave me.

Stay with me.

Follow me.

Marry me.

But the words don't come. They *can't* come. How could I start a life with Mila by undermining her dad? I wanted to be able to win him over—not that there's much chance of that now. I've already lost one dad in my life; I don't want to risk losing another.

I know I'm driving Mila crazy with my silence, but for the life of me I can't think of what to say. "I don't know, Mila."

"You can't think of *anything* we can do?" I'm not sure if I'm reading into it, but her words seem to carry a hint of accusation. Like I'm failing her, which...I am. I just don't know what the alternative is.

I hold up my hands. "I'm sorry." She looks at me for a long time, her expression holding both hope and frustration. What does she want me to do, drop down on my knee right here? Again, maybe I'm reading into it, but there's a discomfort stretching between us, crackling like ice about to break.

"Okay," she says finally, nodding in resolve. I go to reach out to her, but before I get to her, she turns and leaves. And just like that, the ice beneath us has cracked and I'm plunged into the cold.

52

Radical Acceptance?

Mila

I escape to Wellington, to Cyrus, to the only place I know that will calm my anxious mind. The barn is mostly empty—most of the horses are at the horse show this weekend, where I *should* be, but I can't seem to muster the energy to care. When I walk up to his stall, Cyrus gives me a snort like he's resentful of my listless behavior of late. "I'm sorry, buddy," I tell him as I come into the stall and stroke his head. He leans his face into me, a sign of his forgiveness, and I bury my face in his forelock.

I ride for a long time, losing myself in the technicalities of flatting Cyrus—pressing my heels into his sides as we do figure eights, leg yielding, and then flying lead changes. Each exercise forcing me to be fully present, my heels against his sides, my fingers gripping the reins, the tiniest changes in pressure telling him where to go and what to do.

Cyrus, who's gotten the short end of my stick lately, relishes the attention. By the end of our workout, he's lathered in sweat and happily lowers his head, snorting at the ground when I give him the reins, signaling the end of our exercises. I head down the driveway of Zen Elite, out onto the trails that skirt the farms surrounding us. We walk under the quintessential Florida oak trees with their Spanish moss, their shadows dappling the ground.

As we walk the trails, my mind goes back to Alex. Why he wouldn't just marry me to save himself. Why he's pushing me away when all I want is to be with him. The oppressive thoughts threaten to suffocate me. If he'd given me any sort of indication that he'd wanted me to go with him, I would've told him I applied for Cuban *and* Canadian visas last night. As it stands, I just look desperate. I wish I knew what Alex was really thinking.

I lean down, running my hand up and down Cyrus's mane, thinking about that day so many months ago when Alex and I went on a trail ride together on these exact trails. How I'd learned so much about him then—his battle after his dad's death, how he coped with tragedy and yet pushed himself to get through it. It was the first time I'd ever heard the term *radical acceptance*—an idea we discuss with our clients quite a bit. It makes me wonder if Alex is accepting his fate faster than he should, because he thinks that's the right thing.

Then I wonder if this is something I need to accept. What would that even look like? How can I accept that Alex is being deported, while also holding true to the fact that I know I'm supposed to be with him?

I just wish he would *let* me be with him.

53

Can't Sleep

Alex

I float through the next few days like I'm a ghost. And, if Mila's silence is any indication, maybe I am. She hasn't come in to the Center, won't answer my calls or texts. I'm waging a constant battle internally—I'll get the ring and just go propose to her right now. The next minute I realize how selfish I'm being, that I can't look to Mila to solve my deportation problem—it's not fair to her. I'm not willing to use Mila like that. I don't want her to think I would ever put my own happiness before hers.

I throw myself into cleaning and organizing the Center, adding to it in whatever way I can. If we have to sell the place, at least I'll make it the best it can be. Not that anyone is here to notice—even Luke hasn't been here for days. Maybe I *am* dead, and this is my purgatory.

I check my Canadian visa status hourly, sometimes more. I book myself a flight to Cuba, and then, because I have to hope for better, I pay for tickets to Canada, hoping and praying our visas will be approved by then. We can't travel to Canada without the visas approved—unless we want to be there illegally, which we do not. Or, at least I don't. I understand why my parents made the decisions they made, but I'm not going to follow in their footsteps. I search for barns in Canada and reach out to several of them, searching for a job. I even find a few equine-assisted therapy centers around Toronto that I email.

If the visas aren't approved before I have to leave, could I go to Cuba and my mom stay here? I could send her money—if that's even possible. I don't know what life would be like there. My only real memories are of the States.

My aunt and uncle—Tomás's parents—come down from Leesburg. They're picking up Tommy, who's been released on bail. I don't know them well—my uncle is my dad's half-brother, almost fifteen years younger than he was. But they offer to look out for my mom if I have to go back to Cuba. I nod and thank them, but a part of me goes empty at the idea of having no one to care for. No Mila, no mom, no horses. What purpose will I have? I throw myself into the barn's repairs.

During a lunch break, I check my email and find a response to one of my emails to another equine-assisted therapy center in Toronto. It's an automated response that says: *After ten years of serving the Greater Toronto community, we have had to close our doors. If you're looking for equine assisted therapy, we recommend Stable Life Therapy.*

I re-read the short email several times, fear rippling through me. Will we have to come up with an automated email like this? I can't help it; I Google the name of the Toronto center and click on an article about its closing. I scan it, discovering that the center had to close because of a lawsuit in which a teenage girl fell and suffered brain injuries, her parents suing for negligence. It's so eerily like our situation that I have to shut off my phone, putting it away in my desk. *Will this be us?* I keep wondering, and then remind myself: there is no *us* once I leave the States. Whether the Center falls or flourishes, I won't be here to see it. I force myself out of my seat and out into the breezeway, picking all of the horses' hooves until there's not even a speck of dirt in them.

Four days before my flight to Cuba, my mom comes into the barn while I'm fixing an automatic waterer in Don Juan's stall. "*Mi hijo,*" she says, her voice rasping. "Let's go get your ring," she tells me in Spanish. I want to correct her, to tell her it's not mine, but I can't muster the energy. I wash up and change into clean clothes and we drive to the police station.

At the front desk, I tell the officer that I have an item to pick up. He takes us down a hallway and points us to a clerk at another desk. I hand the clerk the property voucher the officer had given me when he refused to give me the ring back when I was released. "You need proof of ownership," the clerk says after glancing at the voucher. "Do you have that?"

My mom steps forward, a few faded pictures clutched in her hand. She shows the clerk the photos of her mother wearing the ring—one on her wedding day where she is seated in front of her husband, the ring displayed on her hand. The clerk stares at the picture for a moment, looks back at the property voucher, and then at my mom and me. "*Este eres tu?*" *Is this you?* He points at my grandmother.

"*No, es mi madre,*" my mom says.

"Ah, *si, si.*" He holds up a finger and says, "*Un momento por favor.*" And then he disappears into the locked room behind him. I watch the closed door nervously, shifting from foot to foot, until my mom takes my hand, patting it.

"*Estara bien*, Alex," she says over and over.

It seems to take the clerk an hour to come back, but when he does, he's holding a clear plastic box. Inside of it is the gray felt bag I'd been holding Mila's ring in. My chest tightens when I realize I've been thinking of it as Mila's ring, and I don't even know if I should.

I let my mom take the box from the clerk, though I want to be the first to grab the ring. She inspects it, nodding to the man and thanking him. "*Esta bien*," she says, handing me the ring. "*Muy bien.*"

I could weep with relief to have the ring back in my hand, and yet a hollowness fills me because I don't even know what to do with this ring. I hand it back to my mom. "It's yours," I tell her. And we leave.

I toss aimlessly in my bed, the image of the ring blazing in my mind's eye. How badly I want to get down on one knee and ask Mila to marry me. Not so I can stay in the States, but so that I can stay with Mila. Forever.

I check my phone—no texts or calls from her. I start to type something into the thread that recently has only filled with blue text bubbles from me. But then, there's a text bubble that indicates she's typing something. I freeze, afraid to breath or move or even allow my heart to beat in case it derails her from communicating with me. I wait an eternity for her to tell me: *Can't sleep.*

It's the best text I've ever received. I even smile. Almost laugh. Mila's talking to me. I want to respond in a thousand different ways: *I love you. I miss you. I don't want to leave you. Please don't leave me before I have to leave you.* A million pathetic thoughts flit through my mind until I type out: *What else is new?*

Mila: *I haven't slept for weeks.*

Me: *Me either.*

Me: *I miss you.*

Mila: *I miss you too.*

Me: *Will you let me come over? I have something for you.*

She seems to type out and then erase a few options, and eventually she says: *yes*.

I'm out of the door in the next breath, before quickly turning around and grabbing a few things to bring to Mila's. Then I'm speeding down the Center's driveway before Mila can change her mind. When I get to her house, she's standing outside in an oversized shirt and pajama shorts that make my heart beat a little too hard. When I get out of the car, I'm not sure what to expect, but she walks right into my arms and holds me like she'll never let me go.

The way Mila's curves melt into me, the scent of her floral shampoo, the thrumming of her heart against my own chest—it fills me and empties me at the same time. It builds me up and utterly dismantles me. How can I live, how can I breathe, if she's not with me? My mother's ring is burning a hole in my pocket, and my heart, and I'm one breath away from getting on my knee right here, right now.

We stay this way—holding each other, not speaking, hearts beating in tandem—for a minute, an hour, a lifetime. My hand finds its way to her hair, tangling in her light brown curls, pressing her gently into my chest. I want to memorize this moment, take it with me the rest of my life. That's when I realize my shirt is wet. Mila is crying. I lean back a fraction, tilting her head up toward me.

"Mila?"

"I'm sorry, I'm just..." she shakes her head, never finishing her sentence. And I get it. What is there to say?

I trace her cheek with my thumb, holding this image of her in my head: her eyes red with tears, her face splotchy from crying. I did this to her, and even though it'll take me some time, I'll fix it. "There is only you for me, Mila Kozak. No matter where I go, or who I meet, it's only you."

Doubt is heavy in her eyes as she looks up at me, and it devastates me. Does she doubt *me*, or herself? I won't ask her to wait for me—I won't do that to her—but I want her to know that this is not the end for me. "I—" she starts to say, but she's crying too hard, her words mangled by tears. I hold her, absorbing her tears and her pain, letting it all fall on my shoulders as it should. I hold her until my feet hurt and my hands are numb, and then I hold her some more. I begin to think we may stay this way until morning, and then I hear her father's gruff voice: "Milochka."

She startles away from me, like she's been woken from a dream. Her father's shadow rests on the doorway to their home, and they speak to each other in clipped Ukrainian. Mila turns back to me and whispers. "It's only you, Alex. I still choose you." She kisses me, light as silk, and then she's gone. I realize then that I never gave her the yogurt and smoothie I'd brought for her.

I leave feeling unsettled, wondering if it's more selfish of me to propose to Mila or to leave. If I had a visa to Canada, or anywhere other than Cuba, I might consider asking her to come with me. But I don't yet. So what should I do? It's this thought that keeps me awake until dawn, not ever coming to a conclusion.

54

Gray Hair

Anya

I'm still in my wheelchair, waiting for Mila to come back inside from her rendezvous with Alex, when I see my dad come downstairs and interrupt them. I thought he was asleep when Mila went out to see Alex, but it's as if *Tato* has a radar when it comes to Mila and Alex. I narrow my eyes at his back as he barks at Mila in his brusque Ukrainian.

Mila comes inside and I can't help but check her left hand—no ring. And the tears streaming down her face aren't happy ones. I'm a little mad at Alex for not proposing to Mila—he's running out of time—but as I watch *Tato* usher my sister inside, I wonder about how much my dad's influenced that. I'd be willing to bet a pretty penny that my dad has interfered in more ways than one when it comes to Mila and Alex. I wonder if he's part of the reason Alex hasn't proposed, even though that's the logical choice in this situation. What else would keep the two of them apart, if not for my brute of a father? I think of my dad's late-night venture a few nights ago, just after Mila declared that she'd hired another lawyer to help Alex. I have no way of proving it, other than a daughter's intuition, but I wonder if *Tato* went to talk with Alex. Did he threaten him? Refuse to give his support if he proposed? I wouldn't put it past my dad.

I wait in the shadows as Mila stomps up the stairs and my dad watches her go with a sigh and a hand through his rapidly graying hair. How many of those grays are due to the two of us these past few years?

"*Tato?*"

My dad startles, not realizing I was in the room. "Anochka."

"He didn't propose, did he?"

"He's not going to," my dad says definitively.

"Is that what he wants?" I arch a brow. "Or what you want?"

"All that matters is Mila," he gruffs.

"Yes, but what does *she* want?"

"A parent's responsibility is to look beyond what your child wants and see what they *need*."

I roll closer to my father, seeing the dark circles under his hazel eyes. "That may have worked when we were toddlers, *Tato*. But Mila is an adult, and she knows better than you what she really needs."

I stare him down, wishing I were able to stand so I could go toe-to-toe with him. He clenches his jaw, and I see the muscle in his cheek twitch. When he doesn't say anything, I tell him, "Maybe if you'd gotten out of the way, Mila wouldn't be crying herself to sleep every night." My words find my dad's weak spot, and he looks away. I turn my wheelchair and head up the stairs, wondering how much damage control I need to do to undo whatever my dad has done to keep Mila and Alex apart.

55

Face This

Mila

"I don't know if I can handle this," I say to Anya when we get out of the car at Alex's going away party. I'm not sure I understand the point of this—a celebration marking the last day of Alex's life in the States. "I just don't see how this ends in anything but sadness."

Anya stops her wheelchair and turns it toward me. "*Sestra.*" She levels me with her gaze. "We've had enough of avoiding sadness and pretending it's not there. Let's just face it head on. Maybe that's our first step in coping better with this tragic life we've got."

I pause, taking in what she said. "Dang, girl, that was profound."

Anya sniffs haughtily. "I've always been profound, Mila."

"I know, but that's a new level, even for you."

I'm making light of it, because that's all I can do right now if I'm not going to break down, but Anya's right. I need to face this.

We keep walking toward the party; I'm tottering on my heels as Anya rolls along beside me as my moral support and, apparently, sadness guru. She convinced me somehow to wear one of her old dresses—a tiny red number that I'm pulling down as I walk. I look at her in mock frustration. "'Give him something to miss,' you said. 'He deserves to see you look good one more time,' you said. Ugh."

The moment we enter the room, my stomach starts wobbling with nerves. I search out Alex while simultaneously wanting to avoid him. I know I'd said I'd face this, but it's a lot harder than I thought it would be. I spot Mrs. Caballero, some of our barn mates from Zen, and a handful of volunteers from the Center. I'm surprised that there are so many people here—Alex is a pretty quiet, painstakingly private person. But he clearly has captured a lot of hearts, including mine.

That's when I see him, across the room, on the other side of the makeshift dance floor in the center of the party. The second our eyes lock, my legs start to shake. I walk slowly, on quivering limbs, toward him. He makes his way closer to me, his eyes ablaze with so much emotion it's hard to sort it out in my mind right now. Because all I see, all I feel, all I can calculate, is Alex. Alex, Alex, Alex. He fills my mind, my sight, my whole self. It seems to take an eternity for us to reach one another, but when we do, we both stop about a foot away from each other.

"Hey."

"Hi." I'm breathless, and I don't know why. I want to reach out, to hold him, to never let him go. But also, *why did I come*? Being here is just too painful.

But then I remember Anya's words. I will face this. For my sake, and Alex's. He deserves that much from me.

"I'm glad you're here," Alex says, as if he doubted I would come.

Several options of how to respond flit through my mind: *Anya made me. I didn't want to come. I'm sorry you thought I wouldn't be here for you.* But I land on, "I don't want to say goodbye to you. It's too hard."

This breaks the tension between us, and Alex bridges the gap, putting his arms around my waist and tugging me into him. I've shared a thousand hugs with Alex, but none like this. I'm so keenly aware of him, of all his edges and boundaries, all that makes him *him*. It's like my body and my mind are holding on to this knowledge, memorizing it, so that I can come back to it again and again when he's not here.

He tangles his hand in my hair, breathing me in, and I know he's doing the same thing I am. Capturing every moment of this in his memory.

I can't stand it. I don't want to let go of him—right now, or ever.

Eventually, Alex's aunt comes up to us, saying a little too loudly, "*Hora de comer,*" and we're forced apart. But Alex doesn't let go completely; he holds on to my hand like it's his lifeline and walks me over to a table where his mom is sitting. When I see her, I realize she's been watching us because her eyes are glassy and she's gripping a tissue in her hand. I bend down to give her a kiss on her cheek, and Alex doesn't let go of my hand the whole time.

We eat a meal catered by Alex's aunt and his mom. The meal consists of empanadas, Alex's favorite dish of *Vaca Frita* (very tender shredded beef tasting of garlic and lime), rice and beans, tostones, and of course, his mom's famous guava cheesecake. This time, his aunt and mom made mini versions of the cheesecake so everyone could have an individual serving.

After dinner, Alex's mom makes a tearful speech in Spanish that his uncle translates into English. I have a hard time sitting through the speech—I want to run, to go to the bathroom and cry, or simply fade away. But I breathe through the pain, accepting its reality and letting it pass in and through me. It's awful.

Then someone turns on music and a few people take to the dance floor. I glance over at Alex to see if he wants to dance but he beats me to it. "You want to go out there?"

"Honestly, not yet."

He squeezes my leg. "Me either." It kind of feels like both of us are having a hard time mustering the emotional energy to dance. It doesn't feel like a dancing occasion.

56

Pathetic

Anya

I'm watching the misery that is Alex's going away party, fiddling with my phone, waiting for a text back from Luke. I texted him hours ago, and I haven't heard a single peep. He still has a few more days left in Colorado, and I'm beginning to think I'm too fragile to withstand the distance much longer. And the thought makes me feel so pathetic. *Luke is a good guy*, I remind myself. *If he hasn't texted you back, there's a good reason for it.* I repeat this in my head several times, but the message isn't getting through to my heart, unfortunately.

When people take to the tiny dance floor after Alex's mom's tearful speech, I'm tempted to hide in the bathroom. Just because Mila needs to face this doesn't mean I have to. Right?

I check my texts once more, then turn my phone off and back on to make sure there's not some weird reason I haven't gotten a text from Luke. Still nothing.

Pathetic, a voice seethes in my brain.

I tuck my phone away and then roll to the bathroom, where I stare at my reflection and fix my makeup needlessly. I can't even use the toilet by myself, so being here is pointless. It's just an escape.

When my phone buzzes, my heart leaps pitifully in my chest. I take a deep breath and force myself to wait several beats before I grab it.

When Luke's name appears on my screen, I scramble to open the text.

Luke: *Where are you?*

The hope that sprouts in my chest is so heady that I can't breathe. Why would Luke ask where I am? Unless...

I turn my wheelchair to the door and try to open it, but it's the heaviest door in the history of doors. Getting inside the bathroom, I'd simply backed my wheelchair in, opening the door with my chair. But since the door opens inward, I have to manually open it to get out. I'm pulling on it, groaning and grunting, but I can only get it open so far.

Tears sprout in the corners of my eyes when I realize this stupid door is going to defeat me. How pitiful am I that I can't even open a door? A *door* is going to keep me from getting to Luke.

No, it's not.

I take another breath, rubbing my hands together. An idea pops in my mind like a glorious bud blossoming. I hold on to the door handle and then back up my wheelchair, using the chair as the catalyst for the door opening instead of my feeble muscles. Once it's open, it takes a few attempts to get through the doorway—and I may or may not leave tire marks on the outside of the door—but I'm finally out.

I scour the room, and it only takes me a moment to find the cowboy hat bobbing in the crowd. Luke catches my eye, and the most dazzling smile spreads across his handsome face.

We wheel toward each other, and I try to compose myself even as my emotions are rioting through me. *Luke is here*. I'm relieved, and somehow scared.

Why is it that I can imagine Luke rejecting or abandoning me—and that's scary—but the idea that Luke might make me his whole world is even more terrifying? Because the way Luke is looking at me right now is alarmingly close to that most frightening L-word.

"Fancy seein' you here," Luke says, and the brush of his knees against mine brings tears to my eyes. How can you miss another person's *knees*? It's just not natural, and yet I've desperately missed Luke's knees boxing mine in.

"You're here," I breathe.

"A thousand cows in football helmets couldn't keep me away a day longer."

A teary laugh bubbles out of me as Luke locks my wheelchair and pulls me into his lap. "Besides, I couldn't let anyone else dance with my girl, could I?"

My girl. I like that a little too much. So much so that the forty percent of my heart that I was holding back slips just a little bit more. I'm at about thirty percent now. Maybe twenty-five. I lean back and look into his bright blue eyes, getting lost there. Staring into his eyes is like drifting along a Caribbean Sea—calm and free. Safe. I wrap my arms around Luke's neck and snuggle against him, breathing in his scent that could never be bottled.

This is the part where I should make some sort of sarcastic comment or witty repartee, but all that comes out of me is, "I'm happy you're here."

Luke chuckles, the vibrations of his chest seeping into mine. "Me too, darlin'."

57

Don't Go Yet

Mila

People filter by our table, slapping Alex's back and giving him hugs. "Gonna miss you, man," Ryan from Zen says. People ask where he's going, and he tells them for now he's heading to Cuba, but he hopes his Canadian visa is approved soon.

"Do you want me to take you to the airport?" I ask, and I don't know what I want him to say. Part of me wants to soak up all of this time with Alex, and part of me wants to do what I do best—bury my head in the sand. Pretend like this isn't happening.

"My aunt's going to take us," he says. "She's taking my car once I'm gone."

His words cut through me. *Once I'm gone.* Alex and I look away from each other, and I choke down a sob that's been building ever since I got here. A few more people come to say bye to Alex, including Trina. She hugs us both tightly, and even she has tears in her eyes, which makes it that much harder for me not to run out of here sobbing. She tells him that she's reached out to a few horse friends in Canada who would love to have him at their barn. "I wish I could've done more," she says in a strangled voice.

Alex takes her shoulders and says, "You've done everything, Trina. More than I ever deserved." And there's that word again: *deserve.* What is with that word and Alex lately? It makes me cringe. Alex *deserves* the world. And this is what he gets instead.

After Trina, a few other people from Halliday, the barn Alex worked at before Zen, come to say goodbye.

"You always had treats for Lokey," one girl from Halliday tells him. She's cute and batting her stubby eyelashes at him even though I'm right here.

"He has treats for every horse," I say, draping myself across Alex's shoulder. "It's an equal opportunity thing for the horses." She's appropriately miffed by this and gives Alex an awkward goodbye and walks away. "I think I'm ready to dance," I say, though I'm not so much ready to dance as I am ready to stop hearing people say bye to Alex. There's a salsa song playing and I let Alex take the lead, guiding me through the steps as he pulls me closer. Our foreheads touch as our feet fall into rhythm with each other. He holds one of my hands in his, the other is around my waist, and it feels like he'll never let go of me. And I hope he never will.

I try to lose myself in the dance, the music, the people around us, and more than that, the person in front of me. Alex is everything. He fills me up, he makes me *me*, he loves me more than any person could.

Another song comes on and I'm not totally sure how to dance to this one, but Alex seems to know, and I follow his lead. And something about this makes me realize that this is how things are with Alex and me—so often, I don't know what to do, where to go. And Alex knows how to lead me. Not that he tells me what to do—ever. But it's as if he knows how to guide me to become the fullest version of myself. Who will I be if he's not there to do that for me anymore?

There's something so melancholy about this song. It tugs at my heart as the bass rattles through my chest. My hands roam up Alex's waist to his chest, where I feel his heart beating against my palm. This heart will still exist in Cuba. And as long as his heart is beating, we will still exist—somehow, someway.

The next song is a Camila Cabello song called "Don't Go Yet." Camila has a special place in my heart—dancing to her song "Senorita" is the first time I really accepted that I had feelings for Alex. I couldn't deny the electricity between us anymore.

When Camila starts singing about just a little more time—*Don't go yet*—Alex's eyes connect with mine, and I'm locked into his gaze. His hands are like fire on my hips as Camila repeats the chorus line over and over. It's like the beating of my heart, the movement of my feet. *Don't go yet.*

Alex reaches a hand into my hair; his lips meet mine as the music moves through us. It's the saddest kiss I've ever had, and it takes me a moment to realize the wetness on my face are tears—his or mine, I'm not sure. Maybe both. We sway in the middle of the dance floor, tears mingling with our kiss, as our friends and family dance around us, and I can't believe it. I'm saying goodbye to Alex. *Alex.* The man who was my rock during the hardest time of my life, who got me to face my fears, who stole my heart even as I grieved Anya and Michael. And now I'm saying goodbye.

Don't go yet.

Panic clutches at my chest as I realize—really realize—Alex is leaving. Tomorrow. For *years*. And he hasn't asked me to come with him, or to marry him. Alex knows that getting married to me would potentially solve all of his problems, and yet he prefers deportation to that? What is wrong with him? Or, better yet, what is wrong with *me* that he doesn't want to marry me?

I shake my head as tears prick my eyes again. I don't get it; I don't get it at all. I know Alex loves me. He's made plenty of allusions to wanting to spend the rest of his life with me. Why not marry me to save himself? To save *us*?

The only explanation I can come up with is that Alex is having doubts about me—yes, he loves me, but maybe that's just not enough. Or maybe he's fallen out of love with me? Though this dance, the way he's holding me, it *can't* be that.

Could Alex really not love me anymore? The idea is preposterous, and yet, here we are. He'd rather get deported than marry me.

The realization hits me like a bullet through the heart, and I'm bleeding out from the heartache of it. I want to yell at him, *Why don't you love me enough? Why am I not enough for you?* For *anyone*? I want to shake him, to rattle his brain until he can't see straight anymore. I want to kiss him and hold him and never let him go. I want to cling to him until someone has to pry my hands away from him.

I pull away, gasping for air, my hands on his chest. "I can't," I manage to get out. "I gotta go."

And before he can stop me, I turn and run.

Because as much as I want to do what Anya said, I can't face this.

So I run like the coward that I am.

58

New Person Mojo

Anya

I'm sitting in my room the day of Alex's departure, thinking about the injustice of this whole situation—the Center getting demolished by one fall that was outside of our control, how everything ended up with Tommy and its effects on Alex, and of course Alex's situation. Why? Alex didn't deserve all of this. He's a genuinely good guy, and my heart aches for him and Mila. I put some music on while I aimlessly style my hair in the bathroom. I have some difficulty reaching my arms up and back—my upper back muscles aren't a hundred percent—so I have to pick hairstyles where I don't have to do that. I try this elaborate fishtail-type braid that I saw on TikTok. Selena Gomez's song "Calm Down" comes on, and there's something melancholy and bittersweet about the song that speaks to me right now. It strikes me then that this is what I do when faced with a hardship—I hide. I did that with my accident—pretending to be asleep when friends came to visit, refusing to go to PT or allowing my mom to do the passive range of motion exercises on me. I just would prefer to check out and act like it didn't happen. Which isn't exactly easy to do when the thing you're trying to avoid has literally taken over your body. But I did it. I checked out for a full year until I had a pulmonary embolism and was forced to change my ways. Even then, my repentance was reluctant at best. The Center gave me something to live for—as long as I was doing it for other people, and not myself.

It was time to do something for me. To fight for *me*.

I start by doing something small but tangible—I grab the TENS unit Katie Jo gave me and put it on my shoulders where I'm sore from trying to open the bathroom door yesterday. I stare at my reflection, my cold blue eyes hardened by the past few years. I almost don't recognize myself. And it devastates me.

How do I undo this person I've become? I start by unraveling the braid, letting my straight hair fall around my shoulders. I want to be able to reach the back of my head—I know, it's such a tiny thing. But if really working hard at PT will make that a possibility, isn't it worth the potential devastation if it doesn't work? Even the thought of having such a hope makes my hands feel shaky as I reach backward toward my crown. I can't reach—my arms just sort of hover around my ears, but that doesn't mean I won't ever be able to reach.

Tears mist my eyes as I think about how much I've held myself back. I think about Luke, how he throws himself into whatever is in front of him. And I realize how much I need him in my life—no, how much I *want* him in my life. To bring out those parts of me that I've kept hidden away for fear of hope. His surprise arrival last night made that abundantly clear, and that scares me like nothing else ever has.

I fold my head into my hands and let the tears collect in my palms. I'm wallowing again, by myself. And that's when I decide: this is the last time.

I'm sitting here, mourning all of our losses, and I keep coming back to this fact: I want to be with Luke. Even though needing him terrifies me, I want him here, right now, while I mope and cry and feel sorry for all of us. At my lowest of lows, I want someone to be with me. And not just anyone: *him*. Is this what Mila had been telling me? It's not that I *need* someone to pick up the pieces—I want him. He doesn't have to fix me—I don't even think this could be fixed—but I could open my grieving heart to let him in. One hundred percent. It's not something that will happen by accident. I have to *choose* to give Luke all of my heart.

So I do.

I pick up my phone and dial. "Hey."

"Anya?"

"Can you pick me up?"

As I get ready for Luke to come get me, with all my new-person mojo, an idea occurs to me. I wheel slowly to Mila's room and hear her in the shower. I sneak in, searching for something. I check her bookshelf, her desk, and then finally find it in her bedside stand.

I'm so occupied with my searching that I don't hear the shower cut off. Mila comes out of the bathroom in her towel and says, "Uh, you need something, *sestra*?"

My back is facing her, and I pray she doesn't see what I'm holding. I lift my leg with one of my hands and tuck the item underneath, shoving it under both thighs until it's hidden. "I was looking for lip balm," I lie. I rotate my wheelchair so I can see her face and see what she saw. She's frowning, but she doesn't look upset with me. Just confused. "Luke is coming over and, uh, my lips are chapped."

Mila laughs, a too-big smile spread across her face, and she heads back into the bathroom to grab lip balm. "Heaven forbid the guy kiss you when you have chapped lips."

"Hey, I have enough working against me," I say. The moment I say it, Mila's demeanor changes.

She drops to her knees in front of me, hand still holding her towel in place. She looks up at me, her eyes serious, almost scolding when she says, "Don't say that, Anya."

I lean forward as far as my straps will let me go, trying to hide the stolen item.

"You have so much to offer. Anyone would be lucky to have you." She puts a hand on my wheelchair. "I know you think this makes you somehow less valuable as a person, but this has also shaped you. It's made you who you are today, and that's a beautiful thing."

I press my lips together and nod. Maybe she's right. Maybe it's a lesson I need to learn, but right now I'm just too focused on what I'm hiding from her. "Thanks, *sestra*."

She sighs, as if she's considering whether to say more, and I quickly add, "Luke will be here soon, so I better get going."

She inclines her head, and I hold my breath, afraid she's going to see it, but she stands up and goes back to the bathroom. "Don't have too much fun," she calls. I breathe a sigh of relief and go downstairs to wait for Luke.

When you're a paraplegic in a wheelchair, getting picked up by a guy who's also a paraplegic in a wheelchair is not as simple as "pick me up" sounds. But Luke is more prepared this time, with the passenger seat removed so I can lock my wheelchair in place there. It still takes a good ten minutes for Luke to get out, me to get in, and then Luke to ramp back up. "Where're we off to?" Luke says with a grin that makes me so glad I called him.

"To the Center."

He quirks an eyebrow at me but doesn't argue as he backs out of my driveway. Once we're on the road, he hands me his phone to play music, and I see that the top playlist on Spotify says, "For Anya." My fingers pause, hovering over the screen. It strikes me that as cool and calm as Luke is, he likes me. A lot, if this is any indication. I imagine him lying in bed, picking out songs on his phone, a smile on his face as he thinks about what snarky comments I'll give him about his beloved country music. I open the playlist and see that the very first song is the song we danced to at the Christmas party, "More Than Friends" by Mad3 for M3. I have to blink back tears—honestly, it's a relief to think that that moment meant as much to him as this seems to suggest. The next song is Keith Urban's "You Look Good in My Shirt," and I have to laugh. I don't recognize the third song, a band called Parmalee's "Girl in Mine," so I click it.

"Ah," Luke says. "You found it."

I wish we weren't in wheelchairs for a moment so I could kiss him. Or at least hold his hand over a middle console—but Luke's truck doesn't have a middle console so his wheelchair can fit, and he needs both hands to drive. As Matt Thomas of Parmalee sings about a girl filling his mind, wearing his shirt and sitting in his ride, Luke glances over at me and winks. And since I can't kiss him or hold his hand, I do something I've literally never done to another human being: I blow him a kiss. And the smile that overtakes his face in response is worth all of my dignity.

When in the world did I get to be so cheesy? But I love it.

For some reason, this compels me to do something even crazier (for me). "I have a song for you too," I tell him, searching in his phone. "I'll warn you now: it's a country song."

Luke gasps. "A country song made you think of *me*?" he mocks.

"What's even more shocking is that I was listening to it voluntarily, and not in your presence."

"That is shocking," he says with a chuckle. "I'm anxious to hear what song was worthy of all that."

I grip the phone, not yet ready to play the song and expose myself completely to Luke. But then I look over at him. We're stopped at a red light, and his blue eyes are dancing playfully, and I know I can fall for him. That I *have* fallen for him. I press the play button and the first notes of Ingrid Andress's song "Feel Like This" comes through the speakers.

As soon as she starts singing about her ex's manipulation and toxicity, the tears come. And I don't try to stop them. We're on the second verse when Luke pulls into a Walmart parking lot and stops the truck. He unlocks his wheelchair and maneuvers it over to mine. "What are you doing?" I ask.

"I have to kiss you."

My face is tear-stained and I'm sure it's red and puffy, but it doesn't stop Luke from taking off my seatbelt and pulling me out of my wheelchair into his lap. This is becoming my favorite place to be.

His thumbs go to my cheeks, wiping my tears. Then he draws my face to his, pressing soft kisses onto my cheek, the tip of my nose, inching closer to my mouth until it hurts that he hasn't connected with my lips yet. Finally, finally, he kisses me, and he does taste of security, and stability, and something akin to magic.

"I have a lot of questions about whatever happened with whatever jerk that song reminds you of," he says in a low voice, "but you don't have to tell me anything you don't want to."

I want to tell you everything, my heart says. And then my lips say it too.

We sit like that, in the Walmart parking lot of all places, for a long time, and I tell him everything about Dan. I'd told Mila a little bit about our relationship a few weeks ago, but I've never really told anyone the whole story. And Luke just listens. A part of me is afraid he's going to pull the therapist card on me, but he just lets me talk. To get it all out. I tell him about the time I caught him in a bar with another girl, and he somehow flipped it around on me like it was my fault. How he made a huge scene at the bar, yelling at me for being too pathetic to stay faithful to.

"One time, I was in the library, meeting with some classmates for a group project. Once we were done with our meeting, everyone got up to leave except this one guy. He was asking me questions about another class we were in together, but it was totally benign. Not even flirting. But when Dan randomly showed up—he tracked me on Find My Friends—he made a really big deal about it. Told the guy off for flirting with his girlfriend, totally belittled me in front of everyone there. It was terrible. It's like he loved doing that—making me seem small. Especially in front of other people, he sought out ways to make me look like an idiot. And I-I just let him do it." My eyes fill with tears again as I think of how weak-willed I was to let this guy walk all over me. "The ridiculous thing is, after my accident, I would daydream about him showing up. That somehow my accident would fix things between us, like he would finally love me unconditionally." I shake my head at how pitiful that was. "I can't believe he was the first guy—the only guy, really—that I fell in love with."

Luke runs his fingers down my hair, smoothing it over my shoulder. "Anya," he says gently. "That's not love. That's a prison."

I nod, trying to hold back the sobs that want to push through.

"You can let go now," he says, and I do. I finally let go—I let go of the tears, but more than that, I let go of the awful memories of Dan, and the shame that kept me tied to him. I let go so that I can really embrace myself—the Anya without Dan haunting her—and the man in front of me—the one who values me, who believes in me, and who makes me feel safe.

When I'm done, Luke kisses away all of my tears, and I lose myself in him.

When we finally get to the Center, my heart drops when I find Alex loading up his car. "Just give me a few minutes to talk with him," I tell Luke.

"Take your time, darlin'," he says, and I smile.

Alex straightens up when he sees me, glancing toward Luke's truck to see if Mila's coming out. "She's not here," I tell him. "I'm sorry. It's in the Kozak blood, we don't say goodbye."

He shrugs, but I can tell he's bothered. "What's your plan, Alex?" I shield my eyes from the sun so I can get a good look at him. He's obviously trying hard to be strong through this, but the guy clearly has the weight of the universe on his shoulders.

"I just need to get my life together, one that's worthy of Mila, and then we can make it work..." He trails off, and I get the sense that he's thinking, *if she's still around.*

"What are we, in the 1800s? News flash, Alex: you don't need to have three hundred heads of sheep to marry Mila. You just need to be a good guy. Besides, Mila is a grown woman with a master's degree and all the gumption in the world. *She* can take care of *you.*"

"I don't want her to have to take care of me," Alex grumbles.

I sigh, reaching out to grab Alex's hand. "It goes both ways, my friend. You take care of each other."

Alex nods, a distant look in his eyes. "I really only saw it go one way with my parents, to be honest." He glances over at his mom and then back at me. "He took care of her so much it's like she didn't know how to survive without him. In a way, she still doesn't."

I sit quietly, waiting to see if he has anything else to add, but he doesn't continue. I'm sure he's lost in thoughts about his dad and his parents' dynamic, whether it was right or wrong. I squeeze his hand to let him know I'm still here and say, "I have something I want you to look at." I grab the item I'd stolen from Mila's room out of my wheelchair pocket. "Mila might hate me forever for handing this over to you, but if it helps you guys work it out, it'll be worth it."

Alex takes it slowly, recognition rippling across his features as he runs a hand over the smooth leather. "The journal I gave her," he says, more to himself than to me. He holds it like it's sacred, and maybe it is.

His mom comes out of the cottage with her bags and speaks to him in Spanish.

"I gotta go," he says. I reach my arms out for a hug, and he bends down to accept. Then he turns away, saying, "*Viene, Mama*?"

"*Si, un momento*," his mom says, holding up a finger.

"I'll get your bags in the car," Alex says, and steps away.

Mrs. Caballero rummages in her purse and pulls out a mailing envelope. She leans down, pressing it into my hands and says in her strong accent, "This is for Mila."

I nod, and somehow I know that whatever is in this envelope might be Mrs. Caballero's offering toward the continuance of their relationship, parallel to my journal offering. I hold it against my chest. "*Entiende*," I tell her.

"*Gracias*." She leans down and kisses my cheek, saying goodbye. And then they're both in the car, rolling down the driveway of the Center. The image burns in my mind and my heart—is this the last time Alex is here? Is this the end of our trio? Our Center quartet, if you include Luke. I can't help it; another tear trickles down my cheek. "Turning into a softie," I grumble to myself.

I call Luke to swing around and pick me up, staring at the package. It's addressed to Mila, with stamps on it already. I bet Mrs. Caballero was going to post it at the airport. I feel a crush of camaraderie with her—we're fighting for Mila and Alex, even though we have no idea how it's all going to work out.

Giving Alex the journal was a crazy gamble—I don't know what's written in it except her original plans for the Center. At the very least, it'll hopefully remind Alex of what he helped her build—even if it was destroyed by Clara's fall. But I'd be willing to bet a good chunk of my inheritance that there's quite a bit written in there about Alex. Things that will make him fall back into Mila's arms.

59

Low-Key Shook

Mila

My best friend, Monica, who's in town for her brother's graduation, abducts me the moment I'm out of the shower. After a long hug with entirely too much squealing, she says, "Come, chica, we're getting our nails done." I mope all the way to her mom's car, which she's borrowing while she visits from New York. Monica was already the height of style, but going to New York has only made her that much more trendy. She's wearing a corset top under a sheer blouse with metallic cargo pants and talon-like nails that look like they could spear my eyes out. I would never, ever in a zillion years think to put all of those things together, but it works for her. I'm certain if I wore her outfit, I'd look like a toddler who got caught playing dress up in my mom's closet, but to each her own, right?

"Why do you even need your nails done, Monica? They look perfectly done to me."

"A good manicure is the only cure-all I know that doesn't add fifteen pounds to your rear." She waves a claw at me, like I should know this already. Which, having lived with Monica for four years, I should. "Now, spill the tea. And I mean *everything*. I'll know if you leave anything out."

I sigh, rubbing my eyes with my fingertips. I don't want to talk about Alex, don't want to tell her about the Center, but she is supposed to be my best friend. She should know what I'm going through. "I'm going to need a coffee for this," I tell her. "And a pastry."

Monica winks at me and shimmies her shoulders, doing what we call the guava dance. "Guayaba, guayaba, guayaba," she chants melodically, and I can't help but laugh.

"I've missed you, Mon."

"Obvi."

Getting a mani/pedi and gorging myself on at least fifteen pounds' worth of guava pastries doesn't make me feel better, but at least I'm not alone. Being here with Monica reminds me of all that I learned last year when I first got together with Alex. I was so devastated by Anya's accident that I was alone, even when I was surrounded by others. But I learned, through Alex, and through time spent healing, that I had to open up, to let people in. And so that's why I *spill the tea* with Monica. I expect her to jump down my throat with a hundred different solutions, but she just listens. She cries with me and hugs me. And even though a part of my heart is being ripped out of my chest and flying off to Cuba today, I'm grateful. Grateful for the lessons I've learned, for the person I've become because of Alex.

When we get back to my house, Luke and Anya are there. They're waiting in the front foyer, wheelchairs as close as two wheelchairs can get to each other, an envelope in Anya's lap. "I have something for you," she says, the moment I walk through the door. "It's time sensitive."

I take the envelope. "Who is this from?" I'm not sure what I'm hoping for—good news from a lawyer? The government? I don't even know what time sensitive thing could be in an envelope that would actually help me right now.

"Mrs. Caballero."

I frown at Anya, trying to understand. She flaps her hands at me. "Open it already!"

I rip it open, sticking my hand down to the bottom, and pull out a red box with faded gold edges. My heart is pounding, like it's already figured it out, even though my brain is three steps behind. I open the box, hinges squeaking, and gasp.

"*Ay dios mio,*" Monica says in hushed tones over my shoulder.

"What is it?" Anya and Luke say at the same time. But I'm not done staring at it: the most beautiful engagement ring I've ever seen. It's a pear-shaped golden diamond with a halo of smaller diamonds surrounding the center stone. Filigree embellishments flow down the side of the gold ring. My mouth is dry, and for a second, I almost take it out of the box to put it on. But I quickly shake my head, telling myself I'm not wearing this ring unless Alex puts it on me.

Anya is across from me, huffing and puffing until I show her what it is. I flip the box around, and she gasps, wide-eyed. She snatches the jewelry box from my hand, eyeing it like she's an expert jeweler.

"Anything else in there?" Luke drawls.

"What? The antique ring worth more than all of your organs on the Cuban black market isn't enough?" Monica teases. "By the way, I'm Monica." She reaches out a hand to shake Luke's.

I put a tentative hand into the envelope, not wishing for more, and yet, wanting more. Mrs. Caballero sending me this ring isn't necessarily proof that Alex wants me to wear it. But there's nothing else in the envelope. Disappointed, I hold it upside down and shake it. A piece of paper flutters to the ground. Monica and Anya gasp like another ring just fell out, but I'm assuming it's simply a note from Mrs. Caballero with some sort of explanation. Instead, it's in Alex's scrawl.

Go back to Maxwell's? Hire Cat & Alex to serenade. Write a song.

Scavenger hunt around WEF?

***Fly in Monica*

Sky writing at beach? Too cheesy? Or message in bottle hidden in the sand?

Horse drawn carriage? Teach Cyrus??

A few are scratched out like:

Ring in guava cheesecake?

Write 'marry me' on Cyrus?

I barely hear Monica, Anya, and Luke discussing around me. I walk to the loveseat in the foyer and sit heavily, handing the note to Anya. She scans it quickly, her jaw dropping the farther she gets. "When was he going to do this?" she asks.

"Obviously not now," I say moodily, glancing at the time on my phone. His flight leaves in two hours. He's already at the airport, I'm sure.

"Maybe he was planning to propose if he won the case?" Anya surmises.

"Hold up," Monica says, her taloned hand extended in front of her. "So he was gonna propose if he won, and he's not because he lost? That doesn't make much sense."

"It's not quite that simple." Anya groans, pinching the bridge of her nose with her fingers. She's never had much tolerance for Monica, and it almost makes me laugh. "He's just got this twisted logic, like he needs to have his life together for Mila. Like it's got to be a certain way so he's somehow deserving of her. I don't know. Luke, therapize him, please."

"Wait, how do you know this?" I ask.

"I talked to him this morning."

"And that's what he told you? He wants to marry me?"

"Well, yes, but it has to be perfect because you're perfect or something." She rolls her eyes, holding up air quotes around the word *perfect*.

"Óyeme, I need to have a talk with this Alex guy. He thinks he can simp on you, but you can't simp on him? That's not what marriage is about. I'm low-key shook right now because you and Alex are goals. Just 'cause your ring is drip don't mean your ship ain't sus, you know what I mean?"

"No," Anya says. "I actually didn't understand a single thing you just said."

Monica closes her eyes and sighs. "What I'm trying to say is that this is what is leading modern marriages to the brink of disaster. We build this idea in our minds of what it's all supposed to be like, and it never lives up to that, and we're disappointed. If the proposal can't be perfect enough, how can the marriage be? Marriage isn't about flashy rings and all those things, it's about relationship, companionship, support. Alex and Mila have always supported one another—that's what makes them so great together. So just because the proposal is a little janky—I mean, not ideal—doesn't mean they're not strong together."

We're all silent, staring at Monica as she finishes her diatribe. "What?" she says, hands on hips. "Just 'cause I'm hella trendy doesn't mean I accept all trends." She smooths her blouse. "I'm trendy where it matters."

"Yeah, okay, thanks for that," Anya says, not at all sarcastically. "What're you going to do, Milochka?"

"I have to go," I say, grabbing my purse and rocketing off the couch before she even finishes her sentence.

"Wait!" she calls out as I throw open the front door. "We'll all come with!"

60

Una Idiota

Alex

I check my email at every red light on our way to the airport. My visa to Canada hasn't been approved yet, and I really don't want to fly to Cuba because I know it'll be next to impossible to get out of there once I'm back in the country. *Please, God, please.* I pray the entire way to the Miami airport. I get an email from one of the equine-assisted therapy centers I'd reached out to in Atlanta for advice. I assume the response is like all of the others—sorry, best of luck—so I don't even bother reading it.

When we pull into the departures tunnel for the United Airlines International check-in area, my phone dings in my pocket. When I park, I see the subject line: VISA AP-PROVED. "Mama!" I cry out, showing her the email. "*Esta aprobado! Podemos ir a Canadá!*"

"Ah, *muy bien*," she says, patting my cheek. Tears threaten, and I get out of the car before they can get any farther. Because this opens a world of possibilities for me. I couldn't possibly ask Mila to follow me to Cuba, but Canada? We could be together. I want to call her, to tell her the news, but a wannabe cop is yelling at me to unload or get moving. I get our bags out, kissing my aunt goodbye, and head inside, gripping both sets of tickets— one singular ticket to Cuba and two to Canada. I'm tempted to dump the Cuban ticket in the trash can on my way inside. I'm just happy my mom had her things packed to go with my aunt so she can come with me to Canada now.

It's strange to carry all of your worldly possessions and yet not have the important things. I might as well be dragging coal behind me, that's how useless I feel like all of this is. But there's a tiny bit of hope welling in me—I'll make this right somehow with Mila. We check in and wait in line at security. The more I think about it, the more I feel like I have to do to fix things with Mila. Finish grad school, get a secure job that can take care of all three of us, and come up with the most spectacular proposal ever. This, of course, assumes that Mila will want to come to Canada—a huge if. All of the hope I'd been feeling fizzles as I wonder if we'll ever have it easy. If we'll ever be together again.

By the time we get to our gate, I'm not even feeling that happy that I'm going to Canada instead of Cuba, because everything with Mila still feels insurmountable. I sigh, rummaging through my backpack for my headphones, when I see Mila's notebook. I take it out, running my fingers across the worn leather. I remember giving this to her, that moment playing in shocking detail in my mind. The way she looked when she realized I wasn't going to tell her how to live her life like everyone else seemed to be doing—that I simply believed in her to make her own way. When she kissed me mid-sentence, shocking me yet again with one of her dazzling kisses. The memory aches within me, and I'm stinging with regret and anguish over the consequences of being an illegal immigrant and falling in love.

I almost don't open the notebook, but I think, *Can it hurt any worse?*

I soak up the first few pages—Mila's initial scribbles about the Center. She wrote them while I was in a detention center and Anya was in the hospital for a pulmonary embolism. She was hurting, yet dreaming. About halfway through her first entry, I realize she's writing *to me.*

You inspired me, Alex. To believe, even when it hurts. And later, *I don't know what's going to happen, Alex, but I hope that whatever happens, it happens with you.*

I flip through the next few pages, detailing our pitch to ViaTech, the purchase of the land, and the groundbreaking of the barn. There's a picture of the three of us—Mila, Anya, and me—in front of the barn during construction, taped to one of the pages. She keeps writing to me: *Can you believe it, Alex? It's all coming true!*

I want to keep reading, to not move from this spot until I've devoured every page of this journal, but my mom is chiding me that it's time to board. I follow her, eyes still on the page, as I read about Mila's entry from her birthday this year. I shake my head when she wrote that she thought I "freaked out" when she joked about marrying her now—as if I didn't want to propose right that second. But a moment later, my breath is frozen in my lungs because she says, I see forever with you. *Every day is magical with you.* And I'm realizing how foolish I was for thinking I somehow needed to measure up to Michael. I'm not Michael, and that's a good thing. Which I suppose was what Anya was trying to tell me when I was stressing about it.

I skim through her recap of the lawsuit from Clara and some details about Luke and Anya, but zero in when she starts discussing my case and the heartbreaking loss. I cringe when I realize that Ann talked to her about us getting married. I read through her conversation with my former lawyer, and I want to throw the journal, I'm so frustrated by it. I don't realize I let out an audible groan until my mom asks if I'm okay.

"Estoy bien, Mama, solo soy una idiota."

She clicks her tongue at me, shaking her head, but I go back to reading, the uncertainty building in me with every word I consume.

61

I LOVE Love

Mila

"I need a ticket to Cuba," I tell the woman at the United counter. She types into the computer without looking up at me.

"Do you have your visa?" she asks in a bored voice.

"I, uh, applied for one."

"Did you receive an approval for your visa?"

"Um, not yet?"

She clicks her tongue and sighs dramatically. "I cannot sell you a ticket until you have an approved visa." She looks over my shoulder and shouts, "Next!"

"Wait! What flights are in the same terminal that don't require a visa?"

She gives me a look like I'm a terrorist and she's not selling me a ticket. "Look." I hold up the ring for her to see. "I'm accepting my boyfriend's proposal. Please, please, help me."

Her demeanor changes immediately. "Oooohhh, Evangeline, come look at this! This girl's boyfriend proposed to her and she's running through the airport to accept!" Evangeline, a woman with a bun so tight it's pulling her eyebrows into a surprised look, glances over.

"Beautiful," she murmurs before turning back to her customer.

"I'll help you," the woman says, all of a sudden chummy with me. "I'll get you a ticket to Panama City. It's across from the Havana gate. But, girl, you better hurry or you'll miss him. Here, take this with you." She gives me a neon slip that says RUSH. "It'll get you right through security."

"Wow, thank you."

She sighs dreamily. "I *love* love." She types furiously into her computer. "Ticket's printing now. Oh my gosh, how did he propose?" She props her head on her hands like we're two BFFs gabbing.

"It's, uh, a long story..."

"Right, right, and you gotta run!" She hands me the ticket and yells, "Go get your man!"

62

Sooooo Scammy

Anya

Luke and I are in short-term parking, trying to make conversation with Monica when we could be alone making a very different kind of conversation. Of course, Luke is a lot more tolerant than I am, and it reminds me why I need someone like him in my life. He manages to pull stories out of Monica that are sort of interesting, if laden with weird Gen Z language that requires Google translate. She's droning on about some Mediterranean restaurant around the block from her neighborhood as I watch a red-hot Porsche pull into the spot in front of ours. A guy gets out of the passenger seat, all suave with his pompadour, and I almost roll my eyes. A girl gets out of the driver's seat, and she looks so familiar—and yet she's missing one very important thing, and it makes me hardly able to recognize her.

"Luke," I say, cutting off Monica. "Isn't that...?" I point at the girl as she sashays across the parking garage. The guy grabs her hand and whirls her into a kiss and then releases her. She staggers, but she's very much on her feet. Not at all paralyzed. Not at all in a wheelchair.

"Clara?" he chokes out, barely able to believe it himself. While he's blinking his eyes in disbelief, I turn to Monica, handing her my phone.

"I need you to follow that girl and film her walking."

She glances from me to my phone to Luke. "Oookay," she says slowly.

"It's of utmost importance to Mila and the Center."

"You got it, boss," she says, taking off out of Luke's truck. "At least she's useful for something," I grumble. Luke grunts, but his eyes are still tracking Clara.

"They scammed us," he says, his voice a low growl.

"Looks like she's putting her money to good use."

We sit in silence, both of us mentally tallying the ramifications of this discovery, which is not at all how I wanted to use my time with Luke sans Monica. And just like that, she's back in the truck, showing us the video she captured. "They met up with this other couple," she says, zooming in on Clara's mom and another person who looks vaguely familiar. I snatch the phone, pausing it as I zoom in on the man's face. "It's Ben!" I shove the phone in Luke's face.

"Who's Ben?"

"Our old volunteer. He was the one who was working with us when Clara took her fall." I think for a moment, trying to remember the event. "He was helping her on the horse. Oh my gosh, he was in on it too." I shake my head. "I bet that's where the recording came from."

Luke is wide-eyed, staring off into space where Clara and her boy toy disappeared a few minutes ago. Monica, however, doesn't understand the meaning of silence and is squawking, "Can someone tell me *what* is going on?"

"These people scammed us." I hold up my phone, shaking the image of the foursome walking through the airport. "And they're not getting away with it."

A few minutes later, as we're rewatching the video of Clara and her "mom"—we're not even sure she's really her mom at this point—I get a call from Mrs. Caballero. I scramble to answer it. "Hello?" I put it on speaker phone in case Monica needs to translate for us.

"*Hola,* Miriam?"

"No, this is Anya."

"*Ah, sí, sí.*" She continues as if she didn't make a mistake calling me. "*Logramos nuestro vuelo a Canadá. ¿Recuerdas? ¡Nuestras visas fueron aprobadas! Solo quería que supieras que no vamos a ir a Cuba.*" I glance at Monica to make sure she's catching all of this.

"Their visas to Canada got approved; they're not going to Cuba," Monica whispers.

"Oh! Oh! Good news, Mrs. Caballero! Thank you!"

"*Le dirás a la familia?*"

"She said, Will you tell the family?"

"She wants me to let Mila know. Okay, Mrs. Caballero, we'll let her know."

"*De inmediato?*"

"Right away?"

"Yes, *sí, sí.*" We say goodbye—with Mrs. Caballero still calling me Miriam, which I think is her sister's name—and I dial Mila.

63

Where's Canada?

Mila

I'm dripping in sweat by the time I get to the gate to Havana, and not altogether certain I put on deodorant after my shower. I scour the seats in front of the gate to find Alex, but he's nowhere to be found. Tears prick my eyes until I see that they're still boarding a trickle of passengers. I steel myself, holding my chin high as I approach the front desk. "Excuse me, ma'am. I need to page a passenger on the flight."

She scrutinizes me, her heavily lined eyes shifting back and forth over my face. "Is there an emergency?"

"Um, yes. Yes, there is. His mom is in the hospital, and he needs to get off the plane. Alex Caballero."

She nods, picking up the phone in front of her. "Right away."

I second guess myself because his mom isn't going with him to Cuba, and she *could* be in the hospital. I don't want to unnecessarily freak out Alex. "Actually, can you tell him that his dad is in the hospital?"

The airline employee gives me an incredulous look. "Which one is it, his mom or his dad?"

I groan. Which one is worse? His mom—who could end up in the hospital for her epilepsy—or his dead father? Both options are horrible. But at least he'll know his dad isn't actually in the hospital. Is that incredibly insensitive? "Actually, can you tell him his cat is in the hospital?" Would Alex get off the plane for Gata? I'm not a hundred percent sure, but it's worth a shot. He *loves* that cat.

The woman slams the phone down. "Ma'am, this is really not appropriate. What is this, some kind of mean prank? What did this guy do to deserve this anyway?"

"No! No! It's not a prank, it's a proposal." As soon as I say it, I cringe. The look she gives me makes me cringe even more. I reach in my wallet and grab the emergency hundred dollar bill my dad insists I keep. "Please?" I squeak out.

She looks left and right, then surreptitiously takes the bill, picking up the phone with a sigh. "Nancy, I've got a passenger who needs to deboard for an emergency. Yes, a Mr. Alex Caballero. Mmhmm. His cat is in the hospital." She glances up at me like I'm the biggest inconvenience of her life, and I smile as pleasantly as I can. "You sure? Can you double check? Sure, I'll wait." She drums her fingernails on the desk. "Okay, thanks." She hangs up. "He's not on that flight, sweetheart."

My heart drops. "Are you sure?"

She types into her keyboard, nodding. "He didn't check in for his flight. He's not on board. I'm sure. Sorry, sweetheart."

I back away from the desk, feeling shaken. Surely Alex isn't running? I try to think of a reason Alex wouldn't be on his flight—could his mom really be in the hospital? I dial Alex, and it rings and rings until I get his voicemail. My heart aches at the sound of his voice, *You've reached Alex Caballero...*I don't hang up until I get to the very end of the message. As soon as I hang up, an incoming call from Anya comes through and I accidentally hang up on her too. When I call her back, it goes to voicemail. She's clearly trying to call me while I'm calling her and the lines are getting crossed. "Ugh!" I groan at my phone, shaking it. Finally, we connect. "He's going to Canada!" Monica screams into the phone. I immediately hang up and run back to the woman at the Cuban departure desk.

"Canada!" I shout at her. "Where's Canada?"

"Uh..." She points up. "North?"

"No, sorry. I mean, where's the gates for Canadian flights? Toronto?"

"Oh! That way." She points to the right, explaining how to get to United's Canadian gates. I sprint away, throwing a "thanks!" behind me.

64

Tengo Que Ir

Alex

There's only three more pages left in Mila's notebook, but I don't know if I can read any more. It's killing me.

"Ladies and gentlemen," a flight attendant comes on the overhead speakers. "Please take your seats and check that your carry on is safely stowed beneath the seat in front of you."

My mom's on the phone with my aunt, telling her we made our flight, but I tune her out as I keep reading.

I applied for a Cuban visa today, and a Canadian one, just in case. My dad will kill me, but I'll be in Cuba, so I don't think he'll be successful. I know it takes like a month or so, so I won't be able to leave with you, but I won't be far behind. I just wish you would give me some indication that you want me with you.

Later, she writes in painful detail about the time we stood outside her house, hugging and crying. *All I wanted to say as we stood there is, Why don't you ask me to marry you, Alex? Why? I'll say yes. I already said yes in my heart.*

I can't read anymore. I snap the journal shut and unbuckle my seatbelt. "*Tengo que ir,*" I tell my mom, before pushing past the passengers still taking their seats.

65

You Forgot Something

Mila

I'm sprinting through the Miami International Airport like I'm a hurdler in the Olympics. I'm shoving past old ladies in their walkers, jumping over fallen suitcases. By the time I get to a departure gate for Toronto, the sweat dripping down my face is burning my eyes, but I can't even wipe it away. I can only look for Alex. But he's not there. No one is. I approach the desk. "Did—they—leave—" I pant.

"We're fully boarded, not an empty seat on the plane."

"I—need—" I can't catch my breath, and the man at the counter is looking at me like I'm about to have a heart attack. "Emergency—"

There's a commotion on the gangway. "Sir! Sir!" someone is yelling, and I glance that way.

And there he is, sprinting around the barrier blocking the gangway, past the ticket checker, and then past me.

"Alex!"

He skids to a stop, turning slowly. He's wide-eyed, as if he's afraid he just hallucinated me. But he must decide I'm too much of a mess to have been hallucinated, and he crosses to me in four long steps. "Mila," he exhales my name like it's a prayer. "What are you—"

"You forgot something," I say, still feeling breathless, but for a different reason.

"You?"

"What?"

"I forgot you," he says, cupping my cheek in his hand. "I'm so sorry, Mila. I've been an idiot, pushing you away, thinking I was doing right by you. I was so wrong. So, so wrong."

I rise on tiptoe and gently kiss him, but when he goes to kiss me more deeply, I pull away. "Well, yes," I say tartly. "You did forget me, but there's something else."

He watches me with an adorable crease between his brow while I dig in my purse. When I pull out the red ring box, he says, "How did you—"

"Your mom gave it to Anya to give to me this morning."

Alex lets out an unsteady laugh, shaking his head. "Apparently we needed help to work this out."

"Oh yes, *we* needed so much help."

"You're right. *I* needed help." He holds up a notebook, and I realize it's *my* notebook. "Anya gave it to me this morning." He shifts from one foot to the other, not looking me in the eye. "I hope it's okay that I read it."

My cheeks heat up, but I tell him, "Well, I did write it to you," my voice like a strangled whisper.

"I figured that out pretty quickly." He licks his lips and opens his mouth like he's going to say something, then closes it. I realize Alex is nervous. My hand goes to his chest, where I feel his heart beating in triple time.

"It's okay, Alex."

He shakes his head. "It's not. Mila, I was so afraid that all of this would be too much for your love to overcome that I didn't even give you the opportunity. That was unfair. I should've trusted you more, trusted *us* more."

"Sometimes our faith just isn't there, and that's okay. I've got plenty of faith for you to borrow." He finally looks at me, and the depth of emotion swirling there catches me off guard. I almost stumble back, but Alex's hand is around my waist, holding me in place. Holding me up.

"Thank you," he says in a whisper. He brushes a kiss against my forehead, and I melt into him. "I don't deserve you, Mila."

I shake my head. "Don't say that. Seriously, I don't want you to say that again. Because it's not true, but I get it. I've felt that way before with you, that I don't deserve you. But what's the point in that thought? Can you just let me adore you? And I'll let you adore me? Let's not think of what we deserve, and just think of what *is*. This, Alex, this is it for me. You are it for me. So let's just enjoy that."

Alex quietly searches my eyes, his lips pressed together. Then he silently hands me the notebook and takes the ring box from my hand. My heart pounds as Alex steps back, and then lowers to one knee. "Mila Kozak," he says. "I don't know what's going to happen one minute or one year from now. All I know is that I want you to be by my side through it. And now I know that you will be at my side, come what may." He sighs as he opens the box, revealing the ring that's glittering more than ever under the airport lights. "Will you marry me?"

I tug him up to standing and throw my arms around him, pressing my lips against his. Several people around us, who clearly saw Alex on his knee with a ring, are clapping. I hear one lady tell someone, "He just proposed to her," and a thrill goes down my spine.

"I take that as a yes," Alex murmurs against my lips.

I pull away and smack my journal playfully against his chest. "I already said yes."

He laughs. "That's true." He takes my hand and slips the ring on my finger, and a shiver trembles through me. He takes the journal from me and wraps his arms around my waist, putting his forehead against mine. "It can't hurt to say it out loud, though."

"Yes, Alex," I say, my hand on his chest. "A million times yes."

66

Almost.

Alex

The moment I realize that my mom is on a flight to Canada by herself, I stumble away from Mila, only to find my mom right outside the gate, recording us on her phone, with the biggest smile I've ever seen on her face.

"*Felicidades!*" she calls out, wrapping us both in her arms, her cheeks wet with tears. "*Déjeme ver,*" she says to Mila. *Let me see.* Mila holds out her hand, diamonds sparkling on her finger, and my mom lets out a strangled sob. She holds us again, kissing our cheeks back and forth again and again.

Once she's out of tears and kisses, she releases us. "So, can we all go home now? Or do we have to go to Canada?" she asks in Spanish.

"I actually don't know," I confess.

"Let's call the lawyer," Mila says. We huddle inside a Jamba Juice, phone on speaker while we talk with Mr. Rodriguez.

"Well, congratulations are in order," he says. "Nothing like a little last-minute engagement to make my job more interesting." He chuckles. "When's the wedding?"

Mila and I glance at each other. "Uh," I say.

"We haven't set a date," Mila says.

"Anytime works," I add.

"The sooner the better," he says. "But if you can make it look like a real wedding and not just show up at the courthouse, that might help your case."

An idea forms in my mind, and I wonder if Mila would like an authentic farm wedding, on *our* farm—a last hurrah if we can't resurrect the Center. "That shouldn't be an issue," I tell him. "It *is* a real wedding."

"Sure, sure," he says. "Well for now, you can stay put in the States and I'll start working on a provisional waiver for you once you get married. You'll get it done this week, yes?" He asks as if we need to send an email or fill out a form—not get *married*. I catch Mila's eye, looking for signs she's overwhelmed, but instead she's got a big, goofy smile on her beautiful face.

"We'll get our marriage license first thing Monday," I tell him.

"Great. You'll have to wait three days once you get the license, but the moment it's official, you send me a copy."

We thank him and say our goodbyes. Mila's eyes linger on mine, and I see the rest of my life in those hazel eyes. And I know that no matter what happens, I'll be safe with her.

Just then, her stomach gives an almighty growl. "I, uh, need to eat. I'll be right back," she says, gesturing to the Jamba Juice counter. I'm about to offer to grab it for her, when my mom puts her hand on my arm.

"I'm proud of you, son," my mom says to me in Spanish.

I grimace. "Why? I almost messed everything up, really bad."

"Almost," she says with a smile. "But the important thing is that you let yourself be loved." She sighs, patting my hand. "I don't know why that's so hard sometimes, but allowing yourself to be fully known and fully loved is one of the most fearful things."

"*Si, mamita.*" We sit like that for a long time as I digest everything that's just happened. I almost left Mila without proposing to her because I felt like I needed to be perfect—or at least pretty darn close to perfect—before I could let her really love me forever. But then Anya, and seemingly my mom, intervened. Mila chased after me, buying a ticket to Panama and running through the airport like a banshee on fire. I proposed to her—in the last possible place I would've picked—and she said yes. I laugh and shake my head.

Mila's marrying me.

Even though I'm a mess, don't have a plan for my life, and we still don't have her parents' approval. But now, all of a sudden, those problems seem very small in comparison to the fact that Mila loves me—even when I'm being a blockhead, even when I'm getting arrested and deported and causing lawsuits. I'm not really sure how or why, but I know without a doubt that she does love me and she's going to fight for me, and me for her. Because that is love—being known for all your flaws, all your shortcomings, and being loved anyway. And I almost let that slip through my fingers.

Almost.

My phone buzzes and I check my email—an advertisement I quickly delete. But then I open the email I'd ignored earlier from the equine-assisted therapy center in Atlanta.

Mr. Caballero,

I'm so glad you reached out to us. Please call me as soon as you can at (786) 555-5555. We actually had a very similar situation which ended up being a mother-daughter team with one of them posing as a paraplegic. They're going around scamming other places like ours, but they haven't been caught yet. I hope if we work together, we can track them down. Hope to talk soon.

-Britney

I drop the phone and it clatters on the table. I don't know whether to be ecstatic or livid. I land somewhere in the middle—someone took advantage of us, which means if we can prove it, we should be able to get our insurance back and save the Center. My heart thrums with the idea. I quickly forward it to Anya, thoughts going in a million different directions so that I can't keep them all straight.

I think about the center in Toronto that had to close for a very similar lawsuit—could they have also been a victim of the same scam? My mind is whirling with the possibilities, and I have to grip the table to steady myself.

Mila comes back with her smoothie bowl, and I show her the email and then explain to my mom what the email said. Mila's silent for a long time—so long, in fact, that I ask her, "Are you okay?"

She lets out a long breath, blinking up at me. "I-I can't believe it."

Our phones buzz simultaneously, and I pull up a video from Anya. It's dark and I have to squint to make out exactly what I'm looking at. "Wait, is that—"

"Clara," Mila breathes, her tone murderous. "*Walking.*"

"So she's not—"

"Nope. Dirty little liar. Greedy badger. Con artist filth."

"*Con las manos en la masa,*" my mom mutters as she watches the video, piecing together what's happening.

"*Exactamente,*" Mila says, and I smile because how could I have ever thought that this girl—*who learned Spanish to talk to my mom*—would just let me get deported. My mom gets up to go to the bathroom, and I scoot my chair closer to Mila's. I watch as she takes another bite of her smoothie bowl and shivers, wrapping her arms around herself.

"Aren't you glad we're not heading to Canada right now?" I say as I put an arm around her waist, tucking her against my side. "You would freeze to death."

She scoffs. "I have Ukrainian blood, Alex. It has been forged in the frozen tundras of—oh my gosh, I would've frozen to death."

"I can keep you warm." I nuzzle into her neck, and she makes a happy sound that goes straight to my heart. "If you ever get cold."

"I'm counting on it," she says before pressing her lips to mine, cold from her smoothie bowl. I kiss her until they're warm and I'm tasting of strawberries.

"I should probably let you finish your bowl so we can get out of here."

Mila makes a little humming sound. "We'll have plenty more time for that later," she says, brushing her thumb across my lips, and it takes everything in me to not throw her over my shoulder and get out of here to make her my wife right this second.

"Where's your stuff?" I ask, looking around for a bag or a purse when it's time for us to head home.

"Psh," she says, flipping her hair over her shoulder. "What do I need stuff for?" Then she smiles at me. "I have everything I need." I smile back at her, leaning down to press a kiss to her upturned lips.

Mila takes my shirt and twists it in her hand, trying to pull me closer, though there's no space between us. I look down at Mila, her beautiful hazel eyes glistening with bands of gold right now, promising me the world with just one gaze. I gently move her hair over her shoulder, cupping the back of her head, tracing circles with my thumb on the soft spot under her ear. She sighs, leaning into my hand. "It's me and you, Mila."

"You're my home now, Alex. My favorite person, place, or thing."

I sigh and kiss the finger Mila put on my lips. "I adore you, Mila Kozak."

"Hmm." She tucks her head into my chest. "I like it when you call me that."

"I won't be able to for much longer," I say, leaning down to whisper in her ear, "Mila Caballero." I smile when she shivers against me.

"I like that even better," she says. "Say it again."

I smile, pressing a kiss to her temple. "Mila Caballero." I kiss her jaw, whispering in her ear. "Mila Caballero."

When she stands on tiptoe to kiss me, I let myself absorb every ounce of her love, and then give it all back to her.

67

Bingo

Anya

We pick up a very engaged Mila and Alex (and Mrs. Caballero—sadly, not engaged) exactly where we'd dropped off Mila a couple hours ago. "Have a nice trip?" Luke jokes, and I actually laugh. I feel unusually giddy—between Mila's engagement, the news from the Atlanta center, and the video in my phone of a very un-paralyzed Clara, I'm practically vibrating with glee. Mila, Alex, Monica, and Mrs. Caballero squeeze into the backseat and we head to the Center.

On the way, Luke, Monica, and I give them the long version of how we discovered Clara in the parking garage. The realization that Ben was in on the whole thing ripples through the backseat.

"I never liked that guy," Alex says.

"You loved Ben," Mila scoffs. "You told me he was the funniest guy you've ever met."

"Yeah, but that was before he recorded our conversations," I say.

"You think it was Ben with the recording?" Mila asks.

"It makes the most sense."

"I guess Tomás was innocent of at least one thing," Alex grumbles. The thought of Tommy's betrayal still stings, and I can tell it's going to take Alex quite some time to overcome that—even if he wasn't the one to record us.

The moment we're in the lounge, we call Britney at the Atlanta center and tell her everything that happened and what we'd just uncovered at the airport, as well as our hunch that the center in Toronto may have suffered our same fate. "I'm glad you called," she tells us. "I've been contacting other facilities like ours, on the off-chance that it really was a scam, and I got a call from a place in Ann Arbor saying they had the exact same experience—a horse that is normally calm is totally freaked out for some unknown reason, a mysterious dog appears, a girl who is hesitant to ride takes a headfirst fall. I'll admit, we didn't try to go to the hospital like you guys did, but this Ann Arbor place did try to do a hospital visit, and they met an angry man in the lobby who turned them away, same as you guys."

"Hmm. Any ideas as to how they're getting the horses freaked out?" I ask. I feel Luke's fingers on my shoulder, pulling on the TENS unit electrode I'd forgotten was there.

"It's falling off," he whispers, peeling the electrode off. When I glance back, Mila's looking strangely at me, her brow furrowed.

"Where'd you get this?" she asks, waving at the electrode.

"Luke's sister," I say briefly, gesturing toward the phone to tell her we have more important things to worry about.

"Who else had one of these recently?" she asks.

"Mila, seriously?" I point at the phone again.

"It was Ben," Alex says. "For his back pain." His dark eyes are hyper-focused on the electrode now too, and I'm about to chastise both of them when Alex leans toward the phone and says, "Britney, we need to test something and we'll call you right back," and before I can say anything else, he hangs up.

"Is anyone planning on telling me what is happening?" I huff.

"May I?" Alex says, pulling the other electrode off of my shoulder.

"Of course," I say sarcastically as I hand him the TENS unit. "Go ahead and do whatever you want. Don't worry about me."

Alex disappears without saying another word and I look at Luke, annoyed to be out of the loop. "Y'know," he says. "I think they're on to something."

"They better be. Or I'm going to kill them."

Luke and I roll out to the breezeway, where we find Alex and Mila in Jet's stall. One of my TENS unit electrodes is on Jet's rump, and Mila is holding the unit while Alex is at Jet's head, holding his halter. "Ready," he says. Luke and I watch silently as Mila turns the TENS unit on, increasing the frequency. At first, Jet doesn't seem to react, but the higher the intensity goes, the more agitated he gets. His skin starts twitching like there's a bunch of flies on him, and he's swishing his tail, his ears going back. "I bet if I turned it all the way up, he'd be even more irritated."

"Bingo," Luke says from beside me.

"I've heard of people using TENS units on horses before, for therapy," I say.

"Yeah, but if they've never felt it before, and then you turn up the intensity all the way," Mila suggests. "It's a little shocking."

I nod, thinking of the first time I put on the TENS unit, how it felt like a million needles on my skin. And horses are even more sensitive.

"How could he have done that without us noticing?" I ask.

Mila's shoulders slump with uncertainty, and she glances at Alex. "Here, let me see," he says. He puts the TENS unit in his pocket and then threads the wires through his shirt and down his sleeve so that the wire is going down his arm. "If he was wearing long sleeves, we might not have noticed the wiring. He could've put the electrode in his palm like this"—he situates the electrode so it's practically hidden in the center of his hand—"and if he put his hand on the horse's rump like this..." He puts his hand on Jet's hind end, and sure enough we can't see the electrode.

"I remember that Ben had his hand on Harley's rump that day," I say, the image coming back to me. "It was weird, which is why I remember it. Like he was bracing himself on Harley. I was going to talk to him about it, but obviously forgot with everything that came after that."

"And that electrode we found," Mila says, eyes lighting up. "Remember that? It was in the trash and it had a bunch of horse hair on it."

I nod, vaguely remembering Mila finding it in the trash that day.

"We've got them," Alex says, a glimmer of a smile on his face.

"We should call Britney back," Mila says.

I press my lips together, saying, "We should call our *lawyer*. I want to bury these people."

Luke takes my hand in his, kissing my knuckles. "I like when you get that murderous look in your eyes."

"I suppose you've seen your fair share of it," Mila teases.

"Haven't we all," Alex says under his breath.

I roll my eyes, but when I glance over at Luke, he's smiling at me. "Ready to slay these con artists?" I ask.

"Time to cowgirl up, baby."

68

Enough.

Alex

I spend entirely too long debating what to wear. I don't even have that much fodder for overthinking my wardrobe choices—I barely have a handful of outfits that would be appropriate for this situation. Do I wear the suit? Is that trying too hard? Eventually I take a pair of chinos and the button-down shirt my mom got me for Christmas out of my suitcase, along with my dress shoes and a watch Mila got me for my birthday this year.

My mom is in the living room, waiting. She looks me over, smoothing my hair needlessly and telling me to tuck in my shirt. I do as she says, and she smiles anxiously at me.

"Eres más que suficientemente bueno," she says, and then kisses me on the cheek. "Your father would be proud."

"Gracias, Mama." Her words stir in me an increased desire to be all that my dad was—but also a peace that I am who I am and that is enough.

I drive to Mila's in silence, my thoughts deafening. When I pull into the driveway, my palms are sweating, and I have to wipe them on my pants. Mila greets me at the door. "He's by the pool," she whispers. Walking into her house feels akin to walking into a funeral parlor.

I take Mila's hand and lean down so our foreheads are touching. "No matter how this goes, I'm marrying you." I say this to her as much as to myself. I want Mr. Kozak's blessing on our marriage—family is so important to both of us—but I'm done letting someone else dictate my love life.

She reaches up on tiptoe to kiss me. "Yes, you are."

Outside, Mr. Kozak is lounging by the pool. He's wearing a pair of absurd Versace swim shorts—I only know they're Versace because he said as much the last time he wore them—no shirt, and a pair of Ray Bans. I feel overdressed standing in front of him, and I'm glad I didn't opt for the suit.

"I thought you would be in Cuba by now," he says as he reaches for his lime water beside him. The drink is sweating, and it drips down his chest and it makes me wish he had a shirt on for this conversation—not that it would make me any more comfortable.

The statement catches me off guard. I'd prepared the whole way here with what I wanted to say, rehearsing it in my mind, but now that I'm here, in front of a shirtless Mr. Kozak and he's said something to me, I don't know where to begin. "I thought so too," I say honestly. "But I had something I need to tell you."

I expect him to say something to this—*what do you want to say*, or even *go on*, or anything to indicate he heard me. But he doesn't. So I launch into my monologue. "I know you think that I'm not worthy of your daughter, and maybe that's true. Maybe no one is good enough for Mila. But there are two things I know for certain: I know I love Mila more than anyone has ever or will ever love her. I've loved her for years—when she wouldn't even look my way, when she was a brat, when she was falling apart. I've loved her on her good days and her worst days. And I'm going to keep loving her until there's no more breath in my body, until I'm dead in the ground—and I'll probably love her beyond that too. Because if there's one thing I know about myself, one thing I'm good at, it's that. I love Mila. And I'm good for her." I take a moment, catching my breath, as I wait for a reaction from Mr. Kozak. But he doesn't respond, doesn't even move. And I can't even see his eyes behind his black Ray Bans. I'm beginning to doubt myself, to doubt my approach. Does what I said mean nothing to him?

"You said there were two things?" he finally says.

"Oh. Yes." I clear my throat, and I'm feeling unbelievably nervous at what I have to say next. My words jumble, but I have to get them out. "Well, because of the, you know, aforementioned love, I want to—I *am* marrying Mila. I've asked her and she said yes."

An excruciating moment passes between us. "I see." He takes a sip of his water and then calls out, "Milochka!"

Mila, who was, of course, standing by the sliding glass door—with the door cracked and her ear to it, no doubt—comes bounding out of the house onto the pool deck. He says something to her in clipped Ukrainian as she comes up beside me and takes my hand, squeezing.

"Yes, *Tato*, it's true," she responds in English, and I'm grateful for it. Mr. Kozak finally takes off his sunglasses, and he's studying us with his intensely guarded hazel eyes. He says something to her again in Ukrainian, and I'm beginning to wonder if Duolingo has Ukrainian.

"It's what I want more than anything in the world," Mila says. She turns to look at me, her soft eyes such a contrast to her dad's. I can't believe I ever thought Mila would want anything other than me—but everything in her eyes tells me that I'm enough. That just like she's my everything, I'm hers too. I realize that as important as her dad's approval is to both of us, we will be okay without it. We can weather whatever storms come our way, even one as massive as Mr. Kozak.

"When will you marry?" he asks.

"In three days," I say. The marriage license we picked up this morning is sitting in my glove compartment—a very surreal reality.

"And I'm assuming you want me to foot the bill?"

"We wouldn't presume that, no."

Mila makes a little squeaking noise that has me thinking that, *yes, she would presume that*. But I squeeze her hand, to tell her we'll figure it out no matter what.

"It's not about the money, *Tato*," Mila says.

Mr. Kozak looks at me pointedly. "That much is obvious." He sighs and wipes a hand across his face. "Well," he says, standing up to face me. "It's not ideal, that is certain." His eyes bore into me. "But you are right. In the end, it comes down to love. This"—he waves a hand around at his house, the pool—"it all fades. It's temporary. But this—" He points a finger from Mila to me. "That has the potential to last. If you let it. You've shown yourself to be faithful, if a bit unlucky with the law." He grimaces. "Welcome to the family, Mr. Caballero." He reaches out his hand.

"Alex," I say.

"Alex," he repeats, and we shake hands. He pulls me toward him, slapping my back with his other hand as he says, "If I could scare you away from my daughter, you would not be worthy of her." His eyes bore into me, and the truth of what he's saying hits me. "Welcome to the family, Alex."

Mila throws her arms around her dad, and he holds her for a moment. I have a glimpse, then, of how challenging this situation is for Mr. Kozak—his daughter, his baby girl, caught in the midst of this less-than-ideal situation. If I were him, I might have acted in the same way, in an attempt to protect my daughter. But he's right—the thing that matters most is love. And Mila and I have that in spades.

69

Two Months Later

Anya

It took a while to get everything straightened out, but as of yesterday, the ViaTech Center for Equine-Assisted Therapy is back up and running. Once we collaborated with the other therapy centers and realized it was the same team scamming all of us, we were able to work with the police to track down Clara and her mom—whose real names ended up being Noemi and Hilda Lopez. Two weeks after they left for their celebration vacation to Greece, they were arrested upon their return to the States. A chunk of the money they'd won in the scam lawsuits was returned to us and the other centers—not all of it, since they'd already spent a pretty penny, but enough to keep our doors open. It took quite some convincing to get an insurance company to back us, but once the Lopezes were charged and we could prove what they'd done, we were able to get our coverage back. My dad even got the ViaTech PR lady to work on our situation, and I've had positive interviews with every news outlet in the tri-county area in the past month. The ViaTech partners apologized to us for settling the lawsuit so hastily and not doing their due diligence in finding the scam. The bad press got to them, which is exactly what the Lopezes were trying to do. The whole situation led to a positive discussion on how we would make decisions in the future—together.

After Mila and Alex's whirlwind wedding, Alex was approved for an immigration visa interview, which is a very good step in the right direction. If he passes the interview, he can be granted lawful residence—permanently. After they got the news, they decided it was as good a time as any to celebrate and go on a belated honeymoon. They're at the Little Palm Island Resort, where we'd gone for our Christmas vacation sans Alex. On my dad's dime, of course, since he owed them one. A fact that I convinced him of—not that it took too much convincing. So I've been running the Center by myself while they frolic in the sun and sand.

Well, *not completely alone*, I think as I glance over at the hulking cowboy in a wheelchair.

Luke and I are working in the Center's office, taking turns playing songs for each other. Luke is working at Alex's desk, which is decidedly less tidy with its current occupant. He's eating his vegan food while I munch on cookies he brought from his mom. "I've got one for you," I say, pressing play on "Cloudy Day" by Tones and I.

At the end of the song, he says, "I like that one. It's not so sad like the other ones you always like." He's wearing a teasing smile and I roll my eyes—a gesture that's dimmed only slightly since Luke and I started dating.

"I'm hanging around you too much," I groan dramatically. "You're making me too happy, Luke."

He wheels his chair closer to mine, eyes crinkling in a smile that still makes my heart jump. "I'm so sorry, darlin'."

"You're not sorry at all." I turn my chair toward his.

"No, I'm not."

I reach out and run my hand across his cheek, his stubble tickling my palm. "You are the sun to my cloudy day."

He sighs happily and then faux-grumbles, "Darn these wheelchairs." He reaches out and pulls me out of my chair with his superhuman strength and into his lap. "Although, they do give me an excuse to do this quite a bit." He cocks his head, dimple on display. "So maybe I should be thankful for them."

"And that revenge machine," I say. "Let's be very grateful for that."

"It's no longer the revenge machine," he says.

"What shall we call it now? Is it just the Smith machine?"

He thinks for a moment, looking sufficiently adorable. "It's the Motivation Machine now."

"Oh?"

He puts an arm under my knees, and the other behind my back and curls me up and down. "Motivation to do this."

I laugh, smacking at him to put me down.

"I think we should also be grateful for the vegan diet you keep giving me a hard time about."

I snort-laugh. "I'm not going to stop making fun of you for that. That would take away, like, half of the fodder I have for teasing you. And I know how much you love that."

"Hmm, good point." He curls me again, just showing off at this point. "It also helps that you're, what? A buck ten dripping wet with a box full of Oreos in you?"

"I've never eaten a box of Oreos," I scoff.

"Oh, pardon me, ma'am. What are those things called that you hide in your desk?"

I sniff and look away. "They're called Milano cookies."

He kisses my cheek and I wrap my arms around his neck. "I like you," he whispers. I turn my head so he'll kiss me, but then he breaks off and says, "I got you something."

"Oh?"

He wheels us over to his desk, where he opens up a drawer and pulls out a sticker. "Cowboy butts drive me nuts?" I raise an incredulous eyebrow at him.

He shrugs, laughing. "I told you that you'd have to make it up to me."

"I can't even see your cowboy butt! You're in a wheelchair!"

"Yes, but if you could see it, think of how nuts it would drive you."

I shake my head, but there's a smile playing on my lips. Because if Luke took all his beloved stickers off for me, I can put *one* on for him. It might be at the bottom of my wheelchair where no one can see it, but he'll know it's there.

"Alternatively," he says with a devilish grin, "you could wear these." He pulls out a pair of teeny tiny cutoff shorts with bedazzled rear pockets.

"I'll take the sticker," I grumble.

He sighs. "I was afraid you'd say that."

"Since we're giving gifts, I have something for you too."

I point toward my desk, and we wheel back over there. "Close your eyes." I pull out the "You're Fired" mug I bought on Etsy. "Alright, open up."

Laughter bubbles out of him as he takes the mug. "I thought we covered this already, darlin'. You can't fire me."

"I just thought it could be a memento of what could've been," I tell him, sighing wistfully. "I was originally going to write all the reasons why I was firing you, but I went with a different approach."

He examines the mug, reading my handwritten phrases:

You're an amazing dancer.

Stronger than Superman.

You make me laugh.

The way you really listen.

How you see the good in everything and everyone.

When you pull me in your lap.

How you save me from storms.

When you call me darling. (Don't you dare tell anyone.)

Your Southern drawl.

When you drag me to church.

Your cooking.

The way you love your family, and mine now too.

How patient you are.

He reads each one, his smile growing with each comment. When he's done, he sets the mug down, running a finger across my cheek. "I don't think I've ever been fired so nicely before."

I thread my fingers through the back of his hair, breathing in his earthy scent that's tinged with the hay he fed the horses this morning. "I love you, Luke Craig," I tell him as I tilt my head toward his.

"I know," he says with that smile I've fallen for, and then closes the gap between us, pressing his lips to mine in the sweetest kiss I've ever had.

70

Bonus Epilogue

Mila

Planning a wedding in two days feels a little like getting thrown into a hurricane as it collides with a tsunami. Thankfully, my mom, Anya, Mrs. Caballero, and Monica are all like worker bees set loose. Anya acts as the Queen Bee, coordinating everyone: Monica works on the flowers, a DJ, and bridesmaids dresses; my mom rents chairs, tables, a tent, and a caterer for a reception; Mrs. Caballero is making the cake. Anya contacts our small list of family and friends that we want to be there for the wedding. Meanwhile, my dad plays his role of the gruff father throwing around money like it's candy. He could get an Academy Award for his performance.

I would've been happy with a courthouse wedding or something simple in my parents' backyard, but every time I voice that opinion, I'm silenced with the reasoning that the lawyer said to make it as "real" as possible. But I know that's just an excuse because they want a *wedding*. I'm just happy to be marrying Alex.

Monica makes a few appointments at bridal shops around Miami to find a wedding dress off the rack. I feel like the star-eyed emoji walking into the first boutique. "Shop" doesn't quite begin to cover it—the store is sprawling, with high ceilings, glass chandeliers, and expansive windows that overlook Biscayne Bay. Wedding dresses are displayed on mannequins throughout the store and in wood-paneled racks.

"When's the big day?" the attendant asks. She's dressed in all-black, which seems a little paradoxical for a bridal shop, with pursed Botoxed lips.

"Tomorrow," I tell her, and I watch as the careful smile she'd plastered on her face slips, and before she can help it, she chokes.

Monica pounds on the woman's back so hard, I'm afraid her model-thin body will break in two. When she finally gets her composure, she says, "I'm sorry. I thought you said tomorrow."

"I did," I say, smiling. "You know, shotgun wedding. Woohoo."

This time, it's my mom's turn to choke. She's clutching her chest and reaching out for Anya, who's looking up at me with a bewildered expression.

"Uh, *sestra*, do you know what 'shotgun wedding' means?"

"Yeah, like it's a super-fast wedding. You have to get married quick, like a shotgun going off."

They all stare at me, as if waiting for more. Laughter bubbles out of Monica as Anya sighs and says, "A shotgun wedding is a quick wedding because the bride is *pregnant*." She eyes my stomach. "So, unless there's something you're not telling us, this is not a shotgun wedding."

Realization dawns as I put together the term I'd misunderstood. "You guys, I've been telling everyone this is a shotgun wedding." I groan and cover my face with my hands. "So everyone thinks I'm pregnant?" I open my fingers to peek out through my hands to find them all nodding at me. "Oh my gosh. That makes a lot more sense why the florist kept touching my stomach. I thought it was a little too familiar..." I groan again and my mom clears her throat.

"You are not, um, pregnant, are you?"

"Mom! No!"

Mrs. Caballero turns to me, gesturing at her belly. "You have baby?" she says.

I shake my head. "*No, por supuesto que no en este momento.*"

The attendant is watching this all with wide eyes, glancing back and forth between all of us. "So...wedding dresses," she says slowly. "What are you looking for?"

"Something that fits," I say with a shrug.

"So you'll need something off the rack? You really are getting married tomorrow, then?"

I nod, and she glances at my belly, as if she doesn't quite believe there's not a baby in there. "Let me measure you and see what your options are."

Monica starts spouting out different styles of dresses and designers she thinks will look good on me, but she might as well be speaking Mandarin because I don't understand a word of what she's saying. But she's clearly done her research, for which I am grateful.

There are exactly eight dresses that are ready-to-go in my size. One is a slinky number with a plunging neckline almost to my navel. "Alex would have a heart attack if I wore this."

"Not to mention *Tato*," Anya says with a glint in her eyes, as if she'd love for me to give our dad a heart attack.

The next dress is a full-skirted princess style gown with off the shoulder sleeves. This one gets my mom's waterworks show going, and the attendant has to rummage up a box of tissues. It's a beautiful dress, befitting of a princess, but it just doesn't feel like *me*. The third dress is too big, and the fourth is too small—unable to even zip all the way. When I put on the fifth dress, it's a whimsical piece with breezy fabric, delicate flowers, and a long train. As my eyes take in the full effect, from the bottom of the dress moving up, I snag on the chest part of the dress. Which is, if I'm not mistaken, ever-so-slightly see through. My eyes widen and I quickly cover my chest with my hands.

"Is it supposed to be like that?" I whisper to Monica, clutching my chest.

She shrugs but says, "It's a work of art."

"Yeah, one that's meant to stay in the *bedroom*," I whisper back. I take off the dress without showing it to everyone else and try on the next few options. Too frilly, too poofy, too sexy. I don't know what I was expecting from wedding dress shopping—I guess the feeling that this is *it*, this is *the* dress. But I don't feel that way in any of the dresses I try on. If anything, I feel uncomfortable. Not myself.

Monica gushes over each dress like the good friend that she is, and my mom's gone through almost the whole box of tissues by the time I'm done, but I don't find the one. I walked in with my hopes so high, and after trying on all those dresses with no luck, I feel more like the red-faced exhausted emoji. I can work out five horses in a row no problem, but try on eight wedding dresses? Whew. Who knew trying on wedding dresses could be so tiring?

We grab a few Cuban sandwiches for lunch, and Monica's looking up another bridal boutique in Coral Gables when my mom says, "You could try on my dress." She clears her throat nervously. "If you want."

I can tell my mom feels self-conscious offering me her dress for some reason, so I reach across the table and take her hand. "I would love that."

"It might not fit," Anya says, and I don't know if she's trying to temper my expectations, or our mom's.

"What do I have to lose?" I say, thinking that I might just have to find a white dress on Amazon that can be here by tomorrow morning. I discreetly text Anya to start working on that.

Back at home, we all gather in my parents' bedroom as my mom takes her dress out of a closet. Mrs. Caballero runs her fingers over the fabric, oohing over it. The bodice is a lace-trimmed sweetheart style with lots of beading and curling designs, whereas the skirt is made of smooth satin with *a lot* of tulle underneath. It has the obligatory 90s long sleeves that make my skin itch just looking at them.

Monica helps me into the dress and surprisingly, it fits really well. I don't have a mirror in here, so I can't see what it looks like, but the dress itself fits me like it was custom-made for me.

"Do I look like Princess Di?" I ask Monica.

She steps back, assessing. "It actually works, chica."

I raise an eyebrow. "Really?" I can't tell if Monica is pulling my chain or not.

"The lines are right for your body," she says, gesturing her hands around my curves.

When I walk out, the waterworks display between my mom and Mrs. Caballero is so massive, they could get inner tubes and sell tickets to the new water park they're forming.

"It's beautiful, you're beautiful," my mom says tearfully. Without even glancing at Mom, Anya hands her a tissue from her stash in her wheelchair pocket.

"You look like a bride," Anya says. "Do you feel like a bride?"

I shrug, not really sure what a bride is *supposed* to feel like. I've never been one before. "I'm just ready to get married," I say.

"In this?"

"In anything." I sigh. "If this doesn't work, I'll wear a paper bag. I am just ready."

"Can we talk about the elephant in the room, though?" Anya says.

She makes eye contact with Monica, and together they say, "The sleeves." My hands go to the poofy shoulders and the long see-through sleeves with so much beading, it's making my arms feel heavy.

"Can we cut them off?" Anya asks.

My mom nods but says, "Where are we going to find a seamstress who can pull this off by tomorrow?"

Mrs. Caballero steps forward, fingering the fabric. "I cut shoulders?"

"You could mend the dress?" I ask her in Spanish. "By tomorrow?"

"*Sí, sí, enseguida, no hay problema.*"

"We have a dress, people!" Monica yells. "Let's get this girl shipped. The wedding is *on*."

71

Bonus Epilogue

Alex

When Anya divvied out wedding planning responsibilities, I thought I'd gotten the easy ones. Now I'm on a mission to find someone to perform our ceremony. And so far, I'm failing miserably. Who knew it would be so hard to find someone to stand in front of you as you say your vows? We don't really need anyone to cue us; why isn't that person optional? And yet, you'd think the demand in this town far outweighed the supply. I was laughed out of our local Catholic church—mainly because Mila was baptized Greek Orthodox, not Catholic, a distinction that feels more like a fifteen-hundred-year-old grudge than a real reason for the priest to not marry us. When I call around to other churches, I can't get anyone to answer their phones—forget *email*—and the few ministers that do answer require premarital counseling. Which I'm not opposed to, but time isn't exactly on our side.

"Could we do a Zoom counseling session tonight?" I ask one minister.

"Our premarital counseling series is an 8-week program."

"And you can't make an exception, just this time?"

"Sorry, son. If you were a member, I might be able to, but our board of directors makes these requirements, not me."

Who knew churches were so...political?

Of course there's a plethora of *weird* options, such as Elvis impersonators who will marry you Vegas-style, a comedian who will make a performance out of your wedding, and even magician officiants. I can't even imagine what Mila would say if a magician performed our wedding vows. Although, now that I think of it, I don't think she'd mind since we're in a pinch.

I'm about to book a wedding illusionist when Luke calls. "Hey, man. Just seeing what you need. Put me to work."

I sigh with relief—it's nice to have someone like Luke in my corner. I tell him about the duties Anya gave me, and hand off some of my load. Then I recount my efforts to find an officiant.

"You know, my dad could marry y'all."

"Really?"

"I'll ask him, but I'm sure he'll be fit to be tied."

I have no idea what that means, but I assume that means he'll be happy to perform the wedding. When I get a confirmation from Luke a few minutes later, I check that off my to-do list and text Mila: *Luke's dad is going to marry us.*

Mila immediately responds with a smiley emoji, and my soul soars. I can't believe I get to marry this girl.

Mila: *trying on wedding dresses. Not going great. Just tried on one that was completely see through.*

I almost drop my phone at the visual that pops in my head, a flush creeping up my neck. I take a deep breath and attempt to re-focus on the to-do list. Tomorrow can't come soon enough.

I hardly sleep the night before the wedding, and when I do, it's with dreams that border on the edge of hallucinations. Mila's before me, shimmering like a specter, but when I reach out for her, she disappears. I wake with a start, only to fall into a similar dream minutes later.

At five a.m., I get up for good, going down to the barn. I'm jittery, as if I'd just downed three espressos and a Red Bull, but being around the horses calms me. I stroke Jet's nose, the softness seeping into my nerves. He nibbles gently at my fingers, and I get him a mint from my pocket, rewarding him for helping me. On a whim, I decide to tack him up and go for a ride through the field where our ceremony will be in just a few hours.

The emotions of the past few weeks swirl through me, and I think of all that happened, all that could've been, and thank God for where we ended up. Where we're going.

I think about how long I hoped for this, for Mila to love me. Years ago, when Mila first came to Zen, I'd been so captivated by her beauty, her humor, her zest for life. I'd been too hesitant to make a move, and Michael swooped in. I watched for years as she danced through life, barely noticing me. And I thought that's just how it would be. But after Anya's accident, as Mila fell apart and it became clear that Michael wasn't capable of putting back the pieces, I was there. And it took some time, but when Mila made the jump, she was all in. And the reality of our relationship has been better than anything I could've dreamed up as I waited from the sidelines.

But I'm not waiting anymore. No more sidelines for me. I've loved every minute of building this life with Mila, putting together the Center and pursuing our dreams together. To be able to continue that dream with Mila as my wife...it's hard to believe that this is my real life. I'm half expecting to wake up, but this is it. And it's even more than I ever could've hoped for.

The past few days, I've thought about my dad quite a bit—what he would say to me now. It hits me like a two-ton weight that my dad won't see me get married, that he won't be here for all that's to come—my wedding, having children one day, all of the highs and lows in between. It's a strange experience when you feel two strong emotions at the same time—insane happiness at the prospect of marrying Mila, while also an immense sadness that my dad is missing all of this.

I'm balancing these two contrasting feelings throughout the day, as I feed the horses, clean stalls, oversee the setup of the chairs, tables, and tent for the wedding, and then finally shower and start getting ready. Luke comes over around noon, dressed in a suit and missing his signature cowboy hat.

"Special delivery," he says, holding out a package to me.

"What's this?"

"From your fiancée."

He hands me a takeout box, and when I open it, it's Panda Express. I laugh and shake my head, remembering our date a few weeks ago when Mila was trying to show me that she was with me no matter what. That she believed in me and was going to be by my side through it all—and here we are. She's proved it to me yet again. And I think that's what love is: when one person is down, you pick them up. It doesn't have to be fifty-fifty all the time; that's just not realistic. Love is carrying the extra weight when your partner is down-and-out. And, sometimes, when you're both laid low, it's laying in the mud together until you can summon the strength to get up. And that's what Mila's showed me through this all. Sometimes I'll pick her up when she's down, and sometimes she'll pick me up. We're in it together, come what may.

Luke hands me a gift bag, and I pull the tissue paper out. There are several individually wrapped items with handwritten notes on each one, and I take them out one by one.

One note says, *If you get cold feet*, and I unwrap a pair of dress socks.

The next one is a tube of lip balm with a note that says, *For a lifetime of kisses*.

I unwrap a portable Bluetooth speaker. *For all the dancing we're going to do.*

A watch with a leather strap has a note, *No more waiting*.

Note after note, package after package, I unwrap little thoughtful and sometimes funny gifts from Mila. She thought of everything, and I wonder how she got this all done with the craziness of the wedding planning.

When I unravel something black and lacy, Luke's eyebrows shoot up, and he quickly scoots away, mumbling something under his breath about needing to check something on his truck. I quickly tuck the item away, my heart beating a little faster than it absolutely needs to at this moment.

One thing is for certain: I'm looking forward to tonight.

I compose myself as much as I possibly can and open the rest of the gifts from Mila, smiling and laughing at each one.

When I'm done, I quickly write a note of my own to Mila, grab something out of my mom's room, and ask Luke for a favor.

"Fine," Luke says with a dramatic sigh. "But when it's my turn, you'll be my errand guy."

"Deal."

It's finally time. I glance down at the watch Mila gave me. *No more waiting*. I head down to the field with Luke and my mom, where the farm has been transformed into something magical. A few rows of chairs are set up in front of an archway of flowers, the farm and oak trees framing the setup. My aunt and uncle smile at me from the second row, and I spot a few of our clients from the Center and barn mates from Zen.

Luke stands beside me as my best man, and when I look out at our friends and family gathered, my eyes catch on a framed photo in the front row. My dad's smiling face is sitting beside my mom. I don't know who put the picture there, but tears prick at the back of my eyes as I think about the fact that maybe my dad is here, after all.

Anya rolls down the aisle, and that's when the tears come. And I let them. It's hitting me that this is *real*, that after years of loving Mila, I'm finally marrying her.

Monica follows behind Anya, walks down the aisle in heels that are way too high for the average human. Trina walks down last, and I'm not sure I've ever seen her in a dress before. Of course she's wearing boots with it, but it wouldn't be quite Trina in heels. I smile at her, wondering if she's ever going to open her heart again. Years ago, she dated my cousin, Victor, and he did a number on her before getting arrested for his involvement in a Ponzi scheme. Trina's always been a bit closed off, and after Victor, she's locked up like Alcatraz. I don't blame her, but I do hope she'll release her heart eventually.

I'm also grateful I don't have any more cousins. Tomás and Victor did enough damage, thank you very much.

In a surprising twist (for me, anyway), one of our clients, Hailey, walks Don Juan down the aisle as a flower pony. Someone's braided flowers into his long mane, and Hailey tosses flower petals as she walks him down the aisle.

Finally, Don Juan and Hailey are down the aisle, the bridesmaids are in place, and my heart is beating its own percussion waiting for Mila. But I don't see her anywhere. Her dad is standing at the end of the aisle, off to the side, like he's waiting for her, but she is nowhere to be found. My heart drops, and I start to think of reasons why Mila could be missing. I'm glancing around, hoping I don't look too frantic—or too pathetic. Is it possible I'm getting left at the altar? But no, Mila wouldn't do that. Not after everything. And not after all of her notes and gifts to me this morning.

Would she?

72

Bonus Epilogue

Mila

Nothing is going right today. The DJ got into a minor car accident on his way up from Miami, which means we're scrambling to find a decent speaker system while Anya cobbles together a playlist.

"How do you feel about the Macarena?" she asks.

"Seriously?"

She shrugs, and I don't even bother responding.

When Monica is doing my hair, she accidentally burns off a chunk of my hair, giving me a weird bang on the right side. My eyes widen in disbelief, staring at the singed piece of hair and then the limp piece that's hanging from Monica's hand. She quickly tosses the hair over her shoulder.

"Not to worry!" She laughs nervously. "I'll just braid it. You won't notice, I promise."

"She won't notice for six months while her hair grows out?" Anya grumbles under her breath, while I try to smile and pretend like I don't care. All that matters is that I'm marrying Alex, even if I'm half bald.

When the flowers show up, they are not the white peonies we ordered, but neon green and hot pink carnations.

Lovely.

Then I go to try on the shoes Monica brought me to wear under my dress, and one of the heels cracks off. I tumble to the ground, bruising my knee.

Anya and Monica exchange glances, and I'm wondering if they think this is all doomed.

I've yet to see my mom's dress that Mrs. Caballero mended, but Anya announces that the Amazon delivery was delayed, so my backup dress won't be here in time for the wedding. I pray that my mom's dress works without sleeves. What if the sleeves are an essential part of holding the dress up? What if it just slides right off of me as I walk down the aisle? The see-through dress would've been better than a dress that falls off, surely.

When Anya sends Monica downstairs on a mysterious mission, I'm on the verge of tears. "We should've just gone to the courthouse," I tell my sister.

Anya takes my hand in hers and levels me with her gaze. "What matters today is that you're marrying Alex. Even if all your hair fell out, or you had the ugliest flowers in the world."

"I *do* have the ugliest flowers in the world."

"Fair enough," Anya says, giving the neon-colored bouquets a grimace. "But who's standing at the end of the aisle is what matters."

I nod, pressing my lips together to keep the tears away. Monica reappears holding a coffee and a bag.

"Alex sent something for you," she says, holding out the bag and an envelope.

I open the bag, taking out a massive guava and cheese pastry from my favorite Cuban bakery, and I know that the coffee is a cafe con leche. My favorite.

In the envelope is a hair tie and a note from Alex: *I'll always be here to keep your blood sugar up with a lifetime supply of pastries, but this is the last time I won't be there to hold back your hair if you throw up.*

I smile, thinking of all the times Alex has been there with me and for me when I've vomited before horse shows. I'm grateful he thought of me, but I also know this won't be one of those days, because I'm not even feeling an ounce of fear or nerves. I am one hundred percent ready to go.

Alex's note does give me an idea of how to make this whirlwind wedding day a little bit more mine—even if my dress is a disaster or my flowers belong in a Rainbow Rangers episode.

"Hey Mom?" I call out. "Can you get me my riding pants and boots?"

I'm alone at the barn. My parents, Anya, and Monica drove down to the field, not wanting to get their shoes dirty on the long walk. I should be nervous, or even excited, but instead

I feel an incredible sense of peace and resolve. I'm doing exactly what I want to be doing, exactly what I *should* be doing. And it's so freeing.

I glance down at my phone, waiting for a call from my mom when it's time. Cyrus snorts and paws at the ground. Trina trailered him down this morning, originally so he could be in our wedding pictures. How could we get married without Cyrus?!

"I know, buddy," I tell him. "Soon. Very soon."

He bends his neck to look at me, sniffing at the poofy wedding dress that's enveloping us both. When he nibbles hopefully at the toe of my boot, I wish I had some peppermints to give him. I try to reach into the pockets of my riding pants underneath my dress, to see if I have any treats left in there, but the dress is just too cumbersome to work around.

When the call comes through from my mom, I press my heels into Cyrus's side. "It's time, big guy."

Cyrus lunges forward, and together we gallop out of the barn onto the path toward the field. Mrs. Caballero did an incredible job, and my wedding dress doesn't move an inch as I canter toward Alex. The dress skirt is hitched up in the middle so I can sit astride the saddle, but it's long enough to flow around my legs on either side. Mrs. Caballero presented me with her veil this morning, so I have bits from both moms on my wedding day. The wind lifts my hair and the veil behind me, and this is the moment, *the feeling*, I was waiting to experience.

This is *it*.

It's not about the dress, or the shoes, or the flowers, or anything else. It's about me being my truest self, on my way to meet Alex. To love him for everything he is, and to be loved for everything I am.

And I wanted to present myself in my truest form today—on horseback. Cyrus and I gallop as one down the field, and when I see Alex's face light up, the biggest smile I've ever had takes over my face too. I feel like I'm smiling all the way down to my toes. In fact, I'm so distracted that I don't pull up Cyrus soon enough, so I have to canter around the whole wedding set up, circling Alex, until I slow Cyrus to a walk at the end of the aisle, never losing eye contact with Alex.

He's all I see, all that consumes my mind in this moment. And I know he feels the same way, because as I stop Cyrus, he's striding down the aisle toward me.

I can feel the collective intake of breath of our small group of friends and family as Alex breaks about a millennium of wedding protocol as he walks to me. His hands find my waist, and he carefully lifts me up and out of the saddle. I swing my leg around, the dress bunching behind me, but I don't even care as Alex's hands are on me, firm yet gentle. And so very *Alex*.

He guides me down, holding me against him in a way that leaves me feeling breathless. When my feet hit the grass, I'm a little disappointed because I wanted that moment to last forever.

"Mila Kozak," he says, his eyes like black holes, drawing me in. "You made it."

I put my hands on his chest, steadying myself. I'm trying to remind myself it's not yet time to kiss Alex, but my heart isn't really listening. Behind us, my dad clears his throat, and Alex smiles.

"I think maybe I wasn't supposed to do this," Alex whispers.

"It's perfect," I say, taking hold of his lapels.

"Should I go back now?" He glances down the aisle.

"I do kind of want to walk down with my dad," I say with a smile and a look at my dad over Alex's shoulder. He's barely containing his patience, and it makes me laugh.

"Right, of course," Alex says, but he's obviously as hesitant as I am to let go. "I'll see you soon," he whispers before leaning down to kiss my cheek. "Oops, not sure I was supposed to do that, either." Everyone seems to hear this, and they're all laughing with us as Alex jogs back down the aisle, and my dad takes my arm.

"You can still get out of here if you want," my dad says to me, but he's got a hint of a smile playing on his lips. I stand on tiptoe and kiss his cheek.

"I'm exactly where I want to be."

Walking down the aisle to Alex, everyone and everything around us falls away. All I can see is him. Tears threaten to blur my vision, but still, he's all clear. The walk to him feels like it takes a million years, and at the same time only two seconds. But finally I'm there, with my hands in his, his eyes on mine. I barely notice Luke's dad beside us, welcoming our guests and giving a short wedding sermon. The moments pass too quickly as we exchange vows and then Pastor Craig announces us husband and wife.

"Now you can kiss your bride," Pastor Craig says with a wink at Alex.

I smile up at my *husband*, and he pulls me against him, cupping my cheek. "Finally," he breathes, and then his lips are on mine, a thousand I-love-yous exchanged in one kiss.

The reception is simple–there are no favors, no fancy place settings, only very basic centerpieces. Simple white tablecloths adorn the same rented tables we used for the Center's Christmas party. But we don't need any of that stuff. We have everything we need—and a lot more.

We spend a lot of time dancing and gorging ourselves on Mrs. Caballero's guava cake. The whole time, Alex's eyes are on me, always finding a way to hold me as if he's afraid I'll evaporate if he lets go. I can tell by the hungry look in his eyes that he's ready to get out of here. But Alex is nothing if not patient as we chat with our friends and family—but if he ever takes his gaze off of me, I'm not aware of it.

Finally, it's time for us to leave, and we realize that we didn't plan any kind of special getaway. There's no sparklers or bubbles or anything for guests to cheer us on with, so they just hoot and holler as we run to the car, laughing.

We drive to the beach, a quiet realization filling the car that we really did this. We're really married. Alex holds my hand, fingers twined in mine. Every once in a while, he lifts my hand to his mouth, kissing my fingers.

When we get to the hotel that overlooks the water, Alex doesn't lead me inside—he takes me out to the water. It's dark, and the nighttime ocean reflects the sky, the moon gleaming off the surface as the waves crash onto the shore.

My heart is racing, ready to be with Alex, but he holds me against him and murmurs in my ear, "I just want to soak this in for a moment."

I relax against his chest, absorbing the vibrations of his heartbeat, strong and steady just like Alex. My arms go around his back, thinking of all we've been through, and how Alex has loved me through every moment of it. He loved me at my worst, after Anya's accident, and he's supported my dreams and lifted me up through it all.

As we stand on the shoreline, our feet in the ocean, it feels like we're standing on the edge of the rest of our lives. And even though I don't know what will happen, I know *who* I'll be doing life with.

In the end, that's all that really matters.

I glance up at Alex and realize he's not looking out at the ocean. He's looking at me. That is Alex's way, isn't it? And it always will be.

"Are you ready, Mrs. Caballero?" Alex asks, his voice a whisper on my neck.

I fist my hand in his shirt, tugging him to me for a kiss. "Always."

I've never been more ready for my forever with Alex. My Alex.

We walk hand-in-hand away from the ocean, toward the rest of our lives. Ready for whatever comes next.

THE END (for now)

Keep reading for a sneak peek of book #3 of the Equestrian Dreams series, SOAR!

And, if you want more Luke and Anya, you'll want to check out this bonus scene:

DOWNLOAD A LUKE + ANYA BONUS SCENE

Scan the QR code or go to the link below to download a bonus scene featuring Luke and Anya on vacation with the Craig family.

tinyurl.com/FALLbonus

Did you enjoy FALL?

I'm on a mission to get 100 reviews of FALL! Reviews are the lifeblood of books and authors. Please support this Indie author by reviewing the novel:

REVIEW FALL

Scan the QR codes or go to the links below to review FALL.

Goodreads:

https://tinyurl.com/
reviewFALLGR

Amazon:

https://tinyurl.com/
reviewFALLamzn

A Sneak Peek of SOAR

Book #3 in the Equestrian Dreams Series

TRINA

For the first time in my adult life, I am in control of my destiny. There are no boyfriends holding me back or dictating my every move. And the mourning period for those guys is long over—I'm a free and independent woman. Heck, Kelly Clarkson could've written that Miss Independent song about *me*. But, wait, doesn't she fall in love and lose her independence in that song? I shake my head. It's not a very aptly named song, then, is it? I suppose I'm the "before" picture of that song—and that's where I want to stay.

I've got an incredible job at Zen Elite teaching riding students. I've got my beloved Chevy Silverado, which only took me oh, you know, a *decade* to be able to afford. And, the cherry on top of the ice cream sundae that is my life, I finally—*finally*—have another Grand Prix horse to ride.

This is no small matter. Since my first Grand Prix horse, Blue Thunder, took me to the top of the show jumping circuit, I haven't been able to find a replacement. That's not to say I haven't tried—oh, I've tried—but disaster always ensues when I try too hard. I learned that lesson the hard way.

My most recent disaster ended when my bank account bottomed out. Since my riding instructor budget couldn't handle a full-fledged Grand Prix horse on its own, I decided to take matters into my own hands. I purchased a young horse from Argentina—an Argentinian thoroughbred mixed with Dutch Warmblood. He had a powerful, scopy back and legs for days. He was smart, motivated, and energetic. The horse could jump a mile high and gallop at top speeds for hours. He was incredible—my dream horse. That is, until he was transported to the States.

It's not uncommon for horses to get sick during transport. In fact, out of 100 horses transported commercially, eleven percent of them will contract pneumonia. Want to guess who's horse landed in that eleven percent statistic? That's right. This girl's.

Pneumonia's not a death sentence by any means. But Lightning—that's what I named my Argentinian dreamboat—developed complications, of course. And those complications led to scar tissue in his lungs. Which led to coughing fits every time he got above a trot. Which led to bleeding lungs. Yeah, not ideal. Especially for an athlete.

So I did what any self-respecting horse woman would do: I spent every dime I had on trying to get Lightning well.

Did it work?

No.

Lightning is now a full-time pasture horse out in Okeechobee. C'est la vie, am I right?

I had all but given up. Resigned myself that I would have to be content to watch my students ride in Grand Prixs but not ever be able to afford it myself. Until Caterina came into my life. She's one of my student's moms—a bonafide horse person herself, though she's a dressage rider and not a show jumper. She obviously thinks I'm crazy—as all dressage people seem to think of show jumpers—but her daughter has the need for speed and height like I do, so I've taken her under my wing. Apparently Caterina has more money than Oprah and likes to live her life like it's her own personal Christmas special. *Heeeeerrrrre's a horse for you! And you! And you!*

I happened to be in the way when she was feeling particularly benevolent one day, and am now a (very) partial owner of a brand spanking new Grand Prix horse, Leonidas. She paid full price for my new bundle of joy, which means she's out a quarter million dollars and, as long as good ole Leo stays healthy, I'm set for the next few years of top level competition.

Oh, and did I mention that the summer Olympics are coming up? I've got as good a chance as anyone to make that team with Leo on my side and Caterina funding the whole shebang. International competitions, here we come.

To say that I love Leo is like saying the sun is a star—it's totally true, but it just doesn't do it justice. I remember reading one time about maternal-fetal microchimerism—where a baby's cells enter a mother's body and stay there. If some part of the mother's body is damaged, the fetal cells will rush to help it heal. I'm not going to lie, when I read about that, I teared up. Not because I ever want to be a mom, but because this is what being a horse rider feels like to me. That this horse is becoming part of me, and he's healing me from the inside out. All by being a part of my life. That's what Leo means to me.

For the first time in forever, I'm letting myself *hope*. And I know, I know. Hope is a dangerous thing. But I'm jumping feet-first into an Olympic-sized pool of it, manifesting the heck out of my Olympic dream.

So even when my feet are about to fall off after walking twenty thousand steps from a zillion lessons at Zen Elite, I ride. I train. I skip the cake pop at Starbucks and opt for a green smoothie at home. I take ice baths and gulp down supplements that are bigger than any horse pills I've ever seen. I ignore the ache in my knees that tell me I'm not a spring chicken anymore. Since when did being in your mid-30s mean you weren't young anymore? But bones don't lie. And mine *hurt*.

Lately, I've decided to take a note from racetrack riders and show up to ride Leo in the pre-dawn hours. Today when I show up to the barn, I'm greeted by Leo's low rumble as he pricks his ears at me. He hasn't eaten breakfast yet, so I bring a bag of carrots—organic, of course—and offer him a handful while I tack him up.

We trot through the early morning mist, his freshness making him bounce. He throws out his legs in extension, making me think he could've done dressage or three day eventing in another life. I sink into my heels, sitting the trot as I push him into a leg yield across the field. My cheeks collect the morning dew under my helmet, and I'm damp by the time we're cantering in figure eights—flawlessly changing leads without me having to ask.

Kane and Katelyn Brown's song "Thank God" pops into my head—I'm thankful for this horse, who fits me like a glove, who fills my days with hope and joy. I couldn't ask for more.

I'm three lessons into the day when someone pulls up in a red Maserati. I internally groan—hoping it's not one of my student's dads coming to complain about how calloused their hands are or some other trifling issue. I scan my brain to think if any of my students have fallen off recently, and can't think of anyone in recent weeks, but you never know. For whatever reason, moms seem to "get it"—they understand the horse obsession, the hard work and the sacrifice it takes in this sport. But dads...dads are difficult. Especially the rich ones. As a rule, I make a point to stay away from guys—been there, done that, don't want the t-shirt thank you very much. So when a man gets out of the Maserati looking too put-together for the barn—with his perfect pompadour and thousand-dollar sunglasses—I hide in the feed room.

I'm measuring out tonight's feed—only four hours too early—when one of the girls finds me.

"Trina? There's some guy looking for you."

"You can tell him I'm busy," I say, not looking up from measuring the super expensive Platinum Performance GI into Leo's feed bucket. "You could give him my number if he insists."

"Oh, okay—"

"I can wait," a male voice calls from the other side of the feed room door. I release the scoop into the supplement tub and glance up at the ceiling. Why, God, *why*? I take a deep breath, trying to summon all of my patience for whatever Mr. GQ wants from me. No one shows up in a Maserati if they don't expect something from someone. And that someone is usually me.

I wipe my hands on my riding pants—my favorite pair of Ariat's TriFactor breeches with their cooling technology, perfect for Florida—and open the door.

Of course Mr. GQ has taken off his sunglasses to reveal piercing blue eyes that could slice through your heart, if you let them. He's clean shaven, not a hair out of place, with light-colored slacks that don't have a single wrinkle in them. His shoes look vaguely expensive in that 'I'm-not-trying-too-hard' kind of way that still costs hundreds of dollars. I've never been very impressed with civilian clothes—show up in a pair of Tucci boots, and I'm here for it. But Mr. GQ is rocking this look. At the first flutter of attraction, I think of Jess from New Girl: *Shut it down*.

"Yes?" I say, exuding a bit of annoyance to cover up the fact that I'd stared far too long at this guy.

"Miss Powers? I'm Grayson. Grayson J. Sterling," he says, as if I should know who he is, and then he extends his hand. I take it, still waiting for him to make clear why he's here. Grayson J. Sterling? Sounds like a lawyer. Am I being sued? "You don't know who I am, do you?" he asks, his mouth tilting into a smile that threatens to wedge into my heart like a dart, but I swat that thing away before it gets too close. *Shut it down*, I remind myself.

"Am I supposed to?"

"I thought Cate would've told you..." He spreads his hands apologetically.

My mind is racing, thinking, *Cate, Cate, Cate*, but I'm coming up short. "Cate who?"

"Caterina," he clarifies. "Our daughter, DeDe, takes lessons here?"

Understanding dawns as I realize Caterina is Cate to him. I'm assuming she's his wife, though she goes by her maiden name. "Did something happen?" I know Leo is fine, I just rode him, so that means this must be about DeDe, which makes my stomach coil in fear. I don't get attached to a lot of my students, but DeDe worked her way into my heart like few can. Her parents strapped her with the name Demetria—far too cumbersome of a name for a seven pound infant if you ask me—but everyone calls her DeDe for short.

"Well, yes. Caterina and I have divorced." He says the word like he's still getting used to it. "I would've thought she would have told you."

Why Caterina would feel like she has to inform me of her personal life, I have no idea. We're business partners, not buddies. And I haven't exactly positioned myself as a beacon screaming, *Come tell me all your problems!* It's just not my style. I realize Mr. GQ—I mean, Grayson—is waiting for me to say something. Should I say 'I'm sorry'? Instead, not wanting to invite more discussion since I clearly don't trust myself with this man, I just say, "Okay."

He's still staring at me, waiting for *something*, I'm not sure what, and I'm losing my already-thin patience—and resolve. "I have lessons to get to," I tell him, looking down at my Rolex. I walk past him, unfortunately too close because I catch a whiff of his scent—warm and spicy, drawing me in when I really should be running away.

Before I can lose my mind, Mr. GQ opens his too-perfect mouth and says the worst words I can imagine, "I'm here to tell you, after the divorce, Leonidas is mine now."

Pre-Order SOAR on Amazon!

PRE-ORDER SOAR

Equestrian Dreams Book 3

Scan the QR code or go to the link below to pre-order the third book in the Equestrian Dreams series.

tinyurl.com/ordersoar

Acknowledgements

Thank you, God, for loving us no matter how broken we are and showing us that we are worthy of love. I hope and pray Anya and Alex weren't the only ones who learned that lesson from this book. :)

To Tyler, who believes in me even more than I believe in myself...thank you. Our life together is a dream come true. Thank you for reading this novel and loving these characters like they were your own. Thank you for making time for my writing, wrangling children and financially backing this questionable venture. Oh, and thanks for letting me steal the 'favorite noun' line. You are my favorite person, place or thing.

My boys, Finn and Justus, who bring me so much joy. I love you so much.

For my mom, horsewoman extraordinaire, who also answered questions about spinal cord injuries and gave me the idea for the TENS unit spooking the horse. She also inspired me to write about the World Equestrian Center in Ocala, which is now my favorite showgrounds. Thank you for your endless love and support and access to horses! ;)

My sister-in-law, Amanda, has been one of my biggest cheerleaders. She's read all the worst drafts of all of my books and still loves me enough to keep reading! She saved Alex and Mila from having a pretty unbelievable miscommunication in this book, so you guys should thank her, too. I'm so grateful we get to do life together and raise our kids together.

My parents have supported me in every way a daughter could be supported and I'm endlessly grateful. You guys make it difficult to write dysfunctional families (which I thankfully did less of in this book) because of how, well, functional you are. I love you both so much, 'individually and collectively' as Dad likes to say.

When I was competing, my dad would always call out, "Looking good, Tiffany Stearns (my maiden name)!" It was slightly embarrassing as a shy kid, but now I treasure those tiny moments and fully plan to "embarrass" my children in similar ways.

Endless thanks to both the Stearns and Chacon families. My in-laws, Jeff and Lisa, are parents to me in their own right. I'm grateful to go through life right beside you guys.

(Literally *right beside*—they are my next door neighbors!) In order of importance (just kidding, in order of age): many thanks to Dorothy and Scotty, Joey and Philippa, Kyle and Amanda, Ryan and Andrea, and Daniel.

My brother, Daniel, is an incredible filmmaker and he created a book trailer for my first novel, JUMP, that is amazing. Thank you, thank you, thank you. Many thanks to Nora Pantoja and Gabriel Jose Bonilla who played Mila and Alex. Y'all are so talented and I'm blessed to have worked with you. (Also, if you haven't seen the trailer, check it out in the QR code below. And follow Daniel's filmmaking projects on Instagram @daniel.filmmaking. You won't regret it.)

Thanks you to my editor, Kat Nics, for your work and seeing this story through.

Many thanks to Tamara Shanaman for all your insight into working at an equine-assisted therapy center!

Kristi Carlo, my dear friend who has been so supportive, helped me make sure the specifics of Alex's degree/practicum were on point. Thank you, my friend!

Joyce Bloemker, who was a vital part of my launch team, gave me valuable feedback as an editor. If you are a writer in need of an editor, definitely look up Joyce (who also happens to be a horse person!). You can find her on Instagram @palomino.and.pinto.

One of the women on my launch team, Ariana, gave me the inspiration for Luke and Anya's bonus scene and I'm so grateful! (If you haven't checked out the bonus scene, please do. It's so fun!)

I'm so grateful for everyone on my launch team who helped spread the word about this book! You ladies are awesome (and you, too, Dad!).

Infinite thanks to Lauren, our babysitter, without whom this book would not have been written. I love and appreciate your enthusiasm for my boys.

To all of the bloggers, podcasters, bookstagrammers, BookTokers and others who helped spread the word about JUMP and FALL, thank you thank you thank you!! You are the lifeblood of this industry and I'm grateful for you.

To all who left reviews and spread the word about JUMP, you have no idea how much that means to me. You are helping my books to find their way into the hands and devices of its ideal readers. Thank you!!!

And thank you, dear reader, for continuing this journey with me and making this dream a reality.

VIEW THE JUMP TRAILER HERE:

Scan the QR code or go to
the link below to see the
JUMP trailer:

https://tinyurl.com/jumptrailer

Follow Tiffany

Sign up for Tiffany's monthly newsletter on her website, TiffanyNoelleChacon.com or scan the QR code below:

@tiffanynoellechacon

@tiffanynoellechacon

tiffanynoellechacon.com

Discussion Questions

1. Throughout the book, Alex battled with feeling like he's not enough for Mila. Those feelings were frequently fueled by his interactions with Mila's father. Have you ever experienced something like this? What could you learn from Alex's story?

2. Do you think Luke's stickers were appropriate? Does your knowledge of why he had those stickers make you feel differently about them?

3. Do you have any rituals (like Mila and Alex's kiss before competing)? Have you skipped your ritual before? How did you feel after?

4. What do you think was the turning point for Anya in her relationship with Luke?

5. In chapter 34, Mila gives Alex a gift that leaves him feeling even more insecure. Have you ever received a gift like this? In retrospect, did insecurity cloud your judgment about the thoughtfulness of the gift, or was it actually an insensitive gesture? What do you think of Mila's gift? Was it thoughtful, or insensitive?

6. Think of the family units within the book. What similarities and differences do they have?

7. Alex had to make a difficult decision in firing Tommy. Should he have done it earlier? Should he have done more? Could you do what he did? Is it easier, or harder, to work with family?

8. Anya feels free in the water. Is there a place you feel like that? How could you incorporate this into your life more?

9. In chapters 36 and 37, Luke and Mila organize outings to lift Anya and Alex's spirits. What's an outing that would encourage you after a hard week?

10. Mila said all important decisions should be made on a tack trunk. Where do you like to make important decisions?

11. Think of Mila and Alex's differing reactions to the court decision in chapter 46. Have you ever been in a situation like this where a loved one isn't reacting the way you want or need them to? What could Mila and Alex have done differently?

12. Anya struggled with not wanting to go to physical therapy because of how it made her feel. Have you ever avoided something you know you need to do because of how it makes you feel? What could you change to make it more palatable?

13. What could Mila and Alex have done differently in their communication about marriage? Who do you think was at fault for their miscommunication?

14. Have you ever felt 'too broken' to be loved? What can you learn from Anya and Luke's story to prove to yourself that everyone is worthy of love?

Author's note: I love book clubs and would love to support yours! If you would like me to send you Equestrian Dreams bookmarks, signed name plates, or if you'd like me to come speak at your book club, reach out to me at tiffany@jumpthenovel.com.